COUNTERFEIT KINGS

COUNTERFEIT KINGS

A Novel

ADAM CONNELL

PHOBOS BOOKS
NEW YORK

phobos

Published by Phobos Books
A Division of Phobos Entertainment Holding, Inc.
200 Park Avenue South, Suite 1109
New York, NY 10003
www.phobosweb.com

Distributed in the United States by National Book Network, Lanham, Maryland.

The characters and events in this book are fictitious. Any similarity to actual persons, living or dead, is coincidental and not intended by the author.

Library of Congress Cataloging-in-Publication Data

Connell, Adam.
    Counterfeit kings : a novel / Adam Connell.
        p. cm.
    ISBN 0-9720026-4-2 (alk. paper)
    I. Title.

    PS3603.O545C68 2004
    813'6—dc22

                                    2004004982

Printed in the United States of America

∞™ The paper used in this publication meets the minimum requirements of American National Standard for Information Sciences—Permanence of Paper for Printed Library Materials, ANSI/NISO Z39.48-1992.

For
Barrie Connell, my compass
and
Keith Olexa, my guide

COUNTERFEIT KINGS

CHAPTER 1

"We're going to have to stand and fight. They're right on top of us," Horrocks said. He gorged the thrusters with power looted from the ship's secondary demands.

His wife toggled through the viewscreens. The perimeter cameras tracked pursuit ships as they weaved through the background. "There's at least twenty," she said. "Closer to thirty. Two dead aft."

"What about the Spot Drive?" Horrocks said.

"It's still cold from the last jump."

"Put your belt on," Horrocks said.

"I hate wearing the belt."

"Sari, put the fucking belt on," Horrocks said.

Sari reached up to the head of her chair and pulled down the Y-shaped harness. Horrocks was already wearing his.

The ship lurched upward, briefly, then shot backward as Horrocks switched to the rear thrusters. Sari's hair flew forward and she cried out. The *Moondrunk* rattled as the twin ships directly behind her broke over her back. Silver and black debris tumbled past the forward viewscreen. "My stomach," Sari said.

Horrocks brought the ship up in a tight arc, trying to flee the cadre of aggressors.

The *Moondrunk* rattled again.

"That wasn't debris we just hit," Horrocks said. "We were rammed. Check the screens. Come on, Sari! Check the screens. Where are they?"

The *Moondrunk* snapped to a halt that nearly dislocated both command chairs from their floor sockets. "They've got hold of us," Horrocks said.

The ship was being forced down. Horrocks applied more pressure to the forward thrusters but couldn't arrest the *Moondrunk*'s descent. Two more tethers punctured the *Moondrunk*'s hull.

"Must be hooked to a winch," Horrocks said. He locked the thrusters on high, reached down to his seat and unlocked the harness. "Get into the bunker. Take the dogs."

"I can't move my arms. I can't get out of the chair," Sari said.

Horrocks leaned over to unstrap her.

"You're wasting fuel," she said. "Should have let me fly. We're still going down. May as well turn it off."

Horrocks nodded. Sari shut the engine. The *Moondrunk* descended quickly and collided with the other ship. Horrocks fell across his wife. Her shoulder hit him in the cheek.

"Sorry," Horrocks said and stood up straight. He helped Sari to her feet and guided her down the hallway outside the cockpit.

"Is it the Bastards?" she asked.

"I'm sure it is. Get into the bunker and stay there."

They both stopped when they heard the magnetic umbilical latch onto their ship. The light above the exit hatch shone green. The locks on the outer door were easily tripped. Two large men stepped inside. A third stayed on the lip of the umbilical. He aimed a rifle at Horrocks. "Tinton wants to see you," the man said. He swiveled the rifle and aimed it at Sari.

The two large intruders lifted their hands to show they were unarmed as they moved toward Horrocks and Sari.

Sari spat in the face of the nearest one. He slugged her in the arm and she fell back against the wall. Horrocks sprang forward. The man removed a steel rod from his pocket and struck Horrocks across the face.

Horrocks staggered but managed to get in front of his wife. The intruder wiped Sari's spittle from his nose and lashed out at Horrocks again. Horrocks grabbed the arm and cracked it over his knee.

"My elbow," he said and doubled over. Horrocks lifted the arm like a crank and threw the goon into his partner.

The man with the rifle stepped through the portal onto the *Moondrunk*. "I hate coming all the way through," he said and pointed his rifle at Sari again. "Sweetheart," he said. Then, to one of the goons: "This ain't no peepshow, Loome. Help your brother up and get these two married cretins under control."

"Calder, my arm."

"Do *something*. And you," Calder said to Horrocks, "you'll let them. That's how this works. Because if it doesn't work, I'll be forced to use my new gun and I'd rather not. Then I'll be forced to fly your ship. So do what I say."

Calder was in his mid-thirties. His beard was as thin as the hair on his crown. He had two black plums for nostrils.

"Are you a Bastard, too?" Horrocks asked.

"Not the king's," Calder said. He licked the corner of his mouth and motioned toward the door with his gun. "Don't want to keep Tinton waiting."

The uninjured goon shoved Horrocks and Sari forward. The other one was propped against a wall, eyes closed, his bad arm held against his stomach like a jumble of frail twigs.

Horrocks noticed that the men were wearing oversized miners' jackets. "You're not miners," Horrocks said.

"And you're not a hero. Not anymore. Not to me," Calder said.

Horrocks and Sari walked through the umbilical. Their footsteps echoed off the gravity generators in the floorboards.

"Mind your step at the end there," Calder said from behind them. "There's a bit of a ridge. You'll trip if you're not careful."

"'Cause you care," Horrocks said.

"Just being hospitable. That's how I am," Calder said and gave Sari a hard push.

Horrocks stepped over the ridge and onto the ship. Sari came in behind him.

"To the right, down the alleyway," Calder said.

The floor was carpeted in blue shag. Horrocks couldn't remember the last time he'd seen a carpeted ship. The air was overly humid and in need of recycling; it smelled of fried food and cinnamon beer.

"Another right," Calder said. "That's it. Big as an auditorium, isn't it?"

Four long tables had been pushed to the walls. Twenty men and women surrounded a raised chair set three-quarters of the way into the room. There was a man in the chair. His hair reached past his shoulders and was exceptionally fine. Much finer than the king's, Horrocks thought. The back of the man's head was reflected in the sloping window behind him. His bald spot gleamed on the surface of the glass like a pink coin. The rest of the window was tenanted with stars that shifted counterclockwise. Jupiter, while absent from view, was present in a haze that colored the stars orange. The man in the chair pushed the sleeves of his suit past his elbows and eased himself forward, one leg crooked behind the other.

"Horrocks," the man said.

"Tinton."

Tinton tried to stifle it, but a smile took the reins of his face. "Didn't think you'd remember me. Me, a worthless Bastard."

"I remember," Horrocks said.

"And your wife," Tinton said. "Of course I—"

"I don't remember you," Sari said. She held her arm where the goon had struck her.

"Welcome to the *Res Nullius*. I had to talk to you both. Face to face. Someone check them for weapons."

Four Bastards strode toward the couple and patted them down.

"Be careful where you touch me," Sari told one of the Bastards as his hands worked up past her ribcage.

The Bastard said, "I wouldn't—"

"Just you mind her delicate areas," Horrocks said.

Tinton turned to the people milling around his chair. "Get back. Give me some room to breathe. You're leeching the air, all of you."

The crowd detached themselves from the throne and loitered by the tables. Some of the Bastards were in their thirties, a few were in their twenties and one was no older than eight. They all shared similar features: light eyebrows, a slender nose, sharp green eyes, weak cheekbones, long limbs. All of them had gray in their hair, even the youngest.

Tinton turned back to Horrocks with an apologetic look on his face. "The king is dead. You know that," he said.

"I know two days ago someone tried to kill him but they got one of his sons instead," Horrocks said. He took a step toward Tinton but his shirt was caught by a guard standing behind him. "One of his *real* sons. The king only had three. Now two of them are dead."

"We're his sons," Tinton said. He sat back in mock relaxation, then inched forward again. "We're all of us his sons and daughters. The king has an enormous supply of children, if he'd only acknowledge us."

"He never will," Sari said.

Tinton sighed through his nose and folded his arms in his lap. "He's dead."

"You need him to be dead. That's the only way you've a claim on his kingdom, if he's dead," Horrocks said.

Tinton's mouth became hard. "He might be alive, though I doubt it. If he is alive, he will acknowledge us as his own. We'll make him see it our way. No father could turn his back on a family so earnestly seeking his favor. Bring out the doctor."

A short man with white hair was escorted to Tinton's chair. There was a deep, shadowy crease down the center of the man's forehead. A baldric of surgical tools hung across his white smock. His left hand was bandaged. He bowed curtly and shuffled backward. The crowd swallowed him whole.

"You kidnapped him?" Horrocks said.

"He came to me," Tinton said. "He knows the king will need immediate care if he's found, and he knows we have the best chance of finding him."

"How?" Horrocks said. "If he's alive, I'm the one who's going to find him. I know him best. I have the experience." Horrocks tried to take another step forward and was again checked by the guard behind him.

"I know about your experience during the Push. Everybody knows. I'm not the one who'll be looking. That would be unseemly. We've hired Guilfoyle."

"Guilfoyle, that fucking grave robber?" Horrocks said.

"Say what you want about Guilfoyle, but he never quits."

Horrocks looked at Tinton in disgust. "Guilfoyle."

"I hear you saved his life," Tinton said.

"During the Push," Horrocks said.

"I understand he's never forgiven you."

Horrocks didn't respond.

"I know the queen engaged you to find the king," Tinton said. "You need to find him more than we do. If you do find him, hand him over. It'll make for a smoother transition."

"Nothing's going to be smooth about this transition," Sari said.

"You need to find him. You have more to gain," Tinton said.

"That's not why we're here. I have nothing to gain," Horrocks said.

"So much to lose, then. Your Furnace. Your insignificant Furnace mine that relies on the king's protection. Without the king, you're naked. We all know what happens to a kingdom without a king. First it goes to shit, then it goes to the strongest person out there. That's me. I'll rape that mine of yours."

Horrocks rushed forward and was met by a tide of Bastards. "You don't know a thing, you brat," Horrocks yelled.

Tinton rose out of his chair and shouted Horrocks down. "I know what you paid for that mine. You will lose it to me."

The Bastards pushed Horrocks back. Sari whispered into his ear.

Tinton sat down.

"The queen," Horrocks said.

"The queen is hiding," Tinton said. "She has no power, no support. Tell her to stay hidden because when she comes up for air we'll choke her." He picked at the armrests. One of them came loose and he jiggled it with his fingertips. "Stay hidden. It suits her and her weak boy. I *am* the king's oldest living son."

"You're an illegitimate hopeful," Horrocks said.

"My mother was a Furnace whore. She serviced the miners," Tinton said. "All of us here have proof the king is our father. If we're hopeful, it's only for what's ours. Acknowledgement, and the inheritance of the kingdom."

Sari squeezed Horrocks' hand. She knew he was out of breath. He could try and hide it but she could always tell; it happened so often.

A few Bastards by the tables were shoving each other. A portion of Jupiter rolled into view, a bright crescent framed in the window behind Tinton. The planet always reminded Sari of a child's arts and crafts assignment. A glass globe filled with layers of colored sand. Somewhere around Jupiter would be his numerous moons, but the windowpane was cheap and made distinction impossible.

Calder came into the room. His rifle was gone. He held a rectangular gray box in both hands. A confusing array of capped wires sagged from the lid.

Tinton got off his seat, took the box from Calder and walked toward Horrocks. "Your Spot Drive," Tinton said. He gripped the wires like a lock of hair and pulled them out. Tinton cocked his head to the side and studied Horrocks' face, then lifted the impotent Spot Drive over his head and dashed it to the floor. "I hope you weren't planning on getting anywhere in a hurry."

CHAPTER 2

Calder walked Horrocks and Sari back through the umbilical. Laughter and poorly hushed whispers wafted through the tube. Calder stayed in the umbilical. Horrocks and Sari brushed past him without a word.

The *Moondrunk*'s cockpit was a dark, glorified closet. The darkness accentuated the fluorescent viewscreen. Two Bastards were seated in the flight chairs. One held an open tin of dog biscuits between his hands like a mug of warm soup. Both of Horrocks' dogs were sitting outside the cockpit, guarding the spiral staircase that led to the next floor. The second Bastard dug through the tin the other man was holding, came up with three biscuits and lobbed them toward the dogs. The biscuits dropped to the floor. The dogs—white Dobermans with blue eyes—remained still.

"I think they're clay," said the Bastard holding the tin. "No way these dogs are that disciplined. They're not real."

"They've been blinking, you fool," the other Bastard said. "That's how you know something's alive. It blinks." He grabbed another handful of biscuits and tossed them into the air.

"So they blink. Maybe they bark. Doesn't make them real. If I nail them in the face with a cracker and they move, they're real."

The dogs' blue eyes widened as Horrocks stepped into the cockpit. The two Bastards spun around to face the viewscreen. The first one dropped the tin as Horrocks lifted him out of the seat and threw him into the hall.

Sari knelt by the dogs and patted their smooth skulls.

"I'll get up myself," said the second Bastard.

"Please," Horrocks said.

Both Bastards hesitated when they passed Sari. She wore no makeup. Her bangs ended just above her eyes. The rest of her straight, black hair grew down to her elbows. A red cotton blouse called no attention to her breasts. It was clear to the Bastards that she took no pride in her appearance, that she looked good in spite of herself. She stared back at them and they turned away.

"You should put the heat on," the second Bastard said. "I can see my breath in here. Nice dogs. They're real, right? Such an unusual color."

"They're real," Horrocks said and escorted the Bastards to the umbilical. Calder was gone.

"Where did you get them, the dogs?"

"Found them. Twins," Horrocks said. "They were just a couple of stray bastards. Nobody wanted them."

"You think you're funny? You think—"

Horrocks forced the Bastards into the umbilical, closed the hatch and watched through the porthole as they scrambled aboard Tinton's ship. "C'mon, already," Calder said and helped them inside. The umbilical demagnetized and was drawn back to the *Res Nullius*.

When Horrocks returned to the cockpit the dogs were eating the loose biscuits off the floor. "No discipline," he said.

"None at all," Sari said. She sat in the pilot's chair and rubbed her sore shoulder.

"How hard did he hit you?" Horrocks kneeled between her legs.

"Not as hard as you hit him. I'm fine. Maybe a little purple."

Tulsa City-County Library
Checkout Receipt

Title: Counterfeit kings : a novel / Adam
Connell.
ID: 32345032886062
Due: Thursday, April 18, 2013

Total items: 1
4/4/2013 8:46 PM

To Renew : 918-549-7444
or www.tulsalibrary.org
Central Library

He touched her shoulder, massaging it lightly with his thumbs. She ruffled his short brown hair, then caressed his chin. Horrocks' face was haggard, yet handsome and serene. It was the face of a statue that had seen generations of torment but retained its hopeful expression; it often calmed Sari just to look at him. His skin was thatched with a dozen white scars that matched his ghostly pallor. Sari usually forgot they were there. She would never forget how he got them.

"Are you still out of breath?" she asked.

"You noticed?"

Horrocks brought his big hands down to her stomach. Sari lifted her blouse so he could touch her bare skin. "I won't be showing for a little while yet. It's only been a month."

"I know. I like to feel it. Like to think I'll feel a little heartbeat in there."

He took his hands away and she put them back, held them there with her own. "We've got to be careful," he said and took his seat.

They watched the Bastard armada pull away. There was a hiss followed by three jolts as the tether hooks embedded in the *Moondrunk*'s hull released their wires. The wires were sucked back into Tinton's ship. They looked like tentacles, swaying slightly at first, then whipping frantically as the loose ends were drawn inside. The armada rotated and flew toward Io. The smaller ships looked like retreating wasps. They formed a protective cloud around Tinton's *Res Nullius*.

"I didn't think they'd get involved so early," Horrocks said.

"It's not like you were avoiding them," Sari said and smoothed out her shirt.

"Wasn't seeking them out, either. They're going to get in the way." He used the cameras to track their departure. "I didn't know there were that many."

"Garbage attracts garbage," Sari said.

"Guilfoyle's not going to make this any easier."

Two of the Bastard ships didn't activate their Spot Drives with the others. They hung 2,000 feet off the *Moondrunk*'s stern like a pair of mismatched eyes.

"They're trying to be discreet," Sari said.

"If there's two we can see I bet there's four we can't."

"We've got a message," Sari said and tapped one of the buttons on the dashboard. A woman's voice came through the speakers above them. It was strong and spoke quickly: "Horrocks, you're taking too long. Where's my husband? The mines are—I'll come see you after you've picked up the Ringers from the Mining Annex." She paused. "We'll discuss further plans once you have the Ringers."

"I always hated that bitch," Sari said. "She's so damned presumptuous. No appreciation for anyone. Except you," she said and faced her husband. "She always wanted you. Even her Ringers wanted you."

"Not true," Horrocks said and grinned. "Taking too long? Doesn't she realize how long this could drag on? It's a fairly big region. If the king wants to stay hidden, I doubt we'll find him."

"You will," Sari said. One of the dogs put his head on her knee. The other was asleep at her feet. "Our biggest worry is not having a Spot Drive."

"We'll try to find another. Until then, we'll have to make do."

"Until then, I'm flying," Sari said.

"I'm a little rusty. It's been a while."

"You were never any good flying," Sari said.

"OK, we'll switch seats. Meanwhile Tinton's winch hooks are still buried in the hull." Horrocks stood up. "Those things are enormous. We'll never get them off."

"Better check the seals, make sure they didn't poke all the way through," Sari said. She used the exterior cameras to locate the hooks. "Got them. First one's outside the kitchen."

The dogs followed Horrocks and Sari out of the cockpit and into the main hallway. The hallway ran the width of the ship from port to starboard, bisecting the entire vessel. The kitchen was opposite the cockpit. It was ten by twelve and modestly old-fashioned. The cabinets and countertops were yellow with a drab steel trim.

"Tinton didn't mention the Ringers," Horrocks said and leaned against the sink. "He's got to be interested in them. They saw the attack. He must know the queen is damned interested in getting them back."

"Tinton may not want you to know he's after them. Maybe he wants them for his own sick reasons. Proxy abuse, murder. They look just like the king. Tinton could use them to beat out his frustrations. The Bastard was right. It is cold in here. Are you cold?"

"A little," Horrocks said. He was freezing. He slid his hand across a stretch of faux-wood paneling. "Heater's a little tender. Where's the scope?"

Sari opened a cabinet and found the device hanging on a hook. The scope was a mechanized monocle attached to a rubber cup. She handed it to Horrocks.

"Where was the first one?" Horrocks asked.

Sari pointed to the blank wall above the sink.

Horrocks pressed the scope's rubber base against the wall, looked through the monocle with his left eye and kept his right eye tightly shut. He adjusted the focus, increased the depth of the image and was able to peer through the first and middle layers of the *Moondrunk*'s hull. "The hook barely missed the middle wall. We're OK." He put the scope in his pocket and kneaded his eyes with his thumb and forefinger.

They left the kitchen, made a right down the hallway toward the exit hatch. The next room on the right was the common room. Horrocks flipped off the lights and did the same for the bathroom opposite the common room. Walking back, they passed the cockpit and stopped at the spiral staircase. "Next one's upstairs?" he said.

Sari nodded and climbed up to the top.

Except for the partial attic, the second floor was the topmost deck. This floor housed the master bedroom and the short hallway that connected it to the stairs. The bedroom door was closed. A few taped boxes were stacked by the wall.

"When are we going to unpack?" Sari asked.

"Why bother? We took too much stuff," Horrocks said. "Where is it?"

"Behind you, I think. Pretty high up."

Horrocks peered through the monocle. He didn't find the hook immediately.

"Are you going to fix it later?" Sari asked.

"Fix what?"

"The heat."

"I'll try. Maybe tomorrow if we have time," he said.

"Should've gotten rid of this ship a long time ago. You never treated her kindly." Sari sat on the floor, her back against the wall. The dogs came up the stairs and used their snouts to nudge open the bedroom door. "Stupid ship. Too many memories," Sari said.

"If we hadn't kept her we'd be stuck on the mine," Horrocks said. "This hook's safe. One more to go."

"It's in the cellar," Sari said and went downstairs. Crammed between the cockpit and the bathroom was a narrow door. Sari opened it and descended a long steel staircase.

"You should have gotten rid of her, but you didn't want to," Sari said over her shoulder. "It's like keeping your first girlfriend around to remind you of your youth. Or how you lost your virginity. Nostalgia. I hate nostalgia more than anything."

"Lissa Elbe," Horrocks said.

"Who?"

"Lissa, my first girlfriend," Horrocks said as he followed Sari down the steps.

The *Moondrunk* was ten years old. Horrocks had paid the shipbuilders a premium so he could watch them work. The premium bought him a perch in the foreman's office, a perch near the window that overlooked the shipyard. Thirty years old, rich enough to afford his own ship. Horrocks didn't want to miss the smallest detail of her construction. He slept in the damp office for months.

"Men think you don't trust them, watching all the time," the foreman said. His hair was parted down the center and he had only one arm. The other had been lost in a welding accident.

"If I didn't trust them, I would've used your competition," Horrocks said. He was captivated by the engineers who floated in the weightless dry dock. The ship's chassis had recently been completed and they had just started partitioning the rooms.

"Staying here again tonight?" the foreman said. "Where's your pretty girlfriend with all the tattoos?"

Sari turned on the cellar's lights. It was twice the size of all the other rooms combined. The floor and walls were lined with metal slats. The amber lights were recessed in the stone ceiling. A clean porcelain toilet squatted in the far left corner. Next to the toilet was a glass shower stall. Behind Sari, below the stairs along the back wall, were three closets.

Sari took the scope from Horrocks, cleaned the eyepiece on her shirt and handed it back. She pivoted to face the wall. "There," she said, pointing to the floor near the trapdoor that led to the emergency umbilical.

Horrocks used the scope on the floor, stood, and smiled. "We're fine." He stretched his arms to the ceiling and yawned. Sari hung the scope around her neck and reached up to kiss him. Her tongue parted his lips. Horrocks rested his hands on her hips.

She backed away. "We're not doing it here. Floor's too cold. I'm going to bed."

"I'll be there in a minute."

"No longer than that," she said and went upstairs. Horrocks took off his shoes and walked barefoot over the metal floor. He always enjoyed the sensation of walking on cold floors.

Back in the cockpit, Horrocks used the viewscreen to call up a broad picture of the Jovian system. Jupiter and, more importantly, Io. Horrocks brought the moon in closer. The king's mines were nine blurs bunched together 200 miles above Io's southern hemisphere. Horrocks' mine was a solitary blur fifty-odd miles from the king's. Got twenty days to find him, Horrocks thought. Twenty days from the *attempt*. That leaves me seventeen days. With a Spot Drive I could be back home in a day. Without it, fifteen, sixteen days, maybe. Have to go to the Annex and get the Ringers first. The Annex is in the opposite direction, even further from home. Almost 250,000 miles from home.

Bet the king hasn't been this scared since the Push, Horrocks thought. Probably reacted to the assassin faster than his bodyguards did. He's seen enough of them. God knows I did when I was guarding him. His Ringers have gone soft, otherwise they'd have prevented all this.

Horrocks set the coordinates for the Mining Annex into the navcom. "Estimated time 12 HRS 43 MIN" flashed across the screen. Horrocks put the rest of the ship to sleep, went up to the bedroom and closed the door behind him. The lights were on their lowest setting, just barely there.

"You didn't have to shut the door. No one else's coming in," Sari said.

"I've been on too many ships, picked up too many habits. This is the least of them." He unbuttoned his corduroy shirt and hung it on the doorknob.

"Get over here already," Sari said. She lay in bed. It was too dark to see her entire face. Horrocks used shadow and memory to decipher her expression. The blanket was pulled up to her navel. The tattoos that covered her exposed flesh were indistinct. They seemed to merge and shift and pool their colors. "I'm still cold," she said.

"That's because you're half naked."

"I'm all naked."

He stripped and joined her in bed. He kissed her ears and neck, ran his hands over her buttocks. Their breathing went up in tempo. She scratched his back, moved in close to him, grazed his thighs with hers. He gently squeezed her breasts. They weren't large, but they were very round and soft like padded globes of silk. He pinched her hard nipples.

She grabbed his left leg, laid it over her hip and stroked his penis. He kissed her shoulder, collarbone, chin, her mouth. She stroked him faster.

Their tongues swirled around each other like mating cyclones. He submerged his fingers in her swampy wetness, found her clitoris and manipulated it. His mouth came back to her bruised shoulder. Even in the dark he knew what tattoo graced the skin there: the face of Medusa, her hair of blue snakes unruly and vicious. Horrocks knew all of Sari's tattoos intimately, had kissed them all countless times, and each time wished that she wasn't so ashamed of them. The robotic joints that transformed her elbows; the flaming sun that warmed her stomach; the constellation of stars on one breast, a ring of moons orbiting the nipple on the other; a waterfall of fire down her right thigh, a cascade of ice down the left; an eyeball whose pupil was her bellybutton; jaguars, hawks, spells and landscapes; the stony arch with the hairy entrance just above her vagina.

He parted that arch and climbed over her. He rocked slowly and lowered his chest onto hers. She clasped her arms around him, twined her legs with his like needy vines. Sari hugged him closer, putting as much of her body in contact with him as possible.

She complemented his rocking with her own. "Slower. Slower, honey," she said.

He kissed her breasts again, entered her again, touched her again.

"Slower," she said.

HORROCKS WAS ASLEEP on the right side of the bed. The covers were clutched in his hands for fear that Sari would once again steal them during the night.

She got up and walked naked to the bathroom. She shut the door and the light came on. The bathroom's sole mirror was a rectangle high on the wall, high enough so she could see her head and little else. It was the only mirror Sari would allow. She despised her body. She hated the myriad interlocking tattoos and wished she had the strength to claw them off. The tattoos had been stained to her skin when she was a child. As she grew into a woman the pictures drifted apart like tectonic plates. Pink gaps divided some of the images. The stars and moons around her breasts suffered the most because she had developed later than most girls. By then those stars and moons had seen many years, and many men.

Why'd she put these things on me? Sari thought. The tattoos ended at her neck, wrists and ankles like psychedelic sleeves. The skin on her face, hands and feet was remarkably smooth.

Sari sat on the toilet-seat cover and removed a pen she kept hidden behind the tank. She used the pen's laser tip to trace the tattoo of a white butterfly, hoping the butterfly would fade.

Her mother had used a needle to put it there. She had been a Longliner maid, cleaning the rooms of families and entrepreneurs on their way to the Deeps. The trips lasted three months in both directions.

Sari's mom lost her job by sleeping through too many shifts. Mother and daughter were demoted to the lowest region of the ship. Most nights they couldn't afford a room and wandered the grimy halls for an unoccupied doorway to sleep in.

Out of desperation Sari's mother resumed practice of the one trade she knew: tattooing. She used her young daughter as a work pad, practiced on her and became quite good again. She stood Sari at busy intersections, laid a battered hat at her daughter's feet and stepped back into the shadows.

The passengers in steerage slowed when they passed by to admire the girl and some threw change at the hat. Sari's mother was soon able to afford high quality needles and ink. As the tattoos became more elaborate the people threw larger coins and sometimes bills.

Sari and her mother eventually saved enough to rent a room by the month. Bored, horny men paid Sari's mother to enter the room and watch Sari disrobe. The men sat on the floor and ogled her, marveling at the colored designs, the way each tattoo blended into the next. Though it was forbidden, the men would often grab her skinny arms and legs, turning them in their hands to see the full tattoos.

The men offered to pay for sex but Sari's mother never allowed it. That came much later, after Sari's mother died in a fight. Then there were no new tattoos, no money. The tattoos became a novelty few noticed anymore. Men and women would only pay to violate her body, not look at it.

Sari jammed the pen against Medusa. She hated Medusa the most because it had taken over a month to apply. "Sit still! Are you hungry? Sit still," her mother had said. They often worked well into the morning. Sari's shoulder bled continuously for thirty-six days and she couldn't move her arm for even longer than that. Medusa was one of the few tattoos unaffected by her growth.

She traced it with her pen but it wouldn't fade. She pressed harder and burned herself. She always burned Medusa. Sari dropped the pen to the floor, dragged her nails over the snakes, picked up the pen and burned herself once more.

CHAPTER 3

Horrocks went down to the cellar's main closet and wheeled out ten folded cots. He opened them up and filled one corner of the room with beds. There were no sheets, pillows, or comforters. Horrocks flushed the toilet, ran the shower for a few seconds, then bolted the locker beneath the stairs.

"We're almost there," Sari said from the top step.

"Be right up," Horrocks said.

SARI TOOK THE CONTROLS off auto and guided the *Moondrunk* manually.

"You should stay here. It'll be less complicated if I go alone," Horrocks said.

The Mining Annex was a hollowed asteroid filled with offices and warehouses that stored the fruit of the mines for exportation. Portable energy encased in man-sized tanks. The mines provided Earth with three percent of its annual power. The king held back his supply in times of surplus and flooded the market in times of want.

Sari flew into the gaping entryway. Metal studs ran the length of the tunnel. They were hobnailed with lights that helped Sari to keep her bearings and showed her where to land.

When they were down Horrocks asked, "How are you feeling?"

"Tired."

"Try and stay awake," Horrocks said from the cockpit's doorway. "I'll need your help to get the Ringers downstairs."

"I'll be here," she said and closed her eyes when he was gone.

Horrocks climbed down the *Moondrunk*'s retractable ladder.

The landing area smelled of sweat and sulfur. Loaded energy caskets were propped in the corners like dejected wallflowers. A grate the size of a tennis court stood to the side of the landing zone. The grate was crowded with miners waiting to be cleaned. Their coveralls and matching hats were thick with grime. The Annex moonlighted as a departure point back to Earth. Horrocks looked around for signs leading to a passenger transport but saw none. The miners stomped their feet, shouted jovially, shoved each other. Horrocks wondered if these men were abandoning the mines. Should I be concerned about my own men? he thought. Are they going to leave, too?

A short, heavy woman approached Horrocks. Her coveralls wept perspiration around her armpits and collar.

"Horrocks?" the woman said.

Horrocks nodded and they shook hands.

"I'm the foreman, Norwick. I'll take you about." She walked toward one of a score of tunnels that branched off the landing zone.

"You guys stockpiling again?" Horrocks said.

"No," Norwick said and laughed. "We had a pretty full crop this last season. Warehouses are sold out, so to speak. No more room so we had to move some caskets out by the landing zone. If we didn't have the laundry plant and water processing—This Annex is too busy."

"The mines are overcrowded," Horrocks said. "Whatever work you can do here—"

"I understand that, Mr. Horrocks. It's just a lot for me to oversee. And we're so far away from the mines. I'd feel safer if we were closer, but Jupiter's magnetosphere's too

21

strong there. Radiation disrupts the crop. How do you get around that?"

"I don't hoard it. I send it off straightaway."

Norwick used a handkerchief to smear the sweat off her forehead.

The tunnel narrowed and, for reasons Horrocks could not guess, it smelled like mud. "So what happened?" Horrocks asked. He wished Norwick would walk faster.

"Couldn't say." She applied the hankie to her forehead a second time. "No one was around to see it. Just the king, his son and the Ringers."

"And the assassin."

"And the assassin," Norwick said. "The king's aide, too. Some fool, but no Ringer. The king took his son and his aide, got on his Gunwitch and left."

"So he's alive, the king," Horrocks said.

"Oh, yes. He was when he left here. He was shot, though. A number of people swore to that. He was shot, but able enough to get on his Gunwitch and go."

"Where was he shot?" Horrocks asked.

"He was moving too fast to tell. Most people assumed he was killed in the attempt, and I haven't corrected them. If we told them he wasn't dead, we'd have a hundred good bounty hunters flooding in from the Deeps. A hundred good ones, and five hundred bad ones."

"We could get them either way," Horrocks said.

"Shame," Norwick said and shook her head.

The tunnel widened into a circular chamber 200 feet high. The perimeter of the room was lined with ten Precious Strongholds, their doors open. Above the strongholds were rows and rows of energy caskets; they wound their way up to the ceiling like the inner shell of a metal tornado.

Norwick led Horrocks to one of the open doors. "We keep the finest crop in these strongholds," Norwick said. "We don't even lock them because there's never any theft. The caskets are volatile so we've rigged these doors to close if the sensors detect any kind of sudden heat. They stay closed six hours."

"The Ringers got locked inside," Horrocks said.

"Yes."

"Why didn't they pull the king in with them?"

"You'd have to ask them," Norwick said.

"Soon as you hand them over," Horrocks said.

Norwick pointed through the doorway. "Here's where they were."

"Were?" Horrocks said and stormed into the room. The floor, walls and ceiling were segmented with hard, reflective tiles. The caskets rested on a rack of shelves in the back. These caskets were fatter than the ones outside, and purple instead of gray.

"You were supposed to hold the Ringers for me," Horrocks said.

"That's what the queen said three days ago." Norwick spoke evenly, trying to deflect Horrocks' anger. "The Ringers got locked in here after the attack, I don't know how. They were probably looking through this room when the shots were fired, and the shots were powerful enough to set off the lock protocol. The king was outside the room when the door closed. I managed to keep the Ringers a little while, let's not overlook that. They only escaped yesterday."

"Escaped," Horrocks said. "What kind of security do you have here? I thought this place was fortified. Your cargo—"

"All of our armaments are to prevent intruders, not escapees," Norwick said. She wrung out her hankie like a wet dishrag. "They got away. Would you rather we shot them down?"

"You could have crippled their ship," Horrocks said.

"This Annex is also maneuverable. We can get up to ten, fifteen miles an hour. Would you prefer I'd given chase?"

"When did you say they left?" Horrocks said.

"Yesterday."

"And you didn't tell anyone? The queen didn't mention this to me. Seems like the kind—"

"I've been trying to get her since then," Norwick said, raising her voice for the first time. She dried her forehead again. "Queen's too busy to hear from me. The day of the attack she told me to keep the Ringers here, to wait for you. Said during the Push you handled this kind of situation all the time. I'm sorry, I didn't think I'd need armed guards to make them stay."

"You think they felt safe here? Did you think they'd want to—"

"I don't—I—Now Mr. Horrocks—"

"Just Horrocks."

"This is no prison and I'm no warden. In my two years here we've never had a situation like this. We hold the crop from the mines. In two years the king never came once. Don't know why he came three days ago. I'd never seen him before then, not that I could tell him apart from those bodyguards. They look so much like him."

"The Ringers are made to look like him," Horrocks said. He paced around the room, knelt down, touched the floor, looking for evidence he could use to locate the king or the missing Ringers. There was nothing; the room was immaculate.

"Made. You mean bred? No one talks about them," Norwick said.

"Surgery, not breeding." Horrocks got to his feet. "You had guards on the door?"

"Unarmed. They had to wait six hours for the automatic lock to fold. I'd already spoken to the queen then. That's when she told me to hold them. My guards stayed with the Ringers, but once the Ringers decided to leave my men were no match. And my men are good." She wiped her face again.

"It's really annoying the way you do that," Horrocks said.

"Why do they make them look like the king?"

"How did they get away?" Horrocks asked. The queen will kill all of us, he thought. Kill us, or lose the mines. There's no difference.

"The lot of them came with the king in six separate Gunwitches. After they got past my guards it was just a short run through the tunnel to their ships."

"Five Ringers managed to knock out your men? After a security alert, it took only five?"

"Five? There were twelve Ringers."

"Twelve! Since when did he have twelve? I have to leave," Horrocks said and blew past Norwick. Last year there were only five, Horrocks thought. Why'd he add so many?

Norwick raced to catch up to Horrocks.

"Did the Ringers say anything to anyone?" Horrocks asked.

"No one. Nothing. Could you tell the queen—"

"I'm not covering your ass, Norwick. It's wide open at this point."

"Mr. Horrocks, please."

They came back to the landing zone. The miners were gone. Horrocks got close enough to Norwick to see the hairs on the tip of the woman's nose. "Which direction did they go?"

Norwick took a step back. "Toward Io. We tracked them for 22,000 miles. That's as far as our sensors go." Norwick's hand brought the hankie back to her forehead. Horrocks batted her hand away.

"They could be anywhere," Horrocks said.

"They probably are," Norwick said.

"What the hell does that mean?"

"I'm sorry, I'm nervous. We have the assassin."

"What were you saving that for?"

"Mr. Horr—"

"Show me," Horrocks said.

Norwick led Horrocks to a cramped bathroom in one of the lesser tunnels. The assassin, a man Horrocks recognized as Kleig, was in a stainless steel bathtub filled with ice and water. His long hair floated on the surface of the tubwater like kelp. There was a purple bruise that stood in bas-relief on his left temple. Horrocks recognized Kleig because they had both guarded the king, years before, well before the advent of the Ringers. Kleig had always been too aggressive and it surprised no one the day he accused the king's eldest son of treason and tried to kill him. The king banished Kleig to the Deeps. Here he is, Horrocks thought. Naked and frozen.

"A bunch of miners cornered him," Norwick said. "He took his shot from the caskets. The fifth or sixth level, fairly high up. Must've been hiding there a day, a week. Knew the king would be here. No, I don't know how."

Horrocks was staring at Kleig; Norwick took this opportunity to mop her forehead once more.

"The son must have inadvertently stepped in front of his father when the shot was taken," Norwick said. "The assassin climbed down to the floor to finish the job, but by then the Ringers were locked in the stronghold and the king was in the tunnel. Some miners got to the shooter first. Hit him in the head. That's the mark you see there. Then they smothered him."

"This is the best place you could keep him?" Horrocks said. "Get him out of here. Put him in a bag. Have two men carry him to my ship."

"I think we should keep him here," Norwick said.

Horrocks gave Norwick a stare that made her feel colder than Kleig. "Straight away," Norwick said.

Norwick and Horrocks parted ways outside the room. Horrocks was nearly at his ship when a man came limping across the grate toward him. "Horrocks! Horrocks!"

Horrocks waited by the *Moondrunk*'s ladder for the man to reach him.

"God, I've wanted to thank you again. Wanted to thank you almost nine years. My name's Aitch," he said and clapped Horrocks on the back. Aitch was bald and short and one of his legs was longer than the other. "I was on a twin-engine sleek loader during the Push. We collided with a five-engine loader. Got fused together tighter than a virgin." He shifted his weight to his right leg. "You pried the ships apart. I was in the boiler room. A column had fallen on my leg. You came down in that gold suit, lifted the column right off. Do you remember?"

Vaguely. Horrocks remembered it had been at the start of the Push, before the violence escalated from erratic raids to open warfare.

"Did you keep the leg?" Horrocks asked.

"This one's fake," Aitch said and lifted his right leg, shook his head, raised the left one, and smiled. "Sorry, I use that joke too much."

Two men carrying a canvas sack emerged from one of the tunnels and approached the *Moondrunk*.

"I'm glad you made it out. Sorry about your leg," Horrocks said.

"Are you kidding? I lost the leg, but you saved my life. Saved plenty of lives. Looked like a big golden angel when you lifted that column off me. A lot of lives. For a while, years, all I heard about was you." Aitch shifted his weight again. "I moved out to the Deeps a couple years after the Push but I came back in on the last Longliner. What're you doing now? Still working for the king?"

"I bought a mine instead."

"Oh. Wow."

"What made you return from the Deeps?"

"One of the Annex's Protocol Inspectors, she's out on maternity leave. I used to be an inspector so Norwick contacted me, asked if I'd come back for six months."

"You have any Spot Drives around?" Horrocks asked.

"*Spot Drives*? I haven't seen a new one since the Push embargo," Aitch said.

"They lifted the embargo a long time ago," Horrocks said.

"Still, they're scarce."

The two men carrying Kleig came up to Horrocks and Horrocks pointed at the ladder. They grunted and heaved the body up the steps.

"I have to go," Horrocks said to Aitch and shook his hand.

"Best of luck, angel."

Before he jumped on the ladder, Horrocks noticed one of the Bastards' winch hooks sticking out of his ship's underbelly. The hook looked like a giant toy jack. Horrocks climbed inside the *Moondrunk* and helped the men carry Kleig down into the cellar. After they laid the bag on the floor the two men stood around, admiring the walls. "Are you waiting for a tip?" Horrocks said. "Get the hell off my ship."

In the right-hand corner of the cellar was a door labeled "Operating Room." Years ago, in a fit of whimsy, Sari had stenciled "Dr. Horrocks' Operating Room of Horrors" on the glass. Horrocks left it up for a few months, then took a razor to the door and removed all the words but the middle two. He brought Kleig in and laid him in the shallow tub at the room's center. The tub was adjustable and had drains at both ends. A set of shelves circled the room, loaded with pure embalming fluid, saws, wax and towels. A glass freezer with ten slots for ten bodies took up most of the right wall.

Horrocks unzipped the body bag, put on a pair of gloves and reached for a drum of formaldehyde. He decided Kleig wasn't worth the effort, put the drum back and shoved the body in the freezer.

Sari woke up when Horrocks came into the cockpit. "Where are the Ringers?" she asked.

Horrocks told her. Sari flew out of the hobnailed tunnel and stopped the *Moondrunk* two miles from the Annex. "Twelve Ringers," she said. "Where do you want to go now? Wait for the queen?"

"She could be the one started all this," Horrocks said. "I'm not waiting for her."

"Why do we have to move so fast?" Sari said. "If the king's in hiding, he's going to stay where he is. He's not liable to move around once he's found a good spot." She played with the dashboard, calling up and canceling various programs. It was more mindless exercise than a search for anything useful.

"Norwick told me—"

"Who?" Sari said.

"The foreman. The foreman said she didn't know how bad the king was hurt."

"And Tinton's got his doctor," Sari said. She started the engine. "What did you do with Kleig?"

"Put him in the cooler."

"I'd like to see him. Been forever."

"He doesn't look too good," Horrocks said.

"Did you drain him? Embalm him?"

"He doesn't deserve it."

"So where do you think the king is?" she asked.

"He's on a Gunwitch. They're exceedingly short range. He'd never make it to Europa. He must be someplace between here and the mines. Between here and Io."

Sari pointed the ship toward Io, 250,000 miles away. "There are plenty of places between here and the mines," she said. "A dozen Ringers. That seems excessive, doesn't it?"

She brought the entire viewscreen back to the Annex. "Did the Ringers have Spot Drives?"

"I don't know, Sari," Horrocks said. He tried to hide his exasperation, but knew he could hide nothing from her.

"The king's hurt, maybe seriously. His Ringers are gone. The king could be *dead*, Horrocks," Sari said. She engaged the throttle and the *Moondrunk* sailed forward.

"The queen's going to want the Ringers, even if we never find the king," Horrocks said.

"What do you owe her? Are we doing this for her?"

"I told you why we're doing this," Horrocks said. He twisted to the side to fall asleep.

The dashboard beeped. Sari increased their speed with one hand, touched the flashing button on the dash with the other. The specs for another vessel appeared in the upper left-hand corner of the viewscreen.

"What's that?" Sari said.

"Guilfoyle. I had the computer scanning for his beacon."

"He's nearby?"

"Too far away to bother us. Looks like he's about where we met Tinton. They're probably catching up with each other."

Sari flipped through the cameras again. It was a nervous habit that Horrocks stopped commenting on years ago. Her sleeve had drawn back to expose the faded tip of a tattoo that wrapped around her wrist. She noticed it immediately, tugged on the sleeve and pulled it up past her knuckles. She cycled through all ten cameras again, then cycled back three. "More Bastards," she said. "They're being less discreet this time."

Horrocks shifted to the center of his chair. "How far behind?"

"Hold on." Sari enlarged the image. Blue circles and lines crossed and carved the ships. "Four of them. Three and a half miles away. Speed's increasing. Are you strapped in? We'll have to outrace them," she said and flooded the thrusters with power.

Chapter 4

Guilfoyle was suicidal. He didn't think about it that often anymore. There was a time, after Horrocks had saved him from the flaming tanker, when suicide was the only line of reasoning his mind could follow with any clarity. Soon he was able to build other thoughts around it, like branches laid against someone to be burned at the stake. In the seven years since his rescue, Guilfoyle had put down so many branches that he hardly thought of suicide at all. He accepted the fact that he was too weak to kill himself, too emotionally weak. But the notion was there, an arrow through everything he did or refused to do. For all the branches, Suicide's peaceful face still rose above the top of the pile. She refused to be buried completely. Sometimes she asked Guilfoyle to light the fire already.

After his recovery, after his salvaging business folded, he took a job in vermin control just to keep his mind off self-destruction.

Rats, he thought. Rats would be better than this. He was standing in his ship's upstairs storeroom, building a cage. He had gotten the parts from a storage shelter in the basement. There were four parts altogether, stacked on the floor. Each one looked like the side of a giant crib.

Guilfoyle scratched his bald head, reached for one of the grates and stopped to wipe his sweaty hands on his denim work shirt. He picked up the first grate and walked to the corner. He lifted the thick slat over his head and smacked it into the corresponding cavity in the ceiling. He jammed the second grate into the ceiling at a right angle to the first. They only came halfway to the floor.

Guilfoyle could see the miniature prison taking shape. It would use the corner of the room for two walls, the grates for the other two. The remaining grates waited to be locked into the floor below their counterparts to complete the prison.

Guilfoyle sat down, leaned back on his elbows. Still have to cover up the tanks, he thought. In a few minutes.

He would much rather think about work than do it, so he stayed there, patient for the inspiration to move.

His sister clanged up the metal steps. "Cleaning out the morgue?" she said.

Guilfoyle got up reluctantly, put one grate under each arm and completed the prison.

"You think that's going to hold the Ringers?" his sister said.

"It's a lot sturdier than it looks." He tugged on the bars, then went over the entire structure with a screwdriver.

"It doesn't look very sturdy," she said.

"Kitsis, don't make me repeat myself."

Kitsis strolled over to the pen. She pressed her head against the bars. "One toilet, that's it? Where are they going to shower?"

Guilfoyle lowered the screwdriver and looked at her as if she was simple. "Shower?" He tossed the screwdriver into the toolbox.

Kitsis smirked. "You actually think you'll find any?"

"I'll catch them."

"You used to be very good," she said. The smirk evaporated. "I won't compliment you for a long while so you might want to savor that."

"It'll keep me going," Guilfoyle said.

"You used to be very good. I wouldn't be surprised if you caught the king. What do you think the Bastards want?" One of the grates had a swing door. Kitsis pulled it open, stepped inside, pretended to be an inmate.

"I'll lock you in there. Money, same as everyone else. Money and legitimacy," Guilfoyle said.

"I'm surprised the Bastards knew where to find us," Kitsis said as she exited the pen.

"Me. They were looking for me," Guilfoyle said.

"People stopped coming for you ages ago," Kitsis said. She leaned her hips against the cage and crossed her arms. "They stopped coming when they found out you had nothing but this rotten ship."

"And a rotten sister."

"This ship is what's rotten. Rotting," she said, "like the corpses you used to steal."

Guilfoyle picked up the screwdriver and threw it at her. Kitsis ducked and it bounced off the bars behind her.

"I never stole one body," he said and kicked the tool-box over to the wall. "I returned the dead to their families. Plenty of dead men and women stuck in their ships. I was helping the families to heal."

"And charging them for the service."

He grabbed her shoulders with the ferocity of an eagle ripping fish from a stream. "I never let the bodies spoil. This ship may be decomposing, but I made sure that every parent got their sons and daughters back in no worse shape than I found them."

Kitsis uncrossed her arms.

Guilfoyle pushed her into the bars, turned around and rummaged through a corrugated box. He removed six iron manacles and dropped them on the floor. He rummaged some more and found a soldering iron.

"No worse shape," Kitsis said. "You're so lazy, I doubt you'd have taken the time to be so thoughtful."

Guilfoyle paused. "I never enjoyed it," he said. He plugged in the iron and began soldering the manacles high on the wall, outside the pen.

"Are those collars or cuffs?" Kitsis asked. "How many Ringers are you expecting?"

Guilfoyle grunted.

"I'm glad the Bastards found us—you," she corrected herself before Guilfoyle had a chance. "Found *you*. I thought we'd die on that moon."

"You would have. I'd have gotten out on my own."

"Sure you would have," Kitsis said. She stroked her stringy hair and checked it for split ends. "How come we didn't take those two boys with us? The ones who'd clean toilets for a buck. They didn't mind getting their hands dirty. You're gonna regret not taking them."

"I don't have the money to feed two more stomachs. You just want them here because you liked watching them touch each other."

"It was entertaining," Kitsis said.

Guilfoyle finished putting up the last manacle. "Maybe you're right. We should've brought them along. They'd have done anything for me. Just like you, Kit. You'd do anything for me, right?"

"Drop dead, Gil."

He chucked the hot iron into the box. He didn't care if it started a fire.

"What are you calling this ship now?" she asked.

"I've renamed her the *Honey Locust*. I like the incongruity."

"Am I supposed to be impressed you know one big word? My vocabulary maybe isn't so grand, but I do know that *honey* and *locust* don't go together."

"Help me move this," Guilfoyle said.

They pushed the box to the wall. "We're going to need the space," she said. "You're not used to live cargo."

"I want you to come up here later, sweep up some."

"What for?"

Guilfoyle shrugged. "Just get ready for dinner, then."

"Can't wait. Don't forget to cover up your morgue," she said and tramped down the stairs.

"Bitch," Guilfoyle said when she was gone. "I can cut you loose anytime. Who's dependent on who?"

He spat on his hands to loosen the dirt, wiped them on his shirt again and walked over to the storeroom's eastern wall. It was partitioned into fifty blue squares. Kitsis called them "Guilfoyle's graves" because she knew he hated that. Morgue is better, he thought, but preservers is what they are. Fifty memory preservers, temporary coffins. It was always very transient. Nobody stayed in here long.

He removed a black shroud from the shelf in the morgue's base. He suspended the shroud from hooks in the ceiling and draped it across the wall. The blue light from the cold drawers lit up the shroud like fifty fluorescent eyes.

Guilfoyle took the quickest route to his bedroom. Fucking ship has too many hallways and not enough rooms, he thought. The walls vibrated and leaked slippery fluid. Whole alleyways were unlit, others baked in hot drafts. Ceilings sagged. Floorboards were uneven. The air had a flavor that Guilfoyle could almost swallow: meatloaf, sour cream and bad fruit. Every inch of available wall space was crowded with crucifixes, empty incense trays and spray-painted saints. Stubborn souvenirs from the ship's past life.

Guilfoyle stomped down some rickety stairs to the next floor. He remembered when things were good, when he had his own fleet of ships and good men to steer them. A successful business, good clothes, all gone. Frustration grew in his chest like a balloon. Guilfoyle wanted to break something besides the ailing machines that surrounded him. He wanted to grab a ceiling pipe and use it to dent the floor, the doors and the crosses. He wanted to go from room to room in a violent fugue and trash every level surface. Only by turning himself into a crazed dervish could he vent his aggression.

Not on my ship, he thought. Cardinal rule. Never wreck anything on your own ship. It's foolish.

He had always been unable to tame his frustration. It was only until he became a salvager that Guilfoyle found a receptacle large enough to contain his anger. The ships. After the bodies had been taken off, and sometimes before, Guilfoyle would succumb to an orgy of vandalism. He tore through walls and floors, set fires, slashed and punched and shouted until whatever vessel he was in had been reduced to an open, smoking wound.

His hands were always bloody afterward. The splinters made his fingers look like fleshy pincushions. When he took his jeans off, he'd find they were filled with sticky semen. He never analyzed this behavior. He never analyzed anything he did. He knew that he felt better immediately following one of these bouts, and that was enough. The terms *motivation*, *repression* and *resolution* meant nothing to him.

Guilfoyle flexed his fingers and tried to exorcise his temper by stamping it out through his feet. He went into his bedroom at the end of the hall and slammed the door. The bed, unmade, was next to the sink which was next to the toilet, tub and shower. Guilfoyle took off his filthy shirt and threw it over his pillow. He washed his hands in the sink. He used only water because soap was too much of a luxury to waste on grease. As the dirty water spiraled down the drain Guilfoyle wondered what it would taste like later, when it was recycled. Or look like when he showered.

Guilfoyle ran his wet hands over his bald scalp. He looked at himself in the mirror, touched his fat hips, turned to the side. His chest and arms were thickly muscled, like a bouncer's. I'll never lose that, he thought. If I was taller, I could hide this fat.

Sometimes the sight of his own body could excite him. He enjoyed masturbating in front of the mirror. He took advantage of sex whenever it was available but he found other people's preoccupation with it mystifying. He never felt better afterward.

Guilfoyle turned on the shower, extended the shower curtain and stood beneath the spray. He used the water to scrub his underarms, neck, back and legs. He used soap solely for masturbation. He plucked the cracked bar of soap from its cradle above the showerhead and sat down on the edge of the tub. After he lathered the soap in his hands, Guilfoyle pumped his penis until he came. He had to reapply the soap four times before he climaxed. The lather turned gray as it cleaned his hand and his groin.

He replaced the soap to its rightful spot and saw that it was nearly used up. What remained looked like a curled yellow toenail. Better find some more soon, he thought.

Some of his frustration was gone. He shifted to face the spray.

The semen and soapy water formed a milky paste on the tub's floor. He angled the showerhead to break up the paste and wash it down the drain. He didn't wonder if the water recycler would filter out the taste. He knew it wouldn't.

Guilfoyle dried himself and put on a pair of boxers. He opened his closet door. Besides the denim shirt and pants, Guilfoyle owned three identical flight suits. They were orange and bulky and had countless pockets filled with nothing. None of the suits fit as well as they used to, when Guilfoyle had worn them to pilot hundreds of merchant missions between Earth and Mars.

He arbitrarily selected the middle suit. His favorite part of the uniform was the round metal collar grooved with treads for the helmet. He had asked permission to take three suits and matching helmets after he was kicked out. The company refused. Guilfoyle took them anyway.

Guilfoyle zipped up the suit and went downstairs. The *Honey Locust*'s cockpit was directly above the kitchen, accessible through a ladder to the right of the dishwasher. Guilfoyle climbed the ladder, checked the telescreen for messages and found none.

When he climbed back down he saw Kitsis sitting at the kitchen table. Everything in the kitchen—the table, the counters—was enameled in charcoal Formica. Guilfoyle took a tray of food from the warmer and sat at the head of the table. He peeled back the tray's foil lid and ate. The soupy meal had a pleasant chicken taste sabotaged by a dozen other gossamer flavors, each one of them stale.

"We need more trays," Kitsis said.

"I'll get them," Guilfoyle said over a mouthful of food.

"Hell, we need a new warmer." Kitsis picked up her glass and held it to the light like a scientist. "Look at this water. It's thicker than syrup and just as dark. Water's not supposed to have texture, Gil. You're not supposed to chew it." She took a big sip and gagged in the middle. Through clenched lips she said, "You can only recycle it so many times."

"Now you're starting to sound ungrateful," he said.

"I should be grateful for dry heaves and it burns when I piss."

"I'll check the filters. Maybe they're clogged."

"You use filters?"

"Enough, Kit." He loosened his belt a notch and scraped the bottom of his tray with his spoon.

"I can't eat with that thing looking down at me," Kitsis said and pointed to the ornamental bleeding Jesus that hung from the wall.

"I tried to take it down when I first got the ship," Guilfoyle said. "Nailed too tight. The whole wall would come with it."

"Lose the wall, then."

"Shut up and finish eating. I won't let you leave the table till you do both."

Kitsis took another drink. Her face screwed up as if she'd swallowed a dead insect. "This crazy fucking ship. The food stinks, the air smells, we can't even get fresh water."

"We can't afford it!" Guilfoyle screamed. "Where's the money? Are you gonna pay for it?"

"How much could it cost? Look at this," Kitsis said. She upended her glass and poured the contents on the table. Small chunks floated in the liquid like watery lint.

"You'd rather I turned us around, moved back to Europa?" Guilfoyle said. "You liked it there? Hunting rats?"

"Conamara City wasn't that bad," Kitsis said. "Generators only broke down once a week. It never got *too* cold. So they had a rat problem. What colony doesn't? Every ship that leaves Earth—Those rats paid for our food. I never said it was glamorous. You make it sound like it was so terrible."

"Hunting rats and laying traps," Guilfoyle said. "That was all good fun. Laying traps all day and drinking all night. That wasn't so terrible, right?"

Kitsis balanced her fork on the edge of her tray, pretending not to listen.

"Passing out in the bathroom of that grimy bar," Guilfoyle said.

"Sometimes I wish you'd lose your voice," Kitsis said.

"Holding court with your fat friends. Begging me for beer money," Guilfoyle said. He threw his tray into the sink without getting up.

"I haven't gotten drunk in two years," Kitsis said.

"That isn't the same as being sober."

"It takes my mind off things," she said. "Don't worry, I didn't bring any. God knows I should have. If anyone at this table needs liquid therapy, it's you."

Guilfoyle looked down at his hands. "You used to be beautiful."

Kitsis' face softened.

"Beautiful, once. For about five years in your twenties, which is a long ways off. Long before your looks drove off a cliff. Look at that," Guilfoyle said and pointed to her blouse.

Kitsis sat up. Her tight nylon blouse showcased her thick waist. Her nipples poked through the fabric like thimbles. There was enough cleavage between her breasts to lose fifty singles. She took her breasts in her hands. "They're still nice, Gil. Sometimes they still get me what I want."

"You're not a size six, Kit."

"Oh yes I am."

"Maybe you were, but you're double digits now," Guilfoyle said.

"I am not fat," Kitsis said.

"Then I guess it's your clothes, they're too skinny," he said and chuckled. "It's gonna take a lot more time exercising if you want them to fit again. I look at your shirts, I feel sorry, they must be in agony."

"What about you? That fucking costume you wear. You're not an astronaut anymore, Gil. They took that—"

Guilfoyle slid across the table and grabbed a handful of Kitsis' split ends. He cocked his fist. Kitsis stared up at him as if she was in control. Her eyes dared him to punch her. Guilfoyle stood like that for a full minute before releasing her. Kitsis fell against the table. She got back into her chair and picked up her fork. She tried to hold it steady but it trembled against her tray.

Guilfoyle sat down. "Don't disparage the suit, Kit."

"Fine, fine."

"I'm the one's looking out for you. I probably shouldn't. Not the way you talk to me. You're only my half sister. I don't know why I'm doing this at all. I could drop you any time, whenever I feel like it. Remember that."

"Sure," she said. "What about Horrocks?"

"He's good," Guilfoyle said. "His ship's in better condition than ours, definitely. I'm confident we'll find the king before him. The Ringers, too. I'm confident the two of us can work together and finish this business. You agree?"

"Yes."

"There are certain things he won't do, and certain things I'm not afraid to."

Kitsis used her fork to trap the last bits of food against the side of the tray and scooped them into her mouth. She walked to the sink and put her empty tray on top of Guilfoyle's. She ran the brown water to rinse them off. "How much are the Bastards going to pay you?" she asked.

"We're supposed to meet with them tomorrow," he said and cleared the crumbs off the table with his hands. "They'll give me some of the money."

"How much is some?"

"I'm going to buy a needleship when this is over. There are some people I want to even up with."

"You've got history with everyone. It's really sad," Kitsis said and mopped the sink with a dishrag. "You should let Horrocks win, stay out of his way to thank him for what he did for you."

"For saving me?"

"That's right," she said.

"For pulling me out of that ship with my face half-melted, my limbs charred?"

"That's right. You owe him," she said.

"He owes me! I wish he'd have let me die."

"Because you're too chicken to do it yourself. And don't ask me to do it for you again," Kitsis said. "I'll keep refusing."

"A year of operations. Stitches and grafts and transplants. You know how painful they were?"

"As painful as listening about this for how many years? Six? And you lost all your hair. Or was that before?" Kitsis said. "He saved your life."

"I'll pay him back."

"You're ridiculous, in that ridiculous jumpsuit."

Guilfoyle jumped her again. He dragged Kitsis from the sink, punched her in the face, threw her in the corner and kept her there.

CHAPTER 5

Horrocks was up inside the brains of the ship, attempting to fix the heating system. He stood in a closet whose walls were veined with a Gordian maze of pipes. A pot-bellied boiler was stuffed in the corner. He singed his hands the first few times he adjusted the boiler's controls so he took off his shirt and used it as a glove.

Even though he tightened three hose clamps and sealed hissing leaks in six pipes, Horrocks was certain the ship would be no warmer tonight. The pipes hated him.

Sari's voice came through the attic's intercom: "Come down to the cockpit, fast as you can manage."

"Be right down," he called out. He put his dirty shirt back on, shut the closet door, climbed down the attic's ladder and ran to the cockpit.

Sari was in the pilot's chair, her bare feet curled around the edge of the dashboard. She wore silver toe rings to divert attention from her overlong toes. That morning she had used her fingers to comb her hair and it had dried haphazardly. Horrocks found it carelessly sexy.

"It's a Gunwitch," Sari said.

Horrocks looked up at the viewscreen. The slender Gunwitch was shaped like a winged arrow. Her brown hull was striped green with oxidized-copper racing lines. The curved windows that girded the bridge were thick with light. Fat cannons were clustered on both wings and under the bow. The cannons were no longer active; at the end of the Push the king castrated all the Gunwitches to show his subjects that the hostilities were over.

"They won't answer me. Her trail's still warm, but she hasn't moved in hours," Sari said.

Horrocks eased himself into his chair. "See any movement?"

"None yet. Could be it's a derelict."

"A derelict Gunwitch?" he said.

"I don't think so, either."

Horrocks zoomed the cameras in. "I'm going to get the suit. I have to board her."

"Look at the exit hatch. No, not there. Angle it down. Further to the right. There. It's been caved in."

"The ship looks safe. If the king's onboard, this is all over. If not, we find some Ringers—"

"Just sitting there?" Sari said.

"No one drives the Gunwitches but the king or the Ringers," Horrocks said. "We're bound to find something useful here."

"Imminent solar storm," an artificially masculine voice announced over the ship-wide intercom. "Please take shelter in the bunker. Imminent solar storm. Duration of storm, thirty-one minutes. Please take shelter in the bunker."

"Fuck," Horrocks said.

Sari put on a pair of slippers. "The Gunwitch'll still be here when we get out," she said but hoped that it wouldn't be.

Horrocks gathered the dogs and met Sari in the kitchen. She opened the midget door next to the stove that led to the bunker. The bunker was a tube-shaped room hidden inside the propellant tank that fed the engine and both exhausts. The dogs followed Sari inside. Horrocks went last and sealed the door behind him. The *Moondrunk* was hardened against standard levels of Jovian radiation; the bunker was padded with expensive but necessary shielding that protected its occupants from less frequent but more serious threats like sun squalls that could churn the lethal magnetosphere into an armor-piercing riptide. The dense fuel in the propellant tank added further insulation.

Stone benches ran down both sides of the room. Horrocks and Sari sat facing each other. Horrocks was too tall for the room and his head scraped the roof. Under the benches were jugs of water, enough canned food for two days, and books. At the bunker's other end was a chemical toilet too small to be used in comfort or privacy.

"Half an hour," Horrocks said.

"These benches hurt my ass," Sari said. "I thought we were getting pillows in here."

"We're not in here that often."

"We're in here now," she said and placed her hands beneath her buttocks.

The dogs lay down in front of the door.

"Maybe we should just go back to the mine," Sari said. She had been agonizing over this statement for a day and a half and felt if she held it down any longer she would choke. Having said it, she was afraid of Horrocks' response. She stared at the bent spines of the novels by Horrocks' feet.

"Back to the mine?" Horrocks said.

"Doesn't the queen have people who can look for the king?"

"She's got us," he said.

"That's not true. Hasn't been true for a long time."

"Name someone else with my experience," Horrocks said. "What if the king's trapped somewhere? What if the Ringers need saving?"

"All they know is safety! The king's, the queen's, their own. It's what they do. Let's make this someone else's problem, baby. I don't want it."

"Who else?"

"Guilfoyle," Sari said.

Horrocks rested his palms on the bench. "That's not funny," he said.

"I get the feeling this is going to turn dangerous. The Bastards. Guilfoyle. All these people are going to collide with us sooner or later."

"Go back to the mine," Horrocks said. "Abandon—"

"Yes, abandon." She gave Horrocks a deep, angry nod. "The mine's never worked a hundred percent, but she's strong. She may not be easy on the eyes—"

"And we could go there and pretend everything's fine."

"We'd be safe," she said. "I'd be there now if you knew how to fly this thing."

"I pilot her just fine. Think about it, if the king's not found in fifteen days—"

"That foreman told you he was shot. You don't know how bad. He could be dead," Sari said.

"He's not dead, but we don't find him in fifteen days he may as well be. Fifteen days they'll declare him dead and the queen's too weak to keep everything together. The Bastards'll take the mines by law or by force." Horrocks put his hands between his knees and leaned forward. His legs were inches from Sari's. "We won't have the king's ships to protect our mine and we'll lose it. We have to find him. If we don't, we'll lose—"

"Stop," Sari said.

"If the Bastards don't come for our mine, Rouen will. He could starve us—"

"Stop!" she said and pulled her legs up on the bench. "Such a dark perspective."

"I've sacrificed more than I'll ever get in return for that mine. I'm going to do everything I can to keep it."

Sari's expression changed from contempt to exasperation. "I've sacrificed plenty myself. You're not the only one."

"I didn't say I was."

"Sounded like it. I hate that fucking mine, Horrocks. I know you don't like to hear it. I fucking hate the mine. The only reason I agreed to it was to stop you from chasing those floating crypts." She brought her legs in closer and put her arms around them. "Crypts that collapse and leak and implode."

"I saved a lot of people during the Push," he said and leaned back so that his neck was against the wall, his legs akimbo. "Worked hard to get that mine."

"Why?"

Horrocks ran his hands down his thighs. "I'm sorry you hate it," he said.

"I don't want to have my baby there. It's not safe."

"You just said it was safe."

"Shut up, Horrocks," she said and put her head on her knees.

They sat in silence. Horrocks listened to the fuel splash against the bunker.

"I wonder how the mine is," Horrocks said.

"Don't you think De Cuir can handle it?" Sari asked.

"It's a lot of responsibility," Horrocks said. He picked up one of the paperbacks and leafed through it.

"Where to next, then?"

"The king felt unsafe, he'd want to leave the area completely. Best bet would be—"

"The Longliner," Sari said.

"Today's the twenty-seventh. Next one leaves in three days, end of the month. We can make it to Longliner Station before then."

"Why do you feel you owe the king anything?" Sari said. "Someone does something nice for you once and you love them forever, no matter what. Porphyria's blackmailing you with guilt, with dead memories."

"I'd still be a drug mule if it wasn't for the king. So would you."

"That doesn't mean he's infallible. Doesn't mean I'd scour the universe to find him."

Horrocks ripped the book in half. "Do you know how many packets I swallowed?"

"They were too big for me to swallow. Guess where I hid them?"

"He got us out of that crappy life. We'd be dead now."

"I'm not denying that, but our debt to him and the queen is over. He saved us, we became their bodyguards. He saved us so that we might someday save them. So we could die protecting them."

Horrocks threw the torn book at the toilet. One of the dogs got up and used the book halves as chew toys. "This is about our mine, not the king," Horrocks said.

"I don't know why everyone calls him *king*. He's no fucking king," Sari said. "And how did he thank you for years of loyal service? He insulted you. Nothing regal about that."

"He didn't insult me."

"Asking you to become a Ringer? That's an insult," Sari said.

"He thought I would've been a good match 'cause we spent so much time together I could imitate—"

"That was just an excuse. He wanted to own you. Sick power play. Wanted you to look like him the rest of your life. Knowing how you feel about anything fake, to ask you that," she said and shook her head.

"I admit I was hurt. I didn't expect that."

"Nobody did. It's medieval. It was a stupid idea from the start."

"They're better bodyguards than we were," Horrocks said.

"It's disgusting. Who would want to look like the king permanently?"

"Or the queen?" Horrocks said. "Although you'd have been better off looking like her."

Sari laughed in spite of her anger, took off one of her slippers and threw it at Horrocks' face. "Porphyria never used her Ringers. We should have gone out to the Deeps.

You did good work during the Push, saved a lot of people, saved some money, but we should have left."

"It was too risky," Horrocks said, though whenever he defended that ancient decision he was shamed into thinking that his attachment to the mine was an overexaggeration. That it was just a ploy drummed up by his conscience to smother the admission that he'd made a mistake for not leaving immediately after the Push. Horrocks feared that he was wrong and Sari was right. They should have left. "Nobody knows anything about the Deeps. We got the mine. We were lucky to get the mine."

"And what did the king make you pay for it?"

"You may safely return to the ship," the intercom said. The door clicked open.

CHAPTER 6

Guilfoyle steered the *Honey Locust* toward Tinton's *Res Nullius*.

"Wouldn't it be easier to call them instead of going over?" Kitsis said. She was sitting in the copilot's chair.

"Tinton's paranoid of electronic snoops. Does everything in person."

The *Res Nullius* extended her umbilical. Guilfoyle climbed down the ladder into the kitchen. He stopped by the hallway mirror to admire his orange flight suit. I still feel like an astronaut, he thought.

Kitsis beat him to the exit hatch.

"You're not coming," Guilfoyle said. "I'm waiting for a response from one of my old contacts. If he gets in touch, someone's got to be here. Tell him you're my sister."

"Half sister," she said.

"Tell him *sister*. Not *half sister*. *Sister*."

Kitsis grimaced. "See if you can get us some water."

The Bastards finalized the umbilical's connection. They banged on the door to let him know, and Guilfoyle stepped through.

"A PLEASURE, FINALLY," Tinton said from his chair. Two women and three men stood behind him.

Guilfoyle's first impulse was to grin, so he grinned because he didn't know what else to do with his face.

"It was a hell of a task finding you," Tinton said. "I almost gave up."

"You won't be sorry," Guilfoyle said.

"What took you so long to get out here? Europa's not that far."

"Me and my sister needed a day to pack, couple days to prime the ship," Guilfoyle said. He played with the zippers on his pockets. "The woman you sent was stunning."

"A beautiful face makes for easy decisions," Tinton said.

Guilfoyle pointed behind Tinton's chair. "Those women there, are they Bastards, too? For some reason I thought you were all men."

"That's naive," Tinton said and bent over to rub his ankle. His eyes never left Guilfoyle. "The king was fully capable of having daughters. Anyone with the genetic credentials is welcome to join us. We're constantly searching for more of the king's children."

"Recruiting," Guilfoyle said.

"Wrong. Locating and verifying."

"You don't look much like your father," Guilfoyle said. "How do you plan to find him?"

"I think I'll have the most success if I can get hold of a few Ringers." Guilfoyle put his right hand into a pocket, found a forgotten pen and twirled it between his fingers. "They were there at the attempted assassination. They may have been behind it."

"That's what I think," Tinton said quickly.

"I'll get the entire story from them. Make them want to tell me. I'm sure the king's alive."

"A positive thinker. Very nice to see."

"I still have decent relationships with plenty of informants. I know how to listen, and what to listen for."

"You can stop tooting your own horn, Guilfoyle."

Guilfoyle's face became a shade darker than his flight suit. "I plan to sweep this whole area."

"That could take months," Tinton said. His tone caught the attention of the Bastards behind the throne. They stopped whispering to each other and focused on Guilfoyle.

"Weeks, in a proper ship," Guilfoyle said. "I need a new one. The only thing keeping mine together is a soldering gun and a light touch. I don't have a light touch. I'm afraid to push her."

"Out of the question," Tinton said.

"I'm only thinking of you."

"Let me think of me. It's all I think about. Worry about yourself."

"You've so many ships," Guilfoyle said. "I counted at least twenty. You can spare—"

"None. We'll need every one of our vessels when this situation comes to a boil. It's going to boil rather quickly." He rolled his head around the pivot of his neck. He stared up at the ceiling. "I'll find someone else to do this."

"No you won't," Guilfoyle said. He took two steps toward the throne. Tinton had forgotten to post guards behind Guilfoyle and now he regretted the oversight. Guilfoyle took another step. His voice grew stronger. "It would take three months to get anyone acceptable to come in from the Deeps. You wouldn't have come to me if you had other options." Another step forward.

"And Horrocks?" Tinton said.

Guilfoyle stopped advancing. "He's good. There's no question he has a talent for this kind of thing. So do I. Have you seen him?"

"Right where you're standing," Tinton said. He winked. "But we let him go."

"You should have killed him," Guilfoyle said.

"We took his Spot Drive."

"Not good enough."

"How do you plan on dealing with him?" Tinton asked.

"In my own way."

"He called you a grave robber. A lot of my brothers and sisters were opposed to your hiring."

"I'm sorry to hear that." Guilfoyle scratched his eyebrow. Suddenly his whole body was plagued with itches.

"They heard you ransomed bodies during the Push. Kept them back from the families, for money."

"That's a lie," Guilfoyle said and feared he'd responded too fast. He slowed down. "There were a lot of companies salvaging ships and bodies during the war. Mine was among the most profitable and that made me a target. A lot of rumors were started back then. That one stuck. I don't know why."

"It's sordid, that's why."

"It's wrong," Guilfoyle said. He took two more steps. "I returned the victims to their families. Some were dead, some weren't. The families paid me what they thought was right. That's how I made my money. This notion of me as a grave robber is completely false."

"But most of the people you found were dead," Tinton said.

"That's the nature of war."

"None of my concern," Tinton said and waved the subject away. "What will you do with the money if you find him?"

"Go to the Deeps," Guilfoyle said. His shoulders bunched with tension. I'm drowning in debt, he thought. Held onto my business after the war and lost a fortune. Lost more than I had to lose. Kept my fleet, hoping for the next wave of conflict, hoping someone else would be brave enough, rich enough to challenge the king for his mines. Waited too long. Sold half my fleet at a loss. A few of my trusted men stole the rest of my ships. Took them to the Deeps. They're rich now, so I'm told. I can't afford passage out there myself, otherwise I'd hunt and kill them. When this is done, what I'll do when this is done is sell everything I have, put all my money in a suitcase and take an outbound Longliner to the Deeps. I hear there's a lot of strife there. And if that's not so, I'll create it. "That's what I'll do. The Deeps," Guilfoyle said.

"What will you do there?" Tinton asked.

"Retire peacefully."

Another Bastard came through the door in the back wall. He handed a small suitcase to Tinton. Tinton put the suitcase on his lap. "Do you want to find the king?" Tinton asked. "My reasons aren't enough. I need you to want him for reasons of your own. A reason besides the money."

Guilfoyle forced himself to look away from the suitcase. "The war was over before I was ready. Still had a couple years left in it. The king ended it prematurely. I could have killed him for that."

"You don't get to kill him," Tinton said.

"I'm over that. If he's found, he'll have to answer to you. That appeals to me." Mostly, he thought, it's the money. "What are you going to be doing through all this? How come you're not looking for him yourself?"

"We're hated as it is. People would question our sincerity. Come here," Tinton said.

Guilfoyle had the irrational expectation that Tinton would slap him when he was close enough, but Tinton merely handed over the suitcase. "Find the king for me. Find him within the twenty-day deadline. He comes forward before then, Horrocks finds him before you, you'll wish you'd stayed on Europa. There won't be enough of you left to fill an urn. Here's a quarter of your salary. And there's a $100,000 bonus for every Ringer."

"Why do you want them?" Guilfoyle asked.

"Good luck to you," Tinton said. He shifted to face the Bastards near his chair and they spoke together in a conspiratorial murmur.

"What about any dead Ringers?" Guilfoyle asked.

Tinton made no reply.

"Thanks," Guilfoyle said and walked out feeling like an old toy.

After Guilfoyle turned the corner Tinton called out: "Hey Gilly, is it true you were hunting rats when we found you?"

The umbilical listed as Guilfoyle walked back to his ship. He looked up through the diaphanous roof. The stars blinked like a field of stuttering flashlights. When he left Earth Guilfoyle assumed that, being nearer to the stars, they would share with him some kind of reciprocal importance. They did not; during his time with the merchant astronauts Guilfoyle felt as insignificant as he had in Minneapolis.

This feeling intensified when he moved to Europa. Jupiter mocked everything, dwarfed everything. That was one of the first lessons Guilfoyle learned when he ended up there. The giant planet colored everything orange. It rendered the rest of the universe, even the almighty king and his mines, meaningless. Nothing compared to Jupiter.

Ransoming bodies, Guilfoyle thought as he continued on to the *Honey Locust*. It's the goddam families started that. Because they were cheap they made me look bad. Their reckless gossip's followed me around like a bad stink. Loose lips sink ships. And reputations. They must have thought I became a salvager because of my good nature.

During the Push Horrocks and his network always beat Guilfoyle to the most critical wrecks. Guilfoyle was left to feed on the hopeless cases. Busted ships filled with scorched bodies. Usually the decedent's relatives transferred generous sums to Guilfoyle when he contacted them. Their boys and girls had come out to the mines looking for excitement. Except it wasn't as romantic as they'd expected. Then came the Push. The king paid out salaries so impressive it made everyone myopic. Guilfoyle arranged to have the bodies shipped to Earth, and he earned a modest commission.

Most families were willing to pay. Others had to be reminded. Guilfoyle complained to the grieving parents about the expensive upkeep of his fleet, the market rates for hazard pay, the high cost of embalming fluid. By the end of the war he was weary and disheartened. When he contacted the families then, he expressed his condolences in a pat speech, showed them the corpse and told them how much it would cost to get back. Guilfoyle didn't think of it as ransom but a capitalist exchange, fair and equitable. Many families refused but eventually broke down. Some held out, and so did Guilfoyle. The war's abrupt end left him with more corpses than interested families. He had felt like a retailer who overestimated the demand for snow shovels. Now, in the heat of summer, he was loaded with useless stock. The bodies resided in the bottom tier of the morgue in a state of suspended decay.

Guilfoyle spun the wheel on the exit hatch and stepped inside the *Honey Locust*. When the hatch was sealed the Bastards retracted their umbilical and flew off.

Kitsis was at the kitchen table. Guilfoyle put the suitcase in front of her.

"No water?" she said, flicked open the locks and hauled the suitcase toward her. She lifted out packets of bills and thumbed them like decks of cards. "You look exhausted."

"We'll buy water, filters, some new food. All kinds of food," Guilfoyle said. He pulled up a chair and fell into it like a sack of flour.

"Look at all this money," Kitsis said. "The Bastards got this rich with their blockades? I never understood how they made it work."

"The second-oldest profession. Extortion. They picked on ships going to and from the Annex, stood in their way till they were paid off. It's all about inconvenience."

"What about guardship escorts?" Kitsis said.

"Only so many to go around."

"Maybe that's something we should've looked into. Blockades." Kitsis used the bills to erect a small green fence that divided the table in half. "You want a drink?"

Guilfoyle nodded. Kitsis went to the refrigerator, found two bottled club sodas and plunked them down on the table. "Been saving these. So all this money's from their blockades?" she asked. The bottles fizzed when she popped them.

"They've been doing it a while, but I think someone's backing them on this. Mining interests on Earth who hate the king is my guess. Same people who financed Rouen and the Push. They all want a piece of the Furnaces but there's absolutely no foothold." He sucked the bottle dry. "Rouen failed. Now they'll try it with the Bastards."

Kitsis took small sips, put the bottle back on the table after each one, savoring the clean taste in her mouth. "You got a call from some pervert named Fingersmith. He told me—"

"He talked to you?"

"If you'd let me finish, I'll tell you what he said. First he hit on me, then he gave me the tag for the *Moondrunk*'s silent beacon. It was so long I didn't write it down but I put it in the navcom. That should be good enough."

"It is."

"Didn't you use Horrocks' tag during the Push?" she asked.

"I never wrote it down either. I can't tell you how many times the navcom's crashed since the Push. Here, I want you to monitor this frequency," Guilfoyle said, wrote a number on one of the green bills and slid it over to her.

"Why?"

"You've proved you can handle responsibility," he said.

"No, why this number?" She allowed herself another sip.

"It's a number the Ringers might use. Their Mayday frequency."

"Who would they call to help them?" Another sip. She protected the bottle from Guilfoyle by grasping the dewy neck with both hands.

"The queen. Other Ringers. Guards from the mines."

"Where'd you find this number?"

"It found me," Guilfoyle said. "I always thought it was just rumor, but maybe it's not."

"And you just remembered about it now?"

"I didn't think I'd have time to fly the ship and concentrate on this. Now I won't have to. You've just proved it to me. Fingersmith never talks to someone he doesn't know. I was hoping he wouldn't call when I was out. He talked to you. It's a sign of good luck. We're leaving," he said, opened the trapdoor in the kitchen's ceiling and climbed the ladder into the cockpit.

"I'll stay down here with the money," Kitsis said. She drained the rest of the bottle in one huge gulp.

Guilfoyle sat in the pilot's chair and used the navcom to access the number Fingersmith had given Kitsis. During the Push so many ships went missing that an edict was passed demanding that everyone equip their vessels with a silent beacon. The beacons could only be purchased from the king and each was unique. They were also sinister; once installed they plundered the host ship's directional capabilities and became the new compass. Clever captains who illegally disconnected their beacons were left with fatally confused navcoms.

Guilfoyle's navcom located Horrocks' ship two hours later. He yelled down through the cockpit's trapdoor: "Kit! Buckle in. Spot Drive in a few seconds."

"I can't right now, Gil. Wait ten, twenty minutes."

Guilfoyle programmed the Spot Drive to leave him near the *Moondrunk* but not on top of her. He sat back. His fancy chair had been salvaged from one of the war's damaged hulks, as had many of the *Honey Locust*'s finer trimmings. The chair was Guilfoyle's favorite acquisition. It had a bucket seat, with black leather that had been broken in by someone else yet fit Guilfoyle's body perfectly. Its safety harness came up between his legs, then around his hips to buckle into the seatback. Guilfoyle hated to have his shoulders pinned; he liked to move from control to control in a crisis.

The Spot Drive engaged silently. Guilfoyle felt a painful urge to urinate. The tiny stars on the viewscreen became bright, quivering flares. The turmoil in Guilfoyle's stomach and throat insisted he was in free fall but Guilfoyle knew the ship was shooting forward because he could feel a horde of invisible hands shoving his shoulders and pelvis into the seat.

The stars faded back into diminutive pinpoints. The pressure in Guilfoyle's bladder was gone. He checked his pants; he always checked his pants after the Drive stopped. They were dry.

Guilfoyle rolled his seat closer to the dashboard and surveyed their new location.

"Are we out yet?" Kitsis said from the kitchen.

The *Honey Locust*'s Spot Drive was poorly maintained and it overshot the destination; it took Guilfoyle half an hour to find Horrocks. Guilfoyle brought the *Honey Locust* in at a safe distance. The *Moondrunk* was approaching another ship, an obvious wreck. A Gunwitch. Guilfoyle's scrotum stirred. Fingersmith, right on the money, Guilfoyle thought. He'll be very demanding next time I see him. That'll be soon. He'll want a percentage.

Guilfoyle ran to the basement and watched Horrocks through the *Honey Locust*'s only full window.

Kitsis was upstairs, screaming, "Where are you? Guilfoyle? Guilfoyle!"

"Shut up!" Guilfoyle said.

Kitsis found Guilfoyle by the window a few minutes later. She stood on her tiptoes to see over his shoulders.

The Gunwitch was inert. The *Moondrunk* circled it once, then a second time more slowly. She stopped outside the Gunwitch's dented exit hatch. "Now that they've spread the Gunwitch's legs, Horrocks is probably suiting up to go inside," Guilfoyle said.

White glare glinted off the *Moondrunk*'s windows. Guilfoyle counted twenty-three of them. What the hell does he need so many for? Guilfoyle thought. One window's enough.

"He'll have to cut his way in. No way an umbilical's going to work on *that*," Kitsis said. "What does Horrocks need all those windows for?"

"That's a stupid question. Now shut up, I want to watch him work," Guilfoyle said.

Sari found Horrocks in the cellar. "I've parked over their bow," she said.

Horrocks opened the tall locker under the cellar's stairs. Sari closed it. "You promised me you'd live carefully. I spent the war afraid you'd die tomorrow."

His fingers remained on the locker's handle. "This isn't nearly as dangerous." He gently brushed her aside.

"I want to give birth somewhere safe," she said, touched his chest and kissed him.

He kissed her back. "I promise," he said.

"I'll get your tools," she said and left.

Horrocks opened the locker. Inside was a spacesuit plated in gold leaf. During the Push Horrocks shined it once a week so that it would be blindingly radiant in the feeblest of light. The clean, golden suit calmed the most tenuous survivor, often shocking them into a peaceful stupor. From their beds on the hospital ships, days or weeks later, they would tell Horrocks that his appearance was like a biblical revelation. He had polished and oiled it before leaving his mine. The cellar's amber lights limned the armor with a string of halos.

Horrocks stepped into the suit, reached around and tightened the clasps. The servos in the gloves and joints whirred like muffled drills. He tipped the helmet off the top shelf, caught it, and walked upstairs.

Sari waited by the exit hatch. "I'll control the wires," she said. He walked over to her and she clipped a wrench, torch and handheld buzz saw to his belt.

"I'll cut a small hole in the hull, above their exit hatch. Angle the ship and put the umbilical over that," he said and fitted the helmet over his head. He rotated it half an inch and it clicked into place.

Sari kissed the bottom of his helmet and left the wrinkled imprint of her lips. Two hooks dangled from wires on the wall. Horrocks crouched down. Sari affixed the hooks to his suit.

"I'll be right back," he said as he got to his feet.

"I'll be right here," Sari said. She closed a seldom-used second door, making a pressure lock of the exit hatch. She winked at Horrocks through the door's small square window.

Horrocks pulled the outer door open and looked out on the Gunwitch. Done this a hundred times, he thought as he straddled the doorway.

The darkness always gave him vertigo. Its lack of substance and texture was disconcerting. The Gunwitch seemed to be fading.

"Honey, could you open the lights?" he said.

Sari responded through the speaker in his helmet: "Got it."

The reflection from the Gunwitch burned his eyes before his visor could compensate. He jumped and sailed in silence for ten seconds, the two wires behind him like marionette strings. The boots gave him purchase on the Gunwitch's hull and Horrocks went down on one knee to kill his momentum.

"Made it," he said.

"I can see."

He walked toward the bow and stopped on the section of hull just above the ship's entrance. "I can feel banging coming from inside the ship. It's vibrating through my boots."

"That's encouraging. Hurry up."

He knelt down, took the buzz saw in his hands and cut a crude hole in the ship's skin. Throughout the Push his diamond saw had minced a hundred hulls with ease. This hull was no different.

Horrocks removed the hooks from his suit and fastened them to the hull. Sari brought the *Moondrunk* around on her side. The umbilical used the wires as a guide; it sidled toward Horrocks like a hollow worm and enclosed him completely. After a few moments Sari said, "It's sealed."

Horrocks put the saw back on his belt and lowered himself through the hole.

"Please hurry up," Sari said. "I've just scanned her. No Spot Drive. Shit."

Horrocks was inside another pressure lock. The walls were bordered with iridescent bars that had lost most of their color. He opened the door, walked into the ship and felt as if he'd entered a haunted house. He didn't see any Ringers but he was uneasy with the dread that they would attack him from behind. The helmet blocked his peripheral vision, forcing Horrocks to turn constantly.

He strode to the command center. Eight Spartan seats ringed the captain's elaborate chair. Each seat was equipped with a console and collision rail. The walls were papered in beige. The room was small enough that Horrocks covered every detail in less than five minutes. Healthy green plants were suspended in pots from the ceiling near a far door.

"How's the atmosphere in here?" he asked.

"Breathable. Fine," Sari said.

He took off his helmet and clipped it next to the saw on his belt. The first thing he heard was a wet punching sound. "My name is Horrocks," he called out. "Can you hear me?"

No one. No answer. That punching sound again.

He walked over to the plants and tried the door. It was locked, or busted on purpose. Horrocks hoped that the king was on the other side of the door. He needed to get back home. It would alleviate some of his tension with Sari. And the mine would not keep long without him. Horrocks knew more about the Furnaces than anyone on his staff. Without his attention, the jury-rigged mine was destined to sputter and collapse. The men Horrocks could afford were loyal but untalented; the king hired the best and kept them close. Horrocks didn't mind the work because it kept him busy. It was dangerous but profitable. *Busy* and *profitable* had no meaning this far from home; *dangerous* was the only word with definition. Horrocks prayed that the king was still alive, but part of him believed he was already dead. It was the part of himself Horrocks hated listening to because it was always right.

Horrocks increased the voltage to his arms. The suit crackled with static electricity. He raised his fists and broke through the door.

Horrocks thought he saw the king and an enormous sigh escaped him. The Ringer was so precise a replica that for a few gleeful seconds Horrocks assumed his task was over. The man looked to be in his early seventies. His hair, steadfastly black, was pulled back in a severe ponytail. He had a slight build, compensated somewhat by a rigorously tailored suit that gave the illusion of bulk. His teeth were all slanted in the same direction, making it appear as if his jaw was on crooked. Then the Ringer spoke and put the charade to bed. No amount of technological wizardry had ever duplicated the king's voice.

"Horrocks," the Ringer said. He was standing in a tight hallway. He had been punching the wall. His knuckles were peeled raw.

"I'm taking you out of here," Horrocks said. "Your ship's crippled."

"Not crippled. She's a piece of junk. Gave out not two days from the Annex."

Horrocks saw a dead Ringer at the end of the hallway. "What happened to him?"

"Last night he starts raving about the Mayday frequency. He'll call for help. I tell him he uses that, we'll both be dead. Wouldn't listen. I had to stop him. I hit him too hard."

"Where are the other Gunwitches?" Horrocks asked.

"The good ones filled up fast and we got stuck with this clunker." He wiped his face and left red streaks on his brow. "This crummy clunker that stalled out."

The Ringer collapsed against Horrocks' leg. "I'm exhausted, Horrocks. Got nothing better to do than punch the wall 'cause it makes me feel better."

The Ringer smudged Horrocks' golden leg, so recently polished and pristine, with fingerprints and blood.

Horrocks pushed the man away. "Which direction did the others take off in?"

"Which direction. Who the hell knows where we're facing?" He used the wall to help himself stand. "You'll protect me, right Horrocks? You will?" He came forward again, as if he would give Horrocks a hug.

Don't have time for this, Horrocks thought. He moved forward in a blur and knocked the counterfeit king unconscious. Horrocks caught the man by the armpits and stumbled into the dead Ringer. This Ringer's skin, once the same ruddy color as the king's, was swollen and purple. His teeth, painstakingly slanted to mimic the king's, were chipped and knocked inward. His clothes, so carefully chosen, were tattered and stained.

I know he isn't the king, Horrocks thought but the sight of the dead Ringer gave Horrocks a hiccup of mourning. He's not the king, Horrocks thought. Only a likeness. It's what his death represents, what the death of the king will bring. Instability, collapse, the inevitability of another war.

He carried the unconscious Ringer to the command center and propped him up in the captain's chair.

"Sari?" Horrocks said. "Hello, Sari?" The Ringer slipped out of the chair. Horrocks put him back and walked deeper into the ship, through the door at the foot of the dead Ringer.

The remainder of the rooms were aligned along the port side of the ship in railcar fashion. Beige furniture was bolted to the floor. Dirty clothes were draped over chairs. One sink was running. There were no clues Horrocks could use. "Sari?" he said. He stood completely still as he waited for her response. None came.

He retraced his steps to the deserted cabin.

"Hey hey, it's Horrocks," Guilfoyle said. He was going through the unconscious Ringer's pockets.

"That's my Ringer," Horrocks said.

Guilfoyle put his hands up defensively and took half a step back. "I'm not going to fight you for him."

Horrocks moved between Guilfoyle and the Ringer.

"I watched you come inside. Terrific work, very fast," Guilfoyle said with genuine admiration. "I could never work that quickly. Not without making careless mistakes."

"You got in here pretty fast," Horrocks said.

"I cheated."

Their eyes locked and neither was willing to break it off.

"You look much better than the last time I saw you," Horrocks said.

Guilfoyle held a finger in Horrocks' face. "A year of operations. One after the other for an entire year. Seven, eight a week. They tore my face apart. The fire took all my hair." His smile was lopsided. "I never thanked you for saving me. It really turned my life around."

Guilfoyle wagged his finger. Horrocks pushed Guilfoyle's hand to the side.

"You fucking sycophant," Guilfoyle said.

"Still in business, undertaker?"

"Don't be flip. It's clichéd. How's the painted lady?"

Horrocks carried the unconscious Ringer over his shoulder and walked toward the pressure lock. "Tell the Bastards they'll inherit nothing." Horrocks slowed at the door and turned around. "There's a dead Ringer in the next room. He's yours. That's what you're good for." He slammed the door.

Horrocks brought the Ringer onto the *Moondrunk*, retracted the umbilical and the wires, and shut the hatch. "Found Guilfoyle?" Sari said. "He came under the keel of the Gunwitch. There was a second exit hatch we missed. He fooled the proximity alert and clogged up my audio. I could hear you. Couldn't respond, though. His ship's in such bad condition when I first noticed her I thought it was a stray derelict."

They both carried the unconscious Ringer downstairs and laid him out on one of the cots. "Want me to stay down here with him?" Sari asked.

"No, you should get us moving."

"Same direction?"

"Toward Longliner Station," Horrocks said. "Go to the cockpit. I'll stay here till he wakes up."

Horrocks removed his suit and locked it in the closet. The Ringer stirred and Horrocks joined him on the cot. "You'll stay down here," Horrocks told him. "It's safe. You'll be home in a couple days. There's the toilet, the shower. I'll get you some books if you like. My wife and I will bring you your food."

"I'm going to suffocate in your cellar."

"I'll find you some fresh clothes."

GUILFOYLE STAYED by the Gunwitch's command center. He felt as if his body was sweating fire. Fuck you, Horrocks, you're so damned smart, Guilfoyle thought. He was standing right here. Right here. I should've hit him. I had every chance.

The muscles in Guilfoyle's arms twitched. He wanted to break every window, pick up the nearest chair and pound the Gunwitch into scrap. Better yet, I should get my tools, he thought. My bats. Shit, I've got no time for this.

He walked through the whole ship and found nothing useful. He considered leaving the dead Ringer to spite Horrocks, but couldn't. He might have future value. Guilfoyle's years as a salvager had taught him that. Plus Tinton's $100,000, he thought. Guilfoyle put the body over his shoulder and carried it back to the *Honey Locust*. The Ringer swayed like a stoned dancer and drooled a mixture of blood and bile.

Guilfoyle stepped over Kitsis who knelt on the floor in a hallway adjacent to the engines. Her hands were smeared with black oil. The wall's outer panel had been removed. Five metal filters were propped in her lap. She scrubbed them with dishwashing detergent because that was all they had.

"If you didn't use such cheap fuel, I wouldn't have to clean these disgusting things every day," she said. "Horrocks left."

"He doesn't have a Spot Drive," Guilfoyle said.

Kitsis stopped for a moment to look up at him. "That's ridiculous."

"Tinton stole it, or broke it. I forget."

Kitsis pointed at a black puddle by Guilfoyle's feet. "Whoever it is you're carrying, he sprung a leak."

"I'll be upstairs," Guilfoyle said and went to the storeroom. He dropped the Ringer on the floor near the cage. He took down the black shroud that covered his morgue, opened a freezer on the highest shelf and pulled out the metal slab. Guilfoyle stripped the Ringer and swung him onto the slab; the cold body stuck to the colder surface. Guilfoyle found a tube of rubber cement and, starting with the mouth, glued the Ringer's orifices shut to prevent leakage. When the cement dried he injected the Ringer with a rapid decoagulant to melt clots and thin the blood.

"Hot up here," Guilfoyle said and randomly opened ten of the morgue's cubicles. A light mist evaporated into the air. He unbuttoned his shirt and wheeled over the embalming apparatus.

The apparatus consisted of two tanks on a rolling dolly. Guilfoyle inclined the slab, used a tube from the larger tank to puncture a vein in the Ringer's ankle. Gravity brought the man's blood through the tube and into the tank. The tank had to be emptied twice. When the body was dry, Guilfoyle plugged the wound in the man's ankle with the cement. He inserted the tube from the smaller tank into the Ringer's neck. Guilfoyle waited a few minutes for the ankle cement to harden, squatted on the floor and cranked the machine's lever. Yellow liquid squirted through the tube to seed the Ringer's deflated body. The liquid was home-brewed embalming fluid. Formaldehyde, glycerin, motor oil, alcohol and pulverized gravel. Guilfoyle used the gravel as filler because the fluid was so expensive and the bodies needed so damn much of it. He justified this necrophilic sleight of hand by arguing that the gravel gave the bodies more substance, made them more lifelike in their death.

One regrettable side effect of this potion was jaundiced skin tone. This discoloring had to be explained to the families. They always acted as if Guilfoyle had delivered them a chipped armoire.

Guilfoyle cranked the lever again. Wish Horrocks would go, he thought. Actually, maybe it's good that he's here. He might find the king before me and then I can steal him away. But I hate to be rushed. I hate competition.

Guilfoyle became aggravated when the tank ran out of fluid. He yanked the tube out, shoved the apparatus toward the closet and refilled the canister with more of his funereal moonshine. When Guilfoyle stuck the tube back in the man's neck he didn't notice that it began to slip out a moment later. Guilfoyle spun the crank and diluted embalming fluid spewed from the neck. Guilfoyle didn't have the energy to clean it up. He jabbed the tube halfway through the Ringer's throat, gave the crank a healthy turn, and left.

AN HOUR LATER Horrocks brought the Ringer up to the kitchen. Sari stood next to the stove and boiled water for tea.

Horrocks said, "What happened at the Annex?"

"Can't we talk about something besides the king?" the Ringer said.

Horrocks seized the Ringer's wrist and pulled him over.

"Ow, fucking hurts."

"The king," Horrocks said.

"The king's gone. Will you let go? He had a six-hour lead. I knew we'd never track him. That's assuming he's still alive, which I'm not so sure."

Horrocks released the Ringer's wrist and took a hot mug from Sari. She offered one to the Ringer. He shook his head, rubbed his tender wrist and said, "Put it on the table."

"Ask me, don't tell me," Sari said. The hot tea in her hands became threatening.

"Could you put it on the table, please?" the Ringer said. He swiveled to face Horrocks. "The king was our first loyalty. He's given us so much in return for this," he said and pointed to his face, "and for some other small sacrifices we've had to make." He arched his back. The bones cracked rapid-fire. "This is our first bit of freedom in years. Some Ringers think he's dead, some don't. Some, like me, see this as termination of services."

"Your duty is to protect the king," Horrocks said. "He'll need you now most of all."

Sari sat down with them. "So you're using the king's disappearance as an excuse to forfeit your debt."

The Ringer's ingratiating smile vanished. "Lady, don't question my loyalty. I've taken three bullets for that man. Been crushed, burned, stabbed, and spat on which to me was the worst of all. A bloody wad of spit in my eye. This time they killed his son. Got close enough to kill *him*. It's a caliber of assassin we haven't seen since the Push. We'd gotten lazy, all of us. Always on the lookout for physical threats, some nut who thinks he's been snubbed by the king, some guy with a handgun or a knife. We didn't think about snipers anymore. Didn't think about anything distant. Even the king was lazy. He used to demand we sweep any locale he was going to visit. I'm scared."

He took a sip of tea and scalded his tongue. "You didn't have to knock me out, Horrocks."

"You're not as helpless as you pretend," Horrocks said.

"I failed the king. I never want to see him again. Not because I wish he was dead, but because I'm ashamed."

Horrocks couldn't tell if that shame was genuine. Sari was certain it was false.

"I'm just rationalizing," the Ringer said. "We know it'll be a week, two at the outmost, before we're hunted down. That's why we couldn't stay at the Annex. Norwick told us you were coming but we just couldn't stay. Some of the Ringers were impatient to find the king themselves, and the rest of us we didn't feel safe. Something like this happens, a king gets killed, his bodyguards are next, especially if they look and act just like him."

Horrocks warmed his hands on his mug. "Where did the other Ringers go?"

"I already said, I've no clue. Toward the mines. We split up so we wouldn't become one big target."

"What did you see? How did the son die?" Horrocks asked.

"Haven't you found any of the others? I'm sure they saw more than I did."

"Tell me how it happened," Horrocks said.

"We'd gone to the Annex because the king got an urgent message the caskets were unbalanced. A new impurity in the crop. Seems that was probably a ploy. King took us all with him, including his son who should have had Ringers of his own but he fancied himself a progressive, was going to rule all different when he took over."

"How'd he die?" Sari asked.

"Sniper put a bullet in the kid's throat. *Kid*. He was twenty-eight. It butterflied his neck. Half of us were already inside the stronghold, which is how we go into any room. Half of us first, then the king, then the rest. All of us heard the shot. I turned and saw the kid's neck explode, saw the king's arm get ripped by a bullet, too."

The Ringer winced, then shrugged his shoulders. "The door started closing. It was very confusing, all of us jammed in that little doorway. Someone yelled 'I got him' but obviously they were wrong. The door started closing and we helped it. Heard the bolts click, realized the king's not with us. He's outside. Door wouldn't open for six hours. Six hours is a big lead."

"What's your name?" Horrocks asked.

"McGavin."

"No, that's the king's middle name. What's yours?" Horrocks asked.

"We gave up our names when we were hired. Someone else is named for the king's father, the king's birthplace . . ."

"How could you do it, let someone take your identity away?" Sari asked.

The Ringer tried his tea again but it was still too hot. "Debt, like most of the rest. The kind of debt I had, it has a way of strapping you down and having its way with your own plans. I was so far under that . . . that and a facial structure similar to the king's."

He pretended to drink from the mug. "I used to go to bed on my side, the only way I could fall asleep. The king slept on his back. That was the hardest part for me, a habit I couldn't acquire. We had to learn all kinds of shit like that. Tried to sleep on my side in the Gunwitch.

Stayed awake five hours trying before I gave up. How's that for doomed?"

"I'd rather be dead than pretend to be someone else," Horrocks said.

"Horrocks, I'd like my identity back. Most Ringers do. It's not something we gave without regret. There are plenty of stories about Ringers mutilating themselves."

Horrocks had heard these stories; they were almost as popular as those of the king's infidelities. Unstable Ringer candidates who fooled the screeners could easily end their careers with an explosive identity meltdown. Too long an association with the king, too long pretending to be someone else, superimposing another personality over their own. Ringer identity meltdowns often led to self-mutilation.

"What for?" Sari said.

"So they'd no longer resemble the king," McGavin said. "So they could feel they had control of their bodies, not the other way around. I've thought about taking acid to my face."

"Mention that to the screeners when you're reunited with the king," Horrocks said.

"You must be deaf, you fucking brute. Listen to me. I've *quit*. The king doesn't exist for me anymore."

"Watch your tone," Sari said. "We've been nothing but civil."

"That's real nice, but it doesn't mean I want to stay here. I never planned on being a Ringer for the rest of my life," McGavin said.

"You're going where I take you, bottom line," Horrocks said. "You're a fool to want out now, after all the surgical hoops you Ringers have to jump through. Show a little fortitude."

"How many times did you go under the knife?" Sari asked.

"A lot less than you for those ugly tattoos. I'll tell you one thing—" McGavin said and flung the tea at Horrocks' face. Horrocks stood in time to catch the hot liquid on his chest instead. McGavin flipped the table over and ran for the kitchen door. Horrocks grabbed McGavin's arm, reeled him in and punched him in the kidney. McGavin shouldered Horrocks into the sink. The Ringer swung for Sari and missed. Horrocks brought a pan around and knocked McGavin off his feet. Horrocks pushed Sari out of the kitchen.

McGavin recovered instantly. He feinted left, then right, left again and caught Horrocks in the face with a solid jab. McGavin threw a chair at Horrocks, missed and searched the room for another weapon.

Horrocks belted him with a haymaker that spun the Ringer around. He kicked the Ringer in the back and sent the man to the floor for the second time. McGavin rolled over, trapped Horrocks' legs with his own and tripped him into the chairs.

McGavin crawled for the cockpit door and pried it open. Horrocks leapt for the door and hit it full force with the Ringer halfway inside.

McGavin REGAINED CONSCIOUSNESS in the cellar. He was lying on a cot, his neck, hands and feet tied to the springs underneath.

"My stomach," McGavin said. "Every organ in my belly's burst open."

"I already checked you out," Horrocks said.

"You caught me. I give up, in, whatever," McGavin said. He tried to sit up and nearly choked himself. "I want sanctuary."

"This isn't a fucking church," Horrocks said. "And I don't want you to look at or talk to my wife ever again."

"I'm sorry, I—"

"Ever again," Horrocks said.

IT TOOK HORROCKS AND SARI three and a half hours to re-assemble the kitchen.

"This means I'm gonna have to lock them up. I didn't think the Ringers were going to be combative," Horrocks said.

"And rude," Sari said. She hadn't looked Horrocks in the face since they had started cleaning. "You didn't hurt him enough."

"That door almost cut him in half."

"Wasn't enough," Sari said.

CHAPTER 8

The kitchen was barely in order when the queen's personal shuttle sailed up alongside the *Moondrunk* and extended its umbilical. After the magnets locked and the lights switched from red to green Horrocks opened the hatch and put his hand out to help the first person across the threshold. A tall, chubby teenager. The prince. He was wearing a pair of miners' coveralls without the typical stripes or badges of rank. The only adornment was his last name printed on the breast. He shoved Horrocks' hand aside and surveyed the hallway.

Horrocks said, "How you holding up, kid?"

"Where's my father?"

"I'll have him soon."

The prince noticed Horrocks' grenade rack above the exit hatch. "Makes me feel welcome," he said, strolled into the common room and tossed it with his eyes.

Horrocks grinned. "This isn't a playdate. And who said you were welcome?"

The prince moved all the chairs, checked under the desk and through the drawers.

"You should really have someone with experience do that," Horrocks said. "You're too young to know what to look for."

The prince stopped his search for a moment. "I turned sixteen in February."

"Old enough to work the mines," Horrocks said.

"I started on my birthday. Right now I'm just a gopher for the Furnace engineers, but they've shown me plenty, and I study at night. I'm not a kid. I bet you were older than me when you started working."

"That's a bet you'd lose. It wasn't some soft job my father got me and I was a lot younger than sixteen."

Sari walked into the common room from the kitchen entrance and sat in one of the striped chairs.

The prince nodded to her, left the room, looked down the umbilical and waved.

"What were you talking about?" Sari asked Horrocks.

"Maturity."

The prince reappeared in the doorway with the queen. Horrocks stepped around the prince and bowed. "My Porphyria," he said.

The queen smiled at him. "Always so formal. I admire your respect for tradition, my Horrocks." The queen stood over six feet tall with the help of subtle heels. Her hair was a combination of dark blonde and light gray intertwined to create a muted yellow. It was combed backward, curled up at her shoulders. Her sharp cheekbones made her seem thinner than she was. The prince took her hand and guided her to the seat next to Sari.

"Horrocks, where is my husband?" Porphyria asked.

"We're looking."

"Sorry for the sudden intrusion but I wanted to see you firsthand. Besides, I hate giving people warning." She crossed her legs. Her dress was green and simple. On the lapel she wore a diamond brooch shaped like a swan. "I like to see their surprise." She laid a hand on her knee. "I've come to see the Ringers."

The dogs ambled into the room and walked up to the prince. When he leaned over to pet them his double chin doubled in size.

"I hate dogs," Porphyria said. "That smell, no matter how clean. Sari, take them away. My son, too."

Sari stabbed Horrocks with a look and followed the prince out of the room.

Horrocks took Sari's seat. "The prince looks a lot like you," he said. "I don't see much of the king in him."

"It's mostly on the inside."

"How's he doing with all this?" Horrocks asked.

"He'll be fine once his father is back," Porphyria said. "Once you've done your job."

"Don't talk to me as if I'm in your pay."

"You're in my debt," Porphyria said.

"The king's, not yours."

"You'll be in his debt forever."

"I haven't seen the king in years. I'm doing this as a favor to your house. Any debt is purely emotional."

"My house!" Porphyria said. "My house is falling apart." She leaned forward and put her hand on Horrocks' leg. Her fingers were delicate and warm. "I'm sorry. You're right. We've asked a favor of you. I shouldn't be so rude. The strain lately is—it's a load greater than I can bear. We're not here to talk about you." She sat up straight and laced her hands together. "The mines are my foremost thought."

"What kind of problems so far? You want a drink?"

"Nothing, thanks. Sari's a good woman."

"She always liked working for you," Horrocks said.

"A bald lie," Porphyria said and they both laughed.

"You mentioned my house. It's nearly empty. Our entire court has found excuse to travel. Loyal Brogue stayed with me, a spattering of others, but the—"

"Hangers-on."

"They've let go," Porphyria said. "They were my support, and in return I used to support them. Pampered them and they made me feel comfortable. I'd like to find and punish them, but that's not your job. I have other people with lesser talents and fewer scruples engaged in that hunt." She thumbed away some hot tears. "I feel naked without my king. I love him."

Horrocks smiled a thin smile.

"He has betrayed me with a hundred women and I love him. Not as a person anymore, not as something capable of loving you back. More like a book, or a necklace. People have abandoned me because the king made them feel safe and I do not."

"I won't feed you lies," Horrocks said. "You aren't safe."

"Neither is my boy. We'd help you in your search, but we have to stay at the mines. Give the veneer of stability. And if not stability, then at least a holding of ground. The mines will only last a few more days, a week."

"You can hold out longer than that," Horrocks said.

Porphyria shook her head. She snapped open her purse, dug through its contents, gave up, turned back to Horrocks. "What?"

"I said you could hold out more than a week."

"The miners are anxious."

"They're always anxious," Horrocks said.

"The foremen have assured the miners they're in no danger, and in so doing have exaggerated their safety."

"Move the mines off the volcanoes. Tell everyone it's only temporary," Horrocks said.

"It would take the foremen to do that and they'll do no such thing. They're hoping for an explosion. An explosion would give them more influence over the miners. They'd blame the explosion on me."

"Now you're exaggerating," Horrocks said.

"They're seditious, Horrocks. Already there've been four work slowdowns. The miners have been destructive. There have been defections and talk of revolution. Defections to Rouen's slush mines all the way on Europa. We could lose our mines overnight, both of us."

"My men are very loyal," Horrocks said.

"But how brave? You're not immune, Horrocks. Your people crave security as much as my own. The king was that security. Rebellion is infectious. Open your eyes and start seeing the situation for what it is, the end of every-thing."

"This is becoming surreal."

"The king used to address his miners the first day of every week. This past Monday is the first time he's ever been absent. You should never have bought that mine, Horrocks. Why did you ever get involved in—You're a salvager."

"I'm a miner now." He paced over to the desk, then back to the chair. "I've got a Ringer."

"One? Just one?"

"They escaped the Annex before I got there. Your woman Norwick—"

"Just one, Horrocks? This is terrible. Let me see him."

As they climbed down into the cellar together the queen thought about her own Ringers. Porphyria had a fetish for everything false that had the appearance of au-thenticity. She believed that earnest imitations often had more character and better craftsmanship than the items they aspired to be. Most of her jewelry was costume glass and metal, yet many of the pieces were more expensive to produce than genuine finery. Her real jewelry was locked in a semi-secret vault.

She supposed this was why she had always loved the chubby prince above her other two sons. Because he was not the king's. He was not the king's yet everyone as-sumed he was.

For all Porphyria's love of falsity, she hated her Ringers because they made her feel unoriginal and dull. The concept of someone else using her identity, even for her own protection, enraged the queen more than the most controversial injustice. She knew they had been mandated to keep her from harm. None of them had come out well because Porphyria's beauty was so diffi-cult to pin down. There was a small dose of the grotesque to her appearance that the flesh artists consistently failed to reproduce.

After the first few hours in their presence the queen had her likenesses locked away. She wanted them destroyed. The king acquiesced to their removal but overruled their demise. The queen reluctantly agreed to dust them off for important galas. One time, drunk at an inauguration, the queen tried to kill one of them. This convinced the king that banishment was the best solution. He sent them to the Deeps with a little money and one big apology.

Before the drunken violence the queen's Ringers spent years in Porphyria's jewelry vault; the vault had been expanded to accommodate them. When the queen was feeling base she would visit them, watch them from behind frosted glass. There was one of the king's Ringers she was particularly fond of. In his past life this Ringer had been an itinerant actor who entertained the miners with passionate soliloquies. On many occasions she brought him down to the vault with her and watched behind the glass as he had sex with her lonely duplicates. Porphyria found these depraved sessions more satisfying than lying in bed alone, waiting for a husband who rarely showed. She knew that the Ringers' appearance was manufactured and she wondered what a child of their union would look like. A few times a month Porphyria arranged encounters between the Ringers and didn't watch at all. Just knowing that it had been arranged was enough to gratify her.

When voyeurism lost its appeal, Porphyria took the king's Ringer, the ex-thespian, to bed herself. The Ringer had the artificial veneer of a man forty years her senior but he moved with the bedroom grace of a thirty-year-old. He made her feel like the queen again. The queen and her king. She seduced him in her pink bedroom and did things to him she would never do to the king. The Ringer did things to her the king wouldn't even have considered. Eventually, inevitably, she became pregnant.

Horrocks stopped at the bottom of the stairs, pointed to McGavin amid the collection of cots and said, "He sleeps a lot."

"Why is he tied to that bed?" Porphyria asked.

"Because he bites," Horrocks said.

"The rest escaped from the Annex?"

Horrocks nodded.

"They know how to flee," Porphyria said as she appraised the king's sleeping surrogate. McGavin's hands and face were mottled with bruises. Medals he had won in the fight he lost against Horrocks. "That's what we paid them for, to look like the king and get out of bad situations."

Horrocks kicked the cot's wheels. "This whole thing's a bad situation."

"That they'll be looking to get out of," Porphyria said.

"How do you know they didn't create this situation? Killed the king and your son?"

The queen swung her palm toward Horrocks' cheek. He caught her wrist easily. "The king is not dead," Porphyria said. She struggled to free her arm and didn't win it back until Horrocks let go. She took a few exaggerated breaths to compose herself. "Find the Ringers, too," she said. "Don't neglect them for the king. Get as many as you can. When the king is found there will be an air of assumed weakness about him. His lesser enemies will come out of the ground and his greater enemies will use the lesser ones as tools. My husband will need all his Ringers right away."

Her breathing became erratic and harsh. "How long will it take you?"

"It's already six days since the attempt and all we've gotten is the one Ringer. I'll keep tracking them—"

"That leaves you two weeks to find my husband, Horrocks. You know the law. Twenty days from his disappearance he'll be declared dead and the Bastards will step in with their cheap parentage cards, begging and bluffing. They might even get the mines. Two weeks are left, Horrocks. This is not a lot of time."

"It's a stupid law," Horrocks said.

"People still remember the time he was kidnapped during the Push."

"We think your husband will try to make for the next Longliner. It leaves in two days."

"I hadn't even considered that," Porphyria said. Her wet mascara left black tracks on her face. "It would take him as far away from this mess as possible. Running away. I suppose if he was scared enough—"

"The threat is obviously real," Horrocks said. "He's not himself. He's just lost his son."

"So have I, and it's not the first."

McGavin woke up, saw the queen and said, "My wife—"

"This one's gone senile," Porphyria said.

Horrocks led the queen into the Operating Room to show her the assassin. He slid Kleig's body out of the freezer and gave the queen enough space to examine it. She stroked the bruise on Kleig's forehead. "It should have been bigger," she said. Her eyes implored Horrocks for a sympathetic response. He said nothing.

"I was hoping this man would have been mangled. He mangled my son," she said, pulled the brooch from her collar and stabbed Kleig in the face. Her hand, white with tension, trembled on the brooch. "When this is over, I want you to give me this body. I'll take back him and my pin."

Horrocks said, "You remember him. His name was—"

"He has no name," Porphyria said and recoiled as if Kleig's body were about to explode. She left the pin in his face, regarded the body again, and walked out.

On their way up the stairs McGavin shouted, "My Queen, how—"

"Shut up," Horrocks said and locked the cellar door.

Sari and the prince were sitting at the kitchen table. Horrocks guessed neither had spoken for a while.

"We need a replacement Spot Drive," Horrocks said.

"Every available craft's patrolling the mines," the queen said. "There aren't any Drives to spare. I need those ships maneuverable."

The prince played with his glass of water. "Horrocks, do you think my father is dead?"

"He is not dead!" Porphyria said. "He's out there, waiting to be found. He is not dead. He can't be dead." She marched to the umbilical.

"Get those Ringers back," Porphyria told Horrocks before she left. "We're working on something else that will help you. Immensely, I think. A gift. Should be ready in a few days. I'll deliver it in person, unannounced."

When the queen's ship was gone Sari followed Horrocks to the cockpit, flopped into her chair and said, "No more guests."

Horrocks brought the telescreen up and dialed the number to his mine.

"Thing takes forever to connect," Horrocks said.

"Aren't we a little far away for a surprise jaunt?" Sari said. "Seems like the queen came a long way for a little something."

"Said she's got a surprise for us." Horrocks tapped the numbers on the telescreen's pad absently. "Whatever it is, maybe she's keeping it out here."

"Like what? What could she possibly have that we could use? Are you calling De Cuir?"

"Porphyria made me nervous. I'm checking in."

"I'm nauseous, fucking *nauseous* hearing about the mines," Sari said and went up to bed.

The telescreen went from black to red. The red faded into orange bars like clouds before a setting sun. Orange to green. De Cuir's face blotted out the green. His head was shaped like a cinder block. His only soft feature was his eyes. They were a blue so light it was impossible to discern the edges of his irises from the surrounding white.

De Cuir's office was lined with filing cabinets, piles of folders, maps of Io. A skewed sign read: "The Singular Mining Co." Horrocks could see through the office window into the mine. Workmen were rolling barriers into place around a tentacled gimbal.

"How's the hunt? Catch any wild geese yet?" De Cuir asked.

"How is it there?"

De Cuir showed Horrocks a chart. "We've exceeded our quota every day since you left. Friday we doubled it. Maybe you shouldn't come back."

"Everyone's safe?" Horrocks asked.

"Everyone's safe. We miss the dogs. The moon's really letting loose. Went over the numbers last night and there's definitely been a sharp increase. We haven't even had to seed the volcanoes."

Horrocks didn't realize how tense his body had been until this moment when it started to relax. It began with the muscles in his face. "This is great news," Horrocks said. "Glad I don't have to worry about you."

"You don't have to worry 'bout me, but it might help if you worried about the mine some," De Cuir said. He turned his back to the screen, watched the confusing activity in the mineshaft for half a minute, then came back to Horrocks.

"I don't have time for you to be theatrical, Dee. What's the problem?"

"I'm thinking of a way to say it so—"

"Say it," Horrocks said.

"We're too busy. It's shaking the mine something awful. I had to switch off the third and fifth plume intakes. The men were pissed about that. Caskets have leaked—"

"Anyone hurt?"

"No. Bryant fell into the upcast shaft but we got him out. There are so many things here we can't fix without you. Our best solution's been to shut off whatever's not working."

Horrocks put his elbows on the dashboard. "Maybe we should move her to a calmer altitude."

"I can't, Horrocks. I swore to the men they've nothing to worry about. We move the mine, what does that say? They want to fill their quotas. Move the mine, we'll lose the miners."

"How could so much change—"

"Well it has," De Cuir said. "Morale is low. The junior foremen are doing what they can, but it's too big a fire to put out. The king's Furnaces are hemorrhaging people and it's starting to happen here. Two men yesterday. They see what's going on. We're too fucking close for them not to. There's talk of revolt on the other mines. It happens there, we're next."

"Where will our men go to, the king's Furnaces? They'll be killed in the turnover. Get them to stay."

"With what?" De Cuir said.

"Offer them . . . give them my share."

"Your share? That's too much, Horrocks."

"My share. Divide it between everyone, yourself included. Tell them my share for the next quarter goes to everyone. I want you to keep them there. They'll be safe there."

"That's a lot of money, Horrocks."

Three men barged into the office and demanded to speak with De Cuir. "I've got to go," De Cuir said and cut the transmission.

CHAPTER 9

"C'mon, you're not that good," Guilfoyle said.

A Gunwitch was 200 feet off the *Honey Locust*'s bow. It swerved to the right, flipped and shot upward. Guilfoyle copied the maneuver and stayed right behind them.

Guilfoyle tried to position the *Honey Locust* for a clean shot. The Gunwitch rolled, banked left, continued ahead. Her exhaust cone went from yellow to red as the Gunwitch's pilot applied maximum thrust. Guilfoyle stayed on top of them. "That's it, Witchy. Use up your fuel." Guilfoyle's sweaty hands slobbered over the steering bar.

Guilfoyle kept the Gunwitch centered on the viewscreen. He felt around for the intercom, thumbed it on and said, "They might try for a Spot jump. Make sure you're tied down, Kit." He used one hand to steer, the other to secure his buckle.

The Gunwitch rolled again, moving laterally.

"Don't you have any other tricks?" Guilfoyle said.

The Gunwitch accelerated and executed a sharp nose-dive. Guilfoyle's dive was even sharper and he came up just below his quarry. "Shit," he said and leveled out behind her. He fired the port grapple. Its pronged head punched through the Gunwitch's left wing.

The Gunwitch veered right. Guilfoyle fired the starboard grapple and pierced the Gunwitch's right side.

Guilfoyle ignited his reverse thrusters and reeled the cables in. The wires stretched as the Gunwitch fought to free herself. The *Honey Locust* shuddered. The wire from the starboard grapple strained, then snapped free of the Gunwitch and collided with the *Honey Locust* like a giant sea serpent.

The Gunwitch listed to port. Guilfoyle impaled her starboard side with another grapple. He switched to a different terminal and aimed its sights on the Gunwitch's exhaust cone. When everything was reasonably lined up he fired an oblong missile that exploded within the cone, choking it with a flame-retardant, expanding glue.

The Gunwitch trembled and moved forward in heroic spurts. You guys better shut her down or you'll explode, Guilfoyle thought. The Gunwitch slowed and Guilfoyle slowed with her. He reeled her in and, not for the first time, felt more like a fisherman than a pilot.

Guilfoyle used all of his exterior cameras to help position himself directly over the Gunwitch. He lowered the *Honey Locust* down, tapping the Gunwitch lightly. He unbuckled his seatbelt and activated the *Honey Locust*'s belly saw to drill a new opening in the Gunwitch's roof.

Guilfoyle jumped out of his chair and passed the kitchen in his race to the basement.

"We got them?" Kitsis said. She was standing over the sink.

"You get sick again?" Guilfoyle said.

Kitsis nodded and wiped her lip.

"We won't be moving for a while. We got them," he said.

The massive drill was encased in a soundproof chamber in the center of the basement. Guilfoyle spent a few minutes admiring the device, then walked over to his favorite part of the ship: the salvager's armory. Various tools of the salvaging trade were suspended from the wall on molded hooks.

The drill's soundproof chamber kept the room quiet but did nothing for the vibration. Guilfoyle checked the drill's progress, saw that it was halfway through the

Gunwitch's roof. Bits of hull whirled inside the chamber like pewter mayflies.

Guilfoyle came back to the wall. Should I take the bats? he thought. They were arranged side-by-side, end-to-end like opposing swords. The king had given them to Guilfoyle as reward for an act of bravery Guilfoyle had falsely claimed; the true hero, one of Guilfoyle's employees, died performing that brave act. The bats, a matte gray, were forged from the same durable material as the king's energy caskets. The grips were covered with friction tape. During the Push Guilfoyle relied on the bats so often he needed to replace the tape once a week. The bats had weathered the Push better than most men; a few scars, four minor dents, no burns.

He reached for them both, then withdrew his hands. Should save them for something special, he thought. He left his guns untouched because they were too risky on an unknown ship; most hulls could stop a stray bullet but a surprising number were deceptively thin in places and couldn't be trusted. Instead Guilfoyle chose a worn blackjack that fit nicely inside his boot.

The drill finished boring through the hull and retreated into the chamber's ceiling. Guilfoyle read the display before opening the door: "Atmosphere: Borderline Safe."

Guilfoyle stepped inside the chamber, closed the door and waited for the three clicks that told him the seal was complete. He climbed down the ladder on the side of the tube and dropped into the Gunwitch.

He landed on a chair that promptly tipped him over. He cut his hands on the loose hull shavings that littered the floor. He was on his hands and knees in the middle of the command center. Guilfoyle used the chair to right himself, then shoved it aside. He thought about Horrocks, about the condescension and scorn the man had shown him on the other Gunwitch. Should've brought the bats, he thought. I should lose control, flatten everything. Pretend I'm on the *Moondrunk*.

He looked around the room. No Ringers. The floor plan was similar to the other Gunwitch except the walls were much closer. "No room to swing in here, anyway," he said to himself.

Guilfoyle picked the chair off the floor and used it to beat his way into the locked quarters. The door came apart in two easy strokes. Fucking disappointing! he thought. Couldn't they have taken the time to reinforce it?

He barged through four empty rooms and found two Ringers in the fifth. One was armed.

"Put that thing away," Guilfoyle said. "It's not loaded."

"How do you know?"

"You're carrying it wrong."

The armed Ringer tossed the gun into the air and both dove for Guilfoyle who twisted to his right to avoid them but caught a Ringer in his side anyway. They all tumbled to the floor in a riot of fists and legs, but Guilfoyle proved too strong for the Ringers. He didn't even need the black-jack. "How did you guys ever protect the king?" Guilfoyle said.

One Ringer sat on the floor, one on the bed.

"What did you do to your face? It wasn't me. We didn't tussle that bad," Guilfoyle said to the man on the floor.

A sloppy X had been carved into the Ringer's right cheek. The left side of his face was pocked with cigarette burns. Three of his teeth had been pulled out.

"You don't look like the king anymore," Guilfoyle said.

"King's gone," said X. "I wanted my body back."

"So you burn yourself? Halfwit."

"No he's not," said the second Ringer. He wasn't scarred, but he was bruised. Welts sat all over his face like purple leeches. Guilfoyle wondered if those bruises were self-inflicted.

"This body is mine," said X. "It's a way to reclaim ownership."

"You were the king's before. You're mine now. No amount of self-torture's going to change that," Guilfoyle said.

THE RINGERS STOOD IN THE CAGE. "It's liable to get real crowded real soon," Guilfoyle said. "I'd think about that. Make the most of it, get cozy with each other, or whatever it is you forgeries do to pass time. I know these aren't the kinds of quarters a king would be used to, but then you aren't kings, are you?"

The Ringers tested the six pulpy cots Guilfoyle had put out the day before. X pulled down his pants and peed all over the toilet in the corner.

"That's brave," Guilfoyle said.

"I don't see a shower," the bruised Ringer said.

"Neither do I," Guilfoyle said.

"So what do we—"

"Use the toilet. Get your friend to quit watering it."

"Where's the seat that came with the toilet?" the bruised Ringer asked.

"And don't be cutting yourself," Guilfoyle said.

"He doesn't want to look like the king anymore."

But you're supposed to, Guilfoyle thought. That's your job. A good Ringer looks a lot like the king. Almost exactly like him. They can fool almost anyone.

The plan came to Guilfoyle fully formed, like a gift shuttled up from his subconscious. I'll get all the Ringers, he thought. Got to be a few in the bunch good enough to fool the Bastards. I'll have to get to them quick, before any others decide to tear up their faces.

And I'll get the king, he thought. Get the king before Horrocks. Sell the fake to the Bastards, keep the king for myself. Feed him, keep him safe. Disappear for a few months and sell him to the Eurasian mining companies. They'd love to know how the Furnaces work. Or take him to the Deeps, sell him out there. Then I can go anywhere. Fuck the Bastards and their measly offer. Have to find him ahead of Horrocks. I don't, all I'll have is good copies of nothing. I can do this. These two Ringers are no good. I can find a decent one. I can. I'll have to look hard and I'll have to look fast.

Guilfoyle felt so good he wondered if he was giving off an aura. If I feel this good, I know I'm right, he thought. I've got two live Ringers, one dead one. Horrocks has a live one. That leaves eight more, plus the king. I should write this down.

"Guilfoyle!" the bruised Ringer yelled.

"What?" Guilfoyle yelled, equally loud.

"I've been talking to you. How did you find us? Can we get some food?"

"We'll see what's left after I eat."

"Give us some food. Don't you want to know where we were going? What happened to the other Ringers? I might tell you."

"Why would I believe you?" Guilfoyle said.

CHAPTER 10

"We've covered 43,000 miles since the Annex but it feels like we're no closer," Horrocks said. He stared at the viewscreen, watched the stars glide past the *Moondrunk* like puffy dandelion seeds.

"We are no closer. No closer to the end of this," Sari said. "Don't you think Porphyria could be the one behind this? Feigning weakness, only wants us to find the king so she can kill him?"

"I don't know," Horrocks said. "We have no other options except the Longliner. We'll find the king there."

"And we're headed back toward Io. We should've started there and worked our way out, not in. Don't touch the navcom. Longliner Station's coordinates are already plugged in," Sari said and went up to the bedroom.

Horrocks spent some time reviewing their barren surroundings. Few ships bothered to traffic this far from the activity around Io. Even Io's Galilean sisters were in hiding.

Horrocks stared at the viewscreen and was lulled by the whirling, cloudy eye of Jupiter. Lulled, but unimpressed. Like most residents of this locality Horrocks had lost the capacity to be awed by the king of planets. When he was a child Horrocks marveled at Jupiter whenever given the chance, which was constant since Jupiter dominated the view from every window and wooed the observer relentlessly. As was the fate of most whirlwind suitors, Jupiter's novel charms became predictably mundane. By the time he was five Horrocks lost interest and Jupiter went from spectacle to scenery.

What remained fascinating was *The Priam*. Horrocks knew his interest in that troubled relic would never wane. *The Priam*, once a giant and noble ship, had been whittled down to its marrow. Despite this violent erosion she was still the biggest derelict of all, adrift off Io 6,000 miles from the mines. An eyesore so familiar no one acknowledged it.

Fifty years ago, *The Priam* was all anyone talked about. A pilgrim ship, the first to leave Earth for the Deeps. Her cabins were sold to explorers, farmers, anthropologists, planetary geologists, entrepreneurs, and persecuted fanatics. The media hailed it as the New Ark and praised its diversity.

Halfway to the Deeps a civil war broke out among the citizens of this new nation. Some wanted to continue the voyage while others decided they never should have left. Homesickness overcame curiosity, some recalcitrant protesters were executed, and the ship was turned around.

A second war erupted when the ship broke down near Io. John Kingston, *The Priam*'s chief engineer and a pacifist, ignored the roving battles as he overhauled the master relay that controlled the ship's ten Spot Drives.

Kingston watched in helpless horror as dozens of combatants stampeded into the control room that housed Drive Six. The farmers and fanatics, fighters none, consistently missed each other, but not the machines. Two burly farmers accidentally initiated the room's coolant procedure. The vent to the exhaust cones was opened and the Whipple shock-shield lowered. It was a full ten seconds before the failsafe recognized that people were in the room, closed the vent and lifted the shock-shield.

Kingston smashed the room's thermostat. Within minutes the combatants were too cold to fight.

"Equipment's broke anyhow," said one farmer on his way out. "If they worked, we'd have been home already."

"Why can't you fools play in the galley?" Kingston said.

Most of the machines *were* broken. Kingston called in his six senior engineers and they started cleaning up and evaluating the damage. Fresh battles roamed through *The Priam*'s nine other control rooms.

Hard glitter was cemented to the shock-shield's middle wall. Kingston tried to scrape the glitter off with a maintenance trowel. The subsequent explosion tilted the ship and put Kingston in the infirmary for two weeks.

The explosion was attributed to a buildup of pressure within Drive Six, but Kingston knew that was wrong. The feeling returned to his legs after the first week in the infirmary, and he spent the second week trying to sneak back to his machines. The nurses grew tired of pursuing him through the alleyways; on the night of the fourteenth day they gave Kingston a mild chase to alleviate their guilt should he reinjure himself, then let him go.

Kingston waded into the wasteland that was Control Room Six and used his hands to trawl the sharp rubble. When he found the black box his fingers were covered with more blood than skin. He fixed the analyzer, connected the box and cycled past reams of useless data until he came to the few paragraphs that recorded the changes in the machinery for the ten seconds when the vent lay open.

The records confirmed the hypothesis that had kept him awake in the infirmary: the explosion had nothing to do with Drive Six and everything to do with the shock-shield.

Because the Spot Drives were prone to overheating, giant vents connected to the exhaust cones were periodically opened to bleed heat from the rooms into space. A Whipple shock-shield was then lowered behind them to prevent debris from striking the vulnerable Drives.

The records in Control Room Six indicated that a gust of Io's corrosive haze penetrated the shock-shield that wasn't built to resist such barrages. Most of this haze was sulfur moving at two kilometers per second. Moon breath from Io's abundant volcanoes.

This haze tore through the shock-shield's first wall, a grounded sheet of magnesium-coated aluminum. The middle wall, a charged aluminum plate, emitted a 50,000amp pulse that created a powerful magnetic field designed to slow incoming debris. Bits of loose magnesium were thrown into the electromagnetic field by the spall of the rampaging sulfur. The magnesium and sulfur were forcibly mated in the crucible of the field's intense heat and pressure. The coerced material was an unstable form of magnesium sulfate.

Kingston traced the glitter's explosive shockwave from Control Room Six all the way to Crossroad Control in the keel. Chunks of the Tandem Fief were embedded in the room's secondary machinery. *The Priam* was nearly paralyzed; the Tandem Fief coordinated the ship's ten Spot Drives, turning them off and on from one to the next to maintain thrust and minimize overheating. Without the Fief's dominance the individual Drives would never be able to work in harmony.

Kingston kept his discovery of the Fief's destruction to himself. He wanted *The Priam*'s passengers to leave, but they had to do so when they felt ready.

Kingston busied his engineers with peculiar tasks while he burned up the ship's limited supply of liquid fuel maneuvering *The Priam* closer to one of Io's volcanoes. This movement revived a sense of hope in the passengers, and they were equally disappointed when Kingston's engineers insisted the shift was the propulsion equivalent of a burp, nothing more.

The Priam drifted into an altitude beyond the lava's reach but still within the bull's-eye of Io's towering gas plumes. Kingston went to Control Room Two, which had survived the roving battles mostly intact. He angled the shock-shield into the haze, tweaked the amperage, and opened the vent.

The crystals that formed on the shock-shield were twenty times the size of the original glitter. They looked like clusters of giant yellow salt. Kingston showed the results of this experiment to his engineers, then ejected the dangerous Shock Salts from the ship.

"I understand what it is, but you haven't told us how you made it," one of them said. "There's plenty you aren't telling us, John. I know I'm not just speaking for myself here. What's the rest of it?"

"Ask me later and I'll tell you," he said, but never honored this promise.

Over the next year the engineers ignored the ship's mobility problems. Instead they perfected a container that could harness power from the salts using a solution of ethoxyethynyl alcohol as a substitute electrolyte.

The Priam's passengers, once hopeful that their ship would take them home (and end their wasted journey on the type of symbolic note textbooks love), lost faith in Kingston's ability to fix the ship. They were also nauseated by the malignant stench of sulfur. Kingston's experiments outpaced the air purifiers. The smell took root in everyone's hair, clothes, and food. The passengers sent clandestine messages to Earth for their families to come get them. Prior to leaving, they sold their shares in Priam Ventures, Inc. to Kingston for next to nothing.

When the ship was deserted of all but the engineering staff, Kingston radioed Earth and contacted the experts he needed: volcanologists, physicists, organic chemists, a horde of interdisciplinary specialists, contractors and welders. Three months later they arrived with their families on two crowded carriers.

It took eight years to dismantle *The Priam* and build the mines. The ten mammoth exhaust cones were clipped from the ship, aimed at the volcanoes. *The Priam* and both carriers were gutted and cannibalized. The material they provided helped form the support facilities above the cones: rotating salt caverns, decompression bells, loading and packaging zones, gentle positioning rockets, dormitories. Each mine was mechanically identical from the waist down, but because supplies were limited their amenities and upper structures varied wildly. The flag-ship Furnace was by far the most elaborate and comfort-able.

The rotating caverns were given the most attention. They were balanced over the exhaust vents and lined with energy caskets whose stomachs were miniature shock-shields that cultivated the salts.

The caskets also reflected the shock-shields' heat. When one engineer said, "Hot as a damn furnace in here," everyone agreed. Within days the term *Furnace* was officially adopted.

During the construction Kingston's demanding side manifested itself. This, coupled with his genius for order, led some workers to refer to him as *the king* instead of *Kingston*. Another aspect of his personality excavated by his sudden power was the king's sexual charisma. He se-duced all his female engineers (many of them married) and, it was rumored, a few male ones as well.

When the mines were completed a blanket call was sent out for manual laborers. More than 30,000 came, Horrocks' parents among them.

Once the defenses were secure the king marketed the caskets to the industrial giants back home. He offered an affordable, powerful energy alternative and the super-companies pounced. The Eurasian mining conglomer-ates became his biggest customers. They were long de-pendant on dirty machines that violated the strict environmental laws, resulting in stiff annual fines. The caskets violated no laws and stored their own waste. Over a two-year trial period the companies converted some of their earthmovers to accept the caskets. When the trial period was over the CEOs converted as well: they abandoned the fossil-fuel industry and became faithful yet jealous clients of the king. They tried to spy on the Furnaces but nothing could be seen from the outside. Infiltrators were quickly unmasked, and these unfortunate spies learned the true extent of the miners' loyalty to the king.

Io, like all of Jupiter's moons, had been named after one of the god's many lovers. The king changed the name of *The Priam*'s cooperative to Lovers Mining, Inc. After the first few shipments the king was wealthy enough to buy a hundred *Priam*s, but he feared if the operation grew any larger he wouldn't be able to rule it alone. His engineers were segregated from the start so that each team had an intimate understanding of only a small fraction of Furnace technology; the king made sure that out of all the engineers he was the only one with total knowledge.

To preserve his technological dictatorship, the king alone built the ten chambers that regulated the Furnace caverns' delicate equilibrium: the density of magnesium in the shields' first barrier, the voltage of the shock current, and the duration of the charge. Each chamber's instruments were independent from the rest of the Furnace, and only the king was allowed inside.

The Furnaces' voracious demands robbed *The Priam* of most of her bulk. Horrocks raided her on occasion but so little of value was left that the trips were usually just an excuse for time alone.

Horrocks brought the cameras back to the mines, shut the lights and went upstairs to Sari.

Although the ship was cold, they made love without blanket or sheets. Horrocks felt he could be more creative without the covers; Sari didn't mind as long as the lights were off.

"Slower," she said. Her breath was hot in his ear as her tongue traced its maze of cartilage. She lay beneath him, her hands on his hips, guiding him as he slid in and out of her. She could feel an orgasm coming at her like a high-speed bus.

Horrocks shifted to take the pressure off his sore elbow and bumped the light switch by accident. "Turn it off!" Sari said. Her hands instinctively covered her largest tattoos. Horrocks killed the light. Sari rolled on her side to face away from him.

"I'm sorry," he said.

She snatched the sheets off the floor. "From now on, we use the covers. It's too cold, anyway."

It's not too cold, Horrocks thought. I wish you weren't ashamed.

He moved next to her, rubbed the nape of her neck, an old favorite. His forefinger played with her sparse down of dorsal hairs. She moaned lightly and her body lost its hostile rigidity. He brought his hands around to cup her breasts. He touched and kissed her until Sari turned to face him.

"Sheets," she said and guided his penis inside her.

"Clothes, if you want," he said and she laughed. "I thought I was going to have to finish myself off."

She bucked against him, showing him he wouldn't have to.

AFTER BREAKFAST the next morning Horrocks said, "I have some work to do in the cellar."

"There was another message from the queen. She'll be coming by."

"Already?"

"What work do you have to do?" Sari asked.

"Reinforcing the cellar. I'm going to put up the mesh."

"There's only the one Ringer," she said.

"There'll be more." He rubbed his eyes with the heel of his hand. "The ones we find later are going to be even more aggressive. Our kitchen can't take that kind of abuse."

"You need help down there?" Sari asked.

"Nah, I'll take the dogs."

Horrocks found both dogs and brought them down into the cellar with him.

McGavin was still flat on the cot, his neck and hands bound to the springs. Somehow he had worked his legs free. He had used them to move the cot across the room and, during the past night, repeatedly slammed the cot against the wall in an unsuccessful attempt to break the bed apart.

He was awake but said nothing as Horrocks wheeled him back into the corner. "Bed's a lot stronger than she looks," Horrocks said. "So's the wall."

The dogs milled around Horrocks' feet. He undid the knots to free McGavin, who rose slowly. "Sit. Watch," Horrocks said to the dogs and motioned toward the Ringer. The dogs sat stiffly.

Horrocks went to the main closet, found a coil of old mesh, put it under his arm and closed the door. He unrolled it on the floor and smoothed it out like a giant flag. The mesh was a steel-cloth hybrid. Horrocks lifted the mesh and hung it from hooks in the ceiling. McGavin and the cots were on the other side. Like Guilfoyle's pen, this cage used a corner of the room for two of its walls.

The mesh had long since faded from black to gray. Portions of it had been mended. During the Push the mesh cage had been up all three years. Horrocks was often forced to transport unruly survivors. The last batch had been the most troublesome. One prisoner, a lieutenant from Rouen's high command, squeezed another man's head through the mesh's tiny gaps and strangled him. Then he chose another victim. Horrocks went inside to subdue them both and all three lost a lot of blood. When Horrocks had the lieutenant on his back the man blamed his behavior on a cocktail of anxiety and rage. Horrocks knocked him out. He returned to the cage every few hours to knock the man out.

The hooks that tethered the mesh to the wall and floor doubled as locks. The locks faced away from the cell and could not be picked. Horrocks' nimble fingers guided the mesh around the hooks. McGavin eyed Horrocks like a clever student who thinks little of his teacher.

"There's no key. Locks with a trick of the finger, right?" McGavin said. "I'm good with tricks."

"You won't get this one."

I shouldn't be enjoying this, but I am, Horrocks thought. There's going to be a lot of hurt before this is all over, but I'm having fun.

McGavin approached the mesh. The dogs let loose a peal of menacing barks. McGavin fell back against the cots. The dogs moved closer and continued their vigil.

The constant strain of reaching up for the ceiling hooks burned Horrocks' shoulders. The dogs and the Ringer watched each other. Shouldn't be having fun, Horrocks thought. I've awakened my younger self in a body too old.

Throughout the Push Horrocks struggled with guilt. As a salvager his profession was steeped in death and sadness. There was danger as well, euphoric danger that teased Horrocks with jolts of worth and invulnerability. No two wrecks were alike and Horrocks reveled in those episodes of misfortune. He was keenly aware that his pleasure was distilled from calamity, but the pleasure was undeniable. When he finally retired from salvaging, Horrocks retired his guilt, too. As he put up the mesh it returned to him like an old coin, perfectly preserved.

"Shit," Horrocks said as he came to the end of the mesh with the second wall of the cage yet to be completed. He had forgotten that a large section had been ripped during his fight with Rouen's lieutenant.

"Watch," Horrocks told the dogs and returned to the closet. He rooted through piles of clutter until he found an unopened coil of black mesh. He hung the new mesh next to the old and locked them together. He finished the job by locking both strips of netting to the floor.

McGavin rolled the cots one against the other to form an enormous bed. There was a narrow aisle between this bed and the mesh.

"I feel like I'm on display in an aviary, sitting behind this screen," McGavin said. His fingers played on the air and picked imaginary locks.

Horrocks stared at him. The Ringer's hands floated down into his lap.

Sari opened the cellar door and said, "She's here."

"Don't worry, I won't figure it out," McGavin said and tapped the mesh.

"Watch," Horrocks said to the dogs and went upstairs.

Sari, the queen and a man Horrocks had never seen before were talking by the exit hatch. The queen wore a heavy black gown.

"Where's your son?" Horrocks said.

"On the flagship Furnace," Porphyria said.

"Good," Horrocks said. "You need to keep him away from all this."

"This is my doctor. Regrettably, a necessity for the time being. I'm epileptic."

"I thought you'd medicated that out of your system," Sari said, her disbelief of the queen's illness evident in her scornful tone.

"The pills no longer work," the doctor said. "Under all this stress, she's prone to attacks."

"Prone," Sari said.

"Very," the doctor said. He was dressed in the gray uniform of the Furnace Surgical Corps. His double-breasted jacket came down to his knees and looked as if it had been tailored from sheet metal. The red sash over his left shoulder was lined with surgical tools. He had chubby cheeks and strong hands.

"Any luck?" Porphyria said.

"I'd rather not say," replied Horrocks. "We're getting closer—"

"You can speak freely in front of the doctor," Porphyria said. "I'm here to reiterate my support. Don't be insulting."

I don't trust you or the doctor, Horrocks thought. We'd be much farther along without these interruptions.

"We're not holding back, my Queen," Sari said. "Actually, I'm embarrassed. We've made so little progress—We don't want you to think we're incompetent."

"Your lack of progress is the other half of my visit. I told you, Horrocks, I had a gift for you." Porphyria turned to the open umbilical. She waved her bag, then she and the doctor moved out of the way.

Three tall men emerged from the umbilical. Three duplicates of Horrocks. Sari grabbed Horrocks' arm. He was too numb to feel her nails digging into his skin.

The duplicates stood shoulder to shoulder.

"Don't look at me, Sari, look at them," Porphyria said.

In height and facial features they were nearly identical to Horrocks. Their body types varied slightly, as did their stance and attitude. No wrinkles radiated from their eyes. Their brows were not worried with lines. It depressed Horrocks to realize they were younger versions of himself.

"The flesh artists had no recent photos or videos of you, so they made do with some older ones. I had them start planning as soon as the king disappeared, right before I called you. The machines in the flesh factory needed to be recalibrated for you, and that takes time."

She circled the Ringers and treated them like plastic mannequins, lifting their arms, adjusting their heads. "I was hoping to have them ready by my last visit, but setbacks. Always setbacks."

"They're quite good," the doctor said. His eyes darted from Horrocks to the duplicates and back. His throat made small approving sounds.

"Did you make them?" Sari asked the doctor.

"I wasn't there, no. But I recognize quality when I see it. Don't you?"

"Why?" Horrocks said. If his voice were a man that man would have collapsed.

"Horrocks, show some gratitude," Porphyria said. "*Why.* What a stupid word, *why.* Because you can't do this on your own. Because you'll need to fool a lot of people to find my husband. Because everyone will be watching you, following you. You're welcome, Horrocks. You're welcome."

Sari said, "Porphyria—"

"The only useful people who didn't leave me were the flesh artists," Porphyria said. "I don't know why I did this. I wanted to help. I wanted to do something to help. The doctors were all I had to use, so I used them. I was quite pleased with myself, so don't be ungrateful. All three of them are excellent pilots." She patted one of the duplicates on the head. "Send them about as you wish. They can be trusted not to flee or betray you. We've bonded their loyalty in a very special way."

The queen continued with her angry explanation. Horrocks didn't listen. He felt as if his soul had been carved up and doled out recklessly. They'll grow into the face I have now, he thought. What would it feel like to have someone else's identity thrust upon you? What does it feel like to have your identity forced on someone else? I feel like I've accidentally raped them, that the queen's raped them in my name.

"How did you complete them so fast?" Horrocks asked. He was unsure if he'd interrupted the queen; the sentence just came out.

"The Push taught us nothing if not the value of expediency. The flesh artists work quickly," Porphyria said. She examined the palm of one of the look-alikes. "Down to the smallest line," she said to herself, then continued louder: "It's only six hours of operations, twelve more healing inside the expediting tanks. A month of intensive mannerism training. Obviously these men skipped that, so don't expect them to act like you."

She let go of the man's hand. "They were miners, incidentally. They're not perfect. We also skipped the setting treatment so the Ringers have probably started to diverge already. But there won't be much of that."

"Oh my God," Sari said.

"The teeth are theirs, not yours. From a distance, they'll do."

"Anyone would be fooled," the doctor said.

"I'm fooled," Sari said. "I'm dumbfounded."

"I have to get back to my son," Porphyria said. "So be frugal and be prudent. You've only the three."

"Just three," Horrocks said. His face was a mask of ice.

"Use them. You have them just in time, dear Horrocks. Remember how I described the temper of the miners? It's much worse now. They're itching to revolt. You have to resolve this quickly."

The doctor and the queen exited through the umbilical and their ship departed.

"She's completely insane," Sari said.

Horrocks said nothing.

His Ringers said nothing.

THE SHUTTLECRAFT WAS SMALL but luxurious. The walls, floor and ceiling were covered with folds of silk and velvet. The warm air was scented with cloves and sandalwood.

"Do you understand how ravishing you are?" the doctor said.

"Do you understand how many hours a day this takes to maintain?" Porphyria said.

"My Queen—"

"When are you going to stop calling me that? I'm no longer your queen until my king is found." And without the king what am I? she thought. What is my son?

They were sitting in the ship's tiny lounge, their oval chairs facing each other. The cockpit was at the end of the rectangular room, its twin doors open. The pilot and copilot heard the conversation behind them but were pretending not to.

The doctor leaned forward and took the queen's hand on the pretense of medical concern. He raised it toward him and kissed it suddenly. The queen pulled away.

"Isn't it enough you have one of my Ringers?" she said.

"It used to be," the doctor said and licked his lips. He wasn't trying to be suggestive or crude; he merely wanted to savor the taste of her skin. He sat back and crossed his legs daintily. "You need to keep him away from all this," he said in a poor imitation of Horrocks' voice.

"I do," Porphyria said.

Long years of practice had taught the doctor never to discuss her pregnancy. Instead he said, "Horrocks seems very concerned about the prince. Called him *your son*, not *the prince* like he should. Does he know?"

"You're reading into it."

"It was very telling," the doctor said.

My son, mine alone, the queen thought. After the king's Ringer had gotten her pregnant, the only person the queen had consulted was a young surgeon named Ableman. The entire court had seen the way he watched her, how awkward he was in her presence, so quick to blush. When she caught him looking at her, he usually looked away.

"I'm pregnant," she had told him.

The doctor looked disappointed. "The king will be ecstatic."

"It's not the king's."

The doctor dropped his pen. He picked it up, put it in his pocket and sat down. "So that's why you've finally come to me, looking for an abortion."

"Imbecile, there'll be no abortion," Porphyria said.

"You'll need an examination. I'll tell your gynecologist."

"We'll both tell no one."

The doctor wheeled in a gynecological exam table. It took up most of his office. "You'd better get undressed," he said.

The queen took off her blouse. "You just want to see me naked."

The doctor felt as if his breath had been vacuumed from his lungs. "Yes," he managed to say. He watched the queen remove her pants. When she bent over to slide off her panties the doctor thought his penis would burst at the slightest friction.

She got up into the chair. The doctor was mesmerized. He said, "If you think I'm being salacious—"

"You are," she said and crossed her legs.

"I could call in another doctor, tell him about your delicate condition."

"I trust you," Porphyria said. She opened her legs and placed them on the stirrups.

The doctor brought over a stool and a tray of gynecological instruments. The speculum rattled in his hand.

"Don't put that in me with your hand shaking," Porphyria said. She knew she would never tire of her effect on men. She dreaded the time when men would become impervious to it.

The doctor slid the stool between her raised legs and took a moment to calm his trembling. Her vagina, black with hair and blisteringly red down the center, was the most captivating work of art he had ever seen. Two gray hairs poked out through her black fur but the doctor chose not to see them. Her lips were partially open; a few strings of clear fluid were strung between them like the first strands of a spider's web. The doctor's hands settled into a mild palsy. He took a deep breath and pretended to sigh but was actually trying to capture her feminine smell: wildflower honey, syrupy liquor and sour milk balanced together. He wanted to taste it. He wanted to do much worse, and forcefully, but he put it out of his mind.

"I'm keeping the baby," Porphyria said during the doctor's tender and protracted inspection.

"That will be complicated," the doctor said. He used some gauze to wipe the sweat from his forehead and neck. "The king will demand the proper tests. I couldn't possibly fake them all."

"Yes you could," she said.

The doctor slipped on some lubricated gloves and performed a bimanual exam. "Your pelvis is bruised."

"Some vigorous entertaining."

"The child might look nothing like the king."

"It will be a boy."

"A boy? You're sure?"

"That's all I'm capable of conceiving."

"Who is the father?" the doctor asked.

"Leydin. A Ringer. He's fairly recent," she said.

"He is, and you're lucky. I was with the flesh artists when Leydin came in. He has a natural resemblance to the king. Your child—"

"My boy."

"Your boy will probably pass." He pulled off the slick gloves and laid them on the tray. "Why should I help?"

"Because you want me."

The doctor wheeled his stool back so he could look the queen in her face. He maintained the stare for a few seconds before his gaze lowered.

"You can't take your eyes off it, but you won't have mine."

"Then what do I get for all this?" he asked.

"I have Ringers of my own, similar in almost every way down to the hair between my legs. You can choose any one you want."

"I wouldn't force myself on any woman."

"They're trained to protect me. She'll be willing. She'll be yours."

"She's not you," he said.

"Not me but very, very close," Porphyria said.

"I want to see them now."

The queen got off the chair. The doctor watched her get dressed and was more aroused than when he'd seen her completely nude.

When shown the queen's Ringers he narrowed his selection down to three and made the final choice at random.

The prince was born in a harrowing eighteen-hour labor; he was so large that the queen's hips had to be broken to allow him passage. The doctor circumvented the foolproof paternity tests with grace and guile. The king took great interest in the child, but his involvement waned with time. The queen wondered if he suspected the truth but the topic was never raised.

She frequently passed the doctor in hallways or meetings, but they never spoke of their conspiracy. He seemed uncomfortable in her presence. Porphyria didn't care. Several times a year he called attention to his state of mind through body language, but the queen turned away from such signs. Leydin, the adulterous Ringer and former actor, died during the Push.

The person who concerned the queen most was the Ringer she'd used to bribe the doctor. Porphyria thought about her a lot but never saw her. She was the only Ringer to stay behind when the rest were banished to the Deeps. Porphyria often imagined her walking the mines boldly, her hair dyed or covered with an exceptional wig. Perhaps she had gained or lost weight to take the edge off the resemblance. Probably dresses differently, Porphyria thought, talks differently, carries herself altogether unlike me.

As she sat in the shuttle and faced the doctor in silence, the queen wondered if he was still fucking her. It was possible that he forbade the woman to act like anyone but the queen and kept her locked in his cabin. In that instant the queen decided that she wanted her lost Ringer found and killed.

"Are you still staying in the Kiln Dormitories?" Porphyria asked the doctor.

"Yes, why?"

"Curiosity."

The doctor found two glasses and poured some wine. He had been daydreaming about their first examination as well. Though there had been no intercourse, he considered it the most precious of all his sexual encounters.

"We'll lose the mines. I'm almost certain we will," Porphyria said.

"I hate all this unrest," the doctor said, drank all the wine in his glass and poured himself another.

HORROCKS WENT BACK DOWN TO THE CELLAR. His personal Ringers followed. "Don't stand too close to me," Horrocks said. He felt as if his identity had been polluted. The most infuriating aspect of their company was their youthful appearance. Horrocks knew they could never pass for him but for the briefest and most distant of exchanges. Any value they had at all would be in fooling Guilfoyle and he would never be taken in by these.

McGavin was asleep behind the mesh. The dogs heralded Horrocks' return by licking his palm. They saw the Ringers the queen had brought, weren't fooled, and trotted upstairs. Horrocks went over the mesh's locks again because he needed an outlet for his nervous energy.

Horrocks' three Ringers stood by the locker. "Are you going to use us?" one of them asked.

"I haven't decided. I don't even know if I want you on my ship."

"We're men, too, Horrocks."

Horrocks stopped working and stared at the mesh. "I know you are. You're also in a situation beyond your control."

"You hate Ringers. Can't even look us in the eye."

"That has nothing to do with you." But I have to get you away from me, Horrocks thought. I feel like I could vanish at any moment. Then these Ringers could step in and assume everything I've got. Sari, the dogs, my ship, my Furnace.

"We don't even know how to treat ourselves. What are we? We were just working in the mines, a little in debt maybe, and someone—"

"I don't want to know," Horrocks said.

McGavin woke up and yawned loudly. "Holy shit, I was fast asleep." He got off the bed and stood with his fingers resting on the mesh. When he saw Horrocks' duplicates he smiled wide enough to show the crowns on the king's crooked molars. "You've been busy, Horrocks. They're pretty good. What're your names?"

"Back to sleep," Horrocks said. "Don't talk to them."

"Who am I supposed to talk to? And I've finally got something to talk about. You didn't have them made, I know that. The queen. I bet the queen gave them to you, thought they might help. Come on guys, step into the light so I can see you, huh? Fine, don't move." He curled his fingers around the netting and tested it surreptitiously.

"It'll hold," Horrocks said. He came to the seam where the used mesh was locked to the new. In his rush to get the divider up Horrocks hadn't realized how awful it looked, how poorly the mesh pieces went together.

Horrocks' Ringers came toward the wiry prison. "Not so close," Horrocks said. He was afraid they would touch him. He realized he was being completely irrational, but he didn't know what would happen if they touched him. I might explode, he thought. Or we'd all melt. Nothing. Nothing will happen.

"Are you scared of them?" said McGavin.

"You should be scared of me," Horrocks said. He turned to face the three men. "I'm going to keep you down here."

"With the rest of your toys?" one of them said.

"I don't know any of you. I think I do, just by looking at you, but I don't and it's disorienting. You'll have to stay down here."

"Fine," they said.

"It won't be forever. Oh, your beds," he said, unlocked a portion of the mesh, removed three cots, and relocked the mesh.

SARI WAS STARING AT IO from the kitchen's only window. Io's surface was spotted with reds, yellows and browns, the colors of sulfur allotropes in different stages of solidification. To Sari this patchwork looked like dead skin, as if the flesh from some immense cadaver had been stretched over the moon. Its pores sweated putrid gases and spewed founts of lava.

Horrocks came up behind Sari and put his arms around her shoulders.

"How much longer till we reach the station?" he asked.

"About ten hours." She rested her head on his forearms. "What did you do with them?"

"Left them in the cellar. I can't have them running around the ship."

"Seeing the king's Ringers was always unsettling. These guys are worse. They spook me."

"I'll keep them downstairs," he said.

"You're afraid I might take one of them to bed, thinking it was you," she said, shifted and kissed him. "Maybe the queen doesn't expect you to use them. Knows you'll keep them. They could be here to kill the king's Ringers when we find enough of them. Or kill the king himself."

"I'm going to put them on the Longliner tomorrow," Horrocks said.

CHAPTER 11

Longliner Station was shaped like a giant clamshell. The ridges on the left half contained spacecraft berths. The right half of the shell was devoted to the type of restaurants and services that milk harried travelers.

Sari requested and received permission to dock. Horrocks went to the cellar, roused his three likenesses and brought them up to the kitchen. Three different sets of clothes were folded on the yellow table. "Change into those," Horrocks said. "I'm sending you on the next Longliner. It leaves today."

The Ringers changed into the new garments, moving so quickly their faces became flushed. This flush highlighted the white scars Horrocks had received during the war. Even the scars, Horrocks thought. These poor sods. Horrocks watched them viciously. You disgust me, he thought. I want you away from me. I hate something that looks like me. What does that mean?

"Why the Longliner?" one of them asked.

Because I want you gone. "Because it's safest. You'll be in the way. You're in more danger than the queen let on. You could be killed by the time this is done and I can't worry about that." Horrocks motioned toward the sink. "I have to shave your heads."

"If that's all it takes to get out of this mess," another one said, "I have no problem with that. You could shave my balls."

Horrocks put their heads in the sink and used an electric razor to shave them. The men cleaned their bald scalps with a dishtowel.

Sari walked into the room with one of Horrocks' sweaters. She tore it into strips and handed them out. "Use them for scarves," she said. "Cover up as much of your face as possible without looking suspicious."

Horrocks went into the hallway outside the kitchen and saw the overhang of their berth. There was a loud crash as the station's arms wrestled the *Moondrunk* into place.

Sari and the Ringers waited by the exit hatch. Horrocks studied them, was satisfied with what he saw and punched the button that lowered the *Moondrunk*'s gangplank.

A teenage guard met them outside the ship. Horrocks handed him some money and said, "Stay here and keep an eye out, squire."

The *Moondrunk* had been brought in on the docking terminal's seventh tier, close to the station's dome of glass—a distorted porthole to the stars. The other berths were stuffed with colorful ships. Round elevators shuttled passengers down to the street.

Horrocks hadn't expected to see this many people. Their elevator was filled with elbows and feet and pardon me's.

"Everyone's going away," Sari said.

Thousands of travelers meandered down an incline toward the departure point across the way. They were burdened with valises and trunks. Many stopped to talk, laugh, hold hands. For most these pauses were an excuse to rethink their decision to leave. The incline led to an arboretum that could accommodate 10,000 people. The arboretum narrowed further on and ended with the Longliner herself. She rocked like a boat on an aggravated lake. Steam gurgled from pressure vents in her tan hide.

Sari and the three Ringers followed Horrocks as he abandoned the crowd and turned right. Restaurants and shops were set back from the sidewalk. The swank shops at the end of the street were crowned with a majestic hotel, The Sundowner.

Passing men and women ogled Sari, coveting her beauty out of jealousy or sexual frustration. Sari was oblivious to their stares; in her previous profession Sari needed to be acutely aware of her own allure, but now, wanting to forget those days, Sari ignored everyone's interest but Horrocks'.

Horrocks went up to a red building bordered with shrubbery. A sign outside the door read: "Custom House: Duties and Collections." They walked inside. The ground floor was an empty space designed to corral the Longliner herds. A plain desk stood along the far wall. Two men sat behind it, reading.

"My name's Horrocks and—"

"Horrocks, yes," one of the clerks said. He removed his bifocals and closed his book with a loud slap. The clerk wore a green suit with a brown vest and purple tie. "Porphyria told me to expect you. I'm Jemes."

The other clerk looked up and Jemes glared at him. "Keep reading," Jemes said. He turned to Horrocks. "Follow me."

Horrocks stepped around the desk with Sari right behind. The clerk raised his small hand. "I was expecting you only," he said, "not your lady-friend or your bald-headed brothers."

"Go on and buy the tickets," Horrocks said to Sari. "I'll look here and meet you outside."

"This is a terrible business," said the clerk as he led Horrocks through an L-shaped hallway decorated with pictures of the king, the mines, and all six Longliners. "I've been through the manifest twice already."

"Since last month's Longliner, have there been any other departures?"

"None. As I said," he turned into an office, "I checked the manifest for today's Longliner and the king isn't there."

"I'd like to look myself just the same," Horrocks said. "He may have booked passage under a different name."

"I've gone through—"

"The queen told you I was coming. She also tell you to give me a hard time?"

"There are 4,300 passengers," the clerk said, powered up the monitor, and left.

Horrocks spent the next two hours scrolling through photographs. At the end his eyes were tearing and the backs of his legs hurt from the hard chair.

Horrocks thanked the clerk on the way out. "Sorry if I was rude. There's a lot—"

"No need," the clerk said. "You're a celebrity around here. Saved my brother during the Push. Don't ever apologize to me. If you'd give me your beacon, I'll let you know if we ever see anything."

Horrocks gave him the *Moondrunk*'s tag and left.

Sari and the Ringers were talking outside. "They've got their tickets," she said. "Steerage was all that was left."

"I don't think he's on the ship, unless he's drastically altered his appearance."

"He's too vain to do that," Sari said.

They walked toward the main avenue that led back to the Longliner. Horrocks turned to say something to Sari and saw that one of his Ringers was racing away.

"Keep an eye on these two," Horrocks said and took off.

The Ringer leapt over a low hedge and disappeared behind the Custom House. Horrocks cleared the hedge full speed and glimpsed the Ringer as the man sprinted around the next building.

Horrocks pumped his arms as he ran. His stiff boots squeezed his feet and caught little traction on the asphalt. Leery travelers veered away from him.

He saw the Ringer again. The man unwound the sweater-scarf from his face and threw it at a young woman. The Ringer weaved through the people expertly and, as the crowd thickened, managed to become one of them.

Horrocks stopped and put his hands on his knees in an effort to control his panting. That fucking bastard, he thought, then corrected himself. That fucking *Ringer*. I've got no time to look. Ship's leaving soon. Got to watch the passengers get on.

He found that if he tilted his head and looked at the side of the road he could breathe more easily. A statue of the king stood on the lawn. It was laden with chains. The king's face was covered with a black hood.

Horrocks straightened up, ignored all the inquisitive stares and made his way back to Sari. Green constellations marred his vision. He was still breathing heavily when he found his wife by the hedges.

Sari felt his pulse. "That was stupid. How do you feel?"

"Win . . . ded," Horrocks said.

"Take a rest. In your condition, running like that," she said and shook her head.

"Over there," Horrocks said and pointed to a sculpture of rock. "A little time before the ship leaves." His breath was coming back. "Watch the crowd. Maybe we'll spot the king."

Sari, Horrocks and his two Ringers sat on the perch of rocks that was part of the phony landscape meant to soothe nervous émigrés. Few travelers knew what the Deeps were really like and they found this replica of nature familiar and comforting.

"His name was Noyes," the Ringer next to Horrocks said. The Ringer played with a shard of chipped stone, moving it from hand to hand. "Emil Noyes. He worked the mines with me, was on my shift. He came in from the

Deeps last year. I got the feeling he didn't want to go back out. He did something there, or it was done to him. Don't know what."

"I'll ask when I find him," Horrocks said.

Sari, Horrocks and the two Ringers studied the crowd. It had grown in density during the last hour, became a pink carpet with an army of expressions, no one sharper than the next. The crowd was almost exclusively comprised of miners and their families. Sari did notice some priests from the Mission. There were a few people who weren't wearing coveralls or habits: ancillary scrabblers who didn't work for the king yet managed to survive in his kingdom anyway.

Horrocks looked for the king and the missing Ringer. There were too many shaved heads. After watching the people too long, Horrocks only noticed their eyes.

The Ringers lay back and dozed.

"We're not going to find the king," Sari said.

"Not here," Horrocks said.

Not anywhere, Sari thought. She leaned back on her hands and rolled her stiff shoulders.

"May as well see them off," Horrocks said and woke the Ringers.

Sari and Horrocks escorted them down into the crowd.

"Good luck on your hunt," the Ringers said. "Thanks for the tickets."

Horrocks gave them a bundle of cash. "Start with that," Horrocks said. "The money's worth ten times more in the Deeps. Split it up. I'm sorry the queen did this. The money's a poor reward for your involvement, so are the tickets, but this—"

"It's all right. I was pretty ugly to begin with, so I don't mind the new face. Might get me laid."

"I'll get used to it," the second Ringer said.

They stood on a gangplank that led to one of the Longliner's orifices. "Take care and lay low," Horrocks said.

He shook the Ringers' hands even though their touch nauseated him. The Ringers handed their tickets to the conductor and boarded the Longliner.

Horrocks and Sari walked against the tide of people coming up to the ship.

"They're on their way. Feel any better?" Sari asked.

"There's still one out there," Horrocks said.

"The king's not getting on that ship. What now?"

"I'm fucking tired," Horrocks said.

Sari held his arm and they went back to the *Moondrunk*. The teenage guard was sitting in front of the ship.

"Can we stay berthed here for the night?" Horrocks asked.

"Sure you can," the young man said and looked at his watch. "But it's after six. In the evening, every vessel's subject to a random search. No amount of money will hide you from that."

HORROCKS AND SARI WERE NAKED, the covers in a heap on the floor. Horrocks made love to her with careful, steady motions. Sari was on her back, her head partially off her pillow. She petted Horrocks' face with both her hands, then held his head tightly when she sensed he was ready to come. She had climaxed twice already.

Sari pulled his face down to hers and kissed him deeply. She enjoyed doing this when he came; it made her feel closer to him, knowing that he was inside her in more than one place.

Their bodies tensed. Sari felt the hot liquid rush into her. The sensation was simultaneously remote and intimate.

Sari lay on her side and Horrocks slid next to her. They were still breathing heavily. Horrocks heard people talking and remembered he had put the scanner on before getting undressed. The scanner jumped from frequency to frequency as it sought voices and keywords. It filled the room with a susurrus of shredded dialogue. Most of the talk was dull, but Sari found it soothing so Horrocks left it on.

"Forgot to tell you," Sari said, "we have about nine messages from the queen."

"I'm not calling her back."

"It's still cold in here."

"After all that, you're cold?"

"A little," she said, craned her head and kissed him. It was an open kiss, though their tongues were dormant; neither had the energy for oral acrobatics.

Horrocks touched her thighs with his fingers, mindful not to trace the outline of her tattoos because she abhorred that. He sketched random patterns on her skin, watched the rise and fall of her chest as her breathing evened out.

Horrocks turned his attention to the window. They were parked well outside the station's jurisdiction but were close enough for a good view. The Longliner was still in the first phase of its complicated detachment from the clamshell. The ship looked like a blunt, brown lance. Its progress the first few days would be imperceptibly slow. Horrocks was no expert on Spot Drives, but he did know that they used warp technology, which required a tremendous build up of potential energy. When enough power was amassed it was released in one explosive burst.

For short trips the Drive needed a minimal amount of time to warm up. Out to the Deeps, a ship the size of the Longliner needed twenty days to accumulate the necessary energy, another twenty at the end to decelerate, and fifty days in between cruising at maximum speed. Horrocks had no clue how fast the Longliner could go, but guessed that, for those fifty days, she was moving somewhere near the speed of light.

Many passengers were irked by their twenty-day incarceration prior to the jump. Longliner stewards responded to complaints with a fabricated excuse that cited a hodgepodge of terms incomprehensible to the layman: body-mass equations, warp tabulations, pre-plotted trajectory corrections. The truth was that management didn't want to lose the revenue from their buffets, bars, dinner theaters and virtual parlors that would otherwise sit vacant while the ship warmed up. The passengers knew that the Longliners were the most convenient way to the Deeps, so they voiced their complaints over mouthfuls of buffet-food.

The Longliners' Spot Drives were vastly different from the originals used on *The Priam*. Breakthroughs in Spot mechanics since *The Priam's* construction led to many advancements, the most significant being that the physical Drives were much smaller now, small enough that Tinton could hold one in his hands and dash it on the floor.

Horrocks thought about that humiliation and wondered if he should have gone to the Deeps after the Push. Only a handful of people who went ever moved back. This made the Deeps mysterious, gave it a malleable character that was easily tailored to anyone's needs.

Sari shifted so that her buttocks and shoulders were pressed against him. Her thighs were still wet, the sheets more so. Horrocks stared at the Longliner again. He reverted to his old mindset and envisioned the ship collapsing, burning, falling into the station. He imagined himself knee-deep in wreckage, sifting through the debris for survivors.

Getting the old mentality back, he thought. Becoming a salvager again. That's what another war will make me. And if the king's not found, that's what we'll have. They'll need me to become a salvager again. I won't do it.

"Did you hear that?" Sari asked.

"What?"

"The scanner. Two people saying goodbye."

Horrocks lay on his back. Sari moved with him, put her head on his chest and her arm over his torso.

If the king didn't make it to the Longliner, he's trapped somewhere nearby, Horrocks thought. Maybe we didn't find him but we've narrowed the search. He built this system. Probably never wants to leave it. Probably knows it better than I do. In a couple days he'll be semi-transparent. In a week he'll be invisible. By then my Furnace'll be a total mess.

The Longliner's stern lights blinked. Horrocks pictured his two Ringers standing in a closet compartment, asleep on their feet. Or wide awake, cursing their new faces. They were doomed to contend with their loss of identity until they could afford to have their old faces reconstituted. Horrocks knew they'd never be able to afford a surgeon skilled enough to do the job right. He wondered if the Ringers carried pictures of themselves to remember what they looked like before. They must have been desperate, Horrocks thought. I know about desperation.

The *Moondrunk* rotated. The Longliner went out of frame and Jupiter came into view. The bedroom was aglow in the spotlight of the tie-dyed gas giant. Sari closed her eyes. She hoped Horrocks wasn't staring at her tattoos.

He was staring at Jupiter. The Great Red Spot stood out on its belly like a planetary pimple.

Sari whispered something unintelligible.

Horrocks looked away from the brightness of Jupiter and, after a few minutes of adjustment, could separate some of the lesser moons from the darkness. Metis, Andrastea, Amalthea, Thebe.

Io was much more imposing. It hung on Jupiter's face like a colorful wart. The volcanic moon reminded Horrocks of a scarred glass eye he'd once seen. He tried to make out his mine, or even the king's mines, but gave up.

Maybe I hate the mine as much as Sari does, he thought. I could never abandon it. Gave up too much to have her. Things I'll never get back.

The king had urged Horrocks to become a Ringer and had never gotten over Horrocks' refusal. Horrocks didn't want to adopt another man's face, to be artificially aged.

He did not take this stance out of vanity; he was afraid if he changed his appearance Sari would no longer love him. That she'd leave him. Their love had proved durable over the years, yet there was an unspoken assessment between them that their love was brittle as well. Neither Horrocks nor Sari could dismiss the fear that their bond would disintegrate under the slightest pressure.

When the Push had been repelled and Horrocks' salvaging business was no longer vital, Horrocks had gone to the king and asked to buy the king's oldest Furnace. It had been built around the cone from Control Room Six. Some called it the Epiphany Mine. The cone had suffered more damage from that first explosion than the engineers realized, and the mine was in constant disrepair. Horrocks had heard it was going to be dismantled, the pieces dropped into one of Io's volcanoes during a grand ceremony.

Before settling on the Furnaces as manual laborers, Horrocks' parents had moved from Nebraska to South Dakota to Iowa. Even though Horrocks was born and reared on Furnace Eight his parents instilled him with a lasting hatred of the nomadic life. When the Push ended, Horrocks had the natural inclination to stay. He saw the king's crumbling mine as an opportunity.

Sari saw opportunity in the Deeps. She would only stay if Horrocks could promise her stability.

Horrocks approached the king about the mine. It was an uncomfortable meeting for both of them. As it progressed, the king's unease was replaced with satisfaction.

"I have plenty of money saved," Horrocks told the king.

"Money I paid you. And how much could you possibly have? A fraction of what the Furnace is worth."

"You were going to throw it away."

"Recent interest has inflated its value," the king said.

"I'll give you all we've got."

"You want that mine, I want you to pay a price you'll remember every morning. Every night, too. It's going to be steep. I can't believe you came to me like this. It'll be steep, and if you don't agree to it I'll make your time here so unbearable you'll have to go to the Deeps to escape me. It'll take more than money. When you refused me, part of me shriveled up. Almost as large a part as when I lost my oldest son. That's how I thought of you, Horrocks, as a son, but you were selfish. Put yourself above me."

"I never did that. I don't want to have this argument again," Horrocks said. "Is the Furnace for sale?"

The king made a face of mock concentration. "I'm chewing it over."

"And you're going to show me everything. I don't want to be calling you over every time something goes wrong."

"I'll show you things my engineers don't even know," the king said. His look of mock concentration was replaced with a belligerent stare. "And don't you dare call me if you have a problem. After your tutorial's over, you're all alone. We'll work something out about protection and crop delivery. You won't last a month when you see how hard it is, and then you'll be gone. Out to the Deeps. That's what I want. I'm going to enjoy this."

"I could use a crew," Horrocks said.

"I'll sell you one Furnace engineer. That'll be enough to start with. The rest you find on your own."

"How much is this going to cost?"

"I like this," the king said. "Here's my price. It's a test of your commitment. You didn't commit before. If I give you my precious mine, I want you to prove how committed you'll be."

Horrocks pulled his arm from under Sari's head and turned over. He touched the controls on the wall to lower the window's tinted screen.

His body felt light, filled with air as it did every night before he went to sleep and again when he woke up. Empty. Empty, because the king had taken one lung and one kidney. And to make sure Horrocks would remember the occasion every time he sat down to eat, the king had also extracted the molars from the left side of his mouth.

CHAPTER 12

"You told me we'd get some new food," Kitsis said. "This slop tastes like armpit. I'm starting to get used to it. You shouldn't get used to armpit."

Guilfoyle sat at the head of the kitchen table. He loaded his fork with chunks of green chicken and swallowed them quickly. "We'll get new food," he said. "When we get time, we can stop by a depot."

"And the meal heater won't heat," Kitsis said over a mouthful of runny meat. "Half my tray is lukewarm, the other half frozen solid." She banged on a brick of icy mashed potatoes. "That's harder than—"

"Enough, already," Guilfoyle said. He walked over to the sink and rinsed his tray.

"It's bad enough the food stinks. What's worse is we're running out. Running out of toilet paper, too. *Ran out* I should say, and that's one item we can't recycle." She shook her head and used her fork to dismantle the potatoes.

Guilfoyle dried his tray and sat down. He checked his orange flight suit to make sure he hadn't stained it. "Have you come across anything on the Mayday frequency?"

"Bunch of static. I gave up on that."

"Keep at it. So fucking lazy. I meant to ask you, what kind of perfume are you wearing? Chlorine?"

"You're ugly and you're bald," she said.

"I shave my head."

"Sure you do. No one's believed that lie for as long as you've been telling it. The fire made your scalp a wasteland, brother. Nothing will ever grow there but dandruff."

The intercom hissed, then screeched. A voice came on and said, "Guilfoyle, it's Tinton. We've nearly caught up to you. Slow down and let me come aboard."

"Right," Guilfoyle called out.

"Spread those cheeks," Kitsis said.

"Fuck off," Guilfoyle said. He reached over to the intercom and shut it off. "Shit. OK, get up into the cockpit and don't make any noise."

"What for?" Kitsis said.

"Don't question me," Guilfoyle said.

TINTON STEPPED THROUGH THE EXIT hatch onto the *Honey Locust*. Two burly Bastards loped behind him like obedient gorillas.

"Kind of soon for a house call, isn't it?" Guilfoyle said and extended his hand.

Tinton ignored the hand. "What kind of progress have you made? We're very eager."

"We can go into the den to talk about it," Guilfoyle said. "You want to sit down?"

"I've been sitting two days straight. My ass is as stiff as my cock and my legs are crying for a stretch." Tinton strode down the hallway. "How many Ringers have you captured so far? Five, ten?"

The Bastards stepped around Guilfoyle to guard Tinton.

"How many?" Tinton asked.

"Three."

"Three? Only three?"

"One of them was dead when I found him."

"Two live Ringers? What have you been doing?" Tinton said and stopped to inspect a gouge in the wall. "This whole section's burned out." Tinton touched the black wires that protruded from the wall like a horse's tail. His fingertips came away coated with soot. He wiped them on Guilfoyle's orange sleeve.

"It's an unnecessary conduit," Guilfoyle said. "Bypassed it already on another floor. If I had a newer ship—"

"No," Tinton said and continued down the hallway.

"It would speed things up for you," Guilfoyle said.

Tinton rounded a corner lit by a flickering lamp. Dizzy gnats butted against the dirty yellow glass.

"You have insects on your ship?" Tinton said. The other Bastards chuckled. "A week and what have you been doing? I'm not impressed, Guilfoyle."

"I started by trailing Horrocks. Since he was on the go first, I thought he might have some leads, but no. I left him back at Longliner Station and I'm making my way inward, toward the Mission, toward the mines. Supposed to hear from a few informants soon. Their information's reliable."

"More reliable than you, I hope," Tinton said. "We'll deal with Horrocks. Don't worry about Horrocks."

"Leave him be," Guilfoyle said.

Tinton whirled around. "Leave him alone?"

"Horrocks might get the king," Guilfoyle said. "And anything Horrocks gets I can steal off him, no problem at all."

Tinton stared at Guilfoyle for a few moments, deciding if he should punish the man for contradicting him. "You make a lot of claims," Tinton said and walked up the stairs to the storeroom.

"Where are you going?"

"It's your ship. Don't you know where I'm going?"

The two Bastards chuckled again. Guilfoyle followed them up the steps when what he wanted to do was hurl them back down.

"To see the Ringers," Tinton said when he reached the top. "All two of them."

The Bastards laughed outright.

"Don't see how it's funny. Not from where you're standing," Guilfoyle said.

"You've got to move faster," Tinton said. "I'm thinking of replacing you."

"Replacing me?"

Tinton blocked Guilfoyle from coming into the room. "You're moving too slow!" he yelled. "The miners are on the cusp of a rebellion."

"I thought you were behind that," Guilfoyle said.

"Behind it? If they take the mines, we'll have nothing to inherit." Tinton walked all the way into the room, his back to the cage. "I have men, catalysts, ready to stir the miners at the right time. *On my schedule*. At this moment those same men are soothing the miners but I doubt they'll be successful. An uprising now would—I'm thinking of replacing you."

Guilfoyle bounded up the last few steps. "With who?"

"Someone."

"Someone. *No one*," Guilfoyle said and walked into the room boldly. "I'm the only one you know can do this."

"Let me see the Ringers," Tinton said.

"Right behind you," Guilfoyle said.

The Ringers were sitting on the cots. They didn't stir when Tinton motioned for them to get up and come closer.

"I've seen better. The one on the left is already disfigured. How do we get them out?"

The two Bastards brandished matching knives.

Guilfoyle intercepted them at the cage door. "I'll see you back to your ship."

"I'll see you open that door," one of the Bastards said.

"I have to be meeting somebody shortly," Guilfoyle said.

"You said you were waiting for calls," Tinton said.

The Bastards crowded Guilfoyle into the bars. They'll cut them, Guilfoyle thought. Slash the Ringers to ribbons.

Ruin my plans. Maybe they've guessed. Bastards, maybe they've guessed. I've got to protect the Ringers.

"Get back. They're still mine," Guilfoyle said.

"You're very protective, Guilfoyle. Why is that? We want to brand the Ringers. It'll simplify things in the end. And do you really care what they look like? Step aside and let my men at the Ringers. We cut them now, it'll save us a lot of confusion later on."

"They're not the king. You'll know him when you see him," Guilfoyle said.

"They all look very much alike," Tinton said.

The shorter Bastard put his hand on Guilfoyle's shoulder. Guilfoyle grabbed the hand and swung the man into the cage. The other Bastard lunged toward Guilfoyle, his knife aimed at Guilfoyle's arm. Guilfoyle stepped aside, chopped down on the man's shoulder. The Bastard moved with the blow, bent low and drove his shoulder into Guilfoyle's stomach. Guilfoyle crashed into the bars.

The Bastard stepped back, pleased with himself. The shorter Bastard came forward and Guilfoyle jabbed him in the face. Guilfoyle punched him in the groin and threw him to the floor. The Bastard's head bounced off the metal plating. Guilfoyle stole the man's knife and pressed it against the Bastard's neck. Blood was coming out the corners of the Bastard's eyes.

"Not so rough, Gil," Tinton said and took a few steps toward the cage.

Guilfoyle thought about cutting the Bastard he was pinning to the floor, but decided if the man died Tinton would never leave. Guilfoyle got up, pulled the Bastard to his feet and shoved him forward.

"Put him to bed," Guilfoyle said. "And stay the hell away. You'll get the Ringers when I'm ready to give them away. And don't threaten me with replacement. You wouldn't have hired me if someone else could do this for you. I'm tired of saying it."

"I'm tired of hearing it," Tinton said as he followed the two Bastards into the umbilical.

Guilfoyle waited until they had flown away before he freed Kitsis from the cockpit.

"What was all that racket?" she asked.

Guilfoyle did some cleaning up, then stalked through the hallways to his cabin. His teeth were killing him. Fight must've jarred them loose, he thought. He stood before the antiqued mirror and took his teeth out. He had lost the originals during his disgrace on Mars.

Growing up, Guilfoyle had taken pride in his smile. He brushed four times a day, flossed zealously, never ate candy. His teeth were the one part of his body that he felt total control over. During puberty, Guilfoyle underwent greater changes than most; each morning he woke up feeling as if he had shed the body from the day before. His teenage years were a dark time when he was often too anxious to exert himself for fear he would come apart. His teeth were the only constant.

As an adult he exhausted his skill and energy only to become a mediocre astronaut. An influenza epidemic left him the sole pilot on a crucial mission from Mars to Chicago. On takeoff the ship rose up a hundred feet, tipped over and crumpled like a paper lantern. As was the case with most disasters, the crash was the result of a slew of mishaps, Guilfoyle's being very minor. Of the hundreds who were injured, Guilfoyle managed to bring a couple to safety. Of his humiliating expulsion from the merchant astronauts, Guilfoyle handled himself with tact and modesty. Of his teeth, Guilfoyle could do nothing. They had shattered like icicles during the crash.

His knees were also damaged in the accident. Since then he kept them wrapped in bandages because they had become abnormally sensitive; the slightest abrasion made his kneecaps chatter. Guilfoyle was more ashamed of his knees than his public disgrace, probably because their spastic response was a totem from his body at puberty. He never took the time to deconstruct this shame. He dealt with it by keeping his affliction secret.

Guilfoyle put two fingers in his mouth and unhooked the dentures. He laid them on the wet sink and rubbed his sore gums with anesthetic cream. He opened a drawer and removed two other sets of teeth. He zipped open their leather cases. The teeth, yellow but straight, rested on half-moons of velvet. The first set of dentures was too small; they had a tendency to float off his gums, causing his mouth to fill with saliva. The second set gave him a terrible overbite. The third set, the one he wore most, was too large. He had no trouble planting them in the cored trench where his roots had been, but they bristled against his gums. There were no good dentists in the Jovian system.

Guilfoyle traded the large set for the small one, tucked them in, winced, and went upstairs again. The two Ringers were whispering to each other. Guilfoyle opened the cage door. He ignored the bruised Ringer who said, "Thanks for protecting us, Gil."

Guilfoyle pulled X out of the cage.

"Finally some fresh air," said X.

Guilfoyle unzipped his flight suit to the navel and tied the loose sleeves around his waist.

"The Bastards would have cut me worse, wouldn't they?" X said. He self-consciously touched the scar on his cheek.

Guilfoyle punched him in the face. I'm gonna have to avoid the Bastards from now on, Guilfoyle thought. Take the back ways, alleyways, the long way around for everything. Going to slow me down. They maim the Ringers, I'll have nothing. Got to keep the pretty ones pretty. I better find the king first. I better make it to the Deeps.

Guilfoyle hated not knowing how much progress Horrocks had made. At that moment, Guilfoyle hated the Ringer in front of him.

The Ringer staggered back. Guilfoyle punched him again. Blood shot from the man's nose. "Better make it to the Deeps," Guilfoyle said.

"Shit, I won't stop you," X said.

Guilfoyle bounded forward, laid a powerful round-house in the Ringer's gut. The Ringer vomited on Guil-foyle's flight suit. Guilfoyle slapped him. He elbowed the Ringer in the stomach, punched him in the kidney. The Ringer spun to the side and Guilfoyle grabbed him by the throat.

"What about the other guy?" X asked.

Guilfoyle threw X against the wall. His fists became bony rockets. He could feel the Ringer's teeth loosen with each blow. The Ringer's cheeks ripped open. Blood freckled Guilfoyle's face and hair, stuck to his knuckles like red phlegm. He wiped his hands on the Ringer's shirt. When the Ringer tilted in an effort to fall Guilfoyle straightened him.

He straightened him a dozen times. The Ringer finally fell over. Guilfoyle clenched his false teeth together so they wouldn't come loose, picked the Ringer up and con-tinued the beating.

CHAPTER 13

Sari flew the *Moondrunk* back to Longliner Station the following morning. The Longliner itself had made little progress. She floated 300 feet off the station's stern. Overnight she had turned toward the direction of the Deeps but the ship was, essentially, motionless.

The station, a month before the next scheduled departure, was nearly empty. Sari was able to dock the *Moondrunk* on the lowest tier. Horrocks held Sari's hand as they walked down the paved road toward the hotel.

"You think he might have stayed behind?" Sari said.

"He's clever enough to wait for the next Longliner, smart enough to linger around until the next one when less people will be interested." Horrocks looked closely at every face that passed them and received some rude stares in return.

A thin crowd walked in and out of the empty cafes that lined both sides of the street. Horrocks wondered how many were undercover security officers. Longliner Station had an excellent reputation for safety.

"We might find him here," Horrocks said.

"Hope so," Sari said and squeezed his hand affectionately. "I'd like to get home."

They went into each of the eleven cafes, spoke to a dozen waiters and waitresses, a few cooks and some maitre d's. No one had seen anyone who looked remotely like the king.

Horrocks and Sari thanked them and moved on. They looked down some trash alleys, talked with a few vagrants and again came up with nothing. Horrocks gave the vagrants some money anyway.

"Drug runners live in the sewers," one of them said. His shoes didn't match, his jacket was inside-out. "Your guy could be with them. I know the tunnels. Describe him again."

"Thanks," Sari said and pulled Horrocks into the street. "No way the king is in the sewer."

"Nobody's down there," Horrocks said. "That guy would've jumped me soon as I got down the manhole. Guess we should check the hotel."

Horrocks was hesitant to go inside. He first met Sari around the corner from The Sundowner twenty-two years ago. It had been toward the end of his career as a drug mule. He was returning from the Deeps with three tubes of barbiturate paste somewhere on the interstate of his digestive system. One of them leaked, supersaturating his system. All Horrocks' senses burned.

Sari recognized his condition and brought him up to her room. She had been booked to leave on the same Longliner Horrocks had come in on. She missed her flight. Marat's going to have me skinned, she thought and put Horrocks in the bathtub. She stripped him down, force-fed him a purgative, followed that with a tall shake of liquid charcoal. Both items had come out of her suitcase. She called the suitcase her *saddle* because it was packed with muling accessories.

Sari turned on the shower, cleaned and dried him. He spent the night in the tub, naked, head propped up on a pillow.

They followed this routine for two days. Sari ignored the angry knocks on the door. On the third day she showered with Horrocks. On the fourth day he slept in her bed and they made love. They made love before Horrocks knew her name. Sari doubted he remembered the experience at all, his body had been in such commotion. She guessed that it was possible he recalled a general intimacy, but she never asked because she didn't want to embarrass him.

Sari remembered how aggressive they both were, how they seldom rested between bouts; Horrocks seemed to have no refractory period.

Horrocks didn't comment on her tattoos and Sari found that incredibly appealing. She felt completely uninhibited with him. She even permitted him to perform cunnilingus, something she had rarely allowed her customers to do. Sari had given up prostitution for muling years ago but her memories of those claustrophobic nights hadn't lost their obscene power to depress her. In bed with Horrocks, those memories became vaporous and impotent. This was the first aspect of Horrocks that Sari was attracted to.

At the week's end they decided to quit muling for their dealers and become self-employed. Their respective pushers would not accept the decision and tried to coerce the couple with violence. Horrocks crippled three negotiators before the pushers gave up.

Horrocks and Sari fell in love much later, while in the employ of the king and far away from The Sundowner.

"Let's see what they know here," Horrocks said. They questioned the concierge and cornered a few redcaps but they were all oblivious.

Horrocks and Sari walked out of the lobby and sat on a sidewalk bench. "Why don't you stay out here, watch the people," Horrocks said. "I'm going to sneak upstairs, go through some of the floors. I might get lucky."

He kissed her on the lips, slipped into The Sundowner and up the stairs. He walked to the top floor, crept down the empty hallway and worked his way down. The carpet, white and coarse, had recently been replaced. A small number of rooms had trays of half-eaten food outside their doors. Horrocks overheard two redcaps complain that the hotel hadn't been this empty since its construction, nor yesterday's Longliner as full.

During his sweep of the fifth floor Horrocks realized he was being followed by two men. They tailed him down the stairs to the fourth floor.

"He's the king's dog. Always was," said a voice behind Horrocks.

"Puppy's more like it," said another.

Horrocks turned abruptly and faced two Bastards in their late twenties. Their hair was prematurely gray. "You children lost?" Horrocks said.

"Tinton wasn't specific enough with you," the man on the left said. His cheeks were horribly scarred, the result of carnivorous acne. His left hand was inside his coat. "Why don't you let Guilfoyle do the work for both of you?"

The man on right grinned. His thin hair was tied in a ponytail. "You should go back to your Furnace. We know you've got plenty of problems there. Why don't you hole up? Wait it out like everyone else."

Horrocks saw a tray of food a few doors down, a glass on that tray he could break and use as a weapon. It was too far. "I thought Tinton said you'd be the ones waiting it out," Horrocks said. "Yet here you are."

"We don't all agree with Tinton," Ponytail said. "Tinton's been trying to make everyone happy. He's not to be respected. Doesn't even resemble our father."

"You fellas do?" Horrocks said.

The Bastards nodded. "Plus Tinton's blind in one eye," said Acne Scar. "He thinks we don't know. Our father's got excellent vision."

"Who cares?" Horrocks said.

"It matters to us."

"I heard the king took one of your testicles along with all the other stuff," Ponytail said.

"I heard he took them both. That true, gelding?" said Acne Scar. "If he didn't, we'll take them both now. Are you gonna go back home or not?" He removed a dagger from his coat.

Horrocks grabbed the man by his knife arm and swung him into the nearest door. The door split open; Acne Scar landed on his back. His torso was twisted in such a way that Horrocks didn't think the man would ever get up. Ponytail punched Horrocks in the back and kicked him into the room. Horrocks tripped over Acne Scar and didn't catch his balance until he reached the two twin beds. He turned and braced himself for the assault.

Ponytail launched himself at Horrocks and they landed on the far bed, punching, rolling, shoving. Horrocks reached for the pen on the nightstand and stabbed Ponytail between the ribs; he used the heel of his hand to shove it in all the way to the cap. The Bastard screamed and tried to retrieve the pen but his clumsy fingers buried it deeper instead.

Ponytail ripped the cheap sconce from the wall, swung it at Horrocks and missed. Horrocks dropped to the floor and threw his shoulder into the bed. Ponytail fell over the nightstand. He lifted his bloody shirt in an attempt to get at the pen once more. "You prick," the Bastard said. His ribs were stained with blood and blue ink.

Horrocks looked around the room quickly. He saw a chair and ran for it. The Bastard intercepted Horrocks and knocked him into a desk. The desktop speared Horrocks in the side. Ponytail balled his fists into a hammer and used Horrocks' back as an anvil. He pounded until there was no wind left in Horrocks' lung.

"Your reputation is such a sham," the Bastard said. His ponytail had come undone.

Horrocks took a deep breath between blows, jumped up and charged the Bastard. The charge ended in the bathroom. Horrocks tried to punch the Bastard in the stomach and face but there wasn't enough room to take a proper swing; his elbows kept hitting the wall and mirror. He used his feet to trip the Bastard instead. Ponytail's head struck the sink on his way down. His left arm spasmed. He got to his knees using his right arm as a pivot.

Horrocks wound a fistful of the man's loose hair in his fingers and smashed the back of the Bastard's head against the yellow porcelain tub. The Bastard clawed at Horrocks' body, finally settling on the face. His hands walked up Horrocks' skin toward his eyes, his thumbs poised to pop them.

Horrocks arched his own head back to shorten the Bastard's reach. He tightened his grip on the Bastard's hair and slammed the man's head against the tub again. Again. Again.

Ponytail's hands fell away from Horrocks' face. The pit of the bathtub was greased with blood.

"Fucking idiot Bastard," Horrocks said. He closed the toilet's lid and sat on it. It was a few minutes before he could see clearly. His lung felt as if it had been raked with a tiger's claw. He coughed up a hunk of blood and spat it into the sink. Horrocks stared at the dead Bastard. The man reminded him of dozens of corpses he had seen during the Push. This entire fight reminded him of the Push. Horrocks' hands shook, not with fear but elated rage. No, fucking no, he thought. His mind recalled all the guilty enjoyment he had gotten out of the war. The part of himself that had been resurrected during the kitchen battle with the Ringer McGavin. The part of himself he had buried but was proving too resilient to die. Horrocks was terrified of that man's fluency in menace and anger.

He felt as if he'd just fallen off a centrifuge.

His arms began to shake.

Horrocks wrapped Ponytail in a cocoon of bedsheets and hid him in the tub.

Acne Scar was gone. He'd left his dagger on the floor. Horrocks took it. He went back into the bathroom and washed the blood from his hands and face. His clothes were wrinkled but mostly unstained.

Horrocks left the hotel calmly and found Sari on the bench where he'd left her.

"Any sign?" she asked. A concerned look twisted her features. "Why are you out of breath?"

"Two Bastards," Horrocks said. "I killed one." He sat down next to her.

"This is out of hand. Are you hurt? Let's get out of this."

"Can't now. We were a nuisance to the Bastards before. Now we're a definite threat. They'll try and put us away. Tinton won't be able to hold them back once they hear of it. We're not safe anymore, not at all."

"Should have thought of that before you went on a killing spree."

"One. Only one. I had no options."

"I know," she said softly. "We'd better leave." She got up and started off down the street.

Horrocks slowed her down. "We'd better not. They'll find the body in a little while. Any ship leaving now or anytime soon will be followed and questioned. We have to stay a couple hours at least. Do I have any blood on my face?"

"This is—Horrocks, the hotel. The Bastard. This is—"

"Relax," he said.

The tremor in his arms receded to his fingers. Horrocks put his hands in his pockets.

They found a cafe near the end of the strip, away from the hotel. Sari chose a table on the sidewalk that afforded them views in both directions. The waitress took their order and walked off in a daze.

"Do you think the king could've gotten on the Longliner? Did we miss him?" Sari said.

"We would have seen him. Even if he was disguised—his ego's too big for him to pretend to be someone else. Everyone knows he's missing. Someone else would've seen him even if we didn't. They would've said something. There would've been a commotion."

Horrocks took a drink of water. His glass was beaded with moisture. He touched his wet fingers to his forehead. "The king's got his dead son, too. I hadn't thought of that before. You can't smuggle a dead body on a Longliner." He brought his wet fingers to his forehead again.

"Stop doing that," Sari said.

"I'm hot. The king has too much baggage to slip away unseen. He's holed up somewhere."

"Unless he's really dead," Sari said. "We'll never find him then."

Horrocks could see into the deserted docking wall where the *Moondrunk* was parked. The empty slots gave him a tessellated view of the stars beyond the station.

"I want a soda. Where's the waitress?" Sari said.

"We should go to the Mission next," Horrocks said.

"We should go back to the mine."

"We've been over this." His hand darted for his glass of water and knocked it over. He righted the glass and said, "What would that accomplish?"

Sari calmly unfolded her napkin and laid it over her knees. "Then we should go to the king's mines and wait there. If he's alive, no way is he going to abandon his company. Sooner or later he's going to wind up back home."

As the waitress passed by Sari tugged on her apron and said, "Diet soda, please."

"It'll take more than a week to get to the mines without a Spot Drive," Horrocks said.

"That's why we should get started right now. Why wait?"

"Because of the Mission," Horrocks said.

"They've got nothing to do with this."

"The king's oldest son is buried there. He lost an arm protecting his father during the Push. The king's not cold enough to dump one of his children somewhere. If he's not on the Longliner, he went to the Mission. Either to inter his son or get him last rites."

"Someone on the run doesn't stop for religion," Sari said. "They keep running."

The waitress returned with Sari's drink and their food.

"It would be foolish not to check. He could be hiding there," Horrocks said and picked up his silverware.

"Didn't they excommunicate him?"

"He built the place. Maybe they showed him a little Christian forgiveness. It's not that far. We have to look."

"And after that? After we find nothing at the Mission?" Sari said.

Horrocks took a moment to chew his food, stalling his capitulation. "After that we'll go back to the mines and wait."

"Finally," Sari said and sighed. She sliced her vegetables into small pieces, became bored and moved on to the chicken.

"On the way to the mines I want to try and find as many Ringers as possible. There's more they can tell us. Help us locate—"

"Is that Wyeth?" Sari said and pointed to a man walking away from them. He had the bewildered gait of a mental vacant.

Horrocks stood up. "Wyeth! Wyeth!" he said. The man turned around and a smile of recognition grew over his face. He approached the table.

"Horrocks. Holy shit, Horrocks," Wyeth said.

"Sit down with us, Wy," Sari said.

"But you're eating."

"Quit fussing and sit down," Sari said. "Hungry?"

"I ate this morning," Wyeth said and sat next to Sari. His thin hair was glued to his head with shiny cream. His blue jeans were stained but his red flight jacket was so brand-new it crackled when he moved. His long teeth were as gray as his T-shirt. He blinked with his whole face.

"What are you doing here?" Wyeth asked. "Wait, I know. Looking for the old taskmaster."

"Without much luck," Sari said.

"That's because he's dead," Wyeth said.

Horrocks put his silverware down. Not true, he said to himself. "Where'd you hear that?"

"I've maintained connections in the Deeps. The king was on last month's Longliner. Not yesterday's, the one before that. Had his son's body with him." He blinked hard and frowned. "They both died in some kind of scuffle. It's true. The king was dressed up as someone else."

"The last Longliner left before all this started," Horrocks said.

"Maybe it wasn't a Longliner. Another ship, then."

"What other ship?" Horrocks asked.

"Give it a rest, honey," Sari said.

"All this makes no difference to me," Wyeth said. He put one hand over Sari's and said, "He's too excitable. Let's get him medicated."

"You didn't come in off the Longliner, did you?" Sari said. "Don't you want to eat?"

Wyeth shook his head. "Came in off a Shortliner from Miami. Saw my wife."

"You got married?" Horrocks said.

"About five years ago. When's the last time I saw you? It's a great setup. She stays in Miami. I see her for a year, come out here for a year. Like that."

"We should try it," Sari said.

"I don't get laid for twelve months at a time, but we make up for it during our reunions. My visitor's visa expired, so I had to come back a few months early this time."

"To do what?" Horrocks asked. He was finished with his food and pushed the plate away. The waitress walked by three times without removing it.

"I don't know. Not to mule again, that's for dead cert. Aren't any ships left to salvage, either."

"Mining?" Sari said.

"I've had it with them. Too fucking deadly. I was thinking of opening a depot somewhere abouts. Plenty of empty space out here with lots of traffic. People love to stop and buy little things they don't really need."

The waitress dropped the check on Horrocks' plate. It soaked up the gravy from his steak.

"I should go," Wyeth said. "I've rented a ship to scout some locations and I want to get started."

"It was good to see you," Sari said.

"And you, m'lady," he said and bowed.

"Good luck," Horrocks said and they shook hands.

"You, too. I might stop by your Furnace sometime, see what it looks like."

Horrocks sat down. He counted out some money for the bill and when he was done, Wyeth was gone.

"He looks terrible," Sari said. "All those creases around his mouth. He got old."

"I think he's still muling," Horrocks said.

"He was pretty good at it. You think he's right? The king is dead?"

"Wyeth loves gossip better than sex. That's why he lives so far from his wife," Horrocks said. He left the money on the plate, on top of the soiled check.

"Shouldn't we wait a little longer?" Sari said.

They both looked at the entrance to the hotel. A redcap stood with his arms relaxed at his side. His lips were pursed and he appeared to be whistling a tune.

Horrocks saw the Bastard he had thrown through the door. Acne Scar. He was standing in the alley next to The Sundowner.

"We can go," Horrocks said and they left the restaurant.

"Could you imagine being a mule all these years?" Sari said. "Makes me almost glad we've got the mine."

"You should be glad. I don't think you're grateful enough."

They walked in silence for a few minutes.

"We should get back and feed the dogs," Sari said.

"And the Ringer."

They mingled with the sparse crowd, glanced toward the hotel to be certain they were under no suspicion, and headed back to the *Moondrunk*. Two junked ships occupied the spaces at the end of the platform. Horrocks knew no one would claim them; they had been parked here to be forgotten.

"Who's standing outside our ship?" Sari said.

The stranger was wearing the official Longliner Station uniform: navy pants, white shirt, striped navy jacket. His hair was combed back, oiled in place, shaved on the sides. His forehead was glassy and his lips looked like a pair of earthworms. The upper lip was darkened with a mustache that was more dirt than hair.

"Mr. and Mrs.—" he paused to consult his brown folder, "Horrocks, yes?"

Horrocks didn't reply. He wasn't sure if this pertained to the dead Bastard in the hotel tub.

"I'll need to inspect your ship."

"No you don't. We're leaving," Horrocks said.

"That's fine," the man said. He trapped the folder in his armpit. "Before you go, I need to make an inspection."

Now Horrocks was sure this had nothing to do with the dead Bastard. The man wasn't treating Horrocks like a threat.

"You've been here more than two hours. According to our regulations, that makes you liable to a random search. Custom House regulations," he said. "Your keys."

"What's your name?"

"Pankras."

Horrocks motioned for Sari to step away.

"Your keys," Pankras said.

"Why don't you bother someone who's actually staying here?" Sari said.

"You're actually staying here until I make my inspection," Pankras said.

Horrocks gave Sari the keys and she walked up the *Moondrunk*'s gangplank.

Pankras tried to push Horrocks out of the way and follow Sari but Horrocks pushed him back.

"Really, let me through," Pankras said. He grasped for Sari's clothes, missed and pushed Horrocks again.

"You're going to want to stop shoving me," Horrocks said.

Pankras said, "I only want to see the—"

"What?" Horrocks said.

"Fuck you, gravedigger," Pankras said and pounced.

Horrocks swung at Pankras' stomach with all of his strength; Pankras collapsed around Horrocks' fist. Horrocks reached over the man's back and pinched his wallet.

Pankras tried to push Horrocks again but Horrocks grabbed the hand, twisted it back and punched him in the chest. Pankras sagged and Horrocks eased him to the floor. "Shave that embarrassing mustache," Horrocks said and, without looking to see if he had any spectators, boarded the *Moondrunk*.

"Take her out easy," Horrocks said when he got to the cockpit.

Horrocks opened Pankras' wallet. "Six dollars. One stale condom. Bet this thing's been here two years. Credit cards in different names, none of them Pancreas, or whatever his name was. Picture of a cocker spaniel. One ID. Shit. I was hoping I wouldn't find this."

"He was not a Longliner employee," Sari said. "Where's the ID from?"

Horrocks showed her. "Rival Mines" was written across the top of the shiny card in gothic script. "One of Rouen's men," Horrocks said. "Is he looking to start another war?"

"Now would be a good time to do it," Sari said.

"That's not funny."

"See if I'm wrong."

CHAPTER 14

Guilfoyle showered, masturbated and dressed. We'd better find a depot soon and get some more soap, he thought. He zipped his orange flight suit up to the neck. A little tight around the waist, he thought. I should ask Kit about her exercises.

He lathered his bald head with shaving cream, took out his razor and shaved with neat strokes that made rows of cream, skin, cream, skin. Kitsis is wrong, he thought. I do shave it. I've got as much hair now as before the accident.

After the accident Guilfoyle slept through two rounds of operations and woke up during the third. The shocked surgeons finally subdued and sedated him, but not before Guilfoyle had wrecked their sewing machines.

The next time Guilfoyle came to he was in a hospital bed, unable to move, tubes threaded in his mouth and out his anus. His bed was fenced in by a gaggle of curious doctors. They told him he was on the triage ship *The Arkhangel'sk*. They explained his condition. Permanent baldness due to Guilfoyle's severe burns was the least significant injury. As the rest of his body healed, baldness became the most traumatic. So traumatic that Guilfoyle refused to believe the doctors were right. He shaved his head every day.

Guilfoyle washed some hairless cream off the razor and continued. Should shave Kitsis' head, see how she likes it, Guilfoyle thought. See how cold it gets. Guilfoyle would never admit to her that he did this every morning hoping the razor would reanimate his follicles. He didn't trust doctors or their flawed diagnoses.

When Guilfoyle was done he burnished his pate with a towel and picked two battered paperbacks off the dresser. He shoved them in his back pocket and locked the door to his room on the way out. Guilfoyle crept through the hallways, avoided his sister and climbed through the cockpit's trapdoor. He locked that door, too.

She'd be smart to leave me the fuck alone, he thought. Nothing short of a fire's going to get me out of here.

He sat in his fancy chair, remembered the books in his pocket and leaned forward to take them out. He chose the one with a grizzly gunfighter on the cover and threw the second book on the floor. He folded the novel so that the front and back covers touched, adding another white crease to the spine.

Guilfoyle backtracked a few pages to reacquaint himself with the story, found where he'd left off, then reclined in the chair and read with relish. Both books had been purchased from a roving depot, and both were westerns. It was the only genre he read because it was the only one he could relate to.

An hour later, suitably relaxed, Guilfoyle turned on the scanner to eavesdrop on the light stream of ships that crossed his path. The *Honey Locust* sat motionless somewhere between Longliner Station and the Mission. The scanner hissed as it probed the passing conversations. Most of it was vapid chitchat. Guilfoyle reserved a small portion of his attention for any drama or, better still, the telltale seriousness of dirty secrets. He picked up the book again, found his place and resumed reading.

Few ships passed in either direction; most were coming away from the mines. As they neared the *Honey Locust* their voices grew louder, faded as they went by.

Guilfoyle turned another page, engrossed in a brawl over a classy whore.

The *Moondrunk* had gone by him yesterday. Guilfoyle knew Horrocks was going to the Mission, and when that proved fruitless the *Moondrunk* would cover the rest of the distance to the mines. Without a Spot Drive Horrocks'll never be too far from me, Guilfoyle thought and smiled.

Guilfoyle planned to stay away from the Mission. When he first moved to the Jovian system, immediately after his disgrace, the Mission had been Guilfoyle's first stop. He counted on them to provide him solace and shelter and brotherhood. The clergymen were aggressively friendly, then just aggressive. Guilfoyle asked them about the tenets of their faith and was told not to ask. "When you're ready," was another favorite response.

They went through his belongings and asked him to strip. The Push had recently been declared. Priests and doctors examined his body, comparing his measurements and features against a chart. The words *transient* and *Ringer* and *incompatible* dropped around him like stones.

His clothes came back bleached with thumb-sized crosses. Servants of the Mission periodically refused Guilfoyle meals without explanation. A week later Guilfoyle escaped on a Parish-class vessel with two other detainees. They had to kill the monk guarding the ship and considered that a worthy trade. Guilfoyle ditched the men at Longliner Station. He kept the ship and modified it with stolen parts. It would become the first in his fleet. It would also be his only valuable possession after his business collapsed. The vessel had seen many names but Guilfoyle liked its most recent—*Honey Locust*—the best.

Guilfoyle flipped another page. The words started sliding apart. He fell asleep and woke up two hours later to a harsh banging. Kitsis, pounding on the trapdoor with a saucepan.

"Are you up there?" Kitsis said. "Get down here, Gil. Quit hiding."

"Fuck *off*," he yelled.

A sleek loader moved past the *Honey Locust*, headed for Longliner Station. Guilfoyle tossed the book and leaned forward to adjust the scanner's volume. Where's she going? he thought. The Longliner's left already.

The scanner, on its highest setting, squawked: "—not here or it would have shown all over my body."

"He's around."

"He isn't. Probably back home with the queen. Just wanted to get rid of us."

Guilfoyle jumpstarted the *Honey Locust* and fired three grappling hooks into the loader. He punched in the code to keep the grapple lines tensed, so if the loader pulled away the *Honey Locust* would pull back. Guilfoyle unlocked the trapdoor and climbed down the ladder to the kitchen.

"What are you doing up there, playing with yourself? Hogging all the soap?" Kitsis said. "I need your help for something."

Guilfoyle shoved her aside, raced to the exit hatch and extended the umbilical because he was in too much of a rush to use the drill. When the umbilical started rolling out he went down to the basement. He skirted the drilling chamber and went to the salvager's armory. He decided to save the bats and instead chose a stiletto strapped to a wrist holster.

The umbilical bridged both ships. The door to the loader was locked; Guilfoyle opened it with a gentle explosive. As the ships exchanged air a frigid breeze chilled Guilfoyle's lungs. He stepped through the umbilical into a lounge with ten chairs and three Ringers. Guilfoyle's bloodstream was bombarded with adrenaline.

Three Ringers, Guilfoyle thought. Like looking at evil triplets, these three.

One had cut his hair short and dyed it indigo. The second had cut his hair even shorter and had shaved designs on his scalp. His ears, nose and brow were thronged with steel piercings, most of them infected. The third Ringer, sitting atop a high desk, looked exactly like the king.

"Instead of impaling us you could've hailed us on the comm," Indigo said.

"Too many people listening," Guilfoyle said. He thought about taking all three at the same time. The Ringers had slight bodies, like the king, and Guilfoyle had no doubt he could overpower them individually. But some were good fighters. Some had been strong before their transformation, before they had been given pills that attenuated their muscles to more accurately duplicate the king's aged frame. On occasion their original strength remained.

A fistfight might not work, he decided. Guilfoyle became purposefully agitated. "I've been tracking you six days. I didn't want to blow this by announcing it over a comm. Then anyone with a scanner could hear it. The king wants you back home." He wasn't sure if they'd believe him. He sensed that the one with all the piercings wanted to.

"You found him?" said Pierce.

"A couple days after the attack. You're the last batch floating around. Come back to my ship and I'll get you where you belong, back with the king."

"He's a bullshitter," Indigo said. "Probably working for Rouen. The king is not safe at home." He got out of his chair and circled Guilfoyle. "I would have felt it."

The untarnished Ringer said, "He's a Gei—"

Indigo silenced him with a glare.

Guilfoyle evaluated the untarnished Ringer. I'm going to keep you, he thought. You'll pass without question.

"What kind of stupid suit are you wearing?" Indigo said. "Are you supposed to be a pumpkin?"

"Are you coming?" Guilfoyle asked.

"I'd feel it if the king was nearby," Indigo said.

"He's not nearby," Guilfoyle said. "He's back at the flagship Furnace, waiting for you." He looked at Pierce. "You ready?"

Pierce started to move and Indigo walked over and pushed him into a chair. "Go away, Guilfoyle," Indigo said. "I know who you are. Body snatcher and rat-catcher."

"If you know who I am then you know I'm the one who should take you back."

"We know where the mines are. Besides, he would've sent Horrocks, not you."

"Horrocks is dead," Guilfoyle said.

"You're terrible at this! A first-year Ringer wouldn't believe you. Are there still bodies in your freezer? Is it true you cook and eat them?"

"Let's go. We have to go now, back to my ship. Right now," Guilfoyle said.

The untarnished Ringer hopped down off the desk. "These two can tell when—"

"Why don't we call him?" Indigo said.

"The mines aren't accepting transmissions," Guilfoyle said. "He's still not safe. Especially not until his Ringers are all back home. We haven't figured out yet who tried to kill him."

"I have," Pierce said. He looked pleadingly at the others. "Let's go with him. We've looked hard enough. No shame in quitting now."

"You don't know who did it," Indigo said.

"Bounty hunters are posted all over," Guilfoyle said. "You're damned lucky I found you."

"Damned stupid is what this is," Indigo said. "Go chase your corpses. We're trying to find the king."

"He's been found. We have to get moving," Guilfoyle said.

Indigo kept the other two Ringers rooted with his oblique stares.

"Hope the bounty hunters get to you next," Guilfoyle said and turned to go. He walked slowly, expecting at least one of them would be frightened enough to follow. His footsteps were the only sound.

Fuck this, Guilfoyle thought, spun around and jerked his arm out. The stiletto sprang from the wrist holster to his hand. In the same fluid motion he stuck it in the untarnished Ringer's neck because the man was closest, may even have been following Guilfoyle off the ship. The stiletto went clear through the Ringer's throat. Guilfoyle ripped the knife out the side of the Ringer's neck and pushed him to the floor.

Guilfoyle ran for Indigo who eluded him by staying just out of reach behind a mob of chairs. Guilfoyle gave up, lifted a chair and hurled it at Indigo as the Ringer turned to flee down another part of the ship.

Pierce hadn't moved.

"Wasted a perfectly good Ringer on you two," Guilfoyle said. Could've used him too, Guilfoyle thought. Stupid and rash. Won't win anything being stupid and rash. I've got to be careful. Fuck careful. I wish all the Ringers were dead. Wish I had my bats on me.

Indigo got to his knees. Guilfoyle was tempted to cut his neck, too.

Guilfoyle had his hands in the man's hair when Pierce said, "Hold off. He's a Geiger."

"What the hell is a Geiger? Don't stammer, you fucking moron. What the hell's a Geiger?"

"His body tells him when the king's close by."

"Now who's lying?" Guilfoyle said. He punched Indigo in the face, twisted the man's collar and pulled him to his feet.

"His body tells him," Pierce said. "And it'll tell you, you know how to read it."

"Do you know how to read him?" Guilfoyle asked.

Indigo shook his head. Pierce ignored him and said, "It works by—"

"I don't care how it works, long as it works. You know how to read this?"

"We all do," Pierce said. "I'm a Geiger, too."

"This is common knowledge?"

"To Ringers."

"How many are there? How many Geigers?"

"Three in total."

"Pick up your friend there," Guilfoyle said. He wondered if his luck could be any better. He didn't think it could.

"He's dead, that one," Pierce said. "Why do you want him?"

"Put him over your shoulder. We're leaving."

"Have you really found the king?" Pierce asked.

"Let's go," Guilfoyle said. He pushed Indigo through the umbilical. Pierce walked behind them, struggling with the weight of the dead Ringer.

Guilfoyle led them to the kitchen. Kitsis was at the table, playing solitaire with a soiled deck of cards.

"Get some food together," Guilfoyle told her.

"Who the fuck are they?" Kitsis said. "They think they're the king?"

"Who are you?" Indigo said. Guilfoyle punched him in the back.

"There is no more food. Almost none at all," Kitsis said. She laid the nine of hearts below the ten of clubs.

"Find some. Find food for two more," Guilfoyle said.

The eight of spades below the nine of hearts. "I've told you how many times?" she said. "The food—"

"I don't care if you have to go through the trash," Guilfoyle said. "Scrounge up some food and heat it."

Guilfoyle took the Ringers up to the storeroom, laid the dead one on the floor in front of the morgue and locked Indigo and Pierce in the cage with the other two. "Get reacquainted," Guilfoyle said and left.

He found some timed explosives, threw them into the Ringer's sleek loader, walked back through the umbilical

155

and closed it off. He brought the *Honey Locust* to a safe distance, then went up to his cockpit to watch. The loader collapsed in three stages, each one more dramatic than the last. Guilfoyle wondered if he should have searched their ship for clues, decided he didn't have the patience today so it didn't matter.

Guilfoyle climbed down into the kitchen and saw that Kitsis was still playing cards. He swiped them to the floor before going back up to the storeroom.

He went over to the morgue, opened an empty slot and pulled the slab out. He lifted the dead Ringer off the floor, laid him on the slab and wheeled over the embalming apparatus. He walked over to the cage while waiting for the blood to drain out of the man's ankle.

"You said you knew who killed the king," Guilfoyle said.

"It was a lie to buy time," said Pierce.

Guilfoyle pointed at Indigo. "How can you tell when the king is nearby?"

"Fuck you. Ask the other one, he was so eager to tell you back on the loader."

"I want to hear it from you," Guilfoyle said.

"It's not that accurate. I'm not a compass."

"The hell you're not. What happens? You get an erection?" Guilfoyle said and snickered. "Your tail wag? You pee on the floor?"

Indigo shook his head. Guilfoyle's hands shot through the cage, grabbed Pierce by his earrings and dragged him up to the bars. Guilfoyle's massive palms tightened around Pierce's skull.

"Won't take me long to crush him," Guilfoyle said.

"I'm not going to tell you," Indigo said. "Thought you weren't interested, anyway."

Guilfoyle squeezed harder. Two of Pierce's cellmates took him by the elbows and pulled him out of Guilfoyle's vise. Pierce thanked them, crawled into the corner and rested his head on the toilet's rim.

"I never heard of Geigers before," Guilfoyle said.

"The king didn't want to repeat the chaos surrounding his kidnapping during the Push," Indigo said. "That only lasted a few days, he was found pretty quick, but the incident left an impression. So he let the flesh artists do some tinkering, and here I am."

"A lot of good it's doing, here you are and where's the king? Tell me what to look for, how it works," Guilfoyle said.

"What's a grave robber want with the king anyhow?" Indigo said.

"You will tell me. I will find out."

"Not from us," Indigo said. "Way you just treated my confederate there, he won't tell you either. The king knew all about you. He admired you, the way you nurtured your salvaging business, even rivaled Horrocks' at one point." He sat on the cot near the toilet and put his hand on Pierce's back to comfort him. "But you let those men cheat you. Ripped off your ships and drove them out to the Deeps, didn't they? Must've been embarrassing."

Guilfoyle would've grabbed another Ringer but they'd all moved out of range.

"King heard about that and lost respect for you. He had someone track those men down in the Deeps and he financed them. Every year they give him a tribute of cash. How does that strike you? Rich, they are. Plenty rich."

"You're smug, but you won't last long," Guilfoyle said. He really wanted to reach into that cage.

"How does it feel to know they're out there, so far away you can't do a thing about it?" Indigo said.

"Feels better knowing you're so close, and I can do what I want with you."

Guilfoyle noticed the bruised Ringer—the one he'd gotten days ago on the Gunwitch—asleep on the floor. The Ringer's welts were gone. His coloring had changed from purple to saffron. Guilfoyle looked away quickly, careful to give no sign of his concern. He's healing incredibly fast, Guilfoyle thought. I could use him. He'll do fine. The other Ringers would maim him if they knew what I had in mind.

He wandered over to the embalming machine, changed the hoses and started the preservative feed.

They could maim him, Guilfoyle thought. They might, anyway, just so he fits in. Guilfoyle went back to the cage, opened the door and dragged Saffron out.

"What, are you gonna hit me?" Saffron said, suddenly awake.

Never, Guilfoyle thought. At least not till I find one better. Guilfoyle bound Saffron to the wall manacle farthest from the cage. Guilfoyle stripped the man of his belt and shoelaces, then decided to take the Ringer's shoes altogether.

Indigo watched this and grinned. "You are so transparent."

Guilfoyle banged on the cage with his hand.

Kitsis came into the room with food. "I managed to cobble enough together for three trays. Just don't ask where I got it." She put the trays down and left.

Pierce crawled toward the bars, sat down and held his head. His right eyeball was completely bloodshot. He said, "The king did admire you."

"Get back!" Guilfoyle said.

"I'm just saying. Can't you let us out of here?"

Guilfoyle banged the cage again. His dentures were digging into his gums. He could taste his own blood.

Indigo pointed to Saffron. "He'll never pass for the king. You're a fool to think it would work."

Guilfoyle tried to look surprised. "Pass for the king?"

"Who would you sell him to?"

Guilfoyle gave one tray of food to Saffron and carried the other two toward the cage.

"Look at him, he's lost too much weight," Indigo said. "He was always the worst of us."

"Not true," Saffron said.

"Too skinny," Guilfoyle said and gave all three trays to Saffron. "Have a feast. I catch you sharing, I'll sew your lips to the floor."

Indigo faced the other Ringers in the cage. "He's going to try and pass one of us off as the king. Sell us to the Bastards or someone else."

"I'm just asking you to impersonate the king. It's your goddam job, isn't it? Has been for years," Guilfoyle said. He switched off the lights, said, "Rest up. Tomorrow you're going to find me the king," and walked out.

"At least send your sister back to service us," Indigo shouted. "I can't do anything when I'm tense. Isn't that what she's here for?"

It was a few minutes before their eyes adjusted to the darkness.

"Give us a bite," Indigo said. He was slumped in the corner of the cage like a sated junkie.

"No way," Saffron said. He was sitting on the floor. One hand was in the air, hanging from the manacle. He attacked the used meals with his other hand. "I'm so hungry. Didn't realize until I started to eat all this."

"You're betraying the king," Indigo said.

"I'm *hungry*. You'll be hungry, too," he said between chews. "You heard Guilfoyle. Not a lot of food on his ship. You should cooperate if you want to eat. I plan to eat and keep on eating."

"Traitor," Indigo said. "The least you could do is shave your head. Cut, burn yourself. Be creative."

"Be quiet," Saffron said.

Guilfoyle had neglected to give them water. He's got to have water, Saffron thought. That he's got in abundance. He forgot to bring some down. I'll remind him.

Pierce had been drinking water out of the toilet, but the toilet was on the other side of the cage. Saffron didn't think they'd share.

"If you don't do something about your appearance, I will," Indigo said.

"So will I," Pierce said. "Soon as we get out of here."

"But you won't," Saffron said. The second tray was empty. He licked the juice off the bottom and started on the third. "Guilfoyle will only let you out for beatings." He inclined his head toward X whose face was knotted with colonies of wart-like lumps. His broken nose rained snot but he was too dispirited to wipe it.

"Don't be a traitor," Indigo said. "You ate, you were hungry. We can all of us understand hungry. Throw it up. Do the right thing. Purge."

"*Traitor*. The king is dead," Saffron said. He polished off the third tray, put his fist against his chest and swallowed a burp. "The king is gone. I'm not going to stay true to him. It was bad enough when he was alive. I hated him. I hate looking like him."

"Burn yourself," Indigo said.

"The king is dead."

"He is not dead," Indigo said.

"Then how long do you think he'll last without us?"

CHAPTER 15

The Mission was thousands of miles from any other satellite, and 150,000 miles from Io. It was as large as Longliner Station but saw far less business even though its orbit was fixed to the transport lanes that led to the Annex.

The Mission had a cruciform ground plan and a severely angled roof made of fortified stained glass. Horrocks couldn't tell which biblical scenes the glass recreated. He was too close; the glass was best viewed from miles away.

Sari parked in the docking dome and exited the ship with Horrocks.

"Are you feeling any better?" he asked as they walked through a tube around the decorative flying buttresses to the Mission's front entrance.

"I was bleeding last night," she said.

"Their doctors are good here," he said.

The Mission's triangular façade was embossed with false wooden doors high enough to admit a Titan. One door was ajar, adding to the illusion of utility. There were imperfections in the grain larger than the *Moondrunk*.

"In here," Horrocks said and pointed to a plain revolving door where the angled roof met the floor.

The Mission seemed even larger from the inside. The first stone of the marbled nave was so distant from the apse that the figures on the pulpit were merely blobs of color. The nave was flanked on both sides by an arcade of intersecting arches. Beyond the arches were 400 rows of pews. The pews were simple and solid, kept in fine repair and at a high gloss. Fifty-eight miners were scattered among the benches in silent prayer. The Jupitershine that filtered through the stained glass colored the miners green and yellow and white.

Above the pews was a second floor, the tribune. Members of the clergy were seated there, clad in dark habits, watching the penitent. Their hoods made a shadow of their expressions but could not mask the threatening glint from their metallic eyes.

Choral music resonated throughout the church from well-placed speakers. The ceiling was crosshatched with rough beams; Horrocks guessed it was 300 feet high.

It took Horrocks and Sari five minutes to reach the transept. Across the transept was the raised apse and the ornate iconostasis. Behind the screen were the silhouettes of nine seated bodies.

Sari leaned on one of the arches while they waited for a member of the church to approach them. The choral music ended. Following a few seconds of silence, an instrumental piece began. The door to a confessional booth opened and a priest walked toward them.

"Father Mackerracher, please," Horrocks said.

The priest nodded and disappeared behind the iconostasis.

"This place always made me feel dirty," Sari said. She held her stomach as if her fingers could numb the pain there.

Another priest descended from the apse two steps at a time. "Horrocks. My God, look at you," he said and took Horrocks' hand. The priest's were twice as big. "Who is this vision?"

"My wife, Sari."

"Your wife," Father Mackerracher said in disbelief. "Hello, I'm Father Mackerracher."

She reluctantly took one hand from her stomach to greet him. "Nice to meet you," she said.

"Horrocks was never good at keeping secrets. You, my dear, are a veritable scandal. Ravishing. I don't know how Horrocks managed." Father Mackerracher was half a foot taller than Horrocks. His hair was a jungle of brown corkscrews. He wore a black velvet habit trimmed with green lace. Forty years earlier he had been a professional athlete in Texas. He never told Horrocks which sport; Horrocks assumed it was football.

"Are you here to convert?" he said and smiled.

"We need to catch up on a few things, but first, my wife is sick," Horrocks said. "Is there someone can take a look at her?"

Father Mackerracher motioned for one of the wandering monks to come over. "Wake Sister Somnus for me."

The monk bowed and walked away. Horrocks heard a fan start up. Suddenly, cloves and incense.

"Anything serious?" Father Mackerracher asked.

Sari said, "I'm pregnant, so everything's serious."

"Indeed. We have the best medical facilities outside the mines," Father Mackerracher said. "Including the mines, actually. The queen visits here often for that reason, and for that reason only, to my dismay. Birthed her three sons in our casualty ward. Which is why you've come, am I right? About the king? Sister Somnus already," Father Mackerracher said, turning to face her.

Sister Somnus was somewhere under five feet tall, and old and gray. Her black wimple was bleached with miniature crosses. She smiled with great effort and said, "Come with me, lass."

"I'll meet you back here, Sari," Horrocks said.

"This way, then," Father Mackerracher said and led Horrocks down a portal left of the apse while Sister Somnus led Sari to a staircase to the right of it.

SARI AND SISTER SOMNUS CLIMBED a tight spiral staircase and came to a brief landing. The landing was bookended by two rooms and topped with another staircase.

The nun beckoned Sari to enter the room on the left. Emaciated medical equipment stood around the room like bored soldiers. Sister Somnus pushed an exam table over to Sari.

"Why don't you undress, dear," Sister Somnus said and closed the door but did not lock it. The door had no lock.

Sari was hesitant to show the nun her tattoos but her fear for the baby was stronger than her embarrassment. As she unbuttoned her shirt Sari had the wild notion of asking Sister Somnus to disrobe as well because it would make her feel better. Sari grinned, folded her shirt on a nearby table, then removed her pants and panties.

Sister Somnus eyed Sari's tattoos. "Those must have taken years."

Sari covered Medusa with her hands. "I'm not proud of them."

"You shouldn't be. Take a seat. You know how."

Sari got into the chair, swung her legs onto the stirrups. At least it's not cold, she thought.

"We keep this one heated so it's more comfortable. Is it OK?"

"It's fine," Sari said.

Sister Somnus put on a pair of gloves and stood between Sari's open legs. "I have to say, I've never seen someone so colorful in this chair before." A bundle of gynecological instruments were in her hands. She put them on a stationary cart. "Your vagina looks very—Were you a Joy Maiden?"

"What's that?"

"Never mind," the nun said. She began the examination with an epidermal thermometer, then switched to a speculum. Sister Somnus did not have a light touch and while the chair was warm her tools were not.

Sari knew she'd be sore in a few hours, for a few hours.

"How far along are you?"

"About a month."

"Horrocks is the father?" Sister Somnus said.

"Yes he is."

Sister Somnus traded the speculum for a tool Sari could not see. It was painful and sharp.

"You've had some spotting, some pressure?"

"That's exactly it. The bleeding was what worried me. It's darker than menstrual blood."

Sister Somnus got to her feet and probed Sari's abdomen with her hands. She moved down to Sari's pelvis and up to her ribcage. "Any pain?"

"None," Sari said. "Pressure, but no pain."

"Then the bleeding's normal. We haven't got any spectrum machines that would show me your insides, but I don't think we'd have needed them in this case." She walked to the sink, ripped off the gloves and washed her hands. "How old are you?"

"Can I get up now?" Sari asked.

"Not yet. How old are you?"

"Thirty-nine," Sari said.

"Then the bleeding's definitely normal." She flicked her hands dry, used a paper towel for good measure, and approached the chair. "Your uterus isn't as sturdy as it was ten years ago. That's when you should have had your baby."

"I was busy doing other things. Can I please get up?"

"You can sit up but stay in the chair," Sister Somnus said. "Busy entertaining boys. A lot of them, by the looks of it." She found a stethoscope, listened to Sari's heart and abdomen.

"Good. Very good," Sister Somnus said. "But your body is incapable of holding all this stress and the baby at the same time. There is a lot of stress, correct? For the sake of this child, you should go somewhere safe and sit in a chair for the next eight months. Can you do that?"

"I don't think I can."

The nun gave Sari a wet cloth. "Clean yourself up down there."

She waited for Sister Somnus to turn aside. When Sari realized the nun wasn't going to, she suppressed her embarrassment once again and used the cloth to wipe her vagina.

"Get dressed, I'll take you upstairs," the nun said.

"YOU'VE COME LOOKING for the king because you think we have him," Father Mackerracher said. "Thought this would be a good place to disappear."

"Never crossed my mind," Horrocks said.

They walked down a series of granite staircases that ended in a hallway lit with blue candles. Father Mackerracher walked in front.

"He's not here," Father Mackerracher said.

"This is a big place."

"It is, and I know every face here. Every face and hiding place. Have you come across the Bastards? I hear they're all over, tracking their kin down. Two of our brothers happen to be Bastards. They've finally reconciled their heritage with their calling, have found and accepted their identities. Some Bastards were here a few days ago, trying to recruit them."

"Was the king here?" Horrocks asked.

"He used to come. We used to pray together every week. No one knew that."

"I thought you excommunicated him."

"Publicly. For his own safety, 'cause he was here so often. This is a place of worship where he should feel safe, not harassed. He asked to be excommunicated. Privately, we embraced him. I've never met a man more bold in vice, nor more earnest in his quest for salvation. In more ways than one, the Mission is his. He built it."

They crossed an arched doorway into another hallway. Purple lights hung down from the ceiling. Transparent curtains divided the hallway from two rooms on the right. Horrocks felt a breeze come through the fabric.

"I want to show you something in the catacombs, but first we have to walk through this regrettable portion of the church," Father Mackerracher said. He spoke as if he was afraid he might wake a sleeping child.

The first room was crowded with beds. Each comforter was thick and red. Some beds were partitioned from the rest with silk screens but most were unobstructed. Two dozen naked women worked and lived there.

"Our Joy Maidens," Father Mackerracher said. His eyes fondled them like the pieces of a cherished menagerie.

"Can they see us?" Horrocks asked.

The Joy Maidens lounged on their mattresses, reading or talking. Some applied cream to their arms and legs, trimmed or shaved their pubic hair. They had bodies, Horrocks thought, meant for sex. Their slender limbs were finely toned, promising passion and endurance. Strong thighs and backs suggested that the Maidens could skillfully manipulate the largest of bulks. Their ivory skin created the illusion that the Maidens had never known sweat, though illusion it was for sweat was all they knew. Their constant smiles were a constant invitation. The women were uniformly brunette; their pubic hair was not. Their nails and lips were painted molten pink.

"We forbid them to wear clothes," Father Mackerracher said. "They must always be ready. Most only last a year, but some have been in the service of God longer than that."

"People pay to be with them, out in the open like that?"

"Most of their clients are too far gone to realize. This is the last room in the vice corridor."

"Couldn't the men—"

"Not all our customers are men," Father Mackerracher said.

"Couldn't they find prostitutes anywhere? What about the Furnace whores?"

"The Furnace whores couldn't compete with the Maidens. Sometimes the king rents the Maidens out and they conduct business at the mines. Then their chore has nothing to do with religion, purely lust, but you'd be surprised how many converts we get that way. Not everyone has the time to go to God, so God comes to them."

The next room was much smaller. Six Joy Maidens were asleep in white bathtubs. A monk replenished their baths with water from a clay pitcher. "The baths ease the discomfort in their genitals. The water's saturated with medicine to fight disease."

"Where are the customers?" Horrocks asked.

"It's Monday. No one has time for sin on Monday. They have to whip up their courage for Thursday or Friday."

"You encourage this?"

"Religion through sin is the foundation of our order."

"That's the foundation for nothing but religious sophistry," Horrocks said. He walked up to the curtain, turned and faced Father Mackerracher. "You're a self-serving her—"

"You might not approve, but most religions have a long history with harlots. The best place to see God is from the bottom of a pit of sin. That's when you need him most. The women are relentless, Horrocks. The pleasure they give won't let up. It becomes frightening. That's when we intervene. A good portion of our clergy are men who once sought sin, then sanctuary, then God."

"Sin for God? Don't you see the contradiction?" Horrocks said. He spun around and pulled the curtains down. "Foundation for your order. That foundation is nothing but ether. You're not serving God, you're bribing sinners."

The Maidens paid no attention to their unveiling.

"My purpose was not to upset you, but to instruct," Father Mackerracher said and ducked into the next corridor. "Down to the catacombs."

SARI FOLLOWED SISTER SOMNUS up to the next landing. The stairs ended beneath a plaque that read: "Casualty Reception." The ward was all white. The wide hallways were filled with roving patients. A man on crutches went around Sari with great difficulty but asked her not to move. Sari noticed five more like him, uneasy on their crutches, making their way up and down the corridor. Nuns in hospital blue escorted men and women who had lost one or both arms. Less fortunate patients were wheeled to their destinations on gurneys.

Most of the doors that lined the hallway were open. Sari looked inside them.

"Don't do that, dear," Sister Somnus said, her hands clasped over her heart, wrinkling her wimple. "Those are burn victims. Their faces will haunt you." She sidestepped a young invalid and smiled at him lovingly. "All the people here are victims of the king's mines."

"Do they make it out of here?" Sari asked.

"This isn't a first stop, dear, it's a dead end."

"What about limb replacement? Donors for—"

"Oh, we don't believe in that. You were given one body and you make do with what the Lord decides to subtract. We'll take the elevator up to the Meditorium."

Sari looked inside the last room before they left. A man was propped on a bed. The sheets were stained a reddish-brown where they touched his skin. Sari searched for the outline of his lower body beneath the sheets but saw none. His arms were folded across his stomach; they looked like shaved pencils. His hair had been completely burned off. His face looked as if it was melting backward into the pillow.

"You'll be sorry you didn't listen," Sister Somnus said. She hiked up her clothes and climbed the steps to the elevator.

THE DOOR TO THE CATACOMBS was engraved with the image of a volcano regurgitating lava. It was a stubborn door and it grated against the floor when Father Mackerracher pushed it open.

The vast chamber was cold and quiet, illuminated along the far perimeter with a flickering orange glow. Horrocks thought they were sconces until they moved clockwise in unison. Monks, Horrocks thought. Monks with torches.

"Inside every coffin here is a miner who died in the king's service," Father Mackerracher said.

The coffins lay together in deep rows, mimicking the pews above. They were constructed of distressed steel with lids of glass. Some of the bodies were merely pale. Many had skin chalked with blue and green. A small number were shriveled and black.

The two men walked deeper into the room, past aisles and aisles of coffins. Horrocks maintained a reverent silence.

Father Mackerracher halted by a group of stacked coffins. There were six in total. Their glass casing seemed cheaper than the rest. The bodies they displayed were severely decomposed. "These are the senior engineers from *The Priam* that helped the king design the energy caskets," Father Mackerracher said.

"I thought they were still with him," Horrocks said. "How'd they die?"

"Mysteriously, and all at once," Father Mackerracher said. "Porphyria's father is in there." Father Mackerracher made the sign of the cross and led Horrocks to the lone coffin at the center of the room. The young man inside was perfectly preserved. His cheeks were still ruddy. Horrocks recognized the king's oldest son, dead more than nine years. His left arm was missing, the empty sleeve tacked to his chest.

The coffin was made of dull gold inlaid with swirls of onyx. It was raised on an ornate bier of red obsidian. Biblical quotes had been etched onto the obsidian's surface.

"He died during the Push. The king was too busy fighting for his own life and property to mourn as he should have. He wanted to build a monument to his son, the brave boy who lost an arm defending his father. The Push lasted two years longer than him, and when the king finally had the time to grieve, he didn't have the emotion. This special casket keeps the boy from decay."

"This is why the king came once a week," Horrocks said.

"It is not," Father Mackerracher said. "He didn't want to be reminded of this room, or that he failed to send his son to the grave in a manner he deserved. He won't last, Horrocks. Our king, he will not last."

Father Mackerracher bent down and picked a wooden box off the floor. He laid it atop the coffin's glass lid and opened it. Inside was a miners' jacket. "Belonged to the king's middle son, the man whose death has caused all this nonsense."

Horrocks touched the uniform. There was dried brown blood on the collar and down the front. Horrocks said, "Upstairs you told me—"

"I lied," Father Mackerracher shouted. "This whole damn situation has got everyone mad." He put his hands on Horrocks' shoulders. "The king was here, briefly. To pray, have his son cleansed and anointed. Left in such a hurry the king forgot the coat. The boy's neck . . . " Father Mackerracher looked as if he had swallowed a jar of bloody pus. "His neck was pulp. We reconstructed it as best we could. The king didn't want us to embalm him, but we shot his body with some fluid anyway. Not a lot. Don't know when he'll get buried."

Mackerracher's fingertips clawed Horrocks' skin. "The man lost a son, his second son. Be decent, Horrocks. Let the man run. The king was hurt, too. I guess the sniper didn't miss completely. Bullet wound in his right arm. He refused to be treated, yelled at us to take care of his son, which we did. We wanted to help the king. He was sweating, always leaning on something. He looked like he might pass out, might die any second. Absolutely refused medical attention. 'My son, that's why I'm here,' he said, again and again, like he'd forgotten he'd already told us twenty times. 'My son.' "

Horrocks broke the priest's grip and pushed him away. "I'm not the only one looking, Father."

"You could convince them—"

"Of nothing! I couldn't stop Guilfoyle, or the Bastards, or whoever it was paid to have the king killed."

"He wants to build a shrine for his son, Horrocks! Let the man build his shrine. Let him grieve now the way he should have nine years ago." The priest pleaded with his hands. "A monument as large as his love. Let him give to the second boy what he denied the first."

"And what about the Ringers?"

"Ach, I'm sick of hearing about those hideous doppelgangers. Them and the Bastards."

Horrocks tried to step around the coffin. Father Mackerracher stood in his way. He removed a knife from the bottom of the wooden box. "You'll stay here until the king is done grieving."

Horrocks could feel the embers of his old self blowing through his body. "Out of my way, priest."

"That's why I showed you the Joy Maidens. You'll be comfortable here. Comfortable till the king's ready to surface. And if not, there are plenty of caskets down here. You'll fit any one."

The torches from the edge of the room drifted inward. Three acolytes appeared behind Father Mackerracher. They shucked their robes. A thick cross was tattooed on their bare chests, from nipple to nipple, sternum to navel. The tattoos depicted three very different crosses: one wood, one steel, one stone. The acolytes' pants looked like crudely woven sacks. Wood, Steel and Stone each held a rope in their hands.

"All we ask is that you do nothing, the easiest thing in the world to do," Father Mackerracher said.

"Put your hands out so we can tie them," Wood said.

The acolytes advanced. Horrocks backed up and bumped into the prince's coffin.

"I'm not going to make this easy for you," Horrocks said.

"Don't make it hard," Steel said. "We'll hog-tie you. Hog-tie you so—"

Horrocks swung for the man's face, missed, took one in the gut and one on the cheek.

The acolytes rushed him. Steel and Stone pinned Horrocks' wrists to the coffin. Wood made a noose of his rope, stepped forward to use it when Horrocks kicked him in the knee. Horrocks slipped away from Steel and Stone, found himself behind the stacked coffins that held the engineers. Wood approached from the left, Steel from the right.

"Put out your hands," Wood said.

"Fuck you," Horrocks said.

"Think of all those Joy Maidens."

"Not every man needs to—"

"Yes, every man, all the time. It's all he wants."

"It's all you want," Horrocks said.

"There's no one can take us both together," Steel said.

Horrocks charged Wood and knocked him down. Steel appeared in front of Horrocks, took him by the arms and spun him off balance. Horrocks gained his footing, kept his momentum and aimed for the prince's coffin. He crashed into the hood and sent the coffin to the floor. The glass shattered and the king's son fell out of his box; the body turned green the moment it hit the air.

"My God, my God," Father Mackerracher said and dropped to his knees next to the body. "Put him back in. Fix the seal." The acolytes attempted to right the coffin but weren't strong enough. "Put the body in first!" Father Mackerracher screamed. Horrocks raced for the door. The torches bobbed toward him, some blew out, but none caught him.

THE MEDITORIUM WAS A SMALL ROOM tucked into the church's roof. Ten clergymen sat on the purple carpet and faced the round windows into space. Sari couldn't understand why their eyes were closed. The view of Jupiter and his attendant moons had never been more beautiful.

Tumultuous Io clamored for attention. She was in chronic pain, ground between the competing gravitational yokes of Jupiter, Europa and Ganymede. This tension fathered steep volcanoes, wandering rivers of lava and deep calderas that overflowed with molten sulfur. She was a hemophiliac moon whose uncontrollable bleeding repaved her surface constantly.

The Furnace mines could be seen with the naked eye as black specks that further marred Io's imperfect face. The mines cast thin shadows on the brimstone moon. Her volcanoes, legion and largely unnamed, spat out umbrella-shaped clouds hundreds of miles tall. Fodder for the hungry mines. The flagship Furnace squatted over Bucephalus, an angry volcano that had been active for more than thirty years.

Sari wondered if the window had smooth pockets of magnification because she could even make out *The Priam*'s frail outline.

"Peaceful here, isn't it?" Sister Somnus said though she no longer believed it. Familiarity had deadened her enjoyment of this room long ago.

"Incredibly peaceful," Sari said.

"This room is more than the view. There's a subliminal recording feeding you bits of scripture, soothing words, serenity." To this Sister Somnus was also immune.

"I feel—"

"I know how you feel." She lowered her voice. "We can stay here a few minutes, then we'll take the lift back down."

Sari sat on the floor and felt the urge to sit there forever.

Sister Somnus stood above her and said, "Your hunt is taking you back toward the mines, correct? Looking to snare as many Ringers along the way as you can."

Sari nodded.

"To go any farther you'll have to use the ferries to pass through the Ash Wreath."

"We passed over it on our way to the Annex," Sari said.

"The ferries leave every three days. The king's son was brought here three days ago."

The nun sat next to Sari and took her hand. "The king's son was here. Whoever brought him will probably be among that group of ships. The king could be there. Leave with them tonight. Find the king."

The serenity was broken. "The king? The king's son?" Sari said. "I was barely listening. I—"

"You heard," the nun said and stroked Sari's hand. "You know this stress will kill the baby, but you love Horrocks too much to choose. You've both given so much for that mine. You want to go there and be safe, but you won't be safe until the king is found. Find the king and make it so."

Sari jerked her hand back.

"Why are you so surprised? Spend a lifetime listening to sinners and you learn to hear what people aren't saying." She grabbed Sari's hand again and squeezed it. "I know a little bit of what's going on. The Ringers, the

Bastards. Save your Furnace, Sari. Make it your child's home. Go there and be safe."

SARI WAITED AT THE ENTRANCE for Horrocks. He trotted down the nave, took her hand without a word and together they ran for the ship.

In the cockpit Sari said, "What's your rush?"

"Get us out of here first," Horrocks said.

When they were a good distance from the Mission, Horrocks told Sari his story, and she told hers.

"How do you feel?" Horrocks asked.

Sari sighed. "Relaxed. I could lie down. How are you?"

"Anxious. I hate the Wreath and I hate those overpriced ferries."

CHAPTER 16

Forty ships waited in line to join the shielded convoy. Sari brought the *Moondrunk* to the end of the queue. She was immediately hailed by a recorded announcement: "This is the Ionian Transport League, a subsidiary of LMI. You are about to journey 260 miles through the Ash Wreath.

"While the particles are too small to be seen, any accumulation will do damage to your vessel. Stay within the field of safety between the two ferries. They will reflect the debris as you cross the Wreath. You may hear the tinkling of dust as it hits your ship. Some particles make it around the safety zone. This is normal. Keep your vessel at 520mph. Please enter your ship's tag now. A fee of $80,000 will be deducted from your account. The trip will last thirty-three minutes."

Sari entered the *Moondrunk*'s tag. Horrocks tried to study the other ships but couldn't see them all due to his poor perspective from the back of the line.

The first ferry interrupted the Ash Wreath's orbit. The ferry was 700 feet tall, slim and square with a convex bulge on the bow. The bulge's vermilion skin glowed with green flyspecks where the grains of ash collided against it. The second ferry, convex bulge on the port side, met the first at a right angle. The Wreath moved counterclockwise; the ferries moved in tandem to create a safe harbor.

The convoy settled into this harbor from right to left. The *Moondrunk*, last to go in, was nudged against the ferries. Lined up as they were, the ships looked like the contestants in a drag race.

"Please remember to keep your vessel at 520mph. Do not run ahead. Enjoy your journey. For those of you who are curious," the voice declared in utter boredom, "the Ash Wreath, discovered over a hundred years ago, is actually a transparent ring of volcanic dust held together by Io's—"

Horrocks hung up.

Sari went to the kitchen for a drink. Horrocks toggled between the cameras.

"Any prospects?" Sari asked when she returned.

"Just a lot of ships with their fat asses in our face. Wish we had the time to go over or under this stupid ring."

Dust hit the cameras and filled the cockpit with the sound of sand falling on glass.

"Let me see," Sari said.

Horrocks stole a few sips from her drink. Sari cycled through the cameras, let them linger on a trio of water-bearers. The vessels were shaped like zeppelins, but filled with water instead of helium. The hollow cone that ran through their center from bow to stern housed the cockpit, recreation rooms and night cabins. Sari knew this floorplan because her mother had driven a water-bearer for a few months, traveling the transport lanes with other provision ships to bring water from the Annex to the mines. Sari's mother found the long hours tedious and took naps throughout the day.

During one of these naps the water-bearer ran right through a Bastard blockade. The Bastards loved picking on water-bearers because they had no Spot Drive and were usually unguarded. The water-bearer ricocheted into the oncoming traffic and collided with a dairy shuttle. Both their hulls were torn open in an innocuous disaster that made a dazzling display. The water and milk froze into an opaque cloud that was demolished by the fleeing Bastards.

Sari and her mother spent two days trapped in the safety of the water-bearer's pressurized hollow cone before they were rescued. Two days later Sari's mother was fired. She spent the next year trying to get pregnant so she could have a second child to exploit. Plenty of men were willing to help her try, but all Sari's mother was able to conceive were diseased lesions. Mother and daughter ended up back on the Longliner circuit. Sari resigned herself to the fact that she was destined to travel that depressing route forever. Her bitter mother chased Sari through their apartment when they had one, through the alleys when they didn't. She berated Sari for failing to support them, and only stopped chasing her when the lesions caught up to her eyes and crippled her feet. Sari often passed the prostitutes when she fled, and sometimes she took refuge with them. The women were never hungry, always well dressed.

"Why are we spending so much time on the water-bearers?" Horrocks said. "Go back one."

Sari spun the knob.

"No, one more. All the way on the right, at the end," Horrocks said. "Zoom in. A little higher. Do you recognize that ship?"

"It's Guilfoyle," Sari said. "I'm surprised his ship's still together. Look at that thing."

"He's moving now," Horrocks said. He sat up and took control of the cameras. "Where's he moving to? He nearly bumped that red ship."

Horrocks went through all the exterior cameras again and finally found the Gunwitch. "That's where he's going," Sari said. Horrocks focused on the *Honey Locust* again. Guilfoyle was pressing his way to the middle of the convoy. Horrocks came back to the Gunwitch. It was larger than the standard Gunwitch. Three engines, not two, sat low in the back where the living quarters should have been. She had a broad beam and shaded windows. On the starboard side was the king's emblem: a black volcano silhouetted on a gold box. The letters LMI were embossed along the bottom. Lovers Mining, Inc.

"You think that's the king?" Sari asked.

"With so many decoy Gunwitches, it could be just a batch of Ringers," Horrocks said.

The *Honey Locust* passed two more ships.

"Guilfoyle's going to get to her first. He's closer than we are," Sari said. She guided the *Moondrunk* around a laundry barge.

Another announcement broke through the intercom: "Five minutes remaining. We hope your trip with us has been a pleasant one."

"Won't that thing be quiet?" Sari said.

"Bring us close aboard the Gunwitch," Horrocks said and primed the *Moondrunk*'s weapons.

"Too many ships between us," Sari said. "Hail the Gunwitch, warn them Guilfoyle's on his way."

Horrocks aimed the comm transmitter at the Gunwitch but received only raucous feedback.

There was little space to move. Sari tried to go over the adjacent water-bearer.

"Where's Guilfoyle?" Horrocks said. "He's not on the cameras anymore."

"Maybe he went underneath," Sari said.

Her drink spilled on the dashboard as the *Moondrunk* was struck from the starboard side. Sari fought with the steering bar. Horrocks cycled through the cameras again in time to see the *Honey Locust* come at them like a speeding shark. The second collision knocked out their engine. The third slammed the *Moondrunk* against the nearest ferry. Guilfoyle fired four volleys of grappling wire that stitched the *Moondrunk* to the ferry's spongy hull.

The other vessels moved out of the way.

"Son of a bitch was coming for us, not the Gunwitch," Horrocks said.

"Thank you for using the Ionian Transport League. We have passed the thickest part of the Wreath. You are free to advance to your destination."

Another voice, unrecorded and obviously bureaucratic, came on next: "What the hell are you doing? Get off that ferry."

Horrocks hurriedly donned his spacesuit so he could go outside and cut the grapple lines. He knew he was rushing for naught. The Gunwitch was gone and, in all likelihood, Guilfoyle had already looted what treasure she had.

CHAPTER 17

The modified Gunwitch was fast but her pilot was careless. Guilfoyle had no trouble divining her moves while simultaneously decreasing their lead. Guilfoyle mimicked her hackneyed strategy; he turned when she turned, dropped when she dropped, and was completely surprised when the Gunwitch reversed unexpectedly and nearly killed him.

The Gunwitch's rear exhausts fizzled out in a plume of brake smoke and the ship reared up like a horse. Guilfoyle could see the lambent glow from the Gunwitch's bow thrusters as she shot backward, her armored stern aimed directly at him.

"You slut," Guilfoyle said and swerved out of the way. The Gunwitch executed a flawless bootleg reverse and took off. The *Honey Locust* was nowhere near as agile. Guilfoyle steered the ship through a careful loop, swiveling at the zenith. He leveled out, spotted the Gunwitch and pursued her full throttle. One hand was on the steering bar while the other fumbled for the seatbelt. After he was secure, Guilfoyle keyed the intercom. "Batten down, Kit. Find a safe spot and stay there."

The Gunwitch veered to the right and so did Guilfoyle. He used his heels to drag his chair closer to the dashboard. The indicator for the engines' coolant arteries blinked red for mercy. Guilfoyle smashed the light with his fist. The Gunwitch banked sharply, twisted in midturn and shot straight up like a beam of light. "You're not going to lose me," Guilfoyle said and stayed behind them.

Kitsis flipped the cockpit's hatch open and climbed in on her hands and knees. "Nothing to hold on to down there," she said. She was tossed into the wall as the *Honey Locust* rolled again.

"Shit, Guilfoyle! What's your hurry?" Kitsis said. She buckled herself into the copilot's chair. "Only a couple worthless Ringers on that Gunwitch, if any. It can wait."

"Didn't you see the insignia on the side of the ship?" Guilfoyle said. He braked, slid out in a wide turn and managed to keep the Gunwitch in sight.

"What insignia? Slow down, you're making me sick."

"The king's standard," Guilfoyle said, his foot heavy on the accelerator, "bold as you please right on the starboard side." He used his sleeve to wipe the perspiration from his cheeks.

"As if a king in hiding would—"

"I'm concentrating," Guilfoyle said.

He fired two bolts at the Gunwitch. The first sailed by her harmlessly. The second caromed off her slick hull without detonating.

"Fucking dud," he said.

"You'll kill them," Kitsis said. "If you ever take a decent shot, which I doubt."

The Gunwitch flipped over and plummeted straight down. Guilfoyle braced one foot on the dash, shoved the steering bar all the way up and followed the Gunwitch into the dive. When both ships evened out he reached between his sister's legs and tore the safety harness from her chair.

Kitsis spat at him and clutched the handrests.

Guilfoyle fired two more bolts, both of them wide.

The Gunwitch changed direction as Guilfoyle was readying the guns for one final attempt. He botched the turn and lost sight of them.

"Watch it!" Kitsis said.

Guilfoyle barely avoided a collision with a water-bearer. Three water-bearers. He recognized the plump ships from the convoy. Guilfoyle sailed between them, spotted the Gunwitch again and gave chase.

The water-bearers ejected a cloud of steam to relieve the pressure on their hulls. The steam froze into a crystal cloud. The Gunwitch aimed directly for it and Guilfoyle followed her in. The cloud expanded as the *Honey Locust* plowed through. It condensed on the cockpit's window, frosting it over. Guilfoyle slowed to avoid a blind collision. The frost took ten seconds to flake and peel free from the glass.

The Gunwitch wasn't there. Guilfoyle slammed the steering bar and stood up.

The water-bearers sailed casually toward Io. "Those fat blimps. Can't the mines make their own damn water?" Guilfoyle said.

Kitsis got to her feet and rubbed her thighs. She tried to pick up the copilot's chair to throw at her brother, wasn't strong enough, gave up, and left the cockpit.

GUILFOYLE WAS SITTING AT THE KITCHEN TABLE, his hands intertwined. He felt as if he was wrestling with a stubborn orgasm that refused to break. He needed to destroy something but there was nothing in the vicinity large enough to accept his rage. Even the *Honey Locust* wouldn't do.

Kitsis came down from the storeroom with four empty food trays.

"You didn't feed all four of them, did you?" Guilfoyle asked.

"You've eaten today, haven't you? Probably not," she mumbled to herself, "sitting in that chair like a statue. The Ringers would starve without my attention."

Guilfoyle unlaced his hands and exhaled toward the ceiling. "Only one of the Ringers is worth the cost of feeding."

"Which one? Should I guess?"

"You're the one complains we have nothing to eat."

"Not since we stopped at the depot and stocked up. I'm thankful for that, Gil. Honest. Real grateful."

Kitsis sat down opposite her brother. She looked at him, waited for his mean expression to change, looked away when it didn't.

"Why aren't we using these Geiger Ringers? You said they could lead us to the king."

"I'm not ready to," Guilfoyle said.

"You're too neurotic to try anything new, even if it'll help," Kitsis said. "If they'll lead you to the king, use them."

"If I knew how. They won't say and I'm tired of hitting them."

"Try being nice," Kitsis said. "Treat them right and they'll lead you—"

"Lead me, lead me, lead me. To a fucking trap they'll lead me. I don't trust them anyway. Forget the Geigers. Have you monitored any more distress calls?"

"Why aren't you upstairs chasing that phantom Gunwitch?" Kitsis said.

"We're flying a random pattern through this region. If we come across the Gunwitch, the navcom'll warn me."

He went to the sink to clean the trays Kitsis had brought down with her.

"We got a message from the Bastards," Kitsis said. She took her greasy deck of cards out of her pocket. "They want another meet, tomorrow. See how you're progressing. They picked out some location. I forget where. Not far."

Guilfoyle soaked and scrubbed the trays. "Don't respond to the message," he said. He dried the trays and piled them up, making as much noise as possible.

Kitsis sorted the cards for a game of solitaire and started cheating at once. "Too late," she said. "Told them we'd be there."

"Why would you tell them that? I don't want to see them again until we have the king. Don't respond to any more messages." He dumped the trays back in the sink. He scrubbed them violently and left shiny scratches on their undersides. "The Bastards are going to spoil the plan."

"What plan? Why do you have to be so cryptic? If you don't want to see them before we have the king, you'll be avoiding them a long time. Like forever." She slapped a black four under a black five. "Think you can hide that long? You can't even catch up to a bunch of scared imposters. The king was not on that Gunwitch, I don't care what you say."

Guilfoyle flipped the switch on the faucet's head; the running water went from clear to brown. "That's what you're going to shower with," he said. "I'm going to fix the pipes so all you get is unfiltered, unrecycled sludge."

"I'll sneak into your room and shower," she said. Red nine below a red ten. Red eight below that.

"You'll regret it," he said, turned the faucet on full blast and stalked out of the room.

"I'll sneak in there and jerk myself off with the soap just like you do," Kitsis shouted. "I know you bought plenty of soap at the depot."

Guilfoyle tried to walk off his aggression by wandering the ship. He was about to stomp a warped floorboard into shape when the lights flickered from white to red three times. He ran back to the kitchen and climbed up into the cockpit.

The modified Gunwitch was hiding with its lights off in the shadow of an old derelict. Guilfoyle sailed in for a closer inspection. He wasn't certain if it was the same ship because he hadn't gotten this close during the chase. He couldn't trust the *Honey Locust*'s visual-recognition devices because they had never been very accurate; the best they could muster was a good approximation.

She looks the same to me, Guilfoyle thought. The Gunwitch rotated slightly and revealed the king's emblem.

Guilfoyle was convinced. Wants to play dead, he thought. He aligned their entrances and extended the umbilical.

Guilfoyle went down to the basement, got his stiletto off the wall rack, raced back upstairs. The green light over the exit hatch told Guilfoyle the connection was sound. He ran across the umbilical and stormed into the Gunwitch.

Guilfoyle turned the lights on. The Gunwitch had no passengers. She seemed much smaller from the inside. Can't be right, Guilfoyle thought. Her layout was similar to other Gunwitches Guilfoyle had seen. The subtle differences were a phalanx of machines along the eastern wall and an additional row of desks and chairs near the command station.

He walked toward the machines when he heard someone shuffle their feet. The sound came from behind him. Guilfoyle looked at the western wall. The tiled floor's meticulous pattern ended too abruptly. He spied a faint strip of light between the wall and ceiling.

He began to sweat. He took his time going back through the umbilical.

"I'm serious about the shower," Kitsis said as he passed through the kitchen.

"Go ahead. I don't care."

Kitsis shook her head and reshuffled her cards. "Manic depressive."

Guilfoyle strolled down into the basement and stood before his weapons rack. He didn't realize he was whistling. His eyes flicked from the guns to the knives to the bats. The bats, he thought. At last the bats. He lifted them from their cradles, walked back through the kitchen, through the umbilical and onto the Gunwitch.

The strip of light above the false wall was gone. Turned it off too late, Guilfoyle thought. He was absolutely sure there was a pack of Ringers hiding there. Such an amateurish trick, he thought.

Guilfoyle quelled his eagerness by dredging up his frustration. He thought about the intrusive Bastards, Kitsis' petty animosity. Horrocks and his mine and his gorgeous wife. The pompous passengers on this ship who thought he was stupid enough to swallow their hoax. He held a bat in each hand. The friction tape gave his palms plenty of traction.

Guilfoyle was both enervated and thrilled. He felt as if he had been up all night in anticipation of his favorite holiday. Now it had come and he feared he wouldn't have the strength to stay awake and enjoy it.

He looked at the bank of machines, the desks, the monitors. And the wall, he thought. The wall and the Ringers last. Plenty of room in here. Finally get to break up a decent ship. An augmented Gunwitch with room to swing freely.

His thoughts settled on Horrocks again. An old competitor once told Guilfoyle that Horrocks used a chemical spray that dissolved glass to make salvage operations less messy. Guilfoyle couldn't understand why anyone would want that. He loved a mess.

He looked at the pebbled glass door that led to the bedrooms. His breathing became heavier. Guilfoyle lowered the bats and closed his eyes. He forced himself to hold back, to stall and enjoy this precious moment before he began. His palms sweated so profusely the bats slipped from his hands.

CHAPTER 18

"Hopeless," Horrocks said. He was slouched over the dashboard, his eyes bloodshot from staring at the viewscreen. Each new ship they passed started out as a Gunwitch but ended up something else. Two hours ago Horrocks convinced himself that the Gunwitch from the ferry was somehow camouflaged against the backdrop of inky space. He pored over the star field, looking for a black shape occluding familiar constellations.

"If they used a Spot Drive, Guilfoyle and the Gunwitch are long gone," Sari said.

Horrocks flashed her with a sarcastic expression of idiocy. She laughed, put her hand on his leg and scratched him playfully.

"What I wouldn't give to have our Spot Drive back," Horrocks said.

"What I wouldn't give to have a functioning heater. The ship's still freezing."

"I've been working on it. It's a complicated system, the fault could be anywhere. I'm in the process of narrowing it down."

"You're lazy," Sari said. She reclined in the chair and stretched out her legs. "You'd rather wear heavier clothes than fix the thing."

"It'd be easier," Horrocks said. He rubbed his eyes, then used his hands to secretly smell his breath.

"You need a mint?"

"Not me, never."

"How long are you going to keep chasing your tail over this Gunwitch?" Sari said.

"A few more hours, just so I don't feel like we've wasted our time."

"And after?"

"I know you want to go right back," he said, "but we've got to find more Ringers. They could be the key to this whole nightmare." He lowered his seat to match Sari's.

Sari rested her ankles on the dashboard. "I know what the priest told you, what the nun told me, but who can we really believe? I'm beginning to accept the fact that the king is dead. Maybe you should, too."

"I'm not ready to do that," Horrocks said. He closed his eyes and drifted toward the colored lights that played on his eyelids.

"Shit," Sari said. The chair squeaked when she sat up.

"What?" Horrocks said. He hadn't moved.

Sari pinched him, then nodded toward the screen. "That's the queen's shuttle."

"Again?"

When the ships were connected the queen and her doctor stampeded through the umbilical. "Where are the king's Ringers?" Porphyria asked. "Tell me you've got more, Horrocks. I know you've been successful. Tell me you've got a *lot* more."

"He's got some," the doctor said. "He's hiding them, he is."

"I'm taking them with me," Porphyria said and walked into the common room. She paced to the northeast corner and paced back. "They're coming with me to the mines. Plenty of trouble in the mines. Where are they?"

Horrocks stood by the exit hatch. She's desperate, he thought. Who knows what she wants them for. I'm not done with McGavin. He might still help. "You're not taking the Ringers," he said.

"They're not yours to keep," Porphyria said.

"He's got them chained in here, I bet," the doctor said. He rushed toward the cellar door but Horrocks got there first. He stared down at the doctor. "It'll be a short fight," Horrocks said.

Sari approached the queen and said, "Why the sudden hostility?"

The queen ignored her, came out of the common room, searched through the kitchen, looked up the spiral staircase. "You haven't been successful, is that a fair assumption? That why you're being so defensive? I thought you had a gift for this type of thing, Horrocks. You're a disappointment. I should've hired Guilfoyle."

"I wish you had," Sari said.

Horrocks hadn't moved from the cellar door. "They're not onboard," he lied. "I've found more, but I left them with someone safe."

"Someone like Rouen?" Porphyria said.

"I've found more, but they'd be useless to you," Horrocks said.

"Have you been using the Ringers I made of you? I don't see them here. I hope they're around somewhere, helping us find the king."

"They're around," Horrocks said.

"Give me the king's doubles, Horrocks," Porphyria said.

"None of them know a damn thing. A few are deformed."

The queen came up to him, tried to reach the doorknob hidden by his body. "There are few deformities so severe the flesh artists can't reverse them."

"They're pretty bad," Sari said. Horrocks wants to lie, she thought, I'll play along.

The queen pulled on her fingers in frustration. "I need to find him. Someone has him, Horrocks. Whatever they want for him, I'll trade. I need him back. I need my King."

"I don't think anyone has him," Horrocks said. "If he's alive—"

"I'm beginning to doubt it," the doctor said.

"So am I," Porphyria said. "But if he is, I'll bargain for his life. I'd trade anything. The mines are a mess. I'd even trade my—"

Son, she thought. I would give up my last son for tranquility.

"Trade what?" the doctor asked.

"All the king's Ringers?" Sari said.

"Don't speak to me, you little Longliner tramp," Porphyria said. "Look at you. You Longliner folk disgust me. Stowed away on that smelly ship like pack animals. You were a terrible bodyguard."

"I should have let them kill you," Sari said.

"I know what's under those clothes," Porphyria said.

Horrocks moved to shut her up but the doctor kept him at bay with the threat of a loaded syringe.

"How could you let someone draw those vulgar pictures on you? A slew of disgusting boyfriends, probably," Porphyria said. "Men with no taste."

Sari charged the queen. Horrocks knocked the syringe from the doctor's hand and stepped between the two ladies. "Go back to the mines. This is my ship. Stay away from us."

"She wants the Ringers 'cause she's got no one left to boss around," Sari said.

"I want the Ringers caught for what they have inside them."

"Inside them?" Sari said.

"What, they're couriers?" Horrocks said.

"Secret couriers. Even they don't know. The king put these things inside them, vials, when they were made into Ringers. Stitched the vials to their insides. The king liked to look at his Ringers and be comforted, knowing the information they carried was secure."

"What information?" Sari asked.

"I don't know! Important. He never told me. Valuable things. Things I can use to get him back, I'm sure of it. Things I can use to rewind all this trouble. Not every Ringer is a walking safe. That's why the doctor's here, to examine them."

"You can tell just by examining them? You have a special tool for this?" Sari asked.

"A scalpel," the doctor said. "The vials resist scanning. I'll have to open the Ringers completely."

"I can't have them traipsing around with this sensitive material in their bodies. I want it *back*, all of it *back*," Porphyria said.

"I won't let you near them," Horrocks said. "You can't just do as you please anymore. You can't expect everything to be like it was before. Don't you realize that's impossible?"

The queen walked down the hall toward the exit hatch. "I'm pulling the guardships off the lesser mines," she said. "That includes yours. Your Furnace is simply too far from the rest to spare the men to watch it. No more free security. Give me the Ringers and I might reconsider. I might not, seeing as how difficult you're being. Things have changed, you're right. Anyone who wants can come right up and steal your precious mine from you. I've just given the order for the guardships to move. The flagship Furnace needs to be protected."

"I had an agreement with the king," Horrocks said.

"That was before," Porphyria said. "You can't expect everything to be like it was before."

Sari said, "You selfish—"

"I told you not to speak," Porphyria said.

"Get off my ship," Horrocks said.

"I'm moving the mines, too. You're not welcome to join us. The mines'll surround me."

"You can't pull them off the volcanoes," Sari said. "What about your crop?"

"We've ceased operations. Until all this business is settled, there'll be no more mining."

"And the union? The miners?" Horrocks said.

"Malleable clay," the doctor said. "We'll get them under control."

"They'll revolt. You underestimate them," Horrocks said.

"You underestimate me," Porphyria said. "Now I see your loyalty to the king was all a charade."

"You'll regret saying that," Horrocks said. "I'll make sure you regret it."

"Do you know how many vessels have been spying on us, calculating our defense for a siege? Scores of them, Horrocks. Interests from Earth, the Bastards, a number of ships we can't even place."

The queen waited for Sari and Horrocks to envision the worst. After a long pause she said, "Give me all the Ringers and I'll include you." She tried to make her tone sound sincere. "I can guarantee your Furnace will be unmolested."

"No you can't," Sari said.

"Think about all you've sacrificed, the both of you. To throw that away for some worthless mannequins? The mine is worth billions. I'll make a trade for its safety. I think this is a fair arrangement."

"Blackmail is what it is," Horrocks said.

"Get off," Sari said.

The doctor protested, but Horrocks convinced them to leave.

Sari landed in one of the common room's plush armchairs. She pulled her shirtsleeves down to her fingertips. "That woman is a cunt," Sari said. "That's a terrible word. It's the worst word I know but it suits her."

Horrocks knelt beside the chair. "She's in mourning. She used to have nothing to do. Now everything's her responsibility."

"Are you defending her?"

"Of course not. She's a bitch."

"That's not what I said."

"That's as close an I'm willing to get." He tickled Sari's chin. "Pulling out on us. Who's advising her?"

"Probably her physician," Sari said. "I remember him. A pervert. Gawked at Porphyria constantly. Didn't see him doing that today, looking at her. Porphyria must've cured him."

"Or had sex with him."

"I doubt that. She's very particular," Sari said. She looked up at the ceiling and became entranced by the lighting tiles. Dead bugs lay on the other side of the glass. They looked like black acne on pale skin.

"I took a knife in the shoulder for her once," Sari said.

"I know. I've seen the scar."

"You've kissed all my scars," Sari said. She kept her eyes on the dead bugs while she palmed Horrocks' cheek.

"Porphyria has no character," he said. "She carries herself like a brat, not a queen."

Sari slid her hand back and rested her fingers in Horrocks' hair. Look at those bugs, she thought. Some of them are enormous. How'd they get behind the glass?

"You're more sophisticated than her," Horrocks said. "More kind, more beautiful."

"Shouldn't you go down to check on the Ringer?" Sari said.

THEY MADE LOVE but neither enjoyed it. Horrocks had initially declined. Sari insisted, and won. The ship was especially cold that evening. Horrocks wondered if Sari was so eager because she needed something to warm her up, like making a pot of coffee or starting a fire. He made love more slowly than usual. Sari didn't notice. Afterward, Horrocks was wide awake. He stared out of the window at the stars.

I did the right thing, didn't I? he thought. Saved the Ringer's life, even if it means I'll lose the mine. I should have given him to her. I'll lose the mine. The mine's strong. It'll be fine. Couldn't give the Ringer to her knowing she'd kill him.

Sari wished he would fall asleep. When he did, or pretended to, she went into the bathroom, closed the door and found her pen.

She slid her panties down to the floor and outlined the tattooed arch around her pubic hair. When she finished with the arch, Sari traced the angry sun on her stomach. Her arms accidentally brushed her left nipple as she traced the ring of moons that orbited her areola. Both her nipples were unusually sensitive that night.

Sari used the pen for two straight hours yet no single tattoo seemed to have faded at all. She went from waterfall to Medusa, jaguar to hawk. The roaming, the feeling of her glass pen on every tattoo, however briefly, was a comfort to her. She gripped the pen like a knife and contorted her arm to reach the remote tattoos that decorated her shoulder blades and spine. A feathery wing sprouted from one shoulder blade, a dense whirlwind of crows taking flight from the other. A vine of ivy wrapped around her spine, creating false depth.

Sari sat down on the toilet seat, pressed the hot pen against her nipples and cried. She used the pen on her nipples until they turned black.

CHAPTER 19

Horrocks showered, dressed and went down to the kitchen. Sari was still asleep in the bedroom. He heated a breakfast tray and downed it quickly. He didn't clean the dirty tray because he was too preoccupied with how much time he had left to find the king: ten days. Horrocks walked into the cockpit to call his mine, then checked himself. His right hand hovered over the navcom, over the default coordinates that would send the *Moondrunk* racing home.

I should go back, he thought. They're going to be totally exposed and I'm 130,000 miles away. Once the guardships pull back the Bastards will invade. Anyone ambitious will invade. I should be there to help, to protect them. I can't let others protect my home. I have to fight alongside any of the miners who'll stand with me. And do what? At most there will be forty-two of us. Forty-two against all the Bastards and who knows how many others. Forty-two against Rouen. Impossible. He'll seize my mine and use it as a lever to move the queen from her kingdom.

Horrocks' hand wavered between the navcom and the vidscreen. I have to stay, he thought. Find the king as fast as I can and replace him to the throne. It's the best solution. The mine will have to hold until then.

Horrocks dialed the number. De Cuir picked up immediately.

"The queen came by to threaten me last night," Horrocks said. "The bitch promised to remove the guardships."

"They're gone," De Cuir said. He sat back in his chair, stretched his arms and yawned. "No one saw them leave. Hollingsworth noticed it first. Woke me up. I've been up since three." He yawned again. "I'm having doubts about your promises, Horrocks."

"She also said she'd be moving the mines. She's going to plant them around the flagship Furnace for protection."

"What about their crop?" De Cuir said.

"You're going to be alone. We'd better prepare for that."

"You'd better prepare for that, Horrocks. Some men think you abandoned them so they're leaving. Some have been destructive on their way out. Pederson took a wrench to the fourth plume intake. Convinced three other deserters to help him. That's a week of repairs right there." He rubbed his eyes, checked his fingers for dried mucus. "I've been up too fucking long. Hold on a sec," he said and left the room. The glass at the far end of the office had been spiderwebbed from a blunt impact. Horrocks thought he saw a group of men walk toward a transit shuttle, shouting.

De Cuir stepped back inside. His collar was askew and his face was red. "More of them leaving. Four just now. Four, Horrocks. We didn't have too many to start with." He saw his reflection on the monitor, noticed the collar and fixed it.

"Then let them go. Try and keep them, but if they want to leave, let them. I don't know where they'll go to. There's nowhere safe anymore, not till I have the king."

"I'm not sure I want to stay. But I will," De Cuir said quickly, before Horrocks had to remind De Cuir of his debt. "They're afraid we'll be boarded. We're a pretty big target now, all by ourselves. There's so much uncertainty.

I know you've invested a lot in this place—try and see it from this end of the phone." He shrugged, fell into his chair and tilted the monitor to face him.

"Buttress the doors," Horrocks said. "Pull down the heavy windows. Lock yourselves in the keep if you have to. You're right, there is a lot of uncertainty. But I'll tell you this for certain, within a week I'll have found the king. A week is all I need. Play this call for the men. They trust me, they know I'm capable. A week. You can hold up that long, can't you? One week. Slow down operations as much as you can."

De Cuir closed his eyes. "You have to come back, Horrocks. Your being here would keep everyone right where they are. It's unfair to leave us out here like this. They'll never forgive you."

"There's nothing to forgive. I come back now, we'll spend the rest of our lives defending the mine."

"Or we could give it up to them."

"To who?"

De Cuir's eyes snapped open. "Whoever comes first." He looked away and said, "Whoever comes first, we see how much they offer."

"No one's taking my Furnace."

"Then come back. How many times do I have to ask you?"

The message "Proximity Alert" blinked over Horrocks' screen, obscuring De Cuir's face.

"I have to go," Horrocks said.

"Don't forget about us. No one needs this place enough to die for it. Only you."

Another message came onscreen, this one below the first: "Urgent: Incoming Broadcast."

"I've got to go, De Cuir."

"One week then. I've got thirty-two men here. I hope we make it that long. One week," De Cuir said and killed the transmission.

"Proximity Alert: Six Ships Within 1,000 Feet."

Horrocks turned on the forward camera. Tinton's ship, the *Res Nullius*, filled the entire screen. Horrocks estimated she was only 150 feet away. The ship rolled end over end until her main window faced the *Moondrunk*'s bow camera. The *Res Nullius* pulled in closer, close enough that Horrocks could see Tinton through the glass. Tinton was smiling.

Horrocks accepted his call. "Horrocks. Horrocks, how are you? I saw you talking to the queen yesterday." He crossed his legs at the ankle and leaned one shoulder on the glass. "I gave her some time to get home. Didn't want her to see us talking. How's the old bitch getting along?"

Horrocks used the cameras to inspect the *Moondrunk*'s perimeter. There was a Bastard ship blocking his escape in all six directions.

"You haven't answered any of my questions," Tinton said. "How are you?"

"Cornered," Horrocks said. "Feel like I'm in the middle of one of your extortion blockades."

"We only do that to hurt the king. We've always left you alone."

"You give all the money to charity," Horrocks said.

"The king would never hire us. He'd rather his children starved. We aren't going to starve. Extend your umbilical."

"I'm not taking any more guests. Say what you have to say."

"I'm saying it. Extend your umbilical."

"Fuck off, Bastard," Horrocks said.

"Then I'll extend my own. Why be so stubborn?" Tinton's smile was breaking apart. "I'll extend ours. It's very simple, Horrocks. I will see you."

"I'll put a bomb down your umbilical's throat," Horrocks said.

Tinton drew imaginary figure eights on the window, feigning disinterest. "You'd ruin your exit hatch. No one would ever get onboard."

"Now I'm getting through to you."

Sari came into the cockpit and sat in the pilot's chair. She looked at Horrocks. He shook his head.

"Your delicious spouse," Tinton said.

"What does he want?" Sari asked.

"Besides coming onboard?" Tinton said. "I want to see the Ringers."

"Him, too?" said Sari under her breath.

"We don't have any," Horrocks said.

"And now you're a liar," Tinton said. "Add that to your list of disagreeable traits. Bullshit, you don't have any. A man of your abilities, c'mon. I'm not asking you to switch sides. I could never respect someone who did that, and I do respect you, Horrocks. So do the respectful thing. Bow out."

"Bow down is more like it," Sari said.

"Your whore's got a big mouth, Horrocks. I'm sure you've been moderately successful. Not as successful as Guilfoyle—who is doing extremely well, by the way—but you've managed to capture a few. Would you like to know how well Guilfoyle's done?"

"I don't care about Guilfoyle," Horrocks said.

"You're afraid I'll kill them," Tinton said. "I won't. I'm not going to steal them, either. We just want to borrow them. They don't even have to leave your ship, Horrocks. Give us a few minutes with them. You can supervise if you like."

"I thought you were staying out of this, that Guilfoyle was doing the work for you," Horrocks said.

"He is. We just want to borrow the Ringers."

"What makes them so interesting?" Horrocks said. "They aren't your father, they can't give you what you want."

"They could stand in the way," Tinton said. He took a step back and pressed his palms against the window. "All we want to do's a little reconstruction, mark the Ringers so they'll never be mistaken for the king again.

I'll be taking over soon and we want to be absolutely certain there aren't any counterfeit kings running around. They don't have to die. We just want to give them a touch-up the flesh artists won't be able to reverse. Keep the Ringers when we're done."

"And this'll solve all your problems?" Sari said.

"The queen's not above putting a Ringer on the throne to end all this," Tinton said.

"She wouldn't do that," Horrocks said. "She needs the real king. He's alive so you're wasting your time."

"If he's alive I'll still find him first and convince him to guarantee our inheritance. Our legitimate inheritance."

"'Cause you're so patient you won't mind waiting for him to die naturally," Horrocks said.

"And if he's already dead?" Sari said.

"Then the queen and her baby had better stay away from what's mine."

"Enough of this. Let me pass," Horrocks said.

"We haven't finished," Tinton said.

"Let us through," Horrocks said.

Tinton's fists were the color of bone. "How many Ringers do you have?"

"All of them," Horrocks said.

Tinton smacked the glass. "I know what you did at the Longliner hotel. Left one of ours dead."

Sari flipped through the cameras. Every ship but the *Res Nullius* was pulling away.

"Let me see the Ringers and I'll guard your Furnace," Tinton said.

"I heard this offer yesterday," Horrocks said.

"Your precious little jewel of a mine left all by itself. We recently acquired a whaleship, nicely armed. We could guard your Furnace for as long as you live. With me on the throne, I guarantee this. We could guard your Furnace, or use the whaleship to take it over. Let me see the Ringers."

"I don't have any," Horrocks said.

"And you have them all. How about you, Sari? Don't you want to go back home and have done with this?"

"Why don't you go begging your stepmother?" Sari said.

"She's not—" Tinton banged the glass with both fists. "Doormats, the both of you," he said.

Tinton's ship backed up and led the others away.

"Why is it every person we meet's an asshole?" Sari said.

CHAPTER 20

Sari went through the cabinets in the kitchen and made a shopping list of supplies. Horrocks was in the cellar with the dogs. He fed McGavin and talked with him on the assumption he'd be more loquacious on a full stomach.

He was not.

The proximity alert dimmed the cellar's lights, then filled the room with a strobing yellow. Horrocks took the dogs and jogged up to the cockpit. The cameras tracked a squat ship with short fins as it strafed the *Moondrunk*'s port side.

Sari came into the room a second later. "Is that the queen? She forget something?"

"It's a Bastard," Horrocks said. "From Tinton's brigade."

Sari jumped into her chair and ignited the thrusters. "He has the wrong chassis for a Spot Drive. We'll outrun him."

The Bastard ship positioned itself on the *Moondrunk*'s port side, lagging but steady.

"They'll try and board us," Horrocks said.

"At this velocity?"

"They want the Ringer. Don't know we've only got one."

"They can have him," Sari said.

"They'll just keep coming. Let them board. I'll put an end to it. They won't come back."

"I can outrun them," Sari said. She angled the steering bar all the way down.

The Bastard ship's second engine flamed to life. They narrowed the gap effortlessly and pulled up alongside the *Moondrunk*.

"If you think you can do it," Horrocks said.

Sari cut the forward thrusters and fired the aft burners. She spun the steering bar to starboard and twisted the *Moondrunk* around. The Bastards hadn't anticipated this move and sailed by them.

Sari doused the aft burners, lit the forward thrusters and took off again. The Bastard ship came up behind them. After a short ballet of pirouettes, parries and feints the Bastards launched a junk missile into the *Moondrunk*'s starboard exhaust cone.

The missile exploded inside the cone, filling it with expanding foam. The *Moondrunk* bucked like an obstinate stallion.

Sari shut the engine.

"Can't go anywhere now," Horrocks said.

"What about the port exhaust?" Sari asked.

"We have to burn off the junk before we move at all. That'll take time," Horrocks said. He unclipped his harness and got up. "Lock yourself in the bunker."

"You're glad they stopped us," Sari said. "You want to fight them."

"The bunker, Sari. Just go hide in the bunker," Horrocks said. He went to the exit hatch and guided the umbilical manually. The Bastards tilted toward the *Moondrunk* like a woman angling her pelvis for penetration.

Horrocks waited for the tube to pressurize. He stole a nova grenade from the rack above the door. The door's warning light switched from red to green. The exit hatch on the Bastard's ship irised open. Two of them came through at once. Horrocks swung the *Moondrunk*'s door open and tossed the grenade inside. It struck one of the Bastards in the chest and dropped to the floor like a bowling ball. The grenade did not explode. It blazed like a concentrated sun.

The Bastards' faces and hands were burned a gangrenous black. They fell to their knees like twin supplicants. The grenade went from star to ash within a few seconds. Horrocks jumped the supplicants and raced across the umbilical. He reached the open door on the other side and, before he could stop them, his dogs beat him through.

"Get back!" Horrocks yelled but the white Dobermans disappeared down a corridor on the right. He knew he would never catch up to them. "Stupid mutts," Horrocks said and ran down the hallway on the left.

The ship was all hallways and closets and cubicles. The cubicles were empty yet they still had the dusty outlines from in-boxes and message boards. Horrocks guessed this had recently been an office ship. The air smelled like fresh copy paper.

Horrocks spotted a Bastard going down the steps to the next floor. The Bastard took the steps two at a time. Horrocks tackled him and they tumbled down to the bottom together. Horrocks was out of breath, his one lung a forest fire. The Bastard got to his knees, tried to use the wall to help him to his feet. Horrocks punched him. The Bastard's head banged into the wall. Horrocks kicked him in the stomach and the Bastard folded over Horrocks' foot like a book.

The Bastard spat out a mouthful of blood. His eyes were closed. "Hope that got on your shoes," he gasped.

Horrocks punched him again. The Bastard put his right hand on the wall and half stood. Horrocks grabbed the Bastard's arms and twisted them back until he passed out from the pain.

Horrocks dropped him to the floor.

Relax, relax, Horrocks thought. He tried to suppress his rage but found he had nothing to suppress it with. Rage was all he had. As he searched through the ship he listened for the dogs but his breathing was out of control again and he couldn't hear a thing.

He stalked up and down narrow passageways, mindful of the open cubicles. The sound of a bark penetrated the din in his head and Horrocks followed the noise to what had once been the manager's office.

"All we came to do is cut the Ringers, nothing more," a Bastard said. He was crouching by the wall, next to a broken chair. Crescent bite marks covered his forearms. One of the dogs growled at the Bastard from the corner of the room, his bloody jaw stark red against his white coat.

The Bastard was holding a dismembered chair leg.

Horrocks' breathing was under control. The dog's growls became a grating bark.

"Shut that monster up!" the Bastard said. "Shut him up or I'll bust his head like the other one."

Horrocks saw the second dog on the floor by the Bastard's leg. It lay on its side, dead. His forehead had been split open.

Horrocks leapt for the Bastard the same time as his dog. The Doberman snapped at the Bastard's hands whenever he raised them to protect his face. Horrocks stole the chair leg and pummeled the man's face until his sleeves dripped with blood and his arms were too sore to raise anymore.

HORROCKS CANVASSED THE SHIP and got lost twice before he found the Bastard with the sprained arms. The Bastard had managed to crawl up to a locked closet. The doorknob was crusted with his bloody fingerprints.

Horrocks set the two Bastards next to each other on the carpet in the main conference room that was the heart of the ship. The Bastard with the sprained arms looked at his partner and said, "What'd he do to your face?"

The Bastard Horrocks had clubbed with the chair leg pretended to be unconscious. The right side of his face was inflated like some grotesque raft. He was afraid to touch it. His teeth were loose. His scalp bled into his eyes. Tears mingled with blood.

"Aren't you going to question us?" said the Bastard with the sprained arms. They lay in his lap like bent hangers.

"What would I ask?" Horrocks said.

The Doberman licked the wounds on his dead brother's face. He nudged the body with his paw, barked twice and lay down. Horrocks had found the dogs on his last salvaging operation, seven years ago on the cusp of the Push's demise. They had been a few months old. Their owner had been quartered by a falling light fixture. Horrocks had taken their unusual color as a good omen. Five weeks later the Push was over.

Now one of them's dead, Horrocks thought. What kind of omen is that?

"You have any fight left in you?" Horrocks asked the Bastard.

The Bastard made a feeble attempt to raise his sprained arms. "Not me," he said.

Horrocks' rage was irrepressible. I've found it again, or it's found me, he thought. It'll put down roots, color all my perceptions. Horrocks wasn't sure how mad he could get. Since he'd made the sacrifice to the king, Horrocks hadn't found the need to rage at anything.

If the king was around there would be no cause for any of this, Horrocks thought. He's gone ten days and look at what I'm becoming.

Horrocks called over his dog. The dog was reluctant to leave his dead brother's side, but came over when commanded a second time. "Watch," Horrocks said and pointed to the Bastards.

"Last thing we want to do is get up," the Bastard said.

Horrocks wandered into the belly of the ship and found the master control panel. He disabled the engines by tearing down three whole conduits. He smashed the conduits with a steel pipe that had been propped against the wall. He found the activity therapeutic. He used the pipe to break all the lights in the room, and after that every light in the entire ship save the one above the entrance to the umbilical.

He figured he would be elated when he was done, but Horrocks felt worse than when he started. My dog is still dead, the king is still missing, he thought. Horrocks threw the pipe into the darkness. He went back to the main conference room, remembered the two wounded Bastards from the umbilical and dragged them inside. The low light from the umbilical's doorway made everything in the conference room look as though it was encased in resin.

Horrocks scooped the dead Doberman in his arms and ordered the dog's brother through the umbilical.

"Who's going to drive our ship?" the Bastard asked.

"You've got kin all over. They'll find you."

Horrocks boarded the *Moondrunk* and rescinded the umbilical. He laid the dead dog on the floor outside the cockpit. "One second, buddy," he said, patted the dog's stomach and sat at the controls. Sari was not inside.

Got to burn off the junk, he thought. Horrocks turned his ship about so that the clogged starboard exhaust cone was poised over the entryway to the Bastard ship. Horrocks flushed the engine with heat, using only the starboard exhaust. He programmed the engine to run at three-quarters capacity for one hour. There would be no propulsion on this setting. The ship's gyro kept the exhaust cone centered on the Bastard's door. Horrocks expected the door would be melted shut at the hour's end.

Horrocks lifted the dog off the floor and carried him toward the cellar door.

Sari stopped him.

"They killed him," Horrocks said and shook the dog gently. "I'm going downstairs. Clean him up, put him to rest."

Sari began to cry.

"I'll be back in a few minutes, honey," Horrocks said.

"Horrocks, we have to go home."

"One thing at a time, Sar. I'll clean him up, we'll talk about—"

"It's not the dogs, Horrocks. I'm bleeding again."

CHAPTER 21

Horrocks and Sari slept late. She raised the comforter and checked the sheets for blood. There was none. She sat on the corner of the bed and was going to pull down her panties when she remembered she had left them on the bathroom floor the night before. Sari spread her legs, used her hands to make an inspection, was pleased to find nothing.

Horrocks rolled toward her and put his arm around her waist. He stroked her stomach. "What are you looking for?" he asked.

"Blood."

"Didn't find any, did you?" His voice was still asleep.

"No, baby. Nothing." She leaned back against him.

"We should go find a doctor."

"Where's there a decent doctor out here? Besides the Mission, nowhere."

"Except maybe the queen's," Horrocks said.

"I'm not letting that pervert near me. I'm not sore. I think the bleeding's stopped. Could've been stress, like the nun said."

"That doesn't mean it's normal," he said.

"No."

"We could go to Earth," Horrocks said.

"It'd take too long. Guess I will have to see the queen's doctor, the perv."

"Right away," Horrocks said and sat up. "Maybe we could catch them before they make it back to the mines."

"They're home already," Sari said. "We're the ones without a Spot Drive. That's the direction we're headed anyway, the mines. We can't rush home. The king could be right here. Rushing back, we could miss him. I'm not in a hurry. I feel OK now."

He cupped her breasts. Sari flinched and pulled away; her nipples were still tender from her session with the pen. She diverted Horrocks' concern by patting him on the ass. "I've got to shower. Hands off."

Horrocks watched her stroll into the bathroom. To Horrocks, her embroidered skin made Sari seem like an alien beauty with the power to camouflage her body, only that power had gone awry and she was dressed in miniature objects from her colorful memory instead. Horrocks wondered how the tattoos would be affected when the baby started to show.

He rolled over to Sari's side of the bed and turned on the scanner but all he got was dead air.

SARI HEATED A TRAY OF FOOD and Horrocks brought it down to the cellar. He passed it through the mesh to Mc-Gavin and sat in silence as the man ate.

"This food is awful," McGavin said. He gave the empty tray back to Horrocks.

"I'll tell the chef."

"Really awful. When are you taking me back?"

"Back? Back where?" Horrocks said. "There's nowhere to go back to."

"The mines, salvager. Take me to the mines."

"You've no idea what's going on, do you?"

SARI WAS IN HER USUAL SPOT, the pilot's chair. "How's our guest?" she asked.

"He'd like to lodge a few complaints with management. How are you feeling?"

"Stop asking me," she said.

They rode in silence for two hours.

"I don't think we'll beat the deadline," Sari said just before Horrocks fell sideways into a nap.

Sari nudged him awake an hour later. "She look familiar to you?" she said and enlarged the image on the viewscreen. A modified Gunwitch rotated in front of them listlessly. She had three engines instead of two. The king's emblem was displayed on the starboard side: LMI.

"The Gunwitch from the ferry," Horrocks said. "Her lights are off."

"Everything's off," Sari said. "I've been watching her twenty minutes now."

Sari circled around the Gunwitch, giving Horrocks the proper angles to make an inspection. He hailed them and got no response. "Have to crack her open and take a look," he said.

"Do it slow," Sari said. She kissed him on the cheek. "And I feel fine. Sorry I snapped."

"You snapped. That's how I know you feel fine," Horrocks said. Sari shoved him out of the cockpit.

Horrocks suited up while Sari aligned the entrances for the umbilical. When the ships were joined Horrocks walked through. He tried the Gunwitch's main hatch, but it was stubborn. He went back to the *Moondrunk* and retrieved his wedge.

The wedge was a memento from his first salvaging mission. His participation in that rescue had been accidental; no one present could have known that the incident would be the first strike of a long war: the Push. A fully stocked LMI sorter had been broadsided, ransacked, set on fire and set adrift. The pirates guilty of this destruction later became Rouen's core group of generals. For months Rouen had tried to approach the king's theoretical engineers but never got close enough to court their defection. The engineers hadn't been seen for years and many were convinced the king had ordered their deaths to preserve his secrets.

Rouen had the backing of the Eurasian mining corporations. They coveted the king's monopoly and were eager to build a rival fleet. Years of reverse engineering led to few innovations, none of which culminated in the blueprint for a working Furnace.

The corporations threw money at Rouen. Rouen threw money at vicious rejects from the mines who bluffed their way onto sleek loaders, relief trams and sorters, all the while looking for the precious engineers.

The Eurasian interests demanded results from Rouen, Rouen demanded results from his thugs and they set fire to the sorter. Turned up the oxygen before they cast it off. There were forty people inside. None of them were engineers.

Horrocks and Sari had been on a relief tram, going from mine to mine, filling out the workforce on whichever Furnace was busiest. It had been ten years since Horrocks started working for the king as his bodyguard, six years since he had refused to become the king's Ringer. Horrocks and Sari had been working the mines since the refusal. Their tram noticed the burning sorter and stopped to help. The tram's three umbilicals latched on to the sorter. Men with rescue experience hurried across. Horrocks and Sari waited behind with the other miners.

"They been in there a long time," someone said.

"Be quiet," was one of many responses.

Ten minutes later four rescuers returned with twelve survivors. The same rescuers went back to the sorter and came out with seven more survivors. The survivors were hustled to the medical ward so quickly Horrocks was unable to see the condition they were in. Sari was among the group of miners that escorted them.

Horrocks stayed with the rescuers.

"How many are still inside?" Horrocks asked.

"Heavy sorters like that usually have thirty, forty. That leaves about twenty."

"Where's De Cuir and Geddis?" Horrocks asked. "Didn't they go with you on the first run?"

"Here they come."

"It's a crematorium down there," De Cuir said. He and Geddis were covered in ash.

"Those people were flash incinerated," De Cuir said. He wiped his face and left streaks of pink through the gray.

"Anybody left?" Horrocks asked.

"Like we could get to them," Geddis said. "Who the fuck is this guy?"

"I heard people yelling down in the lower compartments. But that's where the fire's running to," De Cuir said. "That's where they keep the oxygen stores."

"We have to pull away and fast," Geddis said.

No, Horrocks thought and formed an immediate plan.

"They have another hatch on the underside, too, right?" Horrocks said.

"That's plumb dumb," Geddis said.

"How many times have you done this? Twice?" Horrocks said.

"More than you. What do you know about danger? All you know is stacking energy caskets."

"Extract the umbilicals. Get us under that ship," Horrocks said.

Everyone but De Cuir disagreed with Horrocks. "Can you move us under?" Horrocks asked De Cuir. The other men in the room had ceased to exist.

"I'll meet you in the hold," De Cuir said.

"Stupid," Geddis said.

De Cuir joined Horrocks in the hold three minutes later. In De Cuir's hands were two masks with a twenty-minute oxygen supply.

Horrocks sealed the door to the room, put his mask on, made sure De Cuir had his mask on, and opened the room's control box. De Cuir guided the hold's emergency umbilical toward the damaged sorter. Horrocks used the control box to flush their room of oxygen. When it was completely drained, De Cuir went through the short umbilical, opened the door to the other vessel and dove back into the hold. Horrocks flushed the hold again, drawing a heavy gust of oxygen and fire through the umbilical.

"You have to seal off your room! Reverse your vents!" De Cuir shouted. Horrocks flushed the hold once more. Another wave of fire was siphoned into the room and strangled. Don't want to get overzealous, Horrocks thought. Hopefully people are alive over there but they might not have masks.

But they did. Horrocks and De Cuir crossed the umbilical into the smoky room. The floor crackled. The walls had become brittle from the intense heat; blackened sections dropped loose and broke apart like cheap marble.

Horrocks and De Cuir dragged thirteen people to the safety of the relief tram.

The incident endowed Horrocks with immediate fame and respect. The king was still furious that Horrocks had declined to become a Ringer, but provided him with some ships anyway and kept Horrocks on retainer as a mobile rescue unit. Horrocks, Sari, De Cuir and a few others were given detailed instruction in emergency medicine by the king's ablest doctors.

As the Push escalated so did the size of Horrocks' fleet. Two months later the war really hit its stride and stayed there three years. There were more dead bodies than survivors. The king's doctors supplemented Horrocks' education with lessons in the proper handling of the dead. Horrocks was forced to become an expert undertaker.

During one particularly paranoid stretch of the Push, both sides had decided to leave discarded corpses on stolen vessels. The corpses were stuffed with sensitive explosives and the ships returned as Trojan-horse deathtraps.

The dead bodies taken off the sorter during that first rescue had no such traps. When they closed off the umbilical, Horrocks noticed a wedge on the floor, just inside the door. Why didn't I see that? he had thought. Could we have used it?

Horrocks kept the wedge as a reminder: always be observant.

Hope there aren't any corpses in here, Horrocks thought as he struggled against the wedge and pried open the door to the Gunwitch. Cold air rushed past him and frosted his visor. Horrocks knew what he would find before he turned the lights on.

The first set of switches had been broken. Horrocks groped his way along the wall for the next set. He flipped them on and wished that all the lights had been broken. They were about the only thing that wasn't.

Most of the walls had been razed, transforming the Gunwitch into one crude room. The only evidence that the ship had been partitioned were ragged outlines on the ceiling, and the door to the hold that was hanging from a bent hinge. The floor itself could not be seen. Horrocks walked over a layered wasteland of powdery drywall and twisted metal studs. Plastic chips glinted amid the debris like ocean crests.

Horrocks' suit took a measurement of the air. It was unbreathable. Guilfoyle broke the heater and filters, too, Horrocks thought. A plaque over the helm said this ship was the Gunwitch *Sorcerer*.

He plucked a fang of glass from the bottom of his boot. The glass was unavoidable. He mentally pieced together some fragments and recognized the false wall. The false glass wall that could be programmed to mimic any boundary. Horrocks could see where Guilfoyle had clobbered the larger pieces to smaller ones. What's he got against glass? Horrocks thought.

Desks, chairs, terminals, lamps. Nothing had been spared the brunt of Guilfoyle's assault. Not even the passenger. Horrocks found the body near the eastern wall. A Ringer. His face was caved in, the groove from Guilfoyle's bat down his temple and cheek.

Horrocks carried him onto the *Moondrunk* and embalmed him. He put the body in the freezer below his dog and Kleig.

McGavin saw the body but said nothing.

Horrocks stopped by the cockpit on his way back to the Gunwitch.

"Is it bad?" Sari asked.

"He killed one. Don't know how many he got alive. The whole ship is gutted. I've seen how Guilfoyle left some ships during the Push, but nothing like this. Nothing so completely total."

"It's been forever since he's had the chance," Sari said. "He must've loved it. Can we leave?"

"I want to go through the Gunwitch but we don't have the time to stop and look. There could be something on there we could use."

"A Spot Drive?" Sari said.

"No, but they had a false wall, maybe they were hiding something behind it. That could be why Guilfoyle was so extreme. He was destroying some kind of clue."

"Do you want to stay here tonight and look it over? We'll be passing through a whole lot of nothing for the next day or so. One night, Horrocks. We can spare one night."

"We can't, not one. We should hitch her to the ship, go through it later. Want to spot me?"

Horrocks donned his suit again and went outside. Sari fed him directions, made sure the safety lines didn't tangle, monitored his lifesigns. She piloted the ship directly over the Gunwitch so that the *Moondrunk*'s seldom-used keel-side umbilical was aligned with the Gunwitch's topside hatch. Horrocks drilled winch sockets through the

Sorcerer's stern, midship, and bow, then threaded the sockets with cables.

Sari directed him back to the *Moondrunk* and helped him out of his suit. "Thanks," he said. Sari powered the winches from the cockpit, retracted the cables and lashed the Gunwitch to the *Moondrunk*.

Sari used the cameras to double-check her work. "A nice, tight hug," she said. "I'm exhausted."

"I'm going to talk to the Ringer again. I'll be up in a few minutes."

"I'll be asleep," Sari said.

HORROCKS FINISHED HIS INTERROGATION of McGavin, saw that the cockpit light was still on and went inside. Sari was running six different safety programs and cursing under her breath.

"Thought you were going to bed," he said.

"I was waiting for you. Then I got smart and decided to alter our course a bit to maximize our speed home. Gave the starboard exhaust cone a flash burn to steer, and now it's not getting any juice. It's dead cold."

"I'm too tired for this," Horrocks said.

"I'm sorry," she said.

"Not your fault."

"We're not moving now. I had to kill everything because—"

"You didn't want to blow us up. We have no idea what the problem is," Horrocks said.

Sari nodded. She reexamined the partial data from the safety tests.

"The starboard exhaust. That's the one the Bastards loaded with junk," Horrocks said.

"I thought of that, too," Sari said.

"Those fucking pests. When the junk expanded, it could have fractured the exhaust cone or even the propellant feeder."

"Or exploited an existing fault," Sari said. She put her head on the dash. "I might fall asleep right here."

"Fucking pests," Horrocks said. "I'll suit up again and check it out. If the cone's no good, I'll have to eject it and clip the feeder. Otherwise there's too much danger of an internal spark. There's a lot of propellant in that tank."

Sari played with the cameras. They showed both cones' exteriors but had no way of seeing around or inside them. "Can't watch your progress, but I'll listen and help," she said.

"Then we go to bed," Horrocks said.

"Right after," she said.

HORROCKS' SUIT WAS STILL WARM. He grabbed a flashlight, torch and wrench before he went outside. He clung to the *Moondrunk*'s slim starboard rail and progressed toward the stern going hand over hand. He went too fast and tangled his wrist in the safety lines.

"Shit."

"Take it easy," Sari said through his helmet.

"You saw that?"

"Klutz."

The starboard rail ended where the exhaust cone began. He slowly climbed over the top of the starboard cone, then lowered himself inside. The flared cone was twenty feet in diameter at the outside, two feet in diameter where it connected to the feeder. Horrocks turned his flashlight on and moved deeper inside. The cone's interior was etched with red scoring. Horrocks' boots picked up a film of propellant dust.

"Should I test the engine now?" Sari said and laughed.

"I see it," Horrocks said.

A minuscule black line swirled around the inside of the cone. Horrocks got on his knees to peer into the crack but his helmet was in the way. "It's a bad angle for me. There's definitely a fracture. Big enough for me to see it without a scope."

"Can you fix it?"

"This whole cone's one piece. There's no filler onboard strong enough to do the job."

"There's no filler onboard, period," Sari said.

Horrocks nodded, realized Sari couldn't see him, said, "We'll have to lose it."

He climbed out of the cone, down its back, and stopped where it joined the feeder. The connection was secured by an O-ring with twelve separate bolts. Horrocks heated the bolts with his torch. When they were loose enough he unscrewed them and they tumbled away from the ship. Naked screws poked through the O-ring. It had taken Horrocks an hour to get this far. He had some difficulty around the bottom because the *Sorcerer* was in his way.

Horrocks found his way to the starboard rail. He instructed Sari on how to eject the cone.

"Don't you want to come in first?" she asked.

"I want to watch from out here."

Sari entered the command that retracted the screws and detonated the low-level blast caps hidden in the mooring joint.

The cone was blown from the ship. It drifted in a straight line, rotated, then settled into a wobbly roll. It looked like the fingertip hacked from some giant mechanical hand. Horrocks watched it twirl away toward the Deeps.

"How about a transplant? Take one of *Sorcerer*'s exhaust cones," Sari said.

"Too small," Horrocks said. He used his shoulders to recline the chair.

Sari closed off the engine's starboard spout, recalibrated the port-side exhaust for solitary control. "It's so desolate here. A day at least before we hit civilization again," she said.

"With one exhaust cone, two days. Hooked to *Sorcerer*, maybe three."

"Fucking pests." She reclined her chair to match Horrocks'.

Guilfoyle's got this locked up, Horrocks thought. I've got one Ringer. One live Ringer. We're late to everything. I was sure we'd find more of them. The king is gone. His lead's too big. There's too much to do. With nine days left, I'll never find him. Even if he turns up, it'll be past the deadline. The kingdom will be devoured. My Furnace assumed by someone else. There's too much to do. We'll miss everything.

"Should we cut the Gunwitch loose?" Sari asked. She spoke with a drunken slur. Her body felt light enough to float up to the ceiling.

"I have to go through it first," Horrocks said. He didn't think he would ever have the energy to stand again.

"We'll move faster without it." Sari's eyelids had become heavy shutters. Each blink was harder and harder to recover from.

"How much faster?" Horrocks asked.

"Not much, really."

"We can't chase anything anymore. Plus we'll never get away from anyone with only one exhaust," Horrocks said. His head lay at an uncomfortable angle but he was too tired to move.

Sari mumbled something that sounded like *fomevener*.

"What?" Horrocks said.

"I don't know. It's still cold in here. Are you going to fix the heat?"

"I will. I'm going up to bed," he said.

"Me too," she said.

Neither of them moved. They stared at the viewscreen. The stars blurred and grew larger.

Sari was the first to fall asleep in her chair.

Horrocks fought it, but not hard enough.

CHAPTER 22

Guilfoyle cursed the embalming apparatus, checked the tubes for obstructions, saw none, and pulled the hose from the dead Ringer's neck. He examined the tanks, tightened some connections that didn't need tightening, fiddled with the plugs, and gave up. It's not the machine, Guilfoyle thought.

The Ringer lay on one of the morgue's slabs. Guilfoyle had taken him off the Gunwitch *Sorcerer* the day before and had embalmed him immediately. An hour ago Guilfoyle noticed the Ringer was turning foul. Greenish skin, sunken eyes, wilted limbs. Even the freezer hadn't retarded the decomposition. Guilfoyle assumed the fluid was to blame so he mixed a new batch.

The Bastards aren't going to pay me for a rancid Ringer, Guilfoyle thought. They'll want a fresh corpse, a rosy corpse. He found the hole in the Ringer's neck from the first session and slid the embalming tube back in.

"Would you do something about that? He stinks," someone yelled from the cage.

"Keep complaining," Guilfoyle said as he worked the apparatus' handcrank. "I'll stick him in there with you."

The embalming liquid flooded the dead limbs. The body expanded. The skin was no longer flexible and split open. It leaked fluid from a dozen ragged mouths. The Ringer smelled like a primeval bog.

Guilfoyle shoved the body off the slab. The Ringer landed on the floor and came apart as if he had been made of rotten tomatoes.

"Did you fix him? Smells like shit and cabbage in here."

Guilfoyle's back was turned to the cage but he knew who had said that. The Ringer with the indigo hair. Guilfoyle approached the bars. "Drop dead," he said.

Four Ringers crowded the cage's bars like the blood-thirsty spectators at some brutal sporting event. A fifth man was sitting on the cots, hiding his face.

Saffron sat on the floor, chained to the wall. He used his body to shield a tray of empty food from the others. Guilfoyle wound his fingers in Saffron's hair and forced him to look up. Guilfoyle took Saffron's chin in his other hand and turned his head from side to side like a rough physician. Healing nicely, Guilfoyle thought and released him. Couple days, he'll be ready. He'll be fine.

"Have we reached the mines yet?" Indigo asked. "Down here we've got no sense of direction. I don't know where we are."

"We haven't reached the mines," Guilfoyle said. "We won't for a little while. I'm not done looking for your brothers, your twins, whatever the fuck you call each other. You're in a cage, that's where you are. That's where you're staying. Don't need a sense of direction to appreciate that."

"We'd like to know."

"Not too far from the Mission. Does that make your cage any more bearable?"

"Guilfoyle, I need you," Kitsis yelled from downstairs.

"I'm busy."

She walked halfway up the steps. "There's someone here wants to see you."

"Tell the Bastards to go away. No, don't even answer them."

"Too late for—"

"Later I'm going to clean your ears out with a knife," Guilfoyle said. "I told you not to answer anyone."

"He said he's not going anywhere. His ship's mean-looking. And fuck you. I'd like to see you come at me with a knife," she said and went back downstairs.

"Can't do anything right, can she?" Indigo said.

"I hope you're hungry," Guilfoyle said.

Indigo's tone changed. "I am. We all are."

"I'm not interested," Guilfoyle said, shut the lights and climbed down the stairs.

Guilfoyle peered through the main porthole. He'd never seen this ship before, had never even seen this type of ship. It looked like a gothic cathedral laid on its back. Black, with horizontal spires and vertical ornaments. Guilfoyle was enchanted with her harsh angles and intentional asymmetry. She does look mean, he thought.

Guilfoyle walked into the kitchen. "Tell them to come aboard," he said to Kitsis.

"They won't say who they are," Kitsis said.

"Tell them."

"Screw them. I'm busy playing cards."

"Tell them, Kit. Your hearing problem'll get worse if you don't. I might puncture your eardrums getting the wax out."

Kitsis gave their guests permission to board.

Guilfoyle checked his orange flight suit in the mirror. He zipped all the pockets and snapped all the buttons. He used his pinky to scrub the grit from his dentures.

The dark ship's umbilical connected with the *Honey Locust*. Guilfoyle unlocked the door but didn't open it. He took a few steps back. Kitsis stood outside the kitchen and watched.

The door swung open and a short man in a maroon suit stepped through. "Guilfoyle," the man said. His voice was a bullhorn. Guilfoyle guessed this man was always shouting about something. His small hands surprised Guilfoyle with a powerful handshake. His dark hair was salted with gray at the temples.

"You know me?" Guilfoyle said.

"And you know me, of course," the man said. He raised his eyebrows, waiting for recognition. Guilfoyle gave him none.

"I am Rouen."

"Rune," Guilfoyle said.

"No, Rouen. Pronounce it Row-*En*."

"I should know you," Guilfoyle said.

Kitsis went back into the kitchen.

"Who was that?" Rouen asked.

"My half sister."

"No resemblance. As I said, Rouen. I run Rival Mines out on Europa."

"You started the Push and lost," Guilfoyle said. He stood a little straighter. "Now I know you."

"Very tactful," Rouen said.

"I've never seen your picture."

"I'm very careful about photos. They steal the soul, don't you know."

"What?"

"Mystical crap. Never mind."

Guilfoyle had originally thought Rouen's maroon suit was expensive and new. He gave it a closer inspection and realized that it may have been expensive once but it was far from new. What Guilfoyle had taken for shadowy creases was actually a rampant infection of discoloration. The cuffs were frayed and white. Rouen's fingernails were bordered with a line of black dirt. Brown crescents hung like curtains from his eyes. He gives a great first impression, Guilfoyle thought, but it's all veneer. Not as smart as he seems, either.

"You have somewhere we can sit?"

"My den," Guilfoyle said, walked down the hall and opened a set of double doors.

The den was wallpapered with red velvet. A framed painting of the Virgin occupied most of the far wall. In front of the painting was a silver chair whose cushions were gilded with crosses and stuffed with horsehair. Facing the horsehair throne were two elegant brass chairs made plain by comparison.

"Christian luxury," Rouen said.

On the left wall was a picture of a drugged miner with a needle in his arm. He was looking over his shoulder at an idealized image of the Mission. The caption read: "Shouldn't You?" On the right wall was a pornographic painting of three Joy Maidens spreading their flowers.

Vintage Bibles were displayed in glass niches like museum insects.

"Those must be worth plenty," Rouen said.

"Tried to break them out, sell them to this book dealer in Conamara City. The glass is unbreakable."

Rouen picked a dirty magazine off the horsehair chair and sat down. "That book dealer, he sell you this?"

Guilfoyle took the magazine, slipped it under one of the subordinate chairs and sat facing Rouen.

"I want to trade," Rouen said.

"I've nothing you want."

"Yet. But you will soon," Rouen said. He used the dirty fingernails from one hand to clean the dirty fingernails of the other. "I believe in you where Tinton doesn't. I want the king."

"Haven't got him."

"When you do, he's mine."

"I have a contract with the Bastards."

"A contract!" Rouen said. His bullhorn cackle rattled the brass chairs. Guilfoyle got a good look at Rouen's teeth; they were too large for his mouth and abnormally white. Looks like a mouthful of light bulbs, Guilfoyle thought.

"That's rich. A contract," Rouen said. "Did you have it notarized? No one signs contracts anymore. Least of all with a cult of bitter children. I have plenty, Guilfoyle, to offer you. Much more than the Bastards."

"We have club soda. Do you want a drink?"

"I want you to listen. Passage on a Longliner with a fully-loaded Gunwitch waiting for you in the Deeps, that's what I'm offering. Fully loaded, and five million dollars cash in the hold."

Guilfoyle did a poor job of hiding his eagerness.

"Or a stripped Gunwitch here, and seven million in cash." Rouen smiled his practiced smile. His dimples were like deep wells that had been drilled through his cheeks.

"For the king," Guilfoyle said. His smile was even broader than Rouen's.

"And the condition that when you deliver him to me, you leave this sector for life."

Guilfoyle sensed motion outside the room. He swiveled in his seat to look out the doors, saw the umbilical sway and knew that someone was coming across. Whoever it was kept to the side. Guilfoyle pretended to be oblivious. "My shoulders," he said, turning back. "Helps when I turn around. Why do you want the king?"

"Everybody wants him, don't they? They have their reasons. I have different ones." Rouen put his hands in his jacket pockets and played with an object Guilfoyle couldn't see.

"You going to kill him?" Guilfoyle asked.

"Do you really care?"

"No. Did you have anything to do with his disappearance?"

"Don't you think if I did I'd know where I left him?"

"What about the Bastards?" Guilfoyle said.

"Were they behind the disappearance?"

"No, what do we—"

"Speak clearly, man! You're confusing the both of us," Rouen said. His hands came out of his pockets. On his left wrist he was wearing a silver bracelet with a fat yellow diamond set in the band. Guilfoyle wasn't sure if the bracelet had been there before. "How do we fool the Bastards?" Rouen said. "We furnish them with a good Ringer. Surely you have one by now."

This time Guilfoyle had no trouble hiding his cheerfulness. Don't want him to know I had the same scheme, Guilfoyle thought. The one part of my plan, the greedy benefactor, he came to me. I didn't even have to go look. Now that I've heard the plan echoed by someone else, I know it is sound. Don't let *him* know. Play it dumb. Play it dumb and you'll always surprise them.

"Quit looking so damn neutral, Gil. Do you have any Ringers?"

"I have one. The rest are shit."

Rouen's smile disintegrated. "They've taken to marking themselves, haven't they?"

"How'd you know that?"

"Let's see them." Rouen went out to the umbilical and said, "It's time, Bayswater."

Bayswater stooped to fit through the door. His long hair was too perfect to be natural. It rested on broad shoulders that matched his colossal frame. Guilfoyle thought he looked like a frustrated athlete, a man who had gorged on steroids for years but lacked the sporting prowess no drug could provide. Those guys always become bodyguards, Guilfoyle thought.

"Bayswater," Rouen said and introduced him to Guilfoyle.

Bayswater folded his arms across his chest and nodded. His dense forearms were stenciled with spider veins. A sawed-off shotgun hung from an open holster tied to his thigh.

"He's on a strict diet of protein and testosterone," Rouen said. "A lot stronger than he looks, and he looks like he could bend you in two, doesn't he? Nads the size of chick-peas, though. It's quite disgusting."

"Long as he doesn't show me," Guilfoyle said.

"The Ringers?" Rouen said.

Guilfoyle took Rouen and Bayswater upstairs.

"I know that smell," Rouen said. "Awful smell. Bring them out, one by one."

"You need to see them all?"

"Your incessant chatter is grating on me, Gil. One by one and stand them in front of me. Don't give me dialogue, give me Ringers."

Guilfoyle opened the cage, grabbed the nearest Ringer and pushed him toward Rouen. Bayswater caught Indigo one-handed, stood next to him and pressed his shotgun against the Ringer's temple.

"That should be warning enough, zombie. Don't resist me," Rouen said. He pulled down the skin under the Ringer's eyes to examine his whites. He tilted the Ringer's head back, then side to side.

Indigo said, "Why the hell are—"

Rouen squeezed the man's cheeks so tightly they met across his tongue. "Not a word. Not a syllable. Breathe through your nose."

Rouen felt the man's arms, opened the man's shirt and checked his skin for ridges or protrusions. "Get down on your knees," Rouen said.

Indigo didn't move.

"Pay attention," Rouen barked at Bayswater.

"Yes, sir," Bayswater said and stuck the shotgun's barrel into Indigo's ear. The Ringer knelt.

"Very good," Rouen said.

"Thank you, sir," Bayswater said.

Rouen turned to Guilfoyle. "Bayswater is all manners and no class. You'll see." He addressed the Ringer: "Open your mouth. If your tongue slithers in the direction of my fingers, I'll burn it out."

Rouen pushed Indigo's head all the way back, put his fingers inside his mouth and touched every tooth.

"What do you care about his teeth?" Guilfoyle said.

"You've got a problem interrupting. Bayswater can fix that," Rouen said.

"I'll shut up," Guilfoyle said and turned away.

Rouen passed his bracelet over Indigo's back. Hidden in the clasp was an ultrasound camera that transmitted its picture onto the yellow diamond.

"And the next one," Rouen said.

He repeated the examination three times without deviation until Guilfoyle brought out the last one. Guilfoyle was beaming.

"This looks like a young Horrocks," Rouen said. "What a unique find. Where'd you get him?"

"Hiding on a Gunwitch with some of the king's Ringers. They tried to fool me with a false wall like—"

"You've done a job on him. His jaw's so bruised can he even talk? Who made him?"

"He says the queen did, but I don't believe him."

"The queen. Why?" Rouen said.

"Haven't had a chance to ask her. He's rare, and that makes him valuable."

"Only if somebody wants him," Rouen said.

"Horrocks will want him. You don't think he's curious?"

"I'm only curious about the king. What did you say about a false wall?"

"It's an old cargo scam," Guilfoyle said. "I found two of the king's Ringers with this one. Had to kill them both. Only had time to bring one body back, though."

"I'll want to see the dead one as well," Rouen said.

Guilfoyle showed them his morgue. He had forgotten to scrape the dead Ringer off the floor.

"The smell's much stronger over here," Bayswater said.

"I don't have the stomach for this. Take me downstairs," Rouen said.

Guilfoyle locked the cage and walked them to the umbilical.

"Get the ship ready," Rouen said to Bayswater.

"How much cash will be on the Gunwitch?" Guilfoyle asked.

"Seven million. That's much more than the Bastards offered you."

They aren't paying half that, Guilfoyle thought. "You couldn't know that for sure."

"Don't expect me to wow you with the breadth of my network. I simply know, and that, Guilfoyle, is good enough. This is serious business. This is not hijacking dead bodies and peddling them back to their families. This is not hunting vermin in some filthy city. I expected some ignorance but the least you could do is pretend to understand. Can you do that? Could you pretend for me? I'm severely unimpressed and I impress easy."

Guilfoyle played with the zippers on his uniform. "You said you were confident I could find the king."

"I never said *confident*," Rouen said.

Guilfoyle laughed. Rouen did not. The laugh hung in the air like an embarrassing shirt.

"Until you own the king you'll get no help from me. This partnership must be silent. It will be profitable. We have a deal?" Rouen asked.

"I haven't decided," Guilfoyle said. The words came out too early. He had decided. The arrangement was too rare a gem to ignore. Inwardly, Guilfoyle applauded his own cleverness as a bargainer. He wondered if there was a larger plan buried in his subconscious. But that was introspection and Guilfoyle orphaned the thought before it could take shape.

Rouen pursed his lips and counted to thirty in his head. "Good," he said. "I was afraid you'd jump all over me. That's the sign of a smart thinker. That's what I expected to find." He clapped his hands and grinned. "Forethought is good. Take time to consider it but don't stall me too long. A lot can change before I have the time to come back. The entire neighborhood is in flux. In order to get your answer I have to make another trip out here, and I hate leaving Europa for anything. I come out here in person again and I will be more demanding."

"Do you think the Bastards will be tricked so easy?" Guilfoyle asked. This is the one part I haven't worked out yet, he thought. A good Ringer won't be enough. The Bastards will demand an authenticity test. "The Bastards are focused, Rouen. More than that, they're earnest. How will we fool them?"

"Later, later. It's all been worked out. Now fetch me a Ringer and I'll be gone."

"Fetch you what?"

"A Ringer. A sign of your good faith. I had chosen one in particular, but I'll let you decide. I'm interested to see if we pick the same man. If you do I'll be sure we're of a like mind."

Guilfoyle went up to the storeroom and returned with the Ringer who had scratched the X onto his cheek.

Guilfoyle held the Ringer by the arm. "Is this the one you chose?" Guilfoyle asked.

"I'll keep that a secret," Rouen said and took the Ringer's other arm.

Guilfoyle hadn't let go. "I'd like a third of the money now."

"That is not good faith, Guilfoyle. That's bad faith. I'm disappointed. After all the progress you just made by withholding your decision to say something stupid like that. *A third*. Give him to me freely."

Guilfoyle released his grip on X.

Rouen shook his head more times than necessary and left with his baggage.

BAYSWATER TRAPPED THE RINGER in a full nelson. Rouen's fingernails tore the Ringer's forehead and nose. He stopped by the X on the man's cheek.

"I like the scar," Rouen said, "but you weren't thinking big enough. You should have been more bold."

"I'm only—"

"A Ringer. You look like the king and that's enough. Enough reason for me to hurt you."

Rouen used his nails to gouge X's other cheek. X struggled in Bayswater's grip, flailed his legs, tried to jump up. Bayswater bent forward so X wouldn't have any leverage.

"Midget," X said to Rouen. "You feel better scratching me? Feel taller?"

"I'll feel better when you're in pain. I'll feel better real soon now."

Rouen opened a glass jar. The jar contained an object that looked like a brown straw with arms. "Open up, zombie," Rouen said.

Bayswater tightened his grip and X cried out. Rouen removed the item from the jar and placed it on X's tongue.

"It's a gagroot," Rouen said. He held X's mouth shut and pinched the man's nostrils. "Swallow it. I won't let you breathe until you swallow. Don't try chewing it. The root'll break your teeth."

X turned red, gave up and swallowed. The gagroot slid into his throat. His neck became stiff. Pink vines grew over his Adam's apple. He screamed but all that came out was a low whistle.

"You won't ever speak again," Rouen said. "On his knees," Rouen told Bayswater.

Bayswater forced X down to the floor. He put his meaty fingers around the Ringer's neck.

"Open wide. This'll be the last time," Rouen said.

X's lips parted. Rouen showed the man his gold-plated dental pliers, then went to work. He extracted the front teeth and progressed toward the molars. Rouen dropped the teeth into a silver bowl where they clattered like discarded shellfish. X whimpered as Rouen twisted the teeth, as the grinding noise traveled from his jaw to his ears. The gagroot made it difficult to swallow.

"It's incredible how detailed they get," Rouen said. "As the king ages, the stains on the Ringers' teeth are made darker. That's detail. That's pride in one's work."

"He's passed out," Bayswater said.

Rouen handed the pliers to Bayswater. They were no longer gold. "You finish. My hands hurt," Rouen said.

Bayswater had no skill with tools. He chipped most of the teeth he extracted. The Ringer, unconscious, lay flat on his back. Bayswater found the last molar especially difficult. He straddled X's shoulders, gripped the tooth with the pliers and pulled upward with all his strength. X's head, neck and torso were lifted off the floor.

"Won't come out," Bayswater said.

Rouen stepped on X's chest while Bayswater pulled. The tooth came out.

"Last one," Bayswater said.

"Let's see," Rouen said. The tooth looked like a wishbone left on a slaughterhouse floor.

"I'll clean them up, put them in a new setting for you," Bayswater said.

"Yes you will," Rouen said. "I'll never get tired of doing this to the king."

"But he's not the king," Bayswater said.

"I can pretend. Roll him over so he won't drown."

Bayswater tipped X onto his side.

"We should've put some plastic down," Rouen said.

"Plastic down on what?"

"Clean this mess," Rouen said.

Rouen watched Bayswater mop up the blood.

"You want I should open him up and look for vials?" Bayswater asked.

"I'm not interested in the vials anymore. Is he still breathing?"

"He'll be fine," Bayswater said.

"Should have drawn it out," Rouen said. "I get so eager and now I've got nothing to do before the next stop. I just couldn't wait."

Bayswater wrung the bloody mop over a bucket. "You never wait."

"Guilfoyle's got two Geiger Ringers. I saw the nerve bundles with the camera," Rouen said.

"What does that have to do with waiting?"

"Nothing. Is this pilot any good? I don't feel like we're moving at all."

"We're probably on liquid fuel till the Spot Drive warms up," Bayswater said.

"This pilot's new. Tell him I need to feel it when we move. He's not going fast enough until the ship feels like it's going to shake apart. Tell him that."

"Yes, sir," Bayswater said.

CHAPTER 23

Horrocks climbed down the keel-side umbilical into the Gunwitch *Sorcerer*. Late last night he'd fixed the *Sorcerer's* heating and filtration system so he could breathe without a helmet.

Some of the trash on the floor had shifted, making bald spots and snowdrifts. Horrocks found a pole and used it to stir the debris. He learned nothing new. There had been a wild fight. There was no sign that the king or his dead son had been onboard. No indication of where the *Sorcerer* had been headed. Guilfoyle was the only constant. Frustrated rage grew inside Horrocks and for a full minute he struggled against the temptation to use the pole as a bat. And then what? he thought. Attack the debris? Too much like Guilfoyle. Too weak.

He chucked the pole at the wall and returned to the *Moondrunk*.

"ANYTHING?" SARI SAID. She was reclining in the pilot's chair, mildly engrossed in a paperback novel.

"Nothing but garbage," Horrocks said.

"Check again. We've got the time," she said without looking up. She turned a page.

Horrocks accessed the map to check for upcoming landmarks but there was nothing aside from a few roving depots.

"Could the son have been on the ship?" Sari asked.

"We'll never know."

"Unless you catch Guilfoyle," Sari said.

"How much longer till we reach Hera Station?" Horrocks asked.

"Day and a half. Maybe two."

"I'm going downstairs to autopsy the dead Ringer," he said.

"Disgusting," Sari said. She didn't ask to help. She didn't ask what he hoped to find. She turned another page.

As Horrocks walked toward the Operating Room McGavin called out, "Hey, Horrocks. I could use a stretch."

Horrocks went to one of the closets, got his rifle and then unlocked a portion of the mesh. McGavin bounded into the room and enjoyed ten minutes of spacious freedom before Horrocks herded him back inside.

"Ten minutes. Thanks so much," McGavin said.

"My pleasure," Horrocks said, put the rifle in the closet and went into the Operating Room. He took off his shirt, reached for the sanitary robe and stopped. He touched the scar on his sternum. A couple times a day Horrocks wondered if someone else had gotten his lung and kidney or if the king had just thrown them away. Horrocks could easily have purchased replacement organs but never did. He didn't want to betray his sacrifice. The king had said he never wanted Horrocks to forget. Horrocks agreed. He reminded himself as often as possible.

Horrocks tied the plastic blue robe around his neck and waist and put on a pair of wraparound goggles. He wriggled his fingers into polyurethane gloves and laid a saw with interchangeable heads on the counter beside the tub.

Horrocks could see Kleig and the *Sorcerer*'s Ringer through the freezer's glass door. Horrocks hated to travel with corpses. It had been particularly burdensome during the Push, when ten compartments were rarely enough. He had refused to add more.

He transferred the Ringer to the tub and stripped the body down to its underwear. The embalmed corpse had no smell.

Porphyria had surprised Horrocks with her tale of clandestine surgery and hidden documents. He was intrigued by the concept, disbelieved the queen completely yet was anxious to prove himself wrong. He rationalized the autopsy with the notion that this dead Ringer might have vital information sewn to his stomach or heart.

Before he plugged in the saw, Horrocks inspected the Ringer's arms and legs for bulges that would indicate a hidden capsule. He was less than gentle in his thoroughness as the Ringer was beyond complaint or discomfort. The pale flesh was firm and cold. Where Horrocks pressed it pressed back.

Horrocks plugged the saw into the ceiling outlet, shifted it from hand to hand as he waited for it to warm up. He decided to limit the autopsy to the Ringer's torso. He didn't feel like taking the man's body apart in a savage treasure hunt.

The saw beeped. Horrocks turned it on, pressed it to the corpse's sternum and worked his way down to the man's groin. Dead flesh and reddish-yellow blood were whipped against his goggles and smock. Now the body had a definite odor.

Horrocks yanked on the plug, dropped the saw in the sink and changed his goggles and smock. He squeezed both hands into the cleaved sternum, braced his knees against the tub and cracked the chest. He used pins to keep the dead skin spread apart.

The Ringer's organs had been bleached by the strong embalming fluid. Horrocks ran his gloved fingers over them like a demonic masseuse. Their texture was inhuman. The organs looked smooth but felt as if they had been studded with sharp crystals. Horrocks tried to think of an explanation for this but came up with none that fit. The embalming fluid wouldn't have been responsible.

Another secret procedure, Horrocks thought. Another sick way to use the Ringers.

When he finished this cursory exam, Horrocks dug deeper. He cradled the heart, moved it out of the way. There was a strange clump of gargantuan nerves in the middle of the spine.

Horrocks eased the bleached heart back in place. He searched between the damp organs, fighting his way deeper into the body. Bloody embalming fluid dripped down Horrocks' gloves, filling the tub like an evil bath. Horrocks nudged the organs aside, slashed those that were too stiff to slide out of his way.

A small cylinder had been screwed to the top of the Ringer's pelvis and another to his liver. The cylinders looked like platinum cocktail straws capped at both ends. That's a lot of luggage to carry around, Horrocks thought. How many are the others hiding?

Horrocks placed the straws on a tray and did a poor job of sewing the man back up. The Ringer's chest looked like the seam of a shirt contested by two opposing dogs, the buttons ready to fly off. Horrocks put the body back in the freezer. He made a pile of the Ringer's clothes, topped it with the smocks, goggles, and gloves. I'll burn it later, he thought. I didn't find anything useful. What are the straws going to tell me? Not where the king is. Not where the Ringers are. Not how to save my Furnace. Nothing, nothing at all. A waste of time. Autopsy's just the most perfect metaphor for this, for *everything*. Toying around with something that's already dead.

Horrocks washed out the tub. Need a shower myself, he thought, took the straws with him and went up to the kitchen. He laid a dishrag on the table and lined up the two straws.

Horrocks paused for a moment to enjoy this precious quiet. To sit comfortably, no conflict, no one around. I'm tired of running, he thought. Need to catch my breath, get some real sleep. He closed his eyes. When he opened them, the straws were still there. Horrocks pried them open with a knife. Both straws contained a piece of rolled parchment. Together the sheets formed the single design for a giant new Furnace. The design was so detailed and complicated Horrocks didn't think it would be possible to build. Certain objects were labeled in the king's crisp handwriting.

Probably the only copy, Horrocks thought. Is this related to the assassination attempt? Somebody wants to get hold of the plans for a new kind of Furnace?

Horrocks was studying the miniature blueprints when Sari's voice came over the kitchen's intercom: "Horrocks, could you get in here?" Her voice was clear but worried.

Horrocks curled the parchment back into the straws, hid the straws in the dishrag and the dishrag in a cabinet. He scrubbed his hands with disinfectant, then joined his wife in the cockpit.

"I found the weir—"

"Do you recognize that ship?" Sari asked. The vessel on the viewscreen was entirely black, no windows, very narrow.

"It's too dark," he said. "Sharpen the contrast."

Sari added pink to the star field, causing the ship to stand out like a portrait in an overexposed photograph.

"Gothic church with engines. That's Rouen's ship," Horrocks said.

"So I was right."

"How far back is he?" Horrocks asked. The dog was in his chair. Horrocks shooed him away, sat down. The dog crouched on the floor and pressed himself against Horrocks' ankles. Horrocks scratched him behind the ears. "How far?"

"How close is more like it," Sari said. "Less than 400 feet."

"Have they hailed us yet?"

"They've kept a channel open. No message, though. Waiting till we're ready is my guess."

"We'll never outrun that, crippled as we are," Horrocks said. "He's going to want to come aboard and we're going to have to let him."

"You said you never wanted to meet him, you'd never let that man on your ship or your Furnace," Sari said.

Horrocks stroked the dog's ears harder. "Tell Rouen to come onboard."

Sari reduced their speed gradually. The ships fell into line; Rouen extended his umbilical and came through. Horrocks noticed a second shape coming through the tube. He slammed and locked the exit hatch before Bayswater could follow Rouen inside.

"He'll be pissed when you open that door to let me back," Rouen said.

"So he'll be pissed," Horrocks said. "He's with you, he can't be that smart. Don't be offended I don't shake your hand, but I think you're a slug."

"And you're a fool, but I'd never say it to your face," Rouen said. "Don't you have somewhere we can talk?"

"We're talking," Horrocks said.

"You start with the pyrotechnics and this conversation can go nowhere beneficial," Rouen said. His grin made a display of his perfect teeth. "We've never met. I'd like to do this in a room, not a foyer."

Horrocks shook his head and led Rouen to the common room. Rouen went for one of the chairs but saw that Horrocks had no intention to sit.

"If you're not taking a chair, I'm certainly not going to talk to you sitting down."

"So don't," Horrocks said. He crossed his arms, could feel his cheeks puff with anger.

Rouen dipped his hands into his pockets. "Your patron is gone. The king's either dead or doesn't want to be found. Makes no difference. How do you plan to proceed?"

Horrocks gave Rouen a tiny shrug and an even tinier smile.

"Don't be so stubborn!" Spittle jumped from Rouen's mouth like white ticks. "Who would you have run this kingdom? The queen? She's a hysterical puppet. Her son? He's not even the legitimate heir. If it came to that, I would prove it and disgrace him. There is no legitimate heir. This kingdom is up for grabs."

Through the fabric of Rouen's pockets Horrocks could see the man clenching and unclenching his fists.

"You forgot the Bastards," Horrocks said.

"A sick fraternity, nothing more."

"That leaves you, then," Horrocks said.

"I may be conceited, but it's all true. Me."

"What would you want it for? The Push ended so abruptly, I heard you still had most of the money from the backers on Earth. Billions. Surprised they never tried to get it back."

"Oh, they did. Many times. I used the money to start my own mines on Europa. Real, underground mines. Not those floating contraptions, those ugly Furnaces. They're so passive, aren't they?"

"You've never figured out how the Furnaces work," Horrocks said.

"How do they work?"

"You'll never figure it out, as long as you live," Horrocks said.

"As if you know? The king would never tell you. Just because you own a shitty little mine doesn't make you a Furnace expert. You're just a salvager who got lucky. If I thought you knew Kingston's secret I would've had you in my chair ages ago, but you don't. You're dependent on the king for everything. I know that for a fact."

"You know everything except how the Furnaces work," Horrocks said.

"Probably some cheap trick. Some cheap simple trick. They're heinous contraptions. So ugly."

"Yet you want them," Horrocks said.

"I've never denied I'm ambitious. It's not something to be ashamed of."

"You think you can take the king's place," Horrocks said.

"Half his surgeons seem to agree. They've defected."

"The doctors in this region are notorious cowards," Horrocks said.

"Because there are so few and demand is high. They've learned to pick the winners. They're survivors."

"Weren't you a dentist?" Horrocks said.

"I was the only dentist," Rouen said. His tight expression relaxed. "On *The Priam*, with the king. Only there I never got to practice dentistry. Too many patients. All I did was extraction after extraction. There's no art in that. Fifteen a day. Bloody work, pulling all those teeth."

"You loved it. And now you work for a mine," Horrocks said.

"Mines. More than one, Horrocks. And I don't work for them, I own them."

"I should be impressed you draw water from a frozen moon," Horrocks said.

"Slush, not water. Slush. Europa's not all frozen. Underneath her icy skin's a slushy ocean of pure money. The slush is my secret, something *you'll* never figure out as long as you live."

"Why would I bother?" Horrocks said.

"Because it would astound you," Rouen said. "The precious metals swimming in that ocean—"

"You've had such a busy life yet you found the time to start and lose a war."

"That war is ongoing," Rouen said with conviction.

"From a dentist to this. How does that happen?"

"The way things happen," Rouen said. He took his hands out of his pockets and stroked his mouth to surreptitiously wipe the sweat from his palms. "I'm the only man can glue this system together." His face grew hard again. "You have so much to lose, don't you? Just going to shit all over your accomplishments? I know what that mine cost you. Two organs and six molars."

"You remember how many teeth?"

"My memory's immortal. Screw all this standing," he said and sat down.

"The king's alive," Horrocks said.

"That bullshit again? Do you believe everything everyone tells you?"

"I don't believe a thing you're telling me," Horrocks said. He uncrossed his arms and pulled a card from his back pocket.

Rouen leaned forward, arms on his knees. "Sit down, will you? My neck. What about the Geiger Ringers?"

"Who the hell are they?"

"Later," Rouen said.

Horrocks tossed the card at him. It was the ID he had taken off the false inspector at Longliner Station. Rouen read it, chuckled and slipped it into his shirt pocket. "Not my smoothest operative. I've recently paid Guilfoyle a visit."

Rouen waited for Horrocks to inquire about the meeting. He waited an uncomfortable amount of time before deciding to continue unprompted: "I wouldn't call him refined. Guilfoyle thinks he's clever but he's not. He thinks he's not transparent but he is. For all his faults, Guilfoyle's grabbing Ringers all over, right out of the air."

"So I'm told."

"By who?" Rouen said.

"You're wasting my time."

"Because your ship's so fast with half an engine you could have ended this already? With no Spot Drive? How could Horrocks allow himself to be put in such a position? How many Ringers have you taken?"

"None," Horrocks said.

Rouen laughed. "You're not so poor as that, but not as rich as Guilfoyle. He treats them terribly, you should know. Beats and starves them. Their cage smells like a zoo."

"You're worried sick over them," Horrocks said.

"One of them looks nothing like the king, a lot like a young Horrocks. Honestly, he was the most abused."

Horrocks masked his surprise as best he could but he saw Rouen register the reaction.

Rouen stood up and went to the locked umbilical. "That man is in need of rescue. And by the way, the Geiger Ringers are new. They were created after the Push. I don't know for certain how many there are, but I'm told not more than three. Their nervous systems have a way of leading them to the king in periods of absence. An insurance policy against another kidnapping. A secret policy. Even the queen doesn't know about them. Kingston's so paranoid, isn't he? Guilfoyle has two of these Geigers. How long they'll last in his care—" Rouen threw up his hands in mock dismay. "The door, if you please."

"You're lying," Horrocks said.

"I don't lie. I'm not always completely honest, but I never lie. There's a difference. You're smart enough to know that," Rouen said.

"How come you never commandeered the Geigers before?"

"Never needed to. Up until the incident on the Annex, I *always* knew where the king was."

"But you never acted on it," Horrocks said.

"You know nothing about opportunity, Horrocks. Nothing, truly. Having information and being able to use it, these are two different things."

"Why did you come here?" Horrocks asked.

"To help. Oh, and a warning. There could be trouble on the king's mines soon. Explosive trouble. The door, please."

Horrocks unlocked it. Bayswater was not inside the umbilical. Rouen retracted it and left.

He just wants me to go after Guilfoyle, Horrocks thought. Wants to create as much strife as possible so he can take over at the height of chaos. That's when it'll be easiest.

He thought about the unique talent of the Geiger Ringers. He also pictured his own Ringer being thrashed by Guilfoyle. He knew Guilfoyle would find that activity particularly satisfying. Horrocks checked the lock on the exit hatch then went to the cockpit to share the new developments with his wife. She wasn't there.

SARI HAD BEEN WATCHING THEIR MEETING from the kitchen, through the partially open door that led to the common room. "My memory's immortal." Her waist went cold. Rouen would recognize me, she thought. A different haircut won't matter, faded tattoos, nicer clothes. I don't look all that changed. He'll know, instantly. Recognize me, because I recognize him.

Sari had never run into one of her old clients before. She had made a pact with herself only to work the outbound Longliners because people going to the Deeps rarely returned. Sari was optimistic she wouldn't be hustling for long and didn't want to accidentally meet any of her midnight acquaintances later on in life. On the inbound Longliners Sari rested and took antibiotics. Another set of girls tended to the few returnees.

During one of the outbound voyages Rouen came to Sari every night for two weeks. He preferred to kiss for an hour before having sex. His mouth never left hers and never closed. His tongue mapped the contours of her teeth. Sari found it strange yet tame compared to her other patrons who liked to put their tongues into less savory orifices.

When the clothes were off Rouen would ask for fellatio. "With your teeth," he said the first night. "Don't bite, but use plenty of teeth. As many as you can."

Rouen was a selfish lover who took forever to climax. Sari used her hands and legs to stimulate his body, used all of the shortcuts she had been taught to keep these sessions brief. Two weeks with Rouen and Sari decided he was too much of a chore in bed. She avoided him in pursuit of men and women on the verge of climax before they even saw her naked.

Rouen never commented on her tattoos and that, combined with his dental fetish, made him stick in her mind like a bone in the throat. She had never been positive the Rouen she remembered and the one who started the war were the same man, but looking through the crack of the kitchen door, she was finally sure.

HORROCKS FOUND HER IN THE BEDROOM, the lights already turned off. "Another person threatening us."

"Come to bed," Sari said. She lifted the sheets in invitation, showed Horrocks she was naked.

He unbuttoned his collar and worked his way down the shirt. "Let me un—"

"Come to bed."

He was surprised by her desperate tone. When he was arm's length from her she pulled off his shirt and pants. He tried to help but realized he was in her way and stayed out of it. Sari reached down into his underwear, freed his penis and slammed their pelvises together. She lay on her back. Horrocks made love to her slowly. "Not like that. Harder," she said, grabbed his shoulders and bucked against him.

Horrocks moved faster.

"Not faster, baby. Harder," she whispered in his ear, then bit it.

Horrocks swung his hips into hers but his rhythm was off. Sari established the tempo. Horrocks fell into it easily.

"Like that," she said.

Horrocks used the sheets to wipe the perspiration from his face, could feel rivers of it streaming down the center of his back. Sari was a rocking horse beneath him.

"Why this all of a sudden?" he asked.

Sari responded by grabbing his hair and kissing him so hard their teeth knocked.

After the first round Sari gave him five minutes to catch his breath. Five minutes was all she could stand. She got on her hands and knees, looked over her shoulders at Horrocks and said, "Again."

CHAPTER 24

Over breakfast the next morning Horrocks recounted most of what Rouen had told him. Sari pretended she hadn't been eavesdropping behind the door.

"A little, greedy man," Horrocks said as he reached over the table for more water. His shoulders and hamstrings were sore from last evening's workout.

Sari brought a glass of juice to her mouth, stopped, said, "Why would he tell you these things?" She took a belated sip.

"To mix us up, most of all," Horrocks said. He cut his scrambled eggs into triangles. "He wants chaos. The kind of chaos that can be scattered by his presence. He'll step forward with plenty of support—"

"Not enough, though," Sari said.

"No, but he does make a strong candidate. And if me and Guilfoyle are fighting, it'll take longer to find the king. The longer it takes, the better the odds he won't be found at all." He finished the eggs on his tray but was still hungry. He looked around the table for something else to eat but there was nothing.

Sari protected her eggs with a strategically placed forearm. "Was Rouen behind the assassination attempt?" she said.

"If he was, the king would have died on the spot," Horrocks said. He paused, started to speak, paused again, and just came out with it: "How do you feel about going after Guilfoyle to get these Geiger Ringers?"

"It'll just slow us down. Isn't that what Rouen really wants? And you believe what he told you?"

"Do I have a choice? What do we have? Nothing, nothing," Horrocks said. "If Rouen was telling the truth, I don't want to miss this opportunity. I don't see how we'll find the king any other way. He's not out in the open. He never will be again."

"I thought you gave this up. I thought we were going home. You don't care what I want," Sari said. She put her silverware in the middle of her empty tray. The bottom of the tray gleamed with an oily rainbow. "How would Rouen know Guilfoyle has one of these Geigers? Don't all the Ringers look the same? Isn't that the idea?"

"Nothing is black and white, Sari."

Sari carried their trays to the sink. "Guilfoyle might be as hard to find as the king."

"It wouldn't be that difficult," Horrocks said. "Talking with Rouen, I also got the impression Guilfoyle doesn't realize he has these Geigers. He caught one of my Ringers, Sari, the ones the queen gave us. The one that ran away before the Longliner."

Sari spun around.

"Guilfoyle's got him. He's also abusing the Ringers. Rouen said that. The way Guilfoyle likes to hit things, I'm afraid one of them's going to die."

"He'll murder him, the one looks like you," Sari said. "If you want to do something, we'll have to do it soon."

"Are you sure you don't want to rush home?" Horrocks said.

"We're not rushing anywhere in this thing. I knew we weren't going straight home a while ago. I was hoping, but I knew. If the Geigers are real we might have a shot locating the king. That would put all this behind us sooner. That's what I want."

"You're sure," Horrocks said.

"Of course I'm not, but we have to take care of this soon. Better off doing it out here than trapped on our mine. Should we change direction?"

"No, Guilfoyle will be going the same way. We'll keep on to Hera Station, decide what to do from there."

"Can you do something about this damn heat? There is no heat," Sari said and put her mouth up to his ear so he could hear her teeth chatter.

HORROCKS REREAD THE HEATING SCHEMATICS, inspected the ship for two hours and reasoned the source of their trouble somewhere in the common room. He took down the faux-wood panels, found more problems than he could fix, more broken parts than he had spares. He wiped the oil and dust from his hands, left the panels on the floor and walked down the hall to the cockpit. "We need some equipment the Gunwitch might have," he told Sari. "Before we cut her free I'm going over for another look."

She put her paperback on the dashboard. "Need help?"

"Stay here and fly the ship," Horrocks said.

Sari went back to her book. "Good, because I didn't really mean it."

"I could tell."

She stuck out her tongue.

Horrocks climbed down the emergency umbilical and hunted through the *Sorcerer*. He approximated the location of each necessary part, but Guilfoyle had broken through most of the walls and crushed the machinery they guarded. What a thorough imbecile, Horrocks thought.

He marveled at the carnage once more. How much steam did he have? Horrocks thought. If Guilfoyle had the time, probably would've wrecked the hull, too. Used his ship to do it. All this over a decoy. A decoy. A decoy ship, he thought. That's what we could do. Use this ship how she was meant to be used.

He darted up the umbilical and jogged to the cockpit. "We fix up the Gunwitch, float it by Guilfoyle. Make *Sorcerer* look a little different. Entice Guilfoyle to come onboard. When he does, we grab the Ringers."

Sari didn't put the book down. "How're you going to get on his ship?"

"Not sure. It's only a partial plan. We'll figure out the rest. This way, we'll get all the Ringers and fuck Guilfoyle in the process. Strand him if we want to. We'll need more parts to do it. How long till Hera?"

Sari checked the navcom. "About seven hours."

"I'm going to get McGavin. We'll clean out the Gunwitch."

Horrocks went to the cellar, got his rifle from the closet and used the muzzle to wake the Ringer. "Get up," Horrocks said. "Time for a little exercise."

"I'm too tired," McGavin said.

Horrocks jabbed him in the ribs.

McGavin sat up. "I've got a bad back."

"And I'm deaf," Horrocks said. He took two pairs of gloves from the closet and followed the Ringer down into the *Sorcerer*.

McGavin surveyed the room. "Who went nuts?"

"All this junk on the floor, bring it to the hold in back," Horrocks said.

"I'm swimming in glass here."

Horrocks threw him a pair of gloves.

"Alone? What about you?"

"I decided I can't keep guard and work at the same time."

"You decided," McGavin said, stooped over and shoveled the debris into his arms.

In three hours the floor was clean enough that the tile pattern could be seen. The chairs and stools were righted, the fractured desks and monitors pieced together.

Horrocks ordered the Ringer to turn everything away from the windows.

The hold was so full it took the strength of both men to close the door.

"Nicely done," Horrocks said.

"Nicely done for what? Why'd we do this?"

"Back to the ship," Horrocks said.

McGavin took off the gloves and showed his bare, bloody hands to Horrocks. "Your gloves are for shit," he said.

Horrocks waved his gun. "Back inside."

HERA STATION WAS A MOBILE FLEA MARKET. It had been cobbled together by the families of the specialists who built the mines. At first it was merely a place to pass the time, barter for toiletries and used books, but it soon established itself as an essential though unofficial organ of the Furnace industry. Originally it was known as Trade Station; the old miner who'd dubbed it "Hera" thought that she was Jupiter's wife, not Juno, and didn't realize he was mixing mythologies. Most people had no interest in Greco-Roman parity, and the nickname stuck.

Inside Hera Station were four tremendously long aisles, each aisle a collection of stalls and sellers. The stalls were prefabricated squares packed so close together their roofs were permanently bowed. The station roved through Jupiter's orbit, moving to evade the transient hulk laws, never spending one week in the same location though never very far from the previous one.

The entryway tubes that grew out of the station looked like sprigs from a grapevine. Sari parked in one of the tubes, dropped the *Moondrunk*'s gangplank and left with Horrocks.

The tube was jammed with miners as well as the parasitic chiselers who made their living off the mines without actually working for them. Horrocks and Sari rounded a corner and came to the main auditorium. The room was so crowded Horrocks could see only heads, no bodies.

"What do we need?" Sari asked.

"Some lamps and spare parts. I'll know them when I see them," Horrocks said.

Six children sat on red cartons to his right. Horrocks waved a bill in the air. Two of the children got up immediately, fought, and the victor came strutting over. He shadowed Horrocks and Sari as they attacked the aisles.

The loudest noise in all the depot was not conversation but the shuffling of feet. All the haggling was civil and hushed. The vendors' stalls reminded Horrocks of carnival booths: a ledge with wares at the front, goods suspended on the inside walls. At the center, a bored or overly enthusiastic proprietor.

Horrocks shoved a path through the crowd toward the first stall with lamps and bulbs. He chose four cheap lamps, haggled because it was expected, and paid the owner. "Thanks a bunch," the man said.

Horrocks gave the lamps to the boy.

Sari saw nothing she liked. She took Horrocks' hand and looked at the people instead of the goods. She was a head taller than most of the browsers. A large portion of Hera's clientele drove skims—flat ships that loitered under the mines and snatched the faulty caskets periodically jettisoned from the Furnace exhaust vents to be consumed by Io. These caskets were then sold on the industrial black market at steep discounts. The skimmers were non-aggressive so Horrocks usually left them alone. In return they scraped the stray bits of lava that splashed his mine. The king considered the skimmers a pestilence and had them removed and strung up whenever possible. Sari thought that was the wiser practice.

"Excuse me," Sari said and pushed one of the skimmers out of her way. The man glared at Sari. Horrocks glared back and the man walked off.

Horrocks stopped at ten more stalls, found what he needed at the last three. He held up a metal device shaped like a head of garlic. "For the heat," he told Sari.

"Don't show me. Just fix it," she said.

The crowd thinned by the end of the fourth aisle, then grew dense near the far corner. A man was speaking from a pulpit of red crates. Beside him was a bronze statue of the king. Like the statue at Longliner Station, this one was bound in chains and black cloth.

"Some skimmer demonstration?" Sari said.

"That's Tinton on those crates," Horrocks said.

"I know there's at least one of you here," Tinton said to the crowd. "I can see it around the eyes, the pinch of your nose. You, there. Yes, you right there." Tinton's back was hunched, his hands frantic. "Don't deny your heritage. Don't exclude yourself from your inheritance. Be true to your identity. Don't be swindled from what's rightfully yours." He straightened up, amplified his voice. "Just because your father abandoned you doesn't mean he can abandon his obligations. The man is an irresponsible philanderer. He's had hundreds of affairs, fathered more children then he could know. Why? I know the answer why. He's an egotist. Siring all these children makes him feel like a god. Does anyone respect him?

"Look at this statue." Tinton angled his body to the side so the statue would become the focus of attention. He shook the statue's loose chains. "I've seen a dozen like it. Whoever covered him up—"

"You did it, Bastard," yelled someone from the crowd.

"Not I, sir. You call me a bastard. That is such a foul word to describe an innocent. I've done nothing to deserve so crass a title. We aren't bastards, my good man. The forgotten children is what we are.

"If there are any of my half sisters and brothers among you, give me your parentage cards and come join us. Remember this, the real bastards are the ones who perpetrated the explosion on the mines yesterday."

He spoke some more but no one listened. The crowd expanded and came apart. Horrocks and Sari left with them.

"Rouen mentioned there'd be an explosion," Horrocks said. "I wonder who was actually behind it, him or Tinton."

"I'd guess Tinton," Sari said. "I hope nobody was killed."

Horrocks paid the urchin when they reached the *Moondrunk*. He gave the boy some extra money for the rest of the children, was explicit in his directions but doubted they would be followed.

"That kid's a hustler. Reminds me of someone," Sari said.

Horrocks shrugged and carried their packages inside.

Sari piloted the *Moondrunk* away from Hera's congested traffic. "Far enough?" she said.

Horrocks nodded. He installed the component he had bought for the heater. The ship's pipes shook as if they were being hammered by a troupe of percussionists. Heat blew from the vents. Sari clapped and kissed Horrocks on the forehead.

Horrocks made three trips into the Gunwitch *Sorcerer*, put the lamps near the windows and screwed in the spare parts at the appropriate junctures in the bare walls' circuitry. He went through the pile of debris in the hold, found broken sections of the wall and glued them in place as best he could. He wiped the sparkly dust from the desks and monitors, swabbed the floor and the walls. When he finished, Horrocks extinguished the lamps and sealed up the ship behind him.

Sari was waiting in the *Moondrunk*'s cellar. She helped Horrocks into his golden spacesuit, handed him a torch and a canister of hull polish. At the exit hatch they connected the safety lines to his wrists and ankles.

She went to the cockpit and used the winch to lower the *Sorcerer* a bit so Horrocks would have room to move.

Horrocks left the *Moondrunk* and eased himself down onto the Gunwitch's roof. He sprayed the hull with polish until the canister ran out, then used the canister's edge to score the ship's windows. Horrocks used the torch to etch three jagged burn marks across the Gunwitch's starboard side. Each false scar took an hour. He spent a fourth hour going over his work, deepening and lengthening the scars so they'd look authentic.

Sari helped him shed the suit when he made it back.

"All set?" she said.

"Got to find Guilfoyle now," Horrocks said.

CHAPTER 25

"The Mayday frequency," Horrocks said. "Tell me the frequency."

"The frequency, the frequency," McGavin said. He scratched the stubble that was coming out on his cheeks in unhealthy splotches. "I don't know what *Mayday* means."

They sat in the common room, facing each other in the striped chairs. Sari had locked them in from the outside.

Horrocks' arms rested on his thighs, hands loose but ready. "If you want to fight, we may as well get that out of the way," he said.

"I don't want to fight," the Ringer said.

"Because we should do that first. It'd be a shame I spent my energy talking—"

"It's—What frequency?"

Horrocks flexed his fingers. "The Mayday call. The way you'd let the king or the rest of your coven know there was trouble."

"There was always trouble," the Ringer said. He slapped his knees, stood up, walked around his chair, sat down again. He rubbed the back of his neck.

"The queen will hang you," Horrocks said. Instead of leaning forward for emphasis, he leaned back. "She'll have no use for the king's doubles if the king is dead."

"He's not."

"Give it time."

"She loves us," the Ringer said.

"When things are good everyone's full of love. Things aren't good. There's a lot of undecided ancestry in that family. If Porphyria and her son take power, who'll need the king's surrogates?"

"I hate that term," McGavin said and walked around his chair again. Before McGavin could lower himself back down Horrocks kicked out the chair by aiming between the Ringer's legs. Horrocks jumped McGavin as he fell and pinned the man's shoulders with his knees. "The frequency! Tell me the frequency!" Horrocks shouted into McGavin's face. Horrocks' knees bored into McGavin's shoulders. "The frequency!"

"Get off me!"

"You're worthless if I don't find the king."

"The other Ringers have probably—"

Horrocks shifted his weight to the man's chest, could feel the ribcage give like damp wood.

McGavin spent two minutes thrashing around. Horrocks stood up when McGavin quieted down. Horrocks said, "If you want to fight again, I'd be more—"

"I don't want to fight, for myself or anyone else. Find the king. Leave me alone. It's thirty-two point two. That's the frequency. Thirty-two two."

"WHERE WERE YOU?" Sari said.

"Had to do a little more work on the Gunwitch, some final flourishes."

"Such as?"

"Such as the exit hatch will be easy to open but once it's closed—I played with the tumblers."

They were in the cockpit. The *Moondrunk* was just outside of Hera Station.

"You're ready?" Sari said. She drove the ship 1,000 miles from the station and released the *Sorcerer*. From that position Sari fired off two distress calls along the Mayday frequency. She deserted the *Sorcerer* and reentered the traffic around the station, going one way then turning around and going the other.

"Zoom the cameras out a little," Horrocks said. "It'll help if we see Guilfoyle approach."

"You left a few lights on in there," Sari said.

"I left them all on. Zoom out a little more. There, that's fine."

"What if Guilfoyle comes for us instead of the Gunwitch?" Sari asked.

"He won't notice us. He'll see the Gunwitch first. The Mayday call should have given him the coordinates as well."

"What if a bunch of Ringers come running?"

"I hope they do."

"You're sure he monitors the Mayday line?" she asked.

"I'm hoping."

Sari turned to look at him. "How come we didn't use the Mayday call before?"

"Because no Ringer would actually use it. Least of all the king himself. A code like that's only good when things are calm. Then it means something. To use it now would be redundant. They wouldn't pay attention to it because they know it'd be false. This is the kind of thing Guilfoyle would be watching. He's smart enough to know about the frequency, dumb enough to be fooled by it."

"You hope," she said. "If someone goes near the Gunwitch?"

"We dissuade them."

Horrocks went to the cellar. He opened the locker that contained his armor, separated the legs and put the torso on. He took the handheld battering ram from the floor of the locker and went back to the cockpit. The battering ram was silver in color, made of dense steel, and was very heavy in his lap. It was an uncomfortable weight but it made Horrocks feel prepared.

"How long till he shows?" Sari said.

"A day, probably less. With a Spot Drive, there's no place in the sector will take him more than a day to reach."

Horrocks watched the cameras and wondered how long Guilfoyle could stay away from this sweet trap. Not a whole day, for sure.

"A dancer," Sari said.

"Dancer?"

"You asked me before. We were talking about what we always thought—"

"Right, right," Horrocks said. The battering ram was digging into his legs.

Sari curled against her chair's armrest. "A dancer. They're so fluid. We transported a dance company once, on the Longliner. I watched them practice. I watched them change into their uniforms, then I watched them practice." She drummed her fingers on her calves. "It was so sexual. I was fourteen, fifteen. The way they flew past each other. Men and women, touching, lifting, spreading their arms, gliding in this seamless ballet. It could have been ballet. Their radio was broken. I suppose they had the music in their heads. Long hair, every one of them. They'd fly one way, their hair the other, all sweaty. It accentuated their movements. I thought about going with them."

"Do you regret it?"

"What are dancers going to do out in the Deeps? Out there, who'll pay for that?" she said. They probably all wound up prostitutes, she thought.

She changed lanes and joined the outgoing traffic. No one had approached the Gunwitch. It was a dark speck among nothing, invisible.

"That's it? A dancer?"

"Chef, too," Sari said. "I teased myself with that idea for about two months, but I've no patience with food. A pilot. A bridge engineer. I love bridges."

"I know," Horrocks said. He rested his head against the back of the chair. He felt surprisingly relaxed.

"Original, twisted, modern bridges. A manager of some sort, maybe. Never a bodyguard. Never a miner."

The proximity alert trilled as an unfamiliar ship neared the Gunwitch. Horrocks braced himself to bolt into action. The ship—one of the flat skims Sari despised—passed the Gunwitch without stopping. "Too soon, anyway," Horrocks said. "It's only been a couple hours."

Sari put her hands on the cameras' controls and panned back. "And you?" she said. "Don't tell me a boxer. I've heard that one already."

Horrocks put the battering ram on the floor and rubbed the dents out of his thighs. "Who remembers that far back?"

"You do," Sari said and chortled.

"I've tried to forget it all."

"Not the good parts. You remember something," she said.

"OK, oceanographer. I've never been in the ocean. That's always appealed to me."

"That's one. There's more."

"Boxer. Can't remember another."

"Come on," she said and slapped him on the arm.

"You'd like me to make one up?" he asked.

"If you have to. You suck at this game."

"A poacher. That would've been fun. Never thought of it before. Be pretty exciting, I bet."

"That's good," she said. "One more. Make it interesting."

"I'm all out."

They traveled Hera Station's byways for eleven hours. They took turns making coffee, napping and waking each other up. When the proximity alert flashed again they were both asleep. The *Honey Locust* was on top of the Gunwitch. Sari zoomed the cameras in. Horrocks picked up his battering ram.

Sari magnified the image further. "Looks like something's moving in the Gunwitch. I didn't notice it before."

"The lights are on a pulley I rigged up. It sways, gives the illusion of movement. I also angled the lights away so Guilfoyle wouldn't see how poorly we repaired it."

"The Ringer in there, I can barely see his face," Sari said.

The *Honey Locust* circled the Gunwitch slowly, taking fifteen minutes to orbit the ship completely.

"Bite," Horrocks said.

"He's cautious," Sari said. "He thinks he recognizes the ship."

"I don't know," Horrocks said.

The *Honey Locust* orbited the Gunwitch again, this time completing the circuit in five minutes. It darted away from the Gunwitch, scanned the immediate area and went back. The *Honey Locust* extended her umbilical.

"Wait till it latches on, wait three minutes after that, then move in," Horrocks said.

"Three minutes," Sari said. She was excited and nervous and full of fear. For no reason at all she thought, I could never have been a dancer.

CHAPTER 26

Guilfoyle stood in the *Honey Locust*'s exit hatch and looked through the porthole. The umbilical was slow to reach the Gunwitch. The mechanism that guided the device needed to be cleaned and lubricated; it sent vibrations through the floor that echoed in Guilfoyle's fragile knees. The bats were reassuringly heavy in Guilfoyle's hands. He wore gloves lined with cotton to absorb the sweat from his palms.

He wondered why this Gunwitch had sent the distress call. She *doesn't* look familiar, he thought. The one I ransacked had no scars. What I could see through the windows, she's clean, bright, could be people in there. Someone sitting patient by the window. Mechanical trouble, looks like. Maybe a firefight.

The umbilical creaked like an old tree and finally made the connection. Guilfoyle stared at the safety lights above the door, waiting for the green signal. He twirled the bats by whipping his wrists in a circle. The red safety light stuttered, went out and was replaced with green. Guilfoyle pulled the door open so hard it crashed into the wall and bounced off its hinge. He plunged through the umbilical and stopped at the Gunwitch's entrance. Another set of safety lights. As he waited for the green one, Guilfoyle examined the door. Pretty sure that's a different handle, he thought. Kitsis was wrong. This is not the same Gunwitch.

The light went green. Guilfoyle threw the door open and rushed across the threshold into darkness. He fell ten feet and landed on his hip, one bat smacking his cheek. He got up using the bats as crutches.

The fall didn't mar Guilfoyle's giddiness. The air in the dark space smelled like burnt hair. Definitely a different ship, he thought.

SARI ALIGNED THE *MOONDRUNK'S* MAIN UMBILICAL with the *Honey Locust*'s rear entrance. She made subtle adjustments as the tube bridged the ships. Horrocks flew across the tube and outlined the door to Guilfoyle's ship with pliable explosive clay. He pressed a fuse into the clay, lit it, retreated to the other end of the umbilical and looked away.

The minor explosion rattled both ships but the umbilical remained intact. The *Honey Locust*'s door was hanging open. Horrocks sprinted through the door and met a chubby woman dressed in grossly undersized leotards. She was holding two dumbbells. Dance music pulsed from the room's speakers.

Who the fuck is she? Horrocks thought.

Kitsis threw the dumbbells at Horrocks' face. Her aim was terrible and they dinged off his torso armor as he ran for the stairs. "Gil! Gil!" Kitsis screamed. She tried to tackle Horrocks but he spun out of the way, seized her wrists and tossed her aside.

Horrocks reached the top step when Kitsis jammed a foam exercise block between his feet. He tripped into the kitchen and crashed into the sink. The faucet cracked; water gushed from the base and spout. Kitsis took a handful of dirty trays from the sink and pounded Horrocks on the chest and arms.

Horrocks grabbed the back of her head with his left hand and bounced her face off the counter. She collapsed. A few trays slid over the drain. Water filled the sink and cascaded over the side.

The door to the topmost floor was locked. Horrocks punched it in and took the steps three at a time. The storeroom smelled like a hot sump. Horrocks found the lights and turned them all the way up. The Ringer chained to the wall on the left was pink and well fed. The Ringers behind the cage looked like veteran gladiators, angry and scarred. Horrocks counted four men altogether.

THERE WAS NO LIGHT in the trap basement. Floor must've been weak, that's how I fell through, Guilfoyle thought as he felt his way along the wall. Or they rigged it up to stop intruders. Probably waiting for me when I make it out. Hope they are.

The gloves did a fine job of soaking up his prodigious sweat.

The hallway wasn't straight. Guilfoyle tripped over objects he couldn't see. His eyes colored the darkness in green Rorschach. The complete silence stirred chimes in his ears.

One Ringer, maybe three or four, he thought. Between me and Horrocks that should be about all of them. Hope they're on this ship. Bonus of another $100,000 each. Way my luck's been lately, I wouldn't be shocked. The king might be right here. I'll call Rouen when I'm done, call Tinton after that. Collect from them both. Screw them both, and leave.

And then what? he asked himself in a mock interview. Out to the Deeps, of course. With all that money, out to the Deeps. Give Kitsis just enough so I can ditch her guilt-free.

Guilfoyle rounded a corner, came to a dead end, reached up and pulled down a metal ladder. It clanged as the steps unfolded. He climbed up to the trapdoor in the ceiling. He pulled the latch but the door was locked. Guilfoyle retreated a step, hunched over, bent his legs and put his shoulder to the door. The ladder groaned as he straightened his legs. Guilfoyle groaned. The door burst open.

Rouen'll be pleased, Guilfoyle thought as he stepped up into the bright room. He looked around. The floor was spotless. All the machines were turned away from him but he could hear them humming. Not the same ship at all, he thought.

"Hello?" he said, turning. He approached the Ringer seated by the window. There was a puddle beneath the chair. "Scared?" Guilfoyle said. "All alone, are you? *Are you?*"

HORROCKS FLIPPED THE SWITCH to power his armor, snapped the cage's bars and helped the Ringers through. "Gently, Horrocks," Indigo said. "We're all a little sore."

"We've got to move," Horrocks said. When all three men were out of the cage, Horrocks stopped by the man-acled Ringer and took hold of the chains.

"Leave him here," Indigo said. The others nodded.

"Everyone comes," Horrocks said. He broke the man-acle. Because he was feeling destructive he also broke the other five manacles and the lock on the cage door. "Downstairs," Horrocks said. "All the way down."

He turned off the power to his suit and shoved them through the doorway. "Run. Move," he said.

"It's been days since we—"

Horrocks shouted directions. They passed Kitsis on their way through the kitchen. The floor was covered with half an inch of foul water. She blinked at the pass-ing men but did not move.

Wish I had time to steal or smash Guilfoyle's Spot Drive, Horrocks thought. He led the Ringers through the umbilical, onto the *Moondrunk* and into the cellar. "I'll be down with food in a little while," Horrocks said and locked the door.

He raced back through the umbilical and shut the door to Guilfoyle's ship. It seemed like a good seal. The green light went on. When he was behind the *Moondrunk*'s door he manually retracted the umbilical. His heart was beating so violently his armor sounded like a tin drum.

"Go," he said to Sari when he reached the cockpit.

"You got them all?"

Horrocks nodded.

"And Guilfoyle?"

"Don't know." Horrocks tugged on the armor's clasps. "Got to get out of this damn thing. I'm suffocating."

"ARE YOU HARD OF HEARING, FRIEND?" Guilfoyle asked the Ringer. "Why the Mayday signal? Trouble with the ship?"

He crept toward the Ringer, keeping his eyes on the rest of the room, afraid he'd be taken by surprise. "The bats are for show," Guilfoyle said and flashed a placating smile. The ship rocked—Guilfoyle did not know why—and the Ringer's head lolled like a doll's. Guilfoyle bent at the waist to help the man up and saw that the Ringer's legs and back were stitched to the chair. He realized that the man's skin was far from healthy. His hair was stiff and shiny. Guilfoyle recognized the fluid that leaked from the stitches. Yellow, pungent fluid.

Guilfoyle screamed and brought one of the bats down on the corpse's head. He swung at the corpse's shoulder with the other bat, knocking the chair and the Ringer sideways. The body held the shape of Guilfoyle's bats like a bag of wet rice. Guilfoyle pummeled the body, each time digging a deeper trough. The skin split like a hard-boiled egg, exposing the bleached organs. Guilfoyle flattened the Ringer's waist, made putty out of his face. The stitches ripped as the chair broke apart.

I'm a fool, Guilfoyle thought and trotted over to the machines. He struck them with more passion than he'd shown the body. The desks and monitors toppled easily. Some fell that Guilfoyle hadn't even reached yet.

"This is too familiar," Guilfoyle said. "It's the Gun-witch I wrecked all prettied up. Fucking trap."

He stepped around the hole by the door and pulled the handle. The door was heavier than he remembered. It took five minutes of hearty tugging to get it open. He stormed through the umbilical, closed it off and walked into the kitchen. Kitsis was using a wrench to tighten the bolt at the base of the faucet. Her leotards were drenched.

"Did you get a proximity alert while I was gone?" Guilfoyle asked.

"There's water everywhere," Kitsis said. She was struggling with the wrench, twisting her arms more than the bolt.

"Did we get—"

"What the fuck does a proximity alert sound like, Gil?" Kitsis yelled. She pointed the wrench at him. It was too heavy for her and it dropped into the water on the floor. "Sunk right down," she said. "It's up to your fucking ankles, you louse. See the color? Brown, like shit. All the new water we got at the depot? Gone. It's all run out."

Guilfoyle kicked the water. "I don't fucking believe—"

"He was here and gone," Kitsis said. She fished through the pool for the wrench. "Broke the faucet, too."

"Huh?" Guilfoyle said.

"Horrocks. Here and gone."

Guilfoyle walked up to the storeroom. He moved slowly to postpone his disappointment. The broken cage was empty, the room a mess.

All that time, all that hard work, Guilfoyle thought and hurled one of the bats at the bent cage.

He scared Kitsis by splashing into the kitchen unannounced. He took his other bat in both hands and clove the table in half. He shoved the ends aside and swung for his sister, missed her and caught the sink instead. The mangled faucet erupted in a brown geyser. Guilfoyle smashed their plates and glasses and bowls. He moved out into the hallway.

Horrocks the crook, Horrocks the thief, Horrocks the cheat, Guilfoyle thought. He bent his legs and used the bat to put a hole through the floor. A crack split the floorboards down the length of the hallway. He bashed the ceiling, the lights. He punched his way through the wall and made a crude entrance to the adjacent room. Kitsis' bedroom.

Guilfoyle buried the bat in her dresser and freed a hail of splintered plastic. He shattered her treasured mirror. He got on her bed, spun around, dizzying himself, aiming his bat for anything solid. His armpits were a rainforest of sweat. I've got nothing to show Rouen, he thought. Horrocks stole my fortune.

Kitsis pulled the comforter from under Guilfoyle. He knocked his skull on the headboard going down, bit through his tongue and landed on his back, unconscious. Kitsis pressed his wrists together and pinned them to the box spring with her body.

CHAPTER 27

Horrocks cleared the cellar's floor to make some room. Sari brought down five trays of hot food. Horrocks watched the Ringers eat, chatted with them about nothing important. The Ringers were so eager to use the cellar's shower they stood under the spray together, all of them but McGavin. Sari stood at the bottom of the stairs with Horrocks' rifle.

Horrocks spoke to each Ringer individually. He checked their bodies for trauma, found no wound that couldn't wait a week for a real doctor.

"Broke my cheek. It set all wrong," one of the Ringers said. Steel rings marked all the fleshy parts of his face. Horrocks could tell they had been infected and that the Ringer had scratched the infections hard enough to leave scars. His hair was a sheared mess. He and Horrocks were separated by a card table filled with balls of cotton and old medical equipment.

"What are you going to do with those," Pierce said, "clean our teeth?"

Horrocks smiled weakly. "They're for stitching, mainly. That's about all I can do for you."

"I don't need it. My cheek set all wrong. I can't smile, not that I want to. I'll never guard the king again." Pierce ran his thumb down his rough jawline; he hadn't shaved in the two weeks since the incident.

Horrocks had been dreading these interviews. To sit in the cellar with all these men whose job was pretending to be someone else, something they weren't, made him physically sick. He wasn't sure how long he would last before berating the men for their fraudulence. They silently challenged his bias because most of them didn't even look like the king anymore. Horrocks conceded that he could not hate them the same way as before.

One Ringer, the pure Ringer Guilfoyle hadn't molested, stood out like a luminous angel in a junkyard, his radiance making the others seem dim and worthless. Horrocks had no trouble hating him.

Pierce got up and another Ringer took his chair.

"Did Guilfoyle have any leads?" Horrocks asked.

This Ringer's short hair was dyed indigo, although that color was losing ground to a sneak attack from his brown roots.

"Did he talk to you?" Horrocks asked.

"Mean talk, nothing else," Indigo said. "Never hinted where we were going. He beat us. That's all we ever got out of him, his fists. One Ringer at a time, always. He was careful about that, like you are now." He nodded toward Sari and the gun.

Sari gave the Ringer an indolent grin.

"I don't expect any from you, but one of the Ringers has given me trouble," Horrocks said.

"We're trouble all together like this, no doubt. You've treated us right, so don't expect any from me. Do my best to keep the others calm."

"I need to know which ones are the Geiger Ringers," Horrocks said. He brushed some of the instruments aside and pulled his chair closer to Indigo. "The king's around. The sooner I find him—"

"The sooner we get some rest, the more helpful we'll be. Guilfoyle only fed us when it struck him as funny. Left the lights on for days, off for days. He dickered with the heat. Made a lot of noise. We're useless now. Especially the Geigers. Any change in our—It'll have to be explained, but we're useless as guides right now. Give us some sleep."

Horrocks dismissed him and another Ringer came out from behind the mesh. The junkyard angel. His skin was slightly yellow, his saffron bruises almost fully healed.

"Guilfoyle left me alone," Saffron said. "In comparison to the others, anyway. With me it was all verbal. Sometimes that's worse, don't you think? The only one Guilfoyle went for on purpose was the one who looks like you. We're tired, Horrocks. Need to sleep. Need to get back to normal."

"There is no more normal," Horrocks said. "Go back inside, send out my Ringer, get some sleep."

Horrocks' Ringer came to the table and pulled the chair out; the pain incurred from that simple motion reverberated throughout the man's body. The left side of his face looked like a pink cauliflower. His right eye was a purple slit. Some of his teeth were missing; Horrocks couldn't tell how many because the man's fat lips barely moved.

The rest of his body was equally damaged.

"I'm sorry," Horrocks said. "I know Guilfoyle hurt you because of the resemblance. I wish you'd taken the Longliner with the other two."

"I couldn't go to the Deeps. Go out there and I'm dead." He held his elbows and rocked in the chair. "Had to chance it out here. I didn't volunteer to get your face because I've so many opportunities. It was the only opportunity."

"How did Guilfoyle find you?"

"You mean how did the Ringers find me. Don't know. My memory's only good for certain things now. All those concussions. The Ringers got me, then Guilfoyle got them, and then I'm sitting here. Should've gone to the Deeps, you're right."

This is too dangerous, Horrocks thought. There are too many of them. We're a bigger target than before. Now we've become a destination. Now the *Moondrunk*'s a damn prize.

Horrocks helped the man back to the cage, then joined Sari in the kitchen for dinner. The beef tasted like fish. The vegetables, all different shapes and colors, tasted like broccoli.

"There isn't enough food for all of them," Sari said.

"We'll get more." Horrocks tried to decipher the vegetable on his fork. "Food's not all we need. A few of them could use doctors. Guilfoyle's going to come after us. We couldn't outrun a water-bearer in this ship. We might have to drop them off somewhere safe. Keep the Geigers and lose the rest."

Sari used a knife to scrape half her dinner into the trash. "Somewhere safe? A doctor? I could use these things, too, Horrocks."

WYETH CAUGHT UP TO THE *MOONDRUNK* a few hours after Horrocks and Sari finished their dinner. He parked his small craft inside the *Moondrunk*'s tiny bay.

"Wyeth," Sari said. The two of them joked and reminisced as they waited for Horrocks to come up from the cellar.

"Shit, Wyeth," Horrocks said. "I'm gonna get sick of you."

"Horrocks," Sari said, drawing his name out like taffy.

The three of them went into the common room. "I've got something to do upstairs," Sari said. "Do you want a drink before I go, Wy?"

"Thanks, no. 'Night, gorgeous."

Sari winked at him and left through the kitchen.

Horrocks sank into the nearest chair with the weariness of a man who's been standing for days. "How'd you catch up to us?"

"I've always been good at finding things. Plus you're missing an engine."

Horrocks feigned surprise but couldn't dredge up a laugh. "The Bastards came by to give us a progress report. And it's an exhaust cone we're missing, not an engine."

"Same difference," Wyeth said. He sat down across from Horrocks. "You're still moving half as fast, you still have only one cone left." Horrocks' dog came into the room looking for his master, found Wyeth instead and lay down with his paws in the air. Wyeth stroked its belly. "I love this dog. Where's his brother?"

"The fight with the Bastards. He died."

Wyeth stopped scratching. "I hope you made them pay."

"I left them drifting."

"I would have done worse," Wyeth said. The dog looked at him quizzically. Wyeth cooed and continued scratching.

"How's it going with the depot?"

"The depot," Wyeth said. "The depot was bullshit. I'm still muling, Horrocks. I know you don't care for it, you're too good for it, but it's the only work I can get."

The dog rolled over and licked Wyeth's fingers. Wyeth played with the loose skin around the dog's neck. "He hates this collar. All dogs hate collars." Wyeth burped and the dog jumped.

"Come work for me," Horrocks said.

"I hate the mines worse than muling. All that heat all the time, it's unnatural." He gave the dog a final rub, slouched down and laid his hands on his chest. "Muling's got less drawbacks. I'm amazed you never got sick, all the trips you made."

"Just the one time."

"I'm always sick. Packets of latex. I think I'm allergic. My insides hate me. I've been getting the Liner Sickness lately, too. Must be my old age. The acceleration and deceleration's a bitch."

"Someday one of those packets'll burst inside you, like it did to me," Horrocks said.

"It looks like you made it through."

"I wished I was dead, the whole time and a couple days after."

"The money suits me," Wyeth said. He burped again. "Packets are giving me indigestion."

"How many are you carrying?"

"Six."

"Christ, how do you hold that many?"

"I feel full all the time."

"Where are you headed?" Horrocks asked.

"I just came from the Furnaces. Actually, I couldn't even get close. Guardships chased me down and I spent twenty minutes face to face with their interrogators. Thought I was going to shit my pants. They would've found the packets in my underwear and that would've been it. I've been passing and swallowing these things eleven days straight."

"It's a bad time right now," Horrocks said.

Wyeth stared down at his hands. "Do your miners use?"

"I'm sure they do."

"'Cause that's where I'm headed. I wanted to ask permission first. I didn't see any guardships patrolling her."

"So you're not muling, you're dealing."

"I was gonna go without saying anything, but all we've been through . . ."

"It's a bad time, Wyeth. I think you're going to have to wait a little while."

"What I've brought, it's fancy. They came up with it last year. The wizards in Miami. It'll keep your men happy and it won't make them sloppy. Honest, Horrocks. I can guarantee your production goes up. Guarantee, I swear."

Horrocks got out of his chair.

"My visa didn't expire, Horrocks. They revoked it. They ran me out. I'm trying to scare up enough money to move my wife out here. These packets, they'll bring me just enough."

"My men have enough to worry about clearheaded," Horrocks said. "I'm afraid they start—"

Wyeth clapped his hands. "We're in luck. You can call ahead, tell them I'm coming. This is just what they need. I told you, this stuff won't—"

"No," Horrocks said.

"We're not all as fortunate—" Wyeth stopped himself and fixed his face with a huge grin. "It's all right. Maybe when this is over. I'm only thinking of myself, I know. How's the hunt?"

"Good and bad. We've found some Ringers. We've found too many. I'm flirting with the idea of moving them somewhere else."

"Can I see them, the Ringers?" Wyeth asked. "Where are you hiding them?"

"Basement," Horrocks said.

"Bet no one else's seen them in the state they're in. I love the unusual."

"You better go," Horrocks said. "You're in danger just being here."

"If I'm in danger, so's Sari," Wyeth said. He moved past Horrocks into the hallway. "She always hated conflict. She can't stand any of this, can she? I could do you a favor. A favor I wouldn't want you to forget about. There's room for three in my ship. I could take Sari to Longliner Station, put her in the hotel. You'd have less to worry about that way."

"She does hate all this. I'll ask her."

ONE OF THE BEDROOM'S WALLS WAS FOLDED BACK, exposing a colorful portion of the ship's nervous system. Horrocks watched from the doorway as Sari disconnected a small green cube and flayed it open with a screwdriver. The cube flashed with metronomic regularity.

"Wyeth's leaving," Horrocks said. "I think you should go with him."

"I'm busy," Sari said without looking up. She chose a splicer from the pile of tools on the floor, hunched over the cube and began shaving the wires.

"You should go," Horrocks said. "Guilfoyle's going to catch us eventually. If not him, with all these Ringers—"

"Where's he going to take me?" Sari said.

"Longliner Station."

The cube beeped twice. Sari cursed and traded the splicer for a smaller model. "I can't believe you're asking me this. Go back downstairs."

"I know you don't want to be here. I'm giving you a choice to—"

"There's no choice, Horrocks. What kind of choice? Of course I want to leave, but I'm trapped here."

"Trapped."

"I'm trapped. You aren't good enough to fly the ship. Last time you were at the helm Tinton put his hook in your lip and stole our Spot Drive. If I left—"

"I want you to leave," Horrocks said.

"Do you know what this is?" Sari said and palmed the green cube. "Did you even know it was up here? I'm trying to change the beacon's tag. I'm sure Guilfoyle has it. He can use it to track us down. Didn't think about it until Wy showed up. What I'm doing, it's illegal. Most people don't even know a ship's tag can be changed."

"Then after you're finished, Wyeth—"

"I'm not leaving. I don't want to leave you."

"Wyeth—"

"You were always good for breaking into ships, but you've no talent for fixing them. Or flying them. You're good at so many things, baby, but let me do this. Give me some room. Tell Wyeth to come see us when this is all over."

"I'm sure he will," Horrocks said and went downstairs.

The slim door next to the cockpit was open. Horrocks ducked through the door into the *Moondrunk*'s bay.

Wyeth's ship was little more than an engine with wings. Wyeth was sitting in the front seat; the two behind him didn't look deep enough to accommodate a small rucksack.

"She's not coming," Wyeth said.

"She really appreciated the gesture," Horrocks said.

"Don't forget I asked."

"We won't. Where you going now?"

"I'll go see Mackerracher. The Mission won't pay as much but they're always looking to buy."

"Good luck, Wy. Sorry I couldn't do more for you."

"I see any Ringers, I'll bring 'em back for you. I'm assuming you'd be willing to pay for them."

"If you see any," Horrocks said and nodded.

SARI SEWED THE GREEN CUBE back into the wall and spent four hours in search of a roving market with enough supplies to accommodate their needs. The market—a converted supertram that used to cart energy caskets from the Furnaces to the Annex—extended her umbilical and Horrocks and Sari crossed over. They selected a variety of meals.

"A week's worth is all we need," Horrocks said. "We'll be rid of our baggage by then."

"Or someone will take it from you," Sari said.

They strolled through narrow aisles crammed with food, water, pharmaceuticals, clothing, paper towels and shampoo. Sari climbed a ladder to reach something on the top shelf. Her shirt rode up and Horrocks could see her stomach. Her pants looked tighter than normal. When she got down she walked up to Horrocks and sagged against him. He hugged her. This was all he was going to get by way of apology but they both knew it was enough.

"How are you feeling?" he asked.

"What do you mean?"

He slipped his hand under her shirt, put his fingers on her stomach. "Here. How are you feeling here?"

"Heavier." She hugged him back then pushed him away. She walked down the aisle toward the register, shooting her hips to the side for Horrocks' benefit.

"How much?" she asked.

"That's 1,700 plus 200 for the transfer," said the proprietor from behind the counter.

Three young men, the proprietor's sons, wheeled the food through the umbilical onto the *Moondrunk*. The food came in rectangular holding cabinets. Four cabinets, fifty meals in each.

"By the stove," Sari said.

"This is the *Moondrunk*, right? You're Horrocks, right?" asked the middle son.

"Yes and yes," Horrocks said. "And you are?"

"In awe. We read everything we can get about you. Some great stories there."

"Not all great," Sari said.

The boys laughed to cover their embarrassment. "We're always looking for something new. Something about your past, before the war, before the king."

"I've done a job of burying all that," Horrocks said. "Hope you like digging."

The sons grinned. Horrocks tipped them and said, "Go help your father." He clapped them on the back and shut the exit hatch.

Sari was grinning as well. "There's nothing sadder than little fools," she said.

"The tall one couldn't take his eyes off you," Horrocks said. He used his shoulders to square the cabinets against the wall.

"Two little fools, then. At least one of them has some brains."

SARI HID THE *MOONDRUNK* in the center of three abandoned water-bearers. The water-bearers masked the

Moondrunk while providing an unobstructed view of the region's traffic.

They spent two days warming the trays, feeding the Ringers and doing little else. They made love five times, twice to kill their boredom and three times out of genuine desire. Horrocks hoped to find the adventurous Sari that Rouen's visit had left in its wake, but she was gone.

Jupiter was a good deal closer and very bright. Horrocks went through the *Moondrunk* and darkened her many windows, pausing along the way to count the striped clouds that blew across Jupiter's pastel face. Io was still in view, and so were the mines.

During those two days, they saw Guilfoyle's *Honey Locust* twice. Guilfoyle was in a rush both times.

On the third day Horrocks decided the Ringers should be well enough to help. He got his handgun from the bedroom closet and tucked it into his jeans by the small of his back.

"Going down to see the Ringers again?" Sari said.

Everyone but Saffron looked better. He was sitting on the toilet, fully clothed. He was missing fistfuls of hair and his face was a battlefield of thick black scabs.

"He looked fine yesterday," Horrocks said.

"He fell off a ladder," Indigo said. "Nothing for you to worry about."

"Settle your differences however you want, just so nobody dies. I want to see the Geigers."

Indigo and Pierce came forward and followed Horrocks up to the cockpit.

"We had a third," Indigo said. "He's dead or missing, like the king."

Horrocks remembered the autopsy after the queen's visit, the unusual clump of nerves on the Ringer's spine. "I think your third is long dead," he said.

Sari stayed in the pilot's chair. Indigo sat in Horrocks' seat. Horrocks stood behind them with Pierce.

"You should take us out of here," Pierce said. "It works better if we're in motion."

Sari left the security of the derelict water-bearers. She drove away from Jupiter for three hours, weaving an erratic pattern with no fixed destination.

Horrocks watched the Ringers, looking for any change in their expression, their eyes, a movement, a sound.

"We have to be within 10,000 miles for our bodies to register his presence," Indigo said.

"How?" Sari said.

"The flesh artists put a beacon in the king's chest," Indigo said.

"What, like a ship's beacon?" Horrocks asked.

"It's a whole lot smaller," Indigo said. "Works on a completely different wavelength."

"He got a beacon," Pierce said, "and we got a tiny receiver. A catalyst embedded in the middle of our spinal cord."

"It strums our sympathetic nervous system," Indigo said. "The closer we get, the harder it strums."

"What are the signs?" Horrocks asked.

"They come in stages," Indigo said. "The most accurate from long distance is gooseflesh. The hair on our arms and legs, like static electricity." He toyed with the cameras as he talked. "Then it's cold sweats, arrhythmia, and trembling."

"Hell of a way to spend time apart," Sari said.

"We think of it as incentive to find him faster," Pierce said.

"Guilfoyle didn't know about this?" Horrocks said.

"It was designed to be subtle," Indigo said. "Guilfoyle tried his best to get us to tell him. And there were a couple days we must've been right on top of the king."

"Where?" Sari said.

"Miss, locked in that room, we may as well have been in the Deeps," Pierce said.

"The gooseflesh, the other signs, it's like this for you all the time around the king?" Horrocks asked.

"The receiver shuts off within a hundred yards of him," Indigo said.

Sari turned the ship around and headed back toward the mines. They all agreed this would be the route with the highest probability of success.

A few hours later both Ringers raised their arms at the same time. The hair on their forearms was standing straight up.

"So we're close," Horrocks said. "Thank God we're close."

"Ten thousand miles in any direction?" Sari said.

"Ten thousand miles the way we're headed, since it just happened," Indigo said.

"That's still a lot of distance," Horrocks said. "What did you say the next symptom was?"

"The sweats," Pierce said.

Sari accelerated. She watched the screens while Horrocks watched the Geigers. The Geigers closed their eyes, seemingly the only ones in the cockpit uninterested in the search.

CHAPTER 28

Guilfoyle awoke three hours after his rampage ended. He scoured the ship but couldn't find Kitsis. Must be hiding, the bitch, he thought.

Guilfoyle locked himself in the cockpit and put a chair over the trapdoor. He had taken six trays of cold food with him, a bucket, a vase, and a gallon of water that tasted like the kitchen floor.

Guilfoyle kept himself awake the first day straight thinking how he would treat Horrocks, smug Horrocks, when he found him. Much worse than the Ringers.

Guilfoyle couldn't fall asleep the second day as he pictured the reactions of both Rouen and the Bastards. Neither would believe the truth; they were too cynical. They'd assume Guilfoyle had already auctioned the Ringers to a third party and had planned this ruse from the start.

They'll kill me, he thought. The only way to come out of this clean is find more Ringers. Find some before Rouen or Tinton come calling. How many are left, five? Four? I have to find one the Bastards will believe is the king. With so many Ringers marking themselves—why the hell do they cut themselves? And I have to find the king.

Guilfoyle shat in the bucket, urinated in the vase, ate with his hands. He was afraid to leave the cockpit for a second lest his treasure reappear. The navcom was searching for the *Moondrunk*'s beacon but could find no sign of it. Should've started looking before my rampage, Guilfoyle thought, but that couldn't be helped. He calculated Horrocks' best possible speed, extrapolated some and covered the target area six times in two days. Once he nearly crashed into a trio of derelict water-bearers.

Throughout the search Guilfoyle wanted to masturbate to relieve his tension but was afraid he'd be unable to muster an erection.

Kitsis rattled the trapdoor like a noisy ghost. "You gonna come down and fix these pipes? I'm swimming through the kitchen."

Guilfoyle grabbed the nearest object and bounced it off the floor. He wasn't sure what he had thrown, the bucket, the vase or the water. Kitsis banged persistently. Guilfoyle fell asleep. He woke up sometime the next day, unsure if he was rested or if the stench had roused him. Either way he was ready to leave. He climbed down into the kitchen and left the trapdoor hanging open. The cockpit needed to air.

The kitchen floor was dry. Kitsis opened the stove and took out three trays; one for herself, two for Guilfoyle.

"Ready to eat?" Kitsis said. She slid Guilfoyle's two trays across the table. Her face was a tapestry of bruises. "Sorry about yanking the bedspread. If I hadn't, you'd still be at it."

Guilfoyle nodded, speared some carrots on his fork, shook off their sauce and shoved them in his mouth.

"I was very industrious," Kitsis said. "You'd be proud. Went into the cellar, called up the plumbing schematics. There were a lot of words in there I didn't know, but look around. I fixed the faucet, drained the floor."

She played with her silverware but didn't touch her food. "I even glued some of the floorboards you sma— The ones that needed fixing. I tidied up all around. Don't worry about my room. We'll get me a nicer one. I want to help. I really do. We'll work together. Really we will. I promise you."

Guilfoyle looked as if he would speak but had trouble swallowing his food. He reached for a glass and Kitsis handed him hers. He drank half of her soda, swallowed, and said nothing. Guilfoyle finished both trays of food, took Kitsis', finished that, and left.

"I'll clean up," she said.

GUILFOYLE SOFTENED the cage's broken bars with a blowtorch and used a pair of heavy tongs to bend them back in place. Horrocks and that fucking suit, he thought. The bars would never be straight again, but Guilfoyle was confident they could still keep a man inside. He used another set of tools on the busted lock.

Kitsis came into the room and sat on the floor near her brother. Her dress was showing too much cleavage. Guilfoyle kept his comments to himself.

"I'll keep us going in the same direction, right? That's how I programmed the navcom," she said. "Haven't seen the Bastards in a while. Rouen, either."

Guilfoyle looked at her. Kitsis had the sick impression that she was being watched by two riflescopes.

"I'll keep watch," she said. "I see them, I'll turn everything off, find us a place to hide."

"That may not be enough," Guilfoyle said.

Kitsis was so grateful Guilfoyle had finally spoken she let out a sigh that was vaguely orgasmic. "They won't catch us, Gil. You never let me, but I can fly this ship, too."

Guilfoyle played with the lock; he'd already fixed it but was pretending it was still broken so Kitsis would leave.

Kitsis sat up and nodded vigorously. "We'll get them back."

"We'll never get them back," Guilfoyle said.

"You'll have to find more."

"Do you know how much money Horrocks stole from us, how much each Ringer was worth?"

"You haven't told me any of that stuff. I'm sorry I didn't see—"

"I'm trying my best not to get angry, Kit."

"That's fairly obvious," Kitsis said. "And you're doing a good good job," she added quickly. She shifted to her knees and used her hands to get up. "You left a mess in the cockpit. I already cleaned it. I'll be in the kitchen if you want me."

KITSIS HAD DONE A POOR JOB of repairing the hallway. The wallboards were crooked, some of them upside down. Odd bits of equipment were packed in the corners. Two lights were still broken. Guilfoyle didn't care. On the way to the kitchen for another meal he stopped outside Kitsis' bedroom.

Her back was to the door. She was sitting on her bed, putting the fragments back into the mirror's frame as if it was a sharp jigsaw puzzle.

Guilfoyle skipped the meal, went to his bedroom and disrobed. He thought about his first sexual encounter eighteen years ago back in Minneapolis. It was the only memory that soothed him because the emotions attached to it were so pure. Because of its potency, Guilfoyle reimagined the event rarely. He felt that repetition could diminish anything.

Guilfoyle met her at a This Place Condemned party, an underground youth circuit that staged surreal raves in unsafe buildings. This particular party, Guilfoyle's first, was in a decrepit church scheduled to be torn down the next day. The girl, an amorous waif no older than sixteen, walked up to Guilfoyle and modeled her fur coat like a runway veteran. Then she opened it to show him she was wearing nothing underneath. Every time he pictured that evening he always started by wondering if she ever became the fashion celebrity she thought she already was. This exercise was Guilfoyle's way of hot-wiring the memory.

Her apartment was carpeted with synthetic mink. Her bedcover was a patchwork of used fur coats, some real, some fake. She helped Guilfoyle with his clothes because he found the buttons suddenly complicated. The first time he expected to come soon after penetration and neither of them were surprised when he did. During the second and third times he discovered the ability to stay his ejaculation.

She took control from the start, cajoled him, guided him with tender but insistent directions. Guilfoyle was embarrassed by her aggressive indecency and didn't look her in the eye the entire night.

Toward morning she put his hands on her breasts and said, "Can't you do more?"

"Don't think I can," he said.

They lay together until late afternoon. Neither of them spoke. Guilfoyle was happily exhausted, and he relished the heat from her body like a frostbitten explorer. Yet the weight of their silence seemed to triple every hour. He was unaccustomed to lazy, quiet, blissful moments. As the novelty of their togetherness thawed Guilfoyle felt uncomfortable and unwanted. When the awkwardness became unbearable he picked up his clothes and walked out.

Looking back on it, she'd given him no indication that she wanted him to leave. Two months later, after he'd scrounged up enough courage to visit her again, someone else was living in her apartment and she was gone.

This memory was the unfair barometer against which all his subsequent sexual encounters were measured. He ended the recollection, as always, with regret. I should've stayed, he thought. Should've stayed in that room. Should've stayed in that room and never left 'cause then I wouldn't be here.

Guilfoyle put on earplugs and eyeshades and pulled the sheets over his head. The waif took him into her body again and prevented him from thinking about Horrocks, the Bastards, or Rouen.

CHAPTER 29

The words "Priority Transmission" flashed on the right side of the viewscreen. Horrocks passed his gun to Sari and asked her to bring the Geigers downstairs. The Geigers got up without being told and Sari trailed them out of the room.

Horrocks accepted the transmission. Tinton was laughing. He caught his breath and said to someone off camera, "Wait, he's on."

Horrocks felt as if his chair had plummeted a thousand feet. "You're in my office."

"On your Furnace," Tinton said. "Although your ownership is questionable at the moment. So far away as you are, I'd say your ownership is moot."

"So you got in," Horrocks said.

"Don't make it sound as simple as that," Tinton said, rose from his seat and slammed the desk with both hands. "It was no easy trick getting inside. Inside, we had to spill a lot of blood to capture this office so don't belittle my victory. It was well planned and hard fought."

"Where's De Cuir? How many people stayed with him?"

"I'm so bad with names. They're all dead," Tinton said.

Horrocks felt his chair plummet again.

"There are no hostages to rescue, salvager. Weren't that many people left here, anyway. It wasn't necessary to kill them *all*, but my brothers were angry. They've been angry, and I can't blame them. Nothing I could do."

Tinton scratched his nose and stood fully erect. "Your Furnace has switched hands. It was in dire need of new management, Horrocks. Your bell-wires are stripped. The upcast shaft is completely ventilated and worthless. Where's your Booster Fan? I've never seen a setup more crude. How you farmed any power at all is a mystery to my engineers. The mine's just awful. We burned a lot of it. For fun, and to keep us warm."

Horrocks choked on his rage.

"Nothing to say?" Tinton asked. "I called to see your face but it's not as sweet as I thought. You did this, Horrocks. You could've made it back here straightaway after our first meeting. Even without a Spot Drive you could've been here before the situation demanded we take you over. You made other decisions. Poor decisions."

Horrocks put his hand to his chest in an unconscious motion of despair. Dead? he thought. They were supposed to be safe. They should have been safe there. Everything I gave for that mine. Sacrificed all I had so Tinton could come six years later and steal it from me.

"Bow out," Tinton said. He sat down and plopped his feet on Horrocks' desk. "And if you catch my father, give him to me."

"When I catch him, he'll help me take the mine back in a day," Horrocks said. "Less than a day."

"We've moved into your house, Horrocks."

"I'll get it back."

"Won't want it back when you see how we've redecorated." Tinton cupped his hand over the corner of a filing cabinet and brought it crashing to the floor. "Your office is very cluttered. This is me, signing off."

The screen went blank.

During the Push, Horrocks had saved many amputees who later complained of phantom pain in their missing limbs. The organs the king had taken from Horrocks never came back to haunt *him*. He was always aware of their absence, not a phantom presence. The moment Tinton hung up Horrocks felt as if his missing organs had been suddenly replaced, only they were too large and made of fire. He bent over in pain, the phantom lung and kidney cooking his body from the inside out. In addition to this pain, his heart felt as if it had iced over.

Sari knocked on the cockpit door with one hand and opened it with the other.

"I put the Ringers to bed. Who called?"

"I can't breathe," Horrocks said.

"Your lung?" Sari said. She sat down and swiveled her chair to face Horrocks. His arms were cradled in his belly.

"Tinton took the mine," Horrocks said.

"We'll get it back."

"Not without the king. The queen would never support us. Tinton said he killed everyone there."

Sari gasped. "Even with the king—all those people. You told them to stay, didn't you? This whole fucking—"

"*Sari.*"

"You should never have given the king what you did. It wasn't worth it, baby. None of this is worth anything. Those poor people. We should've gone back home first thing. First thing, Horrocks."

"We'd be dead now," he said.

"You don't know that."

SARI WAS IN THE BATHROOM washing up. Horrocks kicked the comforter to her side of the bed. His right leg dangled off the mattress. He stared at the ceiling. He felt like he'd been crushed under a landslide.

They wouldn't have been there if I hadn't asked them to stay, Horrocks thought. Figured they'd be safer there than anywhere else. Or was I being selfish, didn't want to lose experienced miners? Didn't want to lose the Furnace while I'm out here doing nothing good, making no real progress? I haven't found the king, haven't even seen him.

Horrocks listed his employees in his head, pictured faces for some, parts of their bodies for others. Rystrom's flat nose, Oriana's plump breasts, Glier's wrinkled lips, Lucien's arrogant swagger. Most were old companions who had worked with Horrocks during the Push.

Horrocks couldn't think of anything that would mend his shattered spirit. He thought Tinton's death might help, changed his mind, then changed it again. I'd like to give it a try, he concluded.

Horrocks' grief surmounted him in a succession of waves. He suppressed his tears for ten minutes. When he cried his body did not shake, he did not gasp or choke or clutch at the sheets. The tears left his eyes without commotion and in a minute the well had run dry. He grieved for the dead, not the loss of his mine. This showed Horrocks a depth of feeling he had been afraid to plumb but was glad to find.

Sari came out of the bathroom. He did not rub the wet streaks from his face. Sari lay next to him, put her hand on his stomach and her head next to his on the pillow. She played with the hair on his chest, twirling them in little knots between her fingers, trying to get him to talk. She stared into his blank eyes, smoothed out the knots and turned over to sleep.

An hour later he said, "All those people."

Sari hadn't fallen asleep either. She rolled over to face him but kept some distance. "I know, honey," she said. Her eyes were magnified with tears.

"I wish I'd never been a salvager, never had the mine. Wish I'd never met them. They'd still be alive. I thought they'd be safe. I really thought they'd be safe," Horrocks said. "I should've accepted the king's offer, become a Ringer. Maybe all this shit could've been avoided. All this shit."

Sari blinked to force the ripe tears from her eyes. "Tinton's desperate. And you know he's a liar. What if he still has them? He's lying to put you off, maybe."

"No," Horrocks said. His arms were at his sides. He didn't think he could lift them.

"The mine's gone," Sari said and regretted it instantly.

"The mine is *not gone*. Not forever. We have to get it back. Their bodies. I'm going to find them and return them to the families. If the families are in Virginia or in the Deeps, that's where I'm going." Horrocks found his arms weren't as heavy as he'd thought; he crossed them over his chest. "First thing we do is find the king. Find the king and we—"

She put her forefinger on his lips. "Relax, honey." She pulled herself next to him. They hugged each other and fell asleep.

They woke in the middle of the night and made love. It was their most intense lovemaking since Rouen's visit. They felt guilty, but alive.

Over breakfast the next morning Horrocks said, "That's what I'll do. Get their bodies and deliver them to the families."

Sari nodded and finished her meal.

"Could you help me heat up the food for the Ringers?" he asked.

Horrocks brought the trays down and gave the Ringers half an hour to eat. In the four days they'd been in Horrocks' custody each Ringer had gained a minimum of five pounds. Pierce had gained ten.

Looks cramped behind that mesh, Horrocks thought. Have to move them soon. Hide them on Longliner Station, or on the three derelict water-bearers. Horrocks got out his rifle, told the Geigers to collect the empty trays.

Sari was in the cockpit, fiddling with equations on the viewscreen. "Why don't you leave us alone a couple hours?" Horrocks said.

Sari left the room. Horrocks took her seat. "One of you in the copilot's chair," he said. "The other one stands next to him. And no games."

"Gentle as kittens," Pierce said and took the chair.

"Do you feel anything?" Horrocks asked.

"Nothing different from yesterday," Indigo said.

They watched the forward camera for a few hours.

"Mines look a little closer today. A little larger," Pierce said.

"Queen's got all the mines bunched up around her," Indigo said.

"All except one," Horrocks said. "Are we headed in the right direction? You don't feel any change?"

"Sensation's not getting stronger but it's not getting any weaker," Indigo said. "We're headed the right way."

"Guilfoyle's gonna get mean over this, for you taking us away from him," Pierce said.

"If mean's all you think he'll be, you don't know him," Horrocks said.

"He'll come gunning for us," Indigo said. "We were talking last night, and we don't feel too safe about that."

"Surprised he hasn't come for us already," Pierce said and used the cameras to examine the *Moondrunk*'s perimeter.

"He will," Horrocks said. "Only reason he hasn't found us yet is Sari tampered with our beacon. Right now Guilfoyle's trying to figure out how we disappeared. Things come slow to him. When he finally gets it, he'll be on top of us. You should be scared. No way we can outrun him."

"And then what?" Indigo said.

"I haven't decided the safest place to put you. He comes before then, we all defend this ship."

"Guil—"

"Enough about Guilfoyle," Horrocks said. "Let's find the king. I've just heard some very bad news so let's find the king."

Pierce withdrew his hands from the cameras' controls. "Horrocks, we're trying to help. It's not something we can turn off and on."

"Pay attention to your bodies. Do something."

"We want—"

"Do something. Shut up and do something. Point out the way."

CHAPTER 30

Guilfoyle roamed the ship with a handheld scope. He found what he was searching for beneath the floorboards in the storeroom.

Kitsis came into the room and sat ten paces away from him. She combed her hair back with her hands, then twined her fingers behind her head. "I heard you outside my door. I'm sorry," she said.

Guilfoyle used two screwdrivers to pry up some of the floor's steel planks. "You lied to me," he said. "Right to my face. After all I've given you."

"It was only the one bottle. It's gone now, I swear."

"Drank it all?"

"Poured it down the sink," Kitsis said. She unclasped her fingers; her hair fell over her eyes. "I swear, it was the only one I brought with me."

Guilfoyle's hands burrowed through the ship's innards. "Are you drunk now? Couldn't you show a little restraint?"

"I'm not like you. Drinking is the perfect—"

"I don't want to hear about it," Guilfoyle said. His body was arched toward the floor, his entire left arm swallowed inside.

"Rouen called again. That's what I came up here for," she said and stood.

Guilfoyle's arm swished back and forth. "Ignore him."

"For how long?"

"Until we get some Ringers. Fuck, Kit, don't you ever think? If Rouen or the Bastards find us without any Ringers, they'll kill us. Not just me. Both of us."

"You don't look very threatening down there, your face up against the floor, Gil. Not scary at all."

"I'm not trying to scare—Leave me alone."

"It's gotten so I'm afraid to take any calls," Kitsis said.

"That's how it should have been from the start."

"They'll find us soon. Nothing's to stop them dropping by unannounced. You better do something."

"Ah," Guilfoyle said. He struggled with something unseen, there was a metallic click and he pulled his arm from the hole. In his grimy hand was the *Honey Locust*'s silent beacon. "Like an emerald heart," Guilfoyle said.

"Without that, we'll have no sense of direction," Kitsis said. She followed her brother to the kitchen.

"Not true," Guilfoyle said. He laid the cube on the table. "I can revive part of the old orientation program. The ship'll understand everything within 200 or 300 feet. Beyond that, we go by feel. But no one can trace us."

He smashed the cube with an empty food tray, brushed the pieces into his hand and fed them to the food disposal. "Should've done this days ago."

"By feel," Kitsis said.

"I know this territory," Guilfoyle said.

THEY SAT IN THE COCKPIT, in silence. Seven ships had passed them in the last six hours, none of them likely candidates.

"You're not looking for Gunwitches," Kitsis said just to hear a voice.

"There are only a few Ringers left," Guilfoyle said. He wouldn't have admitted it, but he was just as glad Kitsis had broken the monotony. "The last Ringers'll probably be the smartest. They'll be using something more discreet than a Gunwitch."

The conversation wilted. It was two hours before they spoke again, three before another ship approached them.

"Not her, she's moving too slow," Kitsis said. "Looks like the dumpster we used to put the dead rats in."

Guilfoyle swung the main camera around and focused on the ship. "Laundry barge for the mines," he said. "That's where they'll be."

"Flying with dirty clothes?" Kitsis said.

"The barges go to and from the mines once a week, out to the Mining Annex for fresh uniforms and underwear."

"But they move so slow," Kitsis said. "What a terrible place to hide."

"That's why it's so obvious," Guilfoyle said. "It's too clever."

"It's too something. Stupid, maybe. Which direction is she going? Toward the mines?"

"Toward the mines."

He guided the *Honey Locust* behind her and, the moment the barge shot ahead, filled her exhaust cones with junk bombs. The barge stalled out.

Guilfoyle jumped out of his seat. "You said you can fly. Bring us—"

"I'm coming, too," Kitsis said.

"They might get violent."

"I don't care. I'm bored."

Guilfoyle aligned the ships and extended the umbilical. He got both bats and reluctantly gave one to his sister. Together they crossed the divide between the ships. The light above the barge's door was green.

"Will it be locked?" Kitsis asked.

"You don't have to whisper, they know we're here," Guilfoyle said.

He opened the door and stepped into a huge rectangular room. It smelled, unsurprisingly, like detergent and persistent body odor. Against the western wall were ten carts filled with clean underwear, T-shirts and socks.

Above each cart was an enormous hook used to toss the laundry like dough.

"Come along, little imposters," Guilfoyle said. "The king's been found. We'll take you home. Safely home."

Kitsis stood behind him, both hands on her bat. "I can barely lift this thing."

Guilfoyle passed the first cart, stared at the shadows on either side, shook his head and advanced to the second. He was about to pass the seventh cart when the sixth came shooting out and caught Kitsis in the shoulder. Two of the king's Ringers leapt from the underwear and socks and clubbed her to the floor.

Thank God, Guilfoyle thought. Ringers. Thank God.

He turned around and waited by the disturbed cart, sure that more Ringers would appear from behind it. He was disappointed to see just one more. Guilfoyle planted his bat in the Ringer's stomach. The Ringer high-kicked Guilfoyle in the temple. Guilfoyle spun with the blow, came around full circle and swung at the man's torso. The Ringer stepped out of the way, kicked Guilfoyle in the chest. Even though he was in pain, Guilfoyle smiled. "That all you do is kick?"

Kitsis yelled. You wanted to come, you hold your own, Guilfoyle thought.

The kicking Ringer climbed onto the cart's ledge. He grabbed the laundry hook and launched it at Guilfoyle's head. The hook slid on its track, accelerating as it descended. Guilfoyle blocked the hook with his bat and was thrown off his feet. The Ringer was preparing to use the carts as stepping-stones to get to the umbilical. Guilfoyle scrambled to reach the cart and gave it a healthy push. The Ringer fell into the clothes. Guilfoyle hopped in after him and smothered the Ringer with a T-shirt that read: "LMI: Where Mining Is A Religion." The Ringer ripped the shirt off his face. Guilfoyle choked him with the bat. He put all his weight on the bat until the Ringer passed out.

Guilfoyle lowered himself to the floor and watched Kitsis subdue the second and third Ringers. She punched the second Ringer in the nose and threw him over her shoulder. She stepped on his throat. To the third Ringer she said, "Run and I bust his windpipe."

The third Ringer sighed and sat down.

Kitsis had a fat lip and a purple star above her eye. Her shirt was torn. "I hold my own, Gil. Bet you thought when I yelled, I was yelling for help. Look at me." She swiveled her foot on the Ringer's neck. "I did good."

"They must've been drugged 'cause they didn't put up much of a fight," Guilfoyle said. "Before we go, pick out some fresh clothes in your size. I'll find some in mine."

AT FIVE THE NEXT MORNING Kitsis came to Guilfoyle's bedroom and shook him awake. He rolled over and squinted up at her. "Get out of bed," she said. "Rouen's here."

Kitsis had been considerate enough not to turn the bedroom lights on, but the one from the hallway hit Guilfoyle squarely in the eye. He shielded his face with his forearm and said, "Ignore him. Hide the ship somewhere."

"He's halfway through his umbilical already."

Guilfoyle put on some LMI undergarments, went to his closet and pulled out his last clean flight suit. Hate to put on a clean one before my shower, but I better look good, he thought. He splashed cold water on his bald head.

Guilfoyle walked into the *Honey Locust*'s foyer feeling twenty percent awake. Rouen and Bayswater stood together near the open umbilical. Kitsis was leaning on the doorway to the kitchen, dressed in a sheer negligee that squashed her breasts and hugged the creases of fat on her hips and stomach.

Rouen and Bayswater looked away.

"They're here," Kitsis said to Guilfoyle and closed the kitchen door.

"That's the first time I've seen a woman in her night-gown and wished she was wearing more clothes," Rouen said.

"It's good to see you," Guilfoyle said.

"Don't lie," Rouen said. "It's never good to see me. You've been ignoring my messages. People don't ignore me for long." He went to the chapel and sat in the horse-hair chair. Bayswater flanked him. "What's your decision?" Rouen said.

"My decision about what?" Guilfoyle said.

"The Ringers, the king," Rouen said. He tightened the laces on his shoes, looked around the room absently. "Do we have an agreement? Are we working together?"

"Of course we are," Guilfoyle said. "An agreement. A Gunwitch, the hold filled with—"

"The agreement's changed. You don't get the Gunwitch here," Rouen said. He sneezed into his hands, wiped them on Guilfoyle's chair and asked Bayswater for a tissue.

"Why's it changed?" Guilfoyle asked. "Maybe I won't like the new terms."

"You don't get to like or dislike them. I make arrangements and I change them. That's my role," Rouen said. He leaned forward and spoke in the bored manner of someone who's made the same speech a hundred times. "You accept my changes. That's your role. I told you, the longer you waited, the less favorable the conditions would be. Since you've been avoiding me, I assume the conditions aren't that important to you. They're much less agreeable now. If you hadn't been hiding—"

"I hide from no one," Guilfoyle said.

Bayswater said, "You hide and you lie. Don't lie."

"The only reason we found you this morning is because you trashed your beacon yesterday," Rouen said. "Do you know what happens when you trash a beacon?"

"We lose our sense of direction. I thought the compass was acting funny. It must've been my sister by accident." Instead of fidgeting, which was his first reaction, Guilfoyle remained completely still. He wasn't sure which posture was more suspicious.

"You lose your compass and become invisible to those ships who know your signal," Rouen said. "Before you become invisible the beacon releases a pulse a hundred times stronger than normal. We've been waiting for you to try it. Only a handful of people know about this glitch and no one can fix it. Once we knew your general location you were easy to track down."

"So easy," Bayswater said.

"Lucky thing," Rouen said, "'cause if you weren't here that would mean you'd made a Spot jump. Then I'd think you were running away."

Guilfoyle felt the sweat on his brow, though it could have been the remnants of the cold water he'd splashed on his head to wake himself up. I'm not scared of him, Guilfoyle thought.

Rouen crossed his legs, rested his chin on his hand. "As punishment for your ignorance, for making me wait like some salesman, you'll take a Longliner to the first stop in the Deeps. One of my men will escort you."

"You said you respected my taking time to consider," Guilfoyle said.

"So I did. I'm complicated. Now, the Gunwitch, out in the Deeps. The hold will only be filled with four million."

Guilfoyle closed his eyes and attempted some calculations. He was too tired to see any numbers.

"Fine," Guilfoyle said and thought, It'll still be enough.

"I hear you've been quite successful," Rouen said.

Guilfoyle did not respond immediately. He thought he would have more time to think of the best way to phrase his failure. Now that the confrontation with Rouen had been forced on him, Guilfoyle couldn't find any golden words. He looked Rouen in the face and said, "Horrocks took them."

Rouen delayed his response to compound Guilfoyle's worry. Finally he said, "No bother. He has them, so what? He hasn't found the king." Rouen uncrossed his legs. He put his hands on the armrests to help him out of the chair. Bayswater knew better than to assist.

"I knew this, Guilfoyle," Rouen said. "I knew of Horrocks' thievery."

"That's precisely what it was."

"I'm glad you were honest."

So am I, Guilfoyle thought.

"Sometimes I like honesty," Rouen said. "It won't get you any more money, but it's nice to see once in a while, I come across it so rarely."

Guilfoyle walked Rouen and Bayswater to the umbilical.

"You better find the king soon, Gil," Rouen said. "Four days is all that's left of the deadline. Four days and this turns into a free-for-all. You're running out of places to look."

"I'll start again soon as you leave."

"Are you rushing us out?" Bayswater said.

Guilfoyle shook his head.

"I want another Ringer," Rouen said. "I won't ask how Horrocks made a fool of you. I won't tell you how easy I think that is. To spare you that embarrassment, I want another. Hope you've replenished your stock."

"I have," Guilfoyle said.

"Then please."

"The Bastards will catch up to me soon, just like you have. I need some cargo for show or they'll be—"

"You shouldn't have let Horrocks trick you," Bayswater said.

Rouen said, "You'll give me—"

"If I can keep them awhile—"

"You'll give me another," Rouen said. "One more. Don't force me to make it two. Don't force me to have Bayswater do something drastic to your sister. Don't force me to make it two."

"Oh that's ridi—"

"Two," Rouen said. He sneezed into the tissue Bayswater had given to him in the chapel. "One if you bring him to me within a minute. You were honest before and I'll reward you with a minute's grace."

Guilfoyle brought down one of the laundry-barge Ringers within the time limit. "Be seeing you," Rouen said and pushed the Ringer into the tube.

BAYSWATER HELD THE RINGER while Rouen unscrewed the gagroot jar.

"Wait wait wait," said the Ringer as Rouen approached him. "Why do this? I know so much about the king. I *am* the king. I could be the king. I could be the king for you. I could be useful."

"Useful how?" Rouen said. He put the jar down and hooked his hands in his pockets. "What can you do for me?"

"Find you the king."

"Find me the king. If you haven't already, then you can't." Rouen took the wet gagroot out of the jar. "Right now I find the queen much more interesting anyhow. It seems she and I have a lot in common."

"Why kill me?" the Ringer said.

"Smells like fabric softener, doesn't he?" Rouen said.

Bayswater snorted.

When Rouen was close enough the Ringer slipped out of Bayswater's grasp and knocked the gagroot from Rouen's hand. Bayswater snatched the Ringer's wrists in his giant mitten hands and broke them. He picked the dirty gagroot off the floor, forced the Ringer's mouth open and jammed it in.

The Ringer hunched over and froze. Bayswater straightened him up.

"You look like a mannequin," Rouen said. He breathed directly into the Ringer's stony face. "Why kill you? Didn't say I was going to. I created you, inadvertently. To be more accurate, I'm responsible for your creation.

Three failed assassination attempts long before the Push. The king, or his court, decided you were necessary. And you were. I hate that. I hate being responsible for something I can't control. But I'm not going to kill you."

Bayswater handed the pliers to Rouen.

CHAPTER 31

Horrocks escorted the Geigers down to the cellar. Sari was in the cockpit when he returned.

"So they're not helping?" she said.

"They're helping but it's vague. If we had a faster ship, the changes in their bodies would be more drastic. Right now, the changes are too gradual to notice. That's my theory," Horrocks said. He toyed with the navcom, became frustrated, sat back.

"Should've taken Guilfoyle's ship, too," Sari said. "I wonder how he is?"

The cameras detected a ship coming in and tracked its hesitant approach.

"Looks like a Gunwitch," Sari said.

"Ringers coming to see us?" Horrocks said. He enlarged the image. "Looks like a Gunwitch, but she's not. Definitely part of the king's armada, though. Keep moving. We'll wait for them to—"

"They're hailing us," Sari said.

She routed the call to the viewscreen. It was the queen's youngest son. "I'd like you to come aboard my ship. We've an emergency," the prince said. His tight collar could not contain the excess skin from his loose jowls. His brow was creased with premature worry lines. When he raised his eyebrows to invite a response his worry lines bunched like a wrinkled scrotum.

"An emergency about what?" Sari asked.

"About Rouen," the prince said.

"Where's your mother?" Horrocks asked.

The prince's worry lines grew more distinct. "Safe," he said.

"I doubt that," Horrocks said. "If you need to talk, you come over here."

"I have it all arranged for you to come here. She's a very comfortable ship."

"*Here*," Horrocks said.

The prince hung up.

"We've guests again," Sari said. "I'll go get the gun."

THE PRINCE STEPPED ONTO THE *MOONDRUNK* trailing two duplicates. Ringers of his own. He combed his unruly hair with his fingers, rested his hands on his wide hips and said, "Where are my father's Ringers?"

"I'm tired of that question," Sari said and led everyone to the common room. Horrocks and Sari stayed by the door.

"You have them?" the prince asked.

"Somewhere," Horrocks said.

The prince's two Ringers took the striped chairs, forcing the prince to stand. "How many?" the prince asked.

"I've lost count," Horrocks said.

"But you have them."

"What's this emergency with Rouen?" Sari asked.

"I want the Ringers," the prince said.

"They aren't here," Horrocks said.

The duplicates started from their chairs. The prince threw out his chubby arms to stop them. "My mother was right, Horrocks. You suffer from misunderstanding. I'm not asking you kindly. I demand you give them to me."

"Tough talk for a sixteen-year-old," Horrocks said. "Come back and threaten me when you've hair in your pants."

The prince lowered his arms and his two Ringers advanced.

Sari pointed Horrocks' handgun at the nearest Ringer. "Back in the chairs," she said. The Ringers took another step. Sari straightened her arms and pointed the gun at the prince. "One more step," she said to the Ringers, "and you're unemployed."

The Ringers sat down.

"We need them back. We really do, Horrocks," the prince said.

"What for? Where's the queen?"

"Surrounded by her own guards on the flagship Furnace," the prince said. He leaned on one of the chairs. "Feel like I could collapse. She sent me because she didn't feel safe enough to leave the mine."

"You shouldn't have left, either," Sari said. "The three of you, riding out by yourselves? I'm surprised the Bastards didn't scoop you up. Or Rouen."

"Rouen wouldn't dare," one of the prince's Ringers said.

"I'm worried about my mom, about LMI," the prince said. He rubbed his temples with the heels of his hands. "She wishes I was stronger. You said she's not safe? She's fairly safe now, safer than she was." He looked Horrocks in the eye, tried to maintain the stare but broke it off after a few seconds. "She's made a pact with Rouen."

"A pact!" Horrocks said. "With Rouen? She's decided to just give the mines away?"

"She made it last night. Call her," the prince said.

Horrocks pushed the prince out of his way and activated the monitor on the eastern wall. He got the number from the prince and, after a series of clicks and blue flashes, the queen appeared. She was dressed as if she had just come from a ball. Her loose eyelids exposed the red membranes underneath. She sprayed her face with perfumed vapor, then threw the atomizer on the floor. "Hello, Horrocks," she said. Her voice curdled the words.

"You're a fool," Horrocks said.

"It's a sound agreement." She mustered some energy into her voice, as if conviction was the same as validity. "Only three days left, Horrocks. What can you do in three days? We can't conduct business this way, with everyone harassing us. I don't have the constitution for this. Rouen does. We'll rule jointly."

"What does he know about the Furnaces? About the company?" Horrocks said. His spittle crackled when it hit the screen. "You couldn't have picked a bigger degenerate. Rouen. How many times did he try to kill your husband? One of your sons died during the Push. Rouen's probably behind this current mess. Two of your sons are dead because of this man and you make a pact with him? What can he offer? He can't offer you—"

"Everything. He's offered me everything," she said. The energy she'd so recently mustered jilted her voice and left it limp. "He'll deliver. He promised me so. I'm releasing you from your duty. I absolve you from any debt you had to the king. My king is dead."

"He is not dead," Horrocks said. "Two days, maybe less, and I'll have him."

"Stop looking, Horrocks. Stand down. You know the law. Twenty days presumed dead. The cooperative's assets to be divided according to the charter. The law. Twenty days."

"That law was created during a war Rouen started," Horrocks said.

"The miners may be minority shareholders," the queen said, "but they fought for this amendment and my husband ratified it. When he was kidnapped during the Push—"

"By Rouen's men, probably."

"The miners don't want to live with that kind of uncertainty, not knowing what would happen to the Furnaces if the king went missing again. Twenty days and the king's assets change hands."

"The king's assets—"

"Are mine to inherit," the queen said. "Mine and my son's. If I want to split the kingdom with Rouen, that's my concern."

"Everyone who lives here—"

"There'll be nothing to split if the Bastards barge in here and challenge us before the change is made," the queen said. "You want that? You want the Bastards with a majority say? Horrocks, please listen to me. Rouen's men can't hold the Bastards off indefinitely. We might need what's in the vials. You have to hand them over."

"And if the king's found after twenty days?" Horrocks said.

"He won't be found," the queen shrilled. "He's dead, Horrocks. He is dead. He left me alone and I hate him for it and he's *dead*." Her eyes slanted downward. "We know you stole a good many Ringers from Guilfoyle. Bravo. Return them to where they belong, with me."

Horrocks laughed at her.

The prince moved toward Horrocks but stopped when Sari shook the gun at him.

"You've lost your own mine," Porphyria said. "I understand your aggravation. With Rouen's help I could get it back for you."

"You let it get away."

"Refuse everything else, fine," Porphyria said. "Will you do one thing for me, as your queen, as my servant? Protect my son. Keep him there."

"Mother," the prince shouted.

"Be quiet," Porphyria said. "Horrocks, I sent him to you because I want him away from all this. I want him to survive. The miners are unhappy with my new allegiance. It's a dangerous place here. My son doesn't have the legs to stand up to it. Keep him there. Send the king's Ringers back on the ship he came in."

Horrocks ended the call by punching the monitor's controls.

"The three of you, off," Horrocks said. He had not moved from the monitor.

"I wouldn't stay with you, even if you asked," the prince said. "Her mind's all soft with depression. I'm assuming the *Moondrunk* in the name of the kingdom."

Horrocks whirled around. "What kingdom? What king?"

The prince charged Horrocks, his hands outstretched like a deranged sleepwalker. Horrocks grabbed the prince's wrists and shoved the prince into his duplicates.

Sari said, "I'm not even sure which of you is the real prince. Get out before I kill all three of you."

When they had gone, Horrocks said, "We have to get the Ringers off the ship. They're not safe here."

"If you think of someplace safe, let me know 'cause I'd like to go there, too," Sari said.

CHAPTER 32

Kitsis was sitting in the cockpit but she wasn't flying the ship. She was afraid to touch anything in the room except the chair. Guilfoyle had instructed her to keep watch for any unusual-looking vessels. Kitsis didn't need to press any buttons. The ship was programmed to fly along an elliptical track that brought them a few hundred miles closer to the mines every hour.

One of the red dashboard lights startled Kitsis by blinking insistently. Not going to touch it, she thought.

Guilfoyle sat on the storeroom floor across from the two Ringers that Rouen hadn't taken from him. Two of the laundry-barge Ringers. They fidgeted on the cots behind the bars. "Quit staring," one of the Ringers said. A fuzzy pale scar marked his left cheek. "You're making me nervous."

"There's no shower in here," said the second Ringer. His cheeks were unmarred.

"You can use the toilet for that, too," Guilfoyle said.

"It backs up," the Ringer said.

Guilfoyle responded by bending forward to crack his spine. "I think you folks are responsible. For the king, I mean."

"We tried to have him killed, then locked ourselves in a vault on the Mining Annex? That makes as much sense as using a shitter for a shower," the scarred Ringer said.

"No mystery makes sense without all the ingredients. Most of them do when you've the whole story," Guilfoyle said. He twisted from side to side to crack the difficult bones in his hips. "What's the whole story?"

"Your plan's absurd," said the unmarred Ringer. He sat on his hands and swung his legs back and forth. "No one's going to believe I'm the king. Granted, I'm an excellent likeness, but they'll be too skeptical. The king's been gone a long while, hasn't he? Is it twenty days yet? Whoever you plan on hocking me to—there's no one in this room that good a salesman. What's to keep me from opening my mouth?"

"Who said they wanted the king alive?" Guilfoyle said.

The Ringer's legs ceased their joyful swinging.

"You're convincing," Guilfoyle said. He splayed his hands on the floor and examined his fingers. The creases around his knuckles were grooved with dirt.

"You won't profit from this," the unmarred Ringer said.

"You won't. I will," Guilfoyle said. "Just sit there quiet looking like the king. I'm feeling relaxed. Don't spoil my mood. Don't spoil your face, either."

The unmarred Ringer held up his hands. "With these nails?" he said. The night before Guilfoyle had cut both Ringers' nails down to the cuticles.

"I'm starved," the scarred Ringer said. "How come I don't get fed?"

Kitsis' voice was piped into the room through the intercom: "There are some Bastard ships here, Guilfoyle."

"Ignore them, Kit."

"All five of them?"

"Coming," Guilfoyle said, pointed at the Ringers, smiled, and left.

The largest Bastard ship was shaped like a flattened egg. It was the only one to approach. The other ships blocked the *Honey Locust*'s retreat. The flattened egg extended its umbilical and three Bastards came through the

Honey Locust's exit hatch. The men had the same short gray hair, the same gray suits.

"Hail, hail Guilfoyle," their spokesman said. He shook Guilfoyle's hand and Guilfoyle showed them to the chapel. The Bastard spokesman looked around the room, saw the paintings and Bibles and said, "You must be some religious nut."

Guilfoyle was still in a good mood even though he knew he should be worrying. He beat all three Bastards to the horsehair chair and sat down. The Bastards stayed on their feet. Guilfoyle regretted his haste.

"And the Ringers?" the spokesman said. "The ones Horrocks didn't steal from you? I heard he walked out with them bold as you please."

"The scenario was a little more complicated than that," Guilfoyle said. He picked at the corners of the chair. "How did you hear? He didn't get all that many, anyway. Not all of them. I've replaced the rest."

The two silent Bastards clapped their hands and rubbed their knuckles. The spokesman said, "Tinton sent us over for another review. Incidentally, he's mighty disappointed. Your performance is so far beyond lackluster I can't think of the right word. Lackluster doesn't seem strong enough. We've all been laughing at you."

"Sorry to hear that," Guilfoyle said. He picked at a crease in the chair's cushion and accidentally freed some of the horsehair stuffing. "I'm in a good mood. You won't break that. This affair is long from over. I'll come out in the end."

"But you've got no poise," the spokesman said. "You've no flair. Show me your collection of Ringers. Tinton's filled us up on empty promises but we're still hungry."

The silent Bastards slipped brass knuckles over their hands and flexed their fingers.

"We need the exercise. Show us the Ringers."

"I know Tinton didn't send you here for roughhousing," Guilfoyle said. He couldn't remember if he'd locked the door to the storeroom.

"Tinton's very far away," the spokesman said. He removed a metal rod from his pocket and made a fist over it.

"I'll have to tell him," Guilfoyle said and stood up.

"Then we'll have to beat you, too."

"You think I've never been beaten before?"

"I think that's all you've been," the spokesman said. All three of them laughed. "By Horrocks, by the war, by everyone your whole life."

"Tell Tinton I've got ten Ringers. That's a million dollars he owes me in bonuses."

"Ten Ringers," the spokesman said. He was beaming so hard his cheeks eclipsed his eyes.

"He can have them in a few days. When I'm ready to give them," Guilfoyle said.

The spokesman threw the first punch. It came up short. Guilfoyle punched the man in the stomach so hard the Bastard choked and dry heaved twice.

"Now get out of here before I put the three of you over my knee," Guilfoyle said.

"WE SHOULD GET EVERYONE ON ONE SHIP, go back to Guilfoyle and beat him raw," the Bastard spokesman said.

His two partners were flying the ship.

"Tinton was right," the spokesman said. "Guilfoyle's no pushover."

"Walked right into that punch," one of the pilots said.

"That's when you should've jumped in."

"It would take at least five men to subdue him. You proved yourself useless in a fight. We did the smart thing."

"The cowardly thing," the spokesman said. He rubbed his stomach.

"Can you feel his knuckles there?"

"Fuck both of you. I tried. Couldn't we have hired someone better to find the king? If I was looking—"

"We can't be looking ourselves."

"I said *if*, if I was looking. If it was me, he'd have been found already. Found and questioned. I bet Guilfoyle only has three or four Ringers on his boat. He's a degenerate liar. What do we tell Tinton?"

"I'll tell him," said a voice from the rear of the cabin. The laundry-barge Ringer with the fuzzy pale scar stood up from behind the bucket seat outside the lavatory. "I'll tell him what Guilfoyle's been up to."

GUILFOYLE WASHED HIS HANDS in the kitchen and went upstairs to finish his conversation with the Ringers.

The door to the cage was ajar. The scarred Ringer was gone, the other sprawled unconscious across the cots.

Guilfoyle didn't bother to search the *Honey Locust*. He knew the scarred Ringer was on the Bastard's ship, was on his way to Tinton. As soon as he arrived the Ringer would become a minstrel. He would sing a host of Guilfoyle stories, tales of greed and deceit.

Guilfoyle wondered why the scarred Ringer had knocked out this other Ringer instead of taking him, then decided he probably would have done the same. It was easier to escape alone.

Guilfoyle left the storeroom and locked the door behind him.

He didn't remember the rampage that followed. He woke up in his bed, the sheets smothered with blood. Not all the blood was his own. His flight suit was ripped. He walked the ship to shock his memory into focus. The *Honey Locust* was decimated. Walls lay on the floor. Ceilings had been butchered, furniture smashed.

Kitsis was curled up by the side of her bed, covered in glass and cuts. Her room was a shambles, the mirror broken again.

Guilfoyle went back up to the storeroom. The Ringer was still unconscious but his bruises were new: a deep gash across his forehead, eyes like sunken purple canyons, two gouges down his right cheek. The gouges met near his jaw in a generous delta.

Guilfoyle sat next to him on the cots. Cage won't hold anyone anymore, Guilfoyle thought. I'll have to lock the door to the whole room instead. Shit. Better wake Kit so she can help me clean up.

CHAPTER 33

The Geigers were asleep on the floor of the cockpit, curled up together like dogs sharing a kennel. Half a dozen empty food trays lay by their bare feet. Horrocks' head snapped up and down as he fought the drag of sleep. He tightened his grip on the steering bar, hoping the exertion would keep him alert.

The Geigers grumbled, sat up, thumbed away strands of drool.

"We'd like to sleep," Indigo said.

"You've been sleeping," Horrocks said. "I'm the one's been awake twenty hours."

"On a cot. On a mattress with pillows," Indigo said.

"Can you feel him?" Horrocks asked. "Is he close?"

"We're moving in the right—"

"*Is he close?*" Horrocks asked.

"I can't tell."

"Then we all stay in this little room."

Horrocks sat on the edge of his chair, knowing that if he sat back, if he became the slightest bit comfortable he'd be out for two days. He stomped his feet and drank more coffee. He dug his nails into his neck because his palms were too raw to take them anymore.

Stay awake, he thought. Stay awake stay awake stay awake. He made a song out of it.

The Geigers fell back to sleep.

The king's mines were on the viewscreen, dead ahead, seventy hours away. Horrocks moved the camera left to cover his own mine. He didn't want to dwell on what Tinton could be doing so Horrocks moved the camera again, farther left. It autofocused on *The Priam*. Sunlight and Jupitershine made the dead hulk seem vibrantly alive.

Sari stood just outside the cockpit and coughed. Horrocks didn't have the energy to turn around. She stepped over the sleeping Geigers and leaned against the dash. "You look like a wax dummy," she said. "There's no white in your eyes. You're staring at the screen too much. I'm going upstairs. I don't want to fall asleep alone again."

Horrocks nodded, blinked, and she was gone.

Longliner, he thought. We get on the next one. Sell the *Moondrunk*. Buy two tickets. Or no, we sturdy her up, pad the hull, see if the *Moondrunk* could handle the trip herself. Maybe she could. Out to the Deeps. Try it Sari's way since my way's failed.

He awoke with his chin on his chest. His eyes had been open the whole time; they'd been watching *The Priam*. For the last two hours the *Moondrunk* had veered from the mines in favor of the antique derelict.

The Geigers came awake more quickly than before. Their hands were over their hearts.

Pierce said, "Is your pulse—"

"Did you change direction?" Indigo asked Horrocks.

"I didn't—my hand fell asleep. I don't think I did," Horrocks said.

The Geigers were nodding furiously. Horrocks wasn't sure if this was a Geiger symptom related to the king's nearness or just fervent agreement.

"He's on *The Priam*," Pierce said.

"It's got no atmosphere. She's been dead for years," Horrocks said.

"That's where he is," Indigo said. He was still nodding. His arms were trembling.

"The Priam," Horrocks said. He locked the coordinates into the navcom, brought the Geigers to the cellar and fell into bed next to Sari. She woke up, but only for a second.

CHAPTER 34

"Kitsis," Guilfoyle shouted. "Kitsis. I won't hit you. Kitsis!"

He stopped by her room first, though he knew she wouldn't be there. He checked under the bed, behind the busted sliding doors of her closet. He cupped his hands to his mouth and yelled, "I know I got out of hand. I'm in total control now. There isn't anything left for me to break." He grinned, then decided it wasn't funny.

The hallways were an obstacle course of porous floors, glass splinters and slanted steel studs. Guilfoyle walked the hallways twice, often slipping in the same spot.

Every room was empty, every closet bare.

Guilfoyle cupped his hands to his mouth again. "Don't forget all the things I've done for you." His hands came away from his lips. "All the things I never asked you to do."

He went up to the storeroom but Kitsis wasn't there. Guilfoyle's last remaining Ringer said, "It's awful quiet on this ship." Guilfoyle had been able to fix one of the wall manacles and had chained the Ringer to that. The cage was unusable. The Ringer was sitting on the floor. He picked his teeth with his forefinger. "So quiet. Just you yelling. Where's your sister?"

"You shut up," Guilfoyle said.

"What are you going to do, hit me?" the Ringer said and smiled. The smile rearranged the wounds on his face. The pain it caused him was evident but he fought past it and maintained his ingratiating expression. "I'm hungry, real hungry."

"You'll get no more food. You're useless to me now," Guilfoyle said.

"Shouldn't have done this to my face. Now we're both useless."

Guilfoyle wandered the ship again and wound up in the cockpit. He wondered when the Bastards would show. Not yet, he thought. They'll wait a little while first.

He left the trapdoor open so Kitsis could come disturb him if she wanted.

Guilfoyle sat in the cockpit and thought about death. He thought about the time Horrocks had saved him from death at the end of the Push. At the time Guilfoyle's business was so slow that instead of stockpiling bodies to re-sell he concentrated his time raiding unprotected vessels. The tanker he had been looting collided with a light jit-ney full of mining personnel. The wall in front of Guil-foyle exploded, searing his face and arms with Freon. Horrocks came aboard with his expert crew, dragged Guilfoyle and the other survivors through the umbilical. Guilfoyle wanted to say *Leave me*, but his lips were melted together. He tried to shove Horrocks away but his arms, frayed hoses ready to burst, wouldn't comply.

A year of constant surgery. Guilfoyle was sure he would shed his depression but instead he retreated into a cocoon of suicidal thoughts. When he finally worked up the cowardice to do it he couldn't fit the gun in his mouth he was crying so hard. He sought his half sister, found her in their dead father's apartment in Conamara City on Eu-ropa. Guilfoyle hadn't seen her for six years and the first thing he said at their reunion was, "Kill me, please kill me. I'll leave you everything." Which was nothing.

Kitsis refused. They were both lonely and they stayed together, eventually finding work as vermin hunters. He didn't lift the gun to his mouth again because the shame of his first attempt was too humiliating to survive twice.

He became obsessed with the idea rather than focused on completing the act. Guilfoyle found suicide had romantic appeal.

The *Honey Locust*'s navcom beeped. Guilfoyle stirred in his seat and checked the proximity graph. Still no sign of the Bastards. They'll come, he thought. In their nice ships with their expensive guns.

His limbs felt waterlogged. He chewed his lips. The chair creaked as his body settled into it. He didn't move for an hour.

His mind lit on a dozen topics, none of them related. As they always did, his thoughts returned to suicide. There's always suicide, he thought. I could beat them to it. It'd be less painful. But I don't want to die.

The realization landed on him like a grenade. I wouldn't do it now if I had the strength, he thought. He became instantly aware of the stiff flight suit against his calves, the odor from his dirty dentures, the determined drip from the kitchen's loose faucet. If I wanted to die I wouldn't be afraid of the Bastards, he thought. But I am. They'll want me dead. If this happened last week—it must've been—I'm finally working for something instead of just working. Find the king, get paid, move out to the Deeps. That's where I want to be. The Deeps. Alive and in the Deeps.

"Kitsis, Kitsis," he yelled gaily.

Guilfoyle knew he had a weakness for dark thoughts. In the past this weakness left him with depression hangovers that lasted years. These hangovers varied in intensity and sometimes ended with a month or two of false happiness.

Sitting in the cockpit, the shrapnel from his realization dripping down the walls of his psyche, Guilfoyle was sure there was nothing fake about his joyous mood.

He sat back in the chair, a smile on his ugly face, knowing he would be dead in a few days, content with his rejection of the idea. He wondered who would come for him first, Rouen for more Ringers or the Bastards for revenge. Probably the Bastards, Guilfoyle thought. There are so damn many of them.

KITSIS WAS HIDING IN THE CRAWLSPACE between the second and third floors. The stench from her own body made her dizzy. She used inverted food trays for pillows. She fell asleep to the sound of Guilfoyle calling her name.

The Ringer that Guilfoyle had left to starve in the storeroom died a few days later. Guilfoyle never knew because he never set foot in the storeroom again.

CHAPTER 35

Horrocks woke up the next day and felt as if he was lying on a glacier with snow for a blanket. He breathed cotton balls into the air. His hands were glass claws.

He looked over his shoulder. Sari was still asleep. Her arms were clasped around his waist. His body was so numb he hadn't realized she was attached to him.

Horrocks freed himself from her embrace and padded across the room to the computer terminal on the wall. The icy floor burned the soles of his feet. The terminal was sluggish. It finally told him the *Moondrunk* was a day's ride from *The Priam*. The terminal also relayed the news that a Bastard ship was shadowing them.

"Holy shit, Horrocks," Sari said sleepily. "There's frost on the window, not to mention my skin." She wore the blanket like a cape. "What went wrong?"

"I just got up." He tried to swallow the foul taste in his mouth but it seemed to be reproducing. "Has to be the heater again."

"So you didn't fix it," she said.

"It broke again. Feels like it broke for good." Horrocks hugged himself and sat on the bed. "I'm going to check on the Ringers then take a quick shower."

"That's what I want right now," Sari said. "A nice warm shower." She shivered. The whole bed shook.

"Water's probably freezing," Horrocks said.

Sari launched a pillow at his head, made a cocoon of the blanket, ducked her face inside and whimpered.

Horrocks dressed in his warmest clothes. Sari streaked into the bathroom. Horrocks pillaged his dresser for sweaters and laid them on bed. In the linen closet he found two spare blankets and four towels. All these items hadn't been washed in years, had languished forgotten with the *Moondrunk* in storage. Horrocks carried everything down into the cellar.

The Ringers had pushed the cots against the mesh. They were huddled on the floor like the zealots of some Arctic planet, praying to be smitten by fire. Their chattering teeth sounded like a swarm of bone cicadas.

"About fucking time," Indigo said.

"I know, I'm sorry," Horrocks said, opened the mesh and threw the sheets, towels and sweaters inside. The Ringers snatched them from the air and clamped them over their bodies.

"I'll try to make some hot food. Food, anyway. I'll be right back," Horrocks said.

The Ringers were too cold to respond.

When the stove ignited Horrocks sighed with relief. He filled it with food trays, not caring what meals they were labeled for. While they cooked Horrocks went to the cockpit and called up the ship's schematics. He tried to deduce the source of their heating problem. Yet again, the circuitry in the common room appeared to be the best place to start.

Sari kicked him out of her chair. "Go get washed," she said. "I'll run the program again."

"There's food warming in the oven."

"If it's warm, I might climb in there. Go wash."

The shower was freezing. Horrocks stayed under long enough to work up a mild lather and wash it off. Barely two minutes. He washed his hair in the sink and brushed the taste out of his mouth.

Sari helped Horrocks carry the trays down to the Ringers. After they finished handing out the trays Horrocks and Sari went up to the kitchen to have their own meal. They cherished the warm food.

"It'd be nice if we could leave the oven door open and burn to death. I'd like that," Sari said. Patches of her sweater had been eaten away by bugs with an appetite for cotton. "I can't bend my fingers."

Horrocks touched his hair. He hadn't dried it. He never dried it. It had frozen into stringy icicles. He pushed his empty tray to the center of the table. "I'll start working on it now."

"Can I help?" Sari asked.

"The parts are too small for the both of us to do the job," Horrocks said. He thawed his hands by rubbing them together. "I need gloves. Thin gloves."

"I'll look through the ship, maybe find some more blankets, too," Sari said.

HORROCKS TOOK DOWN THE COMMON room's collapsible wall panels and laid them in the middle of the floor. He stood on a footstool and used a flashlight to examine the exposed circuitry. The wires had melted in three separate spots.

The comm buzzed and Horrocks heard Sari run for the cockpit. After a brief, muffled conversation she came in to see Horrocks.

"It's Wyeth. I told him it was OK to come aboard," she said.

"Hope he brought a jacket."

"Says he's got a surprise for you," Sari said.

Horrocks didn't register her comment right away because he was tracing one of the melted wires to its source. When he finally said, "Surprise?" Sari wasn't there.

She came back five minutes later. Wyeth was behind her, beaming. Behind him were two handcuffed Ringers.

Horrocks didn't get off the stool because in his hands were two more melted wires; he'd found them by accident and didn't want to risk losing them. He craned his neck to see the Ringers and said, "Where'd you find them?"

"They found me. Long story. You transporting ice or something?"

"I'm really busy here, Wyeth," Horrocks said.

"You should come down and take a look," Sari said. "They can't speak and someone pulled all their teeth."

"I'm kind of busy," Horrocks said.

"I'll put them downstairs," Sari said.

"That's good," Horrocks said and turned around to face the labyrinth of wires. "I'll be done here in a minute. Or a hundred minutes."

Sari walked Wyeth and his prisoners to the cellar door. "Those handcuffs look pretty tight," Sari said.

"They're a little ornery," Wyeth said. Horrocks' dog followed on Wyeth's heels, trying to get Wyeth to play with him.

"Here's the stairs. Down there, the Ringers first," Sari said.

"Ringers first," Wyeth said.

HORROCKS' VISION WAS BLURRED. All the colored wires looked gray to him. He sat down for five minutes and flexed his fingers. He went into the kitchen for his tool-box.

A white lump lay in the hallway. The dog. Horrocks bent down and jabbed his fingers into the furry throat. There was a pulse. A small hollow needle stood up from the dog's rump.

Horrocks raced for the open cellar door and flew down the steps. The air smelled like mulched grass. Sari was curled up at the bottom of the stairs, still breathing. Horrocks covered his mouth with his shirt.

The floor was wet. The mesh had been ripped open. The Ringers were strewn about the room like felled trees. Horrocks stepped between their dead limbs, his feet splashing in their blood. The Ringers' throats had been cut. Horrocks stepped on a towel and dark liquid pooled around his shoes. He counted six dead bodies.

The mulched-grass smell was fading. Horrocks knew it was some kind of vapor, some kind of drugged smoke. He saw the slit neck of his own Ringer and gagged.

Wyeth was sitting with his back against the wall. He wore a blue gas mask. His shirt looked like a butcher's apron.

One of the Ringers Wyeth had brought lay in his lap like a reclining lover. Wyeth slit the man's neck before Horrocks could stop him.

CHAPTER 36

Sari regained consciousness as Horrocks was leaving the bedroom. She lay on her back, her head supported by the bed's four pillows. Her skin looked as if it had been dusted with powder. Her hairline was plastered down with sweat. Her arms lay at her sides, palms up. There was no strength in her curled fingers.

Horrocks saw she was awake, came back to the bed and sat near her waist. He was too far away to stroke her face without disturbing her. He smiled as warmly as he could. "You've been out for three hours," he said. "I thought it would be much more than that. He didn't touch you. I looked you over before I put you to bed. No signs of anything."

Horrocks folded his hands in his lap. He studied his fingers. "Shouldn't have let you go down with him alone. I was so preoccupied with the heat. All seven Ringers are dead."

Sari's eyes widened from slits to ovals.

"Seven," Horrocks said, "including the two Wyeth brought with him. Including the one looked like me."

"I don't even have the energy to breathe," Sari whispered.

"Wyeth had a canister of gas and a gas mask for himself," Horrocks said. He lifted Sari's left arm and placed it on her stomach. He slid in closer and stroked her neck. The skin was cold and scaly.

"It was Fescue gas," Horrocks said.

"Thought it smelled familiar." She spoke slowly. "Smelled like cut grass, but that's not what I was thinking at the time. I was thinking of this field—"

Horrocks moved his hand from her neck to her lips. "Sleep some more," he said.

HORROCKS RECOGNIZED the cellar's odor from the war. Stale blood and shit. The real smell of death. He'd been too busy caring for Sari to do anything about the bodies. They lay as he'd found them hours ago.

"Hey, where the fuck have you been, sap?" Wyeth said. He was tied to a metal folding chair in the northeast corner of the room, bound so tightly that his skin between the ropes looked ready to burst. "You left me some slack, Horrocks. I can still feel my eyes."

Horrocks stepped over the Ringers and squatted behind Wyeth's chair. He pulled on the ropes with all his strength and made a new knot with the slack. Wyeth tried to laugh it off but cried out instead. His hands swelled into purple balloons.

"You fell for it like a meteor," Wyeth said.

Horrocks stood in front of the chair.

"I said you fell—"

Horrocks punched Wyeth in the face. Wyeth's mouth filled with blood. His voice became watery.

"I said—"

Horrocks squared his feet, crouched, and punched Wyeth in the nose. Broken bone and mucus slid down the back of Wyeth's throat.

Horrocks surveyed the carnage in disbelief. The first body made a peeling sound as Horrocks lifted it off the floor. He carried the dead Ringer to the Operating Room and laid him in the autopsy tub. He used a scissor to remove the Ringer's clothes. The Ringer's shirt, especially his collar, was thick with congealed blood. Horrocks started a pile of soiled garments. He inclined the tub and used a soapy sponge to clean the naked body. He concentrated on the face and underarms; the rest of the body got a quick brushing. The wound in the neck was short and deep, evidence of a hasty job. Horrocks drained the body of blood, though in truth Wyeth had done most of the work already. Once dry, Horrocks irrigated the corpse with embalming fluid, then placed the Ringer in one of the freezer's ten compartments. He shut the freezer door, washed his hands and refilled the embalming tanks.

Horrocks repeated the embalming process six more times. When he was finished the freezer only had one empty compartment.

Horrocks locked himself in the Operating Room and screamed. He screamed at the top of his voice for as long as he was able. It ended in a hoarse rasp. He wondered if Sari heard him.

Horrocks carried the shredded clothes into the other room and dropped them near the mesh. He dragged over the bloody sheets, blankets and towels, jammed everything into a trash bag and brought it upstairs. He came back down, attached a hose to a spout in the wall and sprayed the room. The runoff, some of it dense and black, washed down through drains along the walls.

Wyeth said, "Nice going. Finally. The smell was—"

Horrocks trained the hose on him. The spray caught Wyeth in the face. He opened his mouth to swallow the torrent. Horrocks was afraid Wyeth would drown himself so he lowered his aim for Wyeth's shoulder. The chair tipped and Wyeth landed on his side. Horrocks used the hose to guide the wet debris past Wyeth's body. Wyeth's curses were muffled by the brown river.

Horrocks turned the water off, drenched the floor with a yellow solvent, then used the hose to give the room a final rinse. He put the hose in the closet, righted Wyeth's chair, lifted it an inch off the ground and slammed it down.

"I've got a mouthful of blood and shit," Wyeth said. His face was speckled with both.

"I wouldn't care if you choked on it," Horrocks said.

"Yes you would. That's why you stopped aiming for my mouth. Afraid I'd suffocate. You're easier to read than a birthday card."

"Rouen tell you that?"

"All that water," Wyeth said. "You should have cleaned yourself. I can't remember what color your clothes were before. They're red and brown now." He wiped his tongue on the roof of his mouth and sucked on his teeth. "Got something caught in here, don't know what it is," he said and smiled.

"Seven men," Horrocks said. "Since when do you have it in you to kill even one?"

"Seven? Closer to fifty. I've been busy these last few years."

"Busy with the Bastards?" Horrocks said. "With Rouen?"

"How's Sari?" Wyeth said. "I spared her but you haven't—"

Horrocks punched him again. Wyeth's head snapped back and sprayed blood on the wall behind him. He lowered his head mechanically. His upper lip was split. One of his front teeth was missing.

"How long did it take to plan this?" Horrocks asked. He boxed Wyeth on the ears. "How long?"

"My chest is itchy. Scratch it for me? I can't reach."

Horrocks slapped him. "This is getting tedious."

"We should switch positions, shake things up."

Horrocks punched him again, this time in the gut. Blood exploded from Wyeth's mouth. "Watch the ropes," Wyeth said.

"Who was it? It wasn't the Bastards," Horrocks said.

"I've always loved Sari," Wyeth said.

"You offered to take her somewhere safe last time. And now this. All this blood."

"I saw her naked once, when she was changing and left the door—"

Horrocks beat him so hard he had to right the chair three times. He became exhausted, pulled up a chair for himself and sat in front of Wyeth.

"Giving your knuckles a rest?" Wyeth said. His mouth looked like a picket fence that had been ravaged by vandals. Every other tooth was gone. Wyeth used his tongue to probe the bloody gaps. "I'm going to have a terrible time passing those. Rouen has the originals somewhere. Every year he gives me new ones, implants, but they never stick. I'm constantly losing them." He tilted his head to the side. "I don't want you to hit me again, Horrocks."

"Was Rouen behind the king's attempted assassination?"

"Nothing to do with it. He'd love to thank whoever was, but Rouen doesn't have the gall to try something like that himself anymore. He's so afraid of failure. It's a complex with him."

"Who, then?"

"I haven't a fucking clue. Whoever it was, they've been quiet about it." Wyeth hawked up an impressive glob of saliva and coughed it onto the floor. A molar surfed toward the drains. "Because they've been so quiet we don't think it was the Bastards. They love a commotion."

"It doesn't rule them out," Horrocks said.

"It doesn't."

"I don't believe a word you're saying."

"Don't."

"So many Ringers," Horrocks said and motioned to the Operating Room. "This was so brutal."

"Rouen knew you'd never give them freely. What have you ever given freely? You think you have this code, that you're so honorable. You're the most selfish person I've ever met. Rouen wanted the Ringers dead because they can be used to fake the king and he wants the throne without complications. Plus he loves hurting them."

Wyeth's lips parted in an ugly smile that showed off his few remaining teeth. "I think the real reason Rouen wants the Ringers dead is he feels they were made 'cause of him. He hates it when things are out of his control, especially things he started. Some shit like that. It's too fucked up to unravel."

"All that horseshit you were slinging about Miami, your wife, asking permission to sell on my Furnace—"

"True, almost every word. I didn't come in on that Shortliner from Miami last week. It was two years ago. Guardships wouldn't let me near the Furnaces, so I went to Europa. Rouen caught me before I could move half my product."

"So the Ringers you brought here were—"

"The price of admission. You wouldn't let me into the basement last time."

Horrocks untied Wyeth's ropes. Wyeth fell to the floor like a toppled statue. Horrocks picked the man up, carried him past the mesh and laid him on a cot.

"Rouen pulled out half my teeth, just enough so I wouldn't talk funny. Pulled them out with the dirtiest set of pliers you ever saw. No sweet air, no foreplay. His ape Bayswater used me as a sparring partner every day for two years. Bayswater and a couple other guys I can't picture they hit me so hard. Snapped off three of my toes with wire clippers. They did all kinds of things you can't tell when I'm dressed. They cracked me like a cast and filled me with bile. 'Brainwashing and leverage,' Rouen would tell me all the time. 'With a little leverage, I could make anyone new.' After all that, Horrocks, you'd have done anything they asked you to."

"I'd have done the sensible thing," Horrocks said. He went to the closet, found the dagger he'd stolen off the Bastard in the hotel and handed it to Wyeth.

"I could tell you more, Horrocks. Then you'd pity me."

"I have trouble believing you," Horrocks said.

"IT'S ALL FUCKING TRUE!" The veins in Wyeth's neck stood out like bamboo shoots.

"Seven men," Horrocks said. He locked the mesh and walked up the stairs.

When Horrocks was gone Wyeth said, "More."

THE DOG WAS ASLEEP on the bed with Sari. He still had the needle in his fur. He woke up when Horrocks removed it, gave Horrocks' face a good tongue lashing and climbed down off the bed. Sari looked much better. Few more hours and she'll be all right, Horrocks thought. He showered and changed.

He saw through the open bathroom door that Sari was up and said, "You look good."

"I feel OK. Actually, I don't feel a thing I'm so tired."

Horrocks came out of the bathroom and told her what Wyeth had said. She nodded when she thought he wanted her to.

"There's still a Bastard ship hanging in our shadow," he said.

"You sure the Geigers are right about *The Priam*?"

"I think so," he said.

"How long till we get there?"

"*The Priam*? Maybe six hours."

But Sari had already fallen asleep.

Horrocks returned to the cellar an hour after he'd left. Wyeth was dead, had been for the better part of that hour. The veins in his forearms had been sliced from wrist to elbow.

Horrocks didn't clean the body. He crammed Wyeth into the freezer's tenth shelf, blood, shit and all.

CHAPTER 37

Guilfoyle was dressed in his orange flight suit. His helmet was on the seat next to him. He was watching the Bastard ship approach the *Honey Locust*; he'd been watching the ship since she'd veered toward him 1,500 miles back. This is no surprise, Guilfoyle thought. Wonder how they'll try to take me.

"Guilfoyle," they said. "We've come for the Ringers."

"Isn't this a little sudden?" Guilfoyle said. He fingered the circular designs on his helmet. "I could have used some notice."

"You haven't heard, we haven't told anyone, the king is dead. We have his body."

"Congratulations," Guilfoyle said. Congratulations on such a terrible lie, he thought.

"We'll take the Ringers now. We have the money for the bonuses, $100,000 for each Ringer."

"I hope you brought a lot 'cause I have over fifteen," Guilfoyle said. He stared at his reflection on the helmet's visor and when he looked back to the screen the Bastard ship was less than a hundred feet away.

"Over a dozen? That's unbelievable. Terrific," the Bastards said. They flew under the *Honey Locust*, emerged behind her and fired a volley of junk bombs into her twin exhausts.

The *Honey Locust* balked as if she were a dog who had run out of leash. Guilfoyle tested the engines with a minimal amount of thrust. They were completely fouled.

The Bastards came close aboard the *Honey Locust* and extended their thick umbilical. "We'll be docked in a minute," they said. "We've got a message from Tinton for you. Give us a few seconds to get the money together. It's very heavy. Fifteen, you said?"

"Make it twenty," Guilfoyle said. "Take your time. If I'm not down to greet you, that means I'm still prepping the Ringers for transit."

The *Honey Locust* recoiled again as the umbilical latched on to her. Don't they have any tact? Guilfoyle thought. He turned on the interior camera, afraid it wouldn't work from years of neglect. He'd never had any use for it. A rectangular box appeared on his viewscreen. Everything was colored a grainy shade of green.

Guilfoyle focused the interior camera on the exit hatch. He put his helmet on, made sure it was properly sealed to his flight suit, then unlocked the exit hatch by remote.

Five Bastards spilled into his ship. They were armed. The first four checked behind doors and in corners. The fifth Bastard followed them casually. They knew exactly where the door to the storeroom was.

Fucking Bastards, Guilfoyle thought and, again by remote, closed the exit hatch. Through a combination of command strokes Guilfoyle created a spike in the ship's air pressure.

Stupid Bastards, Guilfoyle thought and panned the camera to watch each of them pass out.

Guilfoyle climbed out of the cockpit, disarmed the unconscious Bastards and tossed them into the chapel.

Going to have to do this fast, Guilfoyle thought. With the engines fucked, so is the ship. Won't be going anywhere if I stay here. Didn't think they'd junk the exhausts. Got to move.

He ran through the *Honey Locust*'s floor plan in his mind, trying to figure what he'd need from each room that he couldn't live without. He grabbed a trash bag from the kitchen, went to his bedroom and stuffed a week's worth of underwear inside. There was room enough for his other two flight suits. He liberated them from the hamper.

He left the bag by the exit hatch and went to find his sister. She was hiding beneath her bed, fast asleep. Guilfoyle pulled her out by her wrists and laid her on the bed. With both hands Guilfoyle tipped her dresser over, chose some clothes at random and bundled them in his left arm. He carried Kitsis over his right shoulder.

Guilfoyle stuffed her clothes into his trash bag and stopped to say goodbye to his ship. Not going to miss you, you fucking heap, he thought. Have to move quickly. Soon as I open this door the pressure will equalize, the Bastards'll wake up. Race to the other side and retract their umbilical fast as I can. Might be some Bastards on the ship. The pilot, maybe. Better be careful.

Guilfoyle opened the exit hatch and sped across the umbilical. The door to the Bastard ship was open. Once inside Guilfoyle dropped Kitsis and the bag together, then slammed the yellow failsafe knob that closed the hatch and recalled the umbilical.

Something struck his helmet, starring the visor. Guilfoyle ripped the helmet off and flung it at his attacker.

"Grave robber," the man said and put his hands around Guilfoyle's neck.

Guilfoyle elbowed the Bastard in the stomach and tangled their legs together. He tried to throw the Bastard but he had no leverage. The Bastard jabbed Guilfoyle in the face half a dozen times.

Guilfoyle punched the Bastard in the groin, hammered him in the chest. The Bastard moved back and Guilfoyle was finally able to throw him. He landed on his left hip, jumped up and charged Guilfoyle who stepped out of the Bastard's path, caught the man by the head and spun it around until the Bastard's neck cracked. He dropped to the floor. Crippled or dead, Guilfoyle didn't care.

It was a few minutes before Guilfoyle found the cockpit. The main viewscreen showed the *Honey Locust*'s umbilical approaching the Bastard vessel Guilfoyle now captained. Guilfoyle ignited the thrusters and the umbilical connected with nothing. "Good luck," Guilfoyle told the Bastards he'd stranded. "You can have her."

He put his forefinger on his wrist to check his pulse. Just about normal. Not even a trickle of sweat, he thought. Came off better than if I'd planned it for weeks.

A message flashed across the screen: "Horrocks has been tracked to *The Priam*. After you've disabled Guilfoyle, chase and apprehend Horrocks. Please acknowledge this message by deleting it."

The message faded, left a blue residue on the screen, then came back in yellow.

Guilfoyle deleted it.

CHAPTER 38

Horrocks stood in the cockpit doorway and winked at Sari. "I fixed the heat. It won't last forever but it'll do for now. Feel any warmer?"

"No," Sari said and clenched her sweater at the collar. She swiveled to face the viewscreen. "We're here. *The Priam.*"

"Could you magnify it? Seems so dead in there."

"It is dead in there. I think the Geigers were pulling your leg. They told you what you wanted to hear."

The Priam was a giant whale skeleton. Two thousand feet from tail end to skull box. Bone white, bleached by the naked sun and flecked with moles of black lava. All that remained of her underbelly was a ribcage of blunted fangs. Three empty needleships orbited the carcass like desolate moons.

Sari cruised by the ship, searching for a place to dock. She found a port near the tail that looked sound enough to support them.

"Sensors are detecting a breathable atmosphere on the ship," Sari said. "Stale but breathable."

"That means someone's there. Purifier seals don't mend themselves, and they've been broken for years," Horrocks said. "It's still going to be cold in there. I'll get the coats."

"And a couple flashlights," Sari said.

They exited the *Moondrunk* and stood inside the hallway that was *The Priam*'s spinal column. Holding hands, they started forward.

The Priam's frigid air laid siege to their bodies. The coats were useless. Their breath crystallized and reflected the beams from the flashlights.

The empty hallway was haunted with dark patches, the ghosts of missing furniture and equipment. Doors that once led to rooms off the whale spine were melted shut.

"I saw two Gunwitches tucked underneath *The Priam* when I made those passes," Sari said. Her voice carried on the air like a magic carpet. The sound of a woman laughing attached itself to the echo. Sari grabbed Horrocks' arm.

He nodded but didn't reply. His eyes were fixed straight ahead on the set of doors that marked the end of the hallway not fifty feet away. A camouflaged door on their right slid open and Horrocks and Sari were pulled inside. Horrocks was slammed against a wall, his hands trapped behind his back.

"Who are you?" A woman's voice. "Who the fuck are you?"

"Horrocks. My name's Horrocks. I used to—"

"I know what you used to," the woman said and let Horrocks go.

Horrocks turned around. Sari stood by the wall-length window, held captive between two women whose features had been completely smoothed. They looked like blank clones waiting to be struck.

The third woman, the woman who had spoken, was a parody of the queen. She shared the queen's facial structure but was much heavier than Porphyria had ever been, especially around the chin and wrists. Gray hairs peeked out from under her yellow wig. She had wood chips for fingernails. Horrocks could see the queen beneath all these changes, like a palimpsest that had been written over in progressively darker colors. He was disgusted at the charade; he wanted to hate her but his hate succumbed to pity.

Parody stepped forward and said, "We know who you are. We used to work for them, just like you." She waved her thick hands in mock triumph. They were covered in scaly red islands. Psoriasis.

"The queen banished you," Sari said.

"They both banished us," Parody said, "but not before she tried to kill me. Drunken bitch tried to kill me once."

Horrocks realized Parody was wearing a torso of armor similar to his golden spacesuit. Explains her strength, he thought. Parody removed an armplate and showed Sari her scar, an ugly purple ripple. "Stabbed me there." She lifted her wig to scrub her real hair. "We spent months becoming her. Tried our best to please her by *being* her, and she hated us. All those surgeries and she hated us 'cause we made her feel cheap. They kept us in a vault. Comfortable but locked away except for important public events the queen just *had* to attend."

She cracked her knuckles against her hips. The joints in her hands were misshapen, as if one of the many surgeries she'd undergone had been the implantation of rocks under her skin. "Then she tried to kill us and it was decided to send us away."

Horrocks thought he could make it to the door unscathed but he couldn't make it with Sari. "Weren't you given a Gunwitch, and money?" he said.

"A Gunwitch with the steering bar and navcom removed, enough fuel for one way to the Deeps. That was some ride. Gunwitches aren't meant for that kind of trip."

The women with the blank faces holding Sari tugged on her arms impatiently; they wore the same armor as Parody.

"Horrocks," Sari screamed.

"Don't pull on her so hard," Parody said.

"It may not have been fair but they gave you opportunity," Horrocks said.

"The king came to see us before we left and we pleaded to have our faces back. They stole our identities but refused to give them back." She cracked her knuckles again. "The Push was coming. The flesh artists were too busy working on *his* Ringers. He actually said having Porphyria's face might be an asset out there."

"This is a lifetime ago. Ten years before the assassination attempt," Horrocks said.

"What attempt? It succeeded. The son is dead."

"The son?" Sari said.

"You assumed. Everyone assumed," Parody said. She cracked her knuckles a third time. Horrocks didn't think the woman even realized she was doing it. "We've been listening to all your chatter out here. You assumed the king was the target, his middle son the accidental victim. The son was the target." She stroked her cheek, scraping away some of the foundation that masked her face.

"He and Porphyria have taken so much from us. We know he never felt the sting of loss when his first son was killed during the war. They should know loss like we know it. First this son, then the kingdom. We tracked him here from the Annex. You should hear him wail."

"But ten years," Horrocks said.

"Ten years of nonstop manual labor. Practically slave labor. The king was wrong. Having the queen's face out there was no asset. The Deeps is a fantastic place if you have a skill. The only training we had was how to act like the queen."

Parody spat on the floor. "The only work we could get was with hovel crews, building stacked shanties for all the people coming in off the Longliners. Twenty-hour shifts. Mandatory meals laced with stimulants. And there's no such thing as a weekend in the Deeps, not for hovel crews."

"Why didn't you come back?" Horrocks asked.

"You think the king sent us out there with enough money to come back? Anyway we didn't want to come back as much as we wanted our old bodies. There used to be four of us. We roomed together, saved enough money for one of us to see the terrible doctors out there to fix our faces. Fought it out to see who would go first. She died before he sewed her up. We saved some more, looked for a better doctor and then we saw Kleig. After meeting up with him we saved our money for something more satisfying. His fee."

"Kleig's dead," Horrocks said.

"We heard. He took some convincing but we knew he'd do it for us. We'd have done it ourselves but we don't have the talent for it. Kleig's price was high but he'd made a name for himself in the Deeps doing this type of thing. Took almost six years to get the money together."

One of the blank queens released her grip on Sari and came forward. The other took Sari into the corner.

"Where's the king?" Sari asked.

"No one'll see him till the twenty days are up. A day or so from now. Then he'll lose his kingdom, too," Parody said. "Then he'll know loss. Then he's free to go."

"You've put the whole sector in an uproar," Horrocks said.

"Our bodies are in uproar! Look at us! We can't decide who we are. Our bodies haven't stayed true to the queen. Without treatments and follow-up surgery, we hardly look like her at all anymore. What are we? Since our real features started asserting themselves, we don't look like anything at all. I think I've dealt with it rather well," she said and pointed to her wig and makeup. "They," she said and motioned toward the blank Ringer next to her, "just gave up. Used acid to burn all the character from their face."

"Where is he?" Horrocks asked.

"You want to see him?"

"Where is he?"

Parody and the blank Ringer overpowered Horrocks, spun him around and pinned him to the wall once more.

"Open your hand," Parody said.

"Fuck you. Where's the king?"

"Open your hand," Parody said. The motorized joints in her armor whined as she braced Horrocks' wrist against the wall. "Open it," she said but Horrocks' hand was scrunched in a tight fist.

"The other one will cut your wife's throat," Parody said. "She'll do worse, I ask her. Open your hand."

Horrocks flattened his hand on the cold metal. Parody took a knife from its belt sheath, put her lips against Horrocks' ear and said, "The king's nearby. We can't let you leave here without some understanding of what we are. Loss is all we've known. You'll understand that, too. I can't have you thinking we were insane."

She drove the knife into the wall, severing Horrocks' left ring finger.

Horrocks yelled and shoved the Ringers away. He crouched down. The wound where his finger had been squirted blood.

One of the blank Ringers stuffed Horrocks' mouth with a rag. The other tossed Horrocks a cauterizing pad. Horrocks spat out the rag, ripped the pad open with his teeth and slapped it to the wound. Parody injected Horrocks with adrenaline and jumped back.

"How do you feel? Different?" Parody said. "We've been using the adrenaline to keep the king awake. Same needle."

Horrocks lunged for her. The blood in his arm surged down into his hand; Horrocks nearly blacked out from the pain. He fell onto his knees.

"You'll adapt like we did. We've been waiting for you to show. Kind of hoping Guilfoyle would show first. I would've taken his arm. Consider that a kindness, Horrocks."

Sari bent down by her husband, put her arms around his back.

"Where is it?" Horrocks said.

"Where's what?" Parody said.

"What you took from me."

"You won't get that back, Horrocks. Your asking tells me you haven't completely understood this exercise. Maybe we should take another. Ask me again. Maybe I will take your arm."

The second blank Ringer stooped to help Horrocks to his feet. Sari pushed her so hard the Ringer landed on her back.

The adrenaline eroded the pain. Horrocks stood, gritted his teeth and said, "Where is he? Where's the king?"

"He's not leaving till the twenty days are up," Parody said.

"Where is he?"

"Right down the hall."

CHAPTER 39

The queen's banished Ringers escorted Horrocks and Sari to the room at the end of the hallway.

"We'll be waiting," Parody said and flashed her knife.

Horrocks and Sari walked into the room and closed the doors behind them. Along the left and right walls were jeeps and earthmovers secured to an assortment of ramps. Machines for a planetary colonization that never was. They had survived *The Priam*'s looting because the king had long ago declared this one room off limits in honor of the explorers who'd been killed during that first failed attempt to reach the Deeps.

At the end of the room, at the tip of *The Priam*, was the king. He was kneeling before a ramp raised three feet off the floor. On the ramp was a body hidden under a black shroud.

Horrocks felt as if he'd uncovered a priceless tomb. Here was a treasure that could buy them peace. For the second time he had the sensation of falling off a centrifuge. Here's my panacea, Horrocks thought. I *will* get him out of here.

Sari's relief was mixed with anger.

They walked up to the king. The king did not stir. On their left, sitting on the hood of a brown jeep, was the king's aide. He lifted a finger to his lips and shook his head.

They waited ten minutes for the king to rise. He turned with the languor of a man shackled with grief. He didn't wear his customary ponytail, but his hair was creased to show where it had been. His eyelids were veiny and red. His tears chiseled white stripes on his dirty cheeks. He wore the coveralls of a common miner, grimy and brown. His right arm, where he'd been accidentally shot, was in a cloth sling. The hand was swollen and inert, the nails overlong.

The king went to hug Horrocks but Horrocks kneeled first. "My duty has always been to you," Horrocks said.

"Get up," the king said. "I can't hug you down there."

The king looked over Horrocks' shoulders and said, "Sari." He moved past Horrocks to give Sari a one-armed hug. "Sari the beautiful."

"You look just like your Ringers," Sari said.

The king's laugh was sour and short. "Old, that's how I look."

"I'm terribly sorry, John," Sari said.

John Kingston walked over to the body. "He was a good son. Always thought of himself second. I was always first for him. So devoted, so sad."

Horrocks put his hand on the king's shoulder. "You have to come back. Your kingdom—"

The king shrugged Horrocks' arm off. "I don't want my kingdom." He removed two vials from his pocket and threw them over his head. His aide bounced off the jeep and snatched them out of the air.

"You fool," the king said.

The aide hissed.

"A parent should never bury his children," the king said. "It's unnatural. I was ruthless. I created and controlled a kingdom, something to leave my boys. I know it's hard for the children of great men. They seldom outdo their parents." He gripped the shroud to quell his shaking hand. The shroud slipped to the side, exposing the son's rotting elbow. "Doesn't mean they should die before us."

Horrocks stepped toward the fetid body. "Macker-racher said—"

"Don't touch him," the king yelled and blocked Horrocks. "He is," the king paused, "pure. He will stay," he paused again, "pure."

"Your kingdom's in chaos," Sari said.

"I need time to grieve. Now, while my emotions are raw. I'm scraping them, Sari, scraping them to make myself as unhappy as possible. Twenty days is not enough time. I need twenty years. Thank God for those adrenaline shots. I'm too weary to stay up on my own."

He put his back to them and faced his son. The king's tears dripped on the shroud. "My oldest son died during the war, died saving me. There was no time to mourn. Time only to fight, protect myself, my holdings. After the war I had no emotion but relief. Relief, the most potent emotion. I could find no grief. Built him a beautiful coffin because after relief came guilt. Now I have the chance to revel in mourning. No amount of strife will rob me of that. My son—"

"Porphyria thinks you're dead," Sari said.

"I feel dead. That's how I want to feel. Leave me be."

"She's not strong," Sari said.

"Not anymore. She was. I broke her. Had her chemically spayed," the king said and turned to face them. "Should I feel guilty about that? She bore me a son that wasn't my own and passed it off as ours. I have no heirs. All my accomplishments mean nothing. We injected Porphyria's food with specific poisons that murdered her ovaries."

"The king is a bastard," the aide said.

The king threw a loose hubcap at the aide's head. "My parents never married. My father died before they could," the king said. "The Bastards know this, those mongrels. It gives them hope to see someone rise above his tainted lineage. They'd never admit I was a bastard, though. They'd never tell anyone. Afraid it would weaken their creaky platform. They want to be moored to something substantial, not to a ghost ship."

"Why don't you take them in?" Sari asked.

Because I'm a success and I shouldn't be, the king thought. I cheated on my wife to make myself feel base, dirty, real. Sex was the best way to do that. Illicit sex worked even better. The Furnace whores brought me down to where I felt I belonged. But the Bastards are too strict a reminder. I don't need to be reminded.

The king motioned for them to come closer. Horrocks and Sari stepped around the dead body and stood opposite the king. "He was a sweet child, nothing like me. I pared all my traits from him early on. He was stubborn about it. I broke him, too."

The king looked Horrocks in the eye. "When I sold you the mine, when I asked you to pay with—I was asking because I was sure you'd never agree. I was bitter you'd left me. When you agreed to my price I lost all respect for you. Since then I've changed my opinion. You wanted it badly for reasons of your own. You're stronger than me, Horrocks. That was brave."

Horrocks reached across the body and held the king's hand.

"Your finger," the king said.

"Your Ringers are dead," Horrocks said.

"My herd." The king touched his throat. "My voice was the only thing they never got. Did you notice that? No one ever did. Only way you could really tell us apart. The artists couldn't make them sound like me, which was a comfort, actually. I needed to keep something for myself, some individuality. I was wrong to ask you. I hated you for denying me, but I shouldn't have asked. Forgive me."

"I can get you off *The Priam*," Horrocks said. "I'll get us past the three—"

"They want me to suffer. I want to suffer. Leave it alone, Horrocks."

"You're not the only one affected by all this," Sari said, though the last half of her statement was interrupted by six small explosions. Gunshots.

The doors swung open and Tinton strode into the room like the marshal of a parade. "What a lovely little convention. Father, your children have arrived."

Ten of Tinton's half brothers came into the room after him, two of them armed with rifles.

Tinton stopped before the king and got down on one knee. His brothers did the same. Horrocks and Sari were still behind the ramp that held the dead prince. Horrocks moved around to the left, Sari to the right.

Tinton bowed his head. "I offer condolences, father. We grieve for the soul of your son, our brother. Know that we were not behind this. Our indignation would never take us that far."

"Get out of my sight, you worm," the king said. "I'm mourning my *real* son."

Tinton tugged on the king's good hand and said, "Acknowledge us. Give us our due. What we're asking for is such a simple thing. Acceptance, father."

"Coming from you, that word sounds like shit." The king tried to free his arm. Tinton would not let go.

"We're not asking for money," Tinton said. The king stepped back and Tinton crawled forward. "We'd like to see you live a long life."

"I have."

"And when you're gone—"

"Legitimacy," muttered one of the Bastards.

Tinton's head whipped around but no Bastard would look up to claim the remark. "Acceptance," Tinton said. He faced the king. "Acceptance for your actions. Acceptance of your children."

"You are not children," the king said. "You are accidents. The results of loneliness, self-loathing."

Tinton used the king's sleeve to help him rise. He slapped the king across the cheek.

Horrocks darted toward them but was stopped by five Bastards. They pummeled his face and stomach. One man drove both his elbows into Horrocks' back, forcing him to the ground. Horrocks waited for the banished Ringers to show, then remembered the gunshots prior to Tinton's entrance.

Tinton slapped the king again, then shoved him aside like a rack of clothes. Sari caught Tinton before he could reach the dead body. He growled, kicked her in the stomach and handed her to one of his brothers. "It's too crowded in here," Tinton said as he tore off the shroud.

The son was in a state of mild decay. His arms were folded over his chest but his legs had a slight bend to them, a byproduct of the rigor. His body was tinged with green. The flaps of skin around his neck looked like crisp, burned paper. His mouth was distorted with finger indentations where the king had tried to change his son's expression from faded surprise to solace.

"All this drama for one dead child," Tinton said.

"A child!" the king roared. He lunged for Tinton but was dragged to his knees by three Bastards.

Sari lay on the floor, holding her stomach, praying she wasn't bleeding.

Guilfoyle stole into the room unseen. He crouched by the jeeps along the eastern wall and made his way toward the commotion. He heard Horrocks and Tinton arguing but had no interest in their fight. He eased his stiletto out of its wrist holster.

Wish they'd left me on the moon with the rats, he thought. Wish Tinton had never found me. Wish I'd gone to the Deeps.

Guilfoyle watched the action unfold. The king's aide looked as if he would join the fray at any moment. Horrocks was on his knees, struggling to his feet. The king supported himself on the ramp that held his son. Sari was on the ground, crying for Horrocks. Guilfoyle wanted them all dead. Start with the king, he thought. The king's closest. Everyone else can be next.

Guilfoyle sprinted from the jeeps and stabbed the king in the chest. The king groaned and slumped against

Guilfoyle, drenching them both in his blood. Guilfoyle used two hands to work the stiletto around the king's torso.

Horrocks knocked out one of the armed Bastards. He stole the man's rifle, pointed it at Guilfoyle and pulled the trigger.

"Already been emptied into the freak doormen outside," one of the Bastards said and jumped him.

Horrocks' fingers fumbled with the gun and ejected the hidden bayonet. He yanked the rifle upward and sliced the Bastard open from navel to neck.

Guilfoyle lunged for Tinton.

Horrocks stood in front of the ramp; Sari, the king and his son's body were behind him. His lung was ablaze. His legs felt uncertain.

Four Bastards disarmed and subdued Guilfoyle. The rest approached Horrocks. He raised the bayonet.

"The king is dead," a Bastard said. "You want to die protecting him still?"

Tinton held the king's aide by the throat and said, "The king is dead! Kingston is dead!"

The Bastards formed a half circle around Horrocks.

"Forget Horrocks," Tinton said. "The king is dead. The queen and her son are alive." He trotted for the exit, the king's aide in tow. The Bastards left Horrocks and followed Tinton out.

Guilfoyle watched them go, then turned to Horrocks. "People say I'm pathetic. They say you're charmed but I'm pathetic. That I foul everything I'm a part of. I wouldn't trade what little I have to stand in your place. Looking at you, *I* feel like a king. The Bastards'll take the mines, and I'll take what I can from them. But you've got nothing. Nothing but corpses and a bruised wife. That's charmed."

Guilfoyle strolled out of the room.

Horrocks threw the gun at the jeeps. He checked the king. The king was dead. He checked his wife. Sari was alive.

CHAPTER 40

Horrocks didn't want to move; standing still he had the juvenile impression that time had stopped. Nothing could get any worse if time didn't go forward.

Sari groaned and got up on her elbows. She was lying in a puddle of the king's blood. Horrocks ignored the pain in his hand and lifted Sari to her feet.

"Are you OK?" he asked.

"I tried to roll with the kick," she said. She arched her back and winced. "My lower back, that's where it really hurts."

"Not your stomach."

"I don't think so. No cramps, no pain there."

Horrocks went from jeep to jeep until he found one whose battery hadn't dried up. He drove it off the ramp and put Sari in the passenger seat. He picked the shroud off the floor, covered the son's body and laid him in the back. He put the king next to his boy.

Through creative steering Horrocks was able to get the jeep through the doorway. The queen's banished Ringers lay just outside. They had been shot in the head. Parody's wig was in her mouth. Her maquillage had been smeared onto the faces of the two blank Ringers, giving them false life.

Horrocks and Sari weren't molested on their trip down *The Priam's* spine to the *Moondrunk*. Guilfoyle and the Bastards had already started off for the mines.

Horrocks walked Sari from the jeep to the *Moondrunk*'s cockpit. "Can you fly her?" he asked.

"I think I'm OK," she said. But if I lose this baby you will never be forgiven, she thought. No amount of kindness will change that. I'll make your charitable heart turn black.

Horrocks carried father and son onto the ship. Sari backed the *Moondrunk* off *The Priam*.

"I'm taking them into the cellar," he told Sari.

"You're not going anywhere but to bed. Your finger," she said.

"I'm taking them downstairs."

"Horrocks—"

"I'm taking them downstairs. I can't feel that much pain. I want to do this before—"

"Where are we going?"

"The mines. We've nowhere else to go," Horrocks said.

"What do you think you can do there?" Sari said.

"I have no idea. Save Porphyria."

"She doesn't want you to save her, Horrocks."

"Save our mine, then. I don't know. Go down there and get in the way. Make sure the Bastards don't take over. I don't know what we can do. There's nothing we can do. There's no way out of this. No way that's good for any of us."

"If we're going to the mines, we'll be late. They've all got Spot Drives. You'll be too late to do anything at all." A sudden pain pierced her abdomen and, she knew, the baby as well.

Horrocks took a bottle of opiates from the kitchen. His hands were so sweaty he dropped the bottle three times before opening it.

THE KING'S BODY WAS IN THE AUTOPSY TUB, his son's on the floor. Horrocks sat in a chair between them and ran his hands through his hair. He was too feverish to realize the cauterizing pad had come loose. The problem of succession's become unsolvable, Horrocks thought. The true heirs are dead. The queen's loyalties are fickle. There will be no more kingdom. The past is the past and the future is chaos.

Horrocks stopped running his hands through his hair because he was afraid he'd start pulling it out. He lined up the necessary ingredients to care for the bodies.

I can't do this, he thought. Embalming the king is conceding defeat. I won't do it. I won't touch him, won't even clean him. Him or the son.

The freezer was full. Horrocks doubled up two sets of Ringers to free the eighth and ninth slots. He rolled the son in the shroud, placed him in the eighth slot. Horrocks found another dark sheet in the closet, wrapped the king inside it, placed him in the ninth slot.

Horrocks locked the door to the room and sat on the floor. I won't touch them, he thought. He wanted to shout, to rip the tub from its stand, to smash the freezer with his hands. He had the energy for none of these things.

He sat there for an hour. I won't do it, he thought but embalmed them anyway.

HORROCKS STAGGERED UP TO THE COCKPIT. "I—I think I have a fever. My finger, Sari. My fucking finger."

His hand, face and clothes were smeared with blood.

"Oh my God. Where's the cauterizing pad?"

"My finger," he said and passed out.

HORROCKS WOKE UP IN THE BATHROOM. He lay on the floor. Sari was cleaning his hand. She helped him to the bed where he passed out again.

Sari went down to the cockpit and modified their course for the Furnaces. The screen said: "Estimated time 8 HRS 23 MIN."

Sari found some alcohol, gauze, painkillers, a needle and thread and brought them up to the bedroom. She sat cross-legged on the floor and took hold of Horrocks' mangled hand.

"Not the first time I've stitched you up," she said and stroked his bicep.

Horrocks was semiconscious. "We back home yet?" he mumbled.

Sari placed a painkiller on his tongue and closed his mouth. She splayed his fingers and sewed up the gash.

She stopped periodically to calm her trembling hands. She looked out the bedroom window. The Bastards had reached the mines.

HORROCKS WASN'T SURE how long he'd been asleep. He showered, brushed his teeth and dressed. All these chores were complicated by his missing finger.

Sari was in the cockpit, arms crossed over her chest, her gaze fixed on the viewscreen. A crescent of Jupiter occupied one half the screen, Io the other. The king's mines were clustered together for safety but were cruelly outlined by the radiance of the rusty moon. The Furnaces looked like boxy, inverted funnels. The flagship Furnace, the queen's home, was at the center.

Twenty Bastard ships swerved in and out of the mines, firing concussion bombs that threatened to blow the mines off their axes. Guardships challenged the Bastards. Sari noticed some ships from Rouen's gothic fleet defending the mines as well. Yellow entrails laced the tableau. Sundogs of light followed every explosion.

"I called the queen to warn her," said Sari when Horrocks came down. "Obviously she already knows. No one's responded. We'll be there in about two hours."

Horrocks left the cockpit and sat at the kitchen table with a glass of water and the bottle of pills. He emptied the pills on the table. His hand had doubled in size, making a vise of the bandages. He didn't think he would ever adjust to the injury. He swallowed one of the pills. He made a pyramid with the rest, took three off the peak and swallowed them, too.

CHAPTER 41

Sari landed on the covered runway atop the flagship Furnace. There were seven other vessels parked haphazardly on the tarmac. Their doors had been left open, their gangplanks still extended from ship to floor.

"They got out in a hurry," Horrocks said.

"These are Bastard ships," Sari said.

"Take this," Horrocks said and gave her the dagger Wyeth had used to kill himself.

"What about you?" she asked.

Horrocks showed her the butt of the handgun tucked into his waistband.

They walked down a wide staircase that led to the loading/receiving room. A gray-haired woman stood on a crate at the bottom of the stairs and addressed a crowd of hundreds: "The queen has earned your loyalty. Years of silence through all the king's infidelities. Never critical, always the supporter. She knew all your names, did she not? Porphyria never acted as though she was more important than any one of us. Never. We must repel the illegitimate children." Her forefinger jabbed the air. "The Bastards have no claim. They've never worked these mines. None of them ever sweated alongside you, yet they've decided these mines are theirs. Are they? They are not!"

The crowd cheered.

Horrocks and Sari headed for the stairwell on the other side of the room. Another woman addressed a different crowd there. She had a sharp gaze and used it to cut into the crowd. "Porphyria has no leadership ability or experience. This is a woman who allowed her husband to sleep wherever he chose. Allowed him to soil their marriage with scandal. If she won't stand up for herself, will she stand up for you? She will not!"

This second crowd roared and pumped their fists at the ceiling. The speaker put out both her hands to quiet them. "She has no backbone. We need foundation. Tinton is that foundation. He is the king's true son. He's a proven leader. He's the future."

Both crowds walked toward the center of the room. Their walk became a run. They shouted rebukes and threats. They converged in a melee of pipes and fists. The orators, Bastards both, looked over all the heads, nodded to each other and smiled.

One miner grabbed Horrocks' shirt. Horrocks twisted the man's wrist until it snapped.

Another miner threw a hard hat clean across the room. It bounced off the left wall, just missing Guilfoyle.

"Careless morons," Guilfoyle said.

"Let's *go*," Kitsis said. "I don't have anything left. Let's go *home*. We got here too late. You can't stop a riot."

"Fucking guardships," Guilfoyle said. "Wasn't for them, we'd have been here before just about everyone. At least the Bastards landed around the same time as us."

Guilfoyle was holding Kitsis by the wrist. She leaned back as if sitting on an invisible chair. Guilfoyle kept close to the wall and dragged Kitsis deeper into the room.

"I'm gonna throw up," she said. "This smell. Putrid egg smell. The *Honey Locust* smelled better than this." She tugged on Guilfoyle's arm and raked it with her nails. "You don't need me."

"Stop it," he yelled but could barely hear himself above the surrounding roar. "I'm not letting go. I'm only one person, Kit. Together we can do this. Get the queen before the Bastards. Get her son."

"I won't fight for you."

"You did a fine job on the laundry barge," Guilfoyle said.

"A fluke," Kitsis said. "At least ease up with the squeezing. I can't feel my fingers."

Guilfoyle squeezed harder and yanked her forward. Two miners grabbed him by the shoulders and tried to shove him into the fray. "For our queen," one of them said. "Forget the Bastards, forget Rouen."

"She's not my queen," Guilfoyle said.

"Thought so," the other miner said and swung at Guilfoyle's head. Guilfoyle ducked and slugged the man with a hard right. The two miners focused on Kitsis who was crouching down, her free forearm over her face; Guilfoyle was still holding her wrist. He pounded the miners with a barrage of right hooks until the men wobbled and fell against each other. Guilfoyle pushed them into the riot; they were absorbed by the crowd, then sacrificed to it.

Kitsis put her bloody forearm in Guilfoyle's face. "Look. Look at me."

"Why didn't you defend yourself?"

"With one hand?"

Guilfoyle and Kitsis passed a Bastard who was on his knees, screaming, "The king's dead. We saw him on *The Priam*. The king's already dead."

Guilfoyle stooped over and yelled into the man's ear, "No one's listening to you."

Kitsis pointed to a corridor that had opened up on their left. "Through there? Which way are we going?"

"Have you ever been on a Furnace before?" Guilfoyle asked.

"Of course not."

"Louder! I can't hear you."

"No!"

"Me neither. Too confusing here. I don't know how many floors, where the queen is, where Tinton went."

Kitsis tried to sit down, but Guilfoyle didn't give her enough slack.

"We're lost," she said.

"We haven't lost."

"That's not—Let's leave," she said.

"Give me a second."

"Get on the ship, go back to Europa."

"Give me a second!"

Guilfoyle studied the riot, looking for patterns of movement. Bayswater, the tallest person in the room, was at the very center. Men were hanging on his arms and legs. His forehead was perforated with gashes.

Guilfoyle spotted Horrocks and Sari. They went through a door in the far right corner. A matching door was in the far left corner, twenty yards from Guilfoyle.

"This is the way," Guilfoyle said and towed Kitsis behind him. He wrenched open the door and swung Kitsis through first. They were at the top of a staircase leading deeper into the mine.

"Definitely the way," Guilfoyle said.

Kitsis managed to keep up with Guilfoyle without slipping. He stopped abruptly and peered over the railing. Four Bastards were arguing on the next landing. Guilfoyle recognized them. Bastards from *The Priam*.

Guilfoyle squeezed Kitsis' wrist even tighter and dove into the Bastards feet first. He released his grip on Kitsis and lashed out at the Bastards, just trying to connect and not caring with what. He didn't want to kill them; he'd need their patronage later.

When the Bastards were all down Guilfoyle assessed his own damage: some bruised ribs and a bloody lip.

He groped the air to his right for Kitsis' wrist but she wasn't there. He heard her clattering up the stairs.

"Ten minutes," he boomed. "That's all you'll last without me."

He stepped over the Bastards and ran down the stairs. A Furnace-wide explosion knocked him on his ass.

In the opposite stairwell Horrocks caught Sari as she fell. They could see out of the stairwell into the adjacent mines. There was a fire in every window.

Horrocks took Sari's hand and they climbed down to the next level. Sari's thighs felt wet. She knew she was bleeding again.

The stairs ended in a colorful lobby. The walls were decorated with obsidian, olivine and agate. Semitransparent and full of glare, the entire lobby looked like a volcanic hideaway in ruin. The mob lifted slabs of obsidian from their hooks and hurled them around the room.

Rouen's men were wearing red flight jackets. They were outnumbered by miners four to one.

"Where's Bayswater?" Rouen asked. "Get Bayswater down here. Stop fighting! Me and the queen will make you all rich. There's no reason to fight. These are my Furnaces!"

Horrocks was separated from Sari by a stray gang of miners.

Rouen and his entourage surrounded her. "I know you, whore," Rouen said. "Longliner whore. We'll kill Horrocks and take you with us. I still remember your teeth."

Sari sunk the dagger into Rouen's groin. She used the blade to dig a trough down his leg, trying to sever his femoral artery. When the dagger struck Rouen's kneecap Sari shoved him into a passing wave of rioters. His entourage tried to get him back and they were all swept away.

Horrocks put his hands on Sari's waist and turned her around. "More stairs at the end of the room," he said. "Down down down."

They passed through four levels of riots, none as severe as the room that had taken Rouen. The lowest level was nearly deserted. A few wounded miners sat on the floor or strolled aimlessly, holding their heads, arms, sides.

It was quiet and cold. "Was that Rouen up there?" Horrocks asked.

"He threatened to kill you," Sari said. Sweat stood on her face like drops of Vaseline.

"Did he know you? Looked like he recognized you."

"I knew him," she said.

They entered the throne room. The glass from three chandeliers was scattered over a floor checkered with black and gold tiles, the king's colors. Jeweled chairs and love seats had been pushed to the walls.

The twin thrones were raised on three oval steps. They were the simplest chairs in the room. Green silk, high backs, no armrests.

Some chairs had been shoved aside by the wall left of the thrones. Horrocks ran his fingers across the red wallpaper. He felt the outline of a hidden door, saw a maroon tiara embossed on the wallpaper and banged on the wall.

"It's Horrocks," he said. "Porphyria, open the door. It's Horrocks and Sari."

The secret door swung inward. The prince pulled them inside. He peered into the throne room then shut the door.

"You remembered my safe-chamber," Porphyria said. She was sitting at a vanity. The mirror was draped with a black sheet. All the safe-chamber's mirrors were covered. Porphyria's circular bed was unmade. Her son stood behind her, arms crossed defiantly. Behind him were ten of his own Ringers.

Horrocks walked over to the queen. "The king's dead."

"I know he is," she said. She put her hand on Horrocks' cheek. "I've known. I've told you. My son and I have accepted it."

Sari said, "We were there. We tried to—on *The Priam*, not more than a day—"

"Don't tell me it was so recent. I couldn't bear to think he was alive some of this time when he could have been with me. I have to believe he's been dead since the start.

Tell me I wasn't wrong, Horrocks. I couldn't bear it any other way."

Horrocks looked at Sari, then back to the queen. "All along," he said.

"Where are the Bastards?" Sari said. "I don't think I've seen one. Their ships upstairs—"

"They're dressed as miners," the prince said. "They're stoking the crowds, moving from riot to riot."

Horrocks pointed at the prince's fat Ringers. "Two of you, guard that door."

"Why bother?" the queen said.

The Ringers followed Horrocks' orders.

"There another way out of here?" Horrocks asked. "The riots'll move into the throne room soon."

"Over here," the prince said and walked toward the northeast corner. "Another door. It leads—"

"I don't care where it leads long as it gets us out of here," Horrocks said.

Sari joined the prince in the corner. Eight of his Ringers formed a protective semicircle around them.

Horrocks put his hand out to the queen. "Now. We have to go now."

"I'm staying," Porphyria said.

A chair crashed through the throne-room door with Guilfoyle behind it. The two Ringers guarding the door ducked out of surprise. Guilfoyle stabbed them in the neck and threw one of the Ringers at Horrocks. Guilfoyle snatched the queen off her stool and put his bloody stiletto against her stomach.

"Smart work, leaving a gap of chairs right in front," Guilfoyle said.

"What are you going to do? Kill her?" Horrocks said.

"If it hurts you I might." Guilfoyle put his other arm around Porphyria's neck. "What are you here for? What are you gonna do here? I have a plan. At least I have a plan."

"Sell her to the Bastards. Because that plan worked so well with the king," Horrocks said.

"Tinton wants them to himself, all these stupid confusing mines," Guilfoyle said. "He'll want the queen and her son dead. Has to get them, first. That's where I get paid. Only need one."

Guilfoyle and the queen shuffled a few feet toward the broken door. "I'm taking her off the mine. The queen goes on sale tomorrow. Maybe you want to get some money together."

Porphyria tried to slip from Guilfoyle's arm. He prodded her with his knife.

"No one's going to pay for her dead," Horrocks said.

The riot outside grew louder.

"That's the Bastards coming this way," Horrocks said.

"Bull*shit*," Guilfoyle said. "I didn't see any down here."

"Go out there and you'll have no deals to make," Horrocks said. He didn't think he'd be able to draw and fire his gun in time. Horrocks looked at the queen. "He killed your husband."

Porphyria shrieked. Guilfoyle cut her out of instinct but withdrew the blade before it went too deep.

Tinton was standing in the unguarded doorway. A dozen Bastard faces loomed over his shoulders. He raised his gun. "Thanks for holding her," Tinton said and shot the queen through the face. "Now where's the prince?"

"Horrocks! Horrocks!" Sari yelled.

Horrocks fired two shots at Tinton, then spun around to get to his wife. He was blocked by the tide of Ringers rushing to meet the Bastard swarm.

Sari and the prince were already through the second door. Horrocks saw the prince's chubby hands trying to pull the heavy door shut.

Guilfoyle sprinted toward the door and threw his foot out to stop it from closing. He screamed in pain and wedged the door open with his hands. He didn't know how many bones were in his foot, but he was certain more than a few were broken.

One of the prince's Ringers stole Horrocks' gun and started shooting at the Bastards point-blank.

Horrocks reached the door after Guilfoyle made it through but before it closed. Horrocks turned around, grabbed the crossbar and pulled the door shut. The automatic locks fell into place with such force Horrocks felt the vibration in his joints.

He heard five more gunshots but the sounds were remote, like soft echoes. Bodies thudded against the door. Rust sparked from the hinges but Horrocks didn't think anyone else would get through.

Horrocks turned around. He was in a dank tunnel that had once been a stateroom on *The Priam*. Guilfoyle limped around a curve twenty feet away.

Horrocks chased Guilfoyle, ran him into the wall, punched him in the kidneys, hammered him in the spine.

Guilfoyle swung his elbow back and cracked Horrocks across the jaw. Guilfoyle swiveled and put his back to the wall. His face was hidden under debris from the queen's head. "Sneaking up, that's the only way you can beat me."

Horrocks didn't see Guilfoyle's stiletto. Must've lost it, he thought. His grin turned into a snarl. "You won't get the prince."

Guilfoyle punched Horrocks, threw him to the floor and tried to land on him with his knees. Horrocks rolled out of the way. Guilfoyle had completely forgotten about his bad knees, and when they hit the floor he screamed so loud Horrocks felt something in his ear pop. Guilfoyle fell over onto his right hip.

Horrocks couldn't remember which foot Guilfoyle had injured stopping the door, so he stomped on them both.

Horrocks left him there. He loped after the others, panting louder than Guilfoyle, and saw the prince holding a door open at the tunnel's end.

"Where's Sari?" Horrocks asked.

"In here, in here," the prince said.

The narrow room was cluttered with five operating bays: table, lamp, instrument tray, and medcom. Reinforced shelves sagged with chemical drums. All the delicate machines, even the overhead monitors, were papered with photos of the king's face and body. On the far side of the room, next to a black door (Another door, Horrocks thought) were full-body healing tubes.

Sari walked over to Horrocks, stared up at his face but said nothing.

"Did you see my mom?" the prince asked. "Ringers pushed us through before the shooting."

"Where are we?" Horrocks asked.

"Did you see her?"

"Last I saw, Guilfoyle let her go."

Two short, balding men stood next to the prince.

"Who're you?" Horrocks asked.

"Surgeons. Flesh artists," the prince said. "This is The Studio."

Horrocks shut the door he'd just come through. "How do you lock it?"

"It doesn't," the prince said. "My mom liked to come here unannounced, watch the operations."

"Horrocks," Sari said.

Horrocks put his shoulder against the door. "Go hide behind those tanks on the other end."

"Is Guilfoyle dead?" she asked.

"Almost. Didn't have anything to do it with. Couldn't do it with my bare hands. I wanted to make sure you were OK. Go with them. Go hide."

Horrocks pressed his ear to the door and didn't hear a thing. He walked over to the nearest table. It had no wheels. He shoved it in spurts. The door creaked open before the table was in place.

Guilfoyle came into the room and grabbed a lamp. He jerked the plug from the wall and wound it over his fingers. "So where is he?" Guilfoyle said.

Horrocks stayed on the other side of the table. "They're gone," he said. "Went out through the door in back. Just you and me."

"You and me. Two old friends. Happy together," Guilfoyle said and smashed the head of the lamp against the table. Horrocks was sprayed with metal and hot glass.

"Where is he? In this room. I know he's in this room," Guilfoyle said.

Horrocks backed away. He picked glass out of his cheek. "He's gone, Gil. As far as you're concerned, he's gone. It won't work."

"Yes it will," Guilfoyle said and used the decapitated lampstick to split the shelves.

Horrocks reached the center of the room and stopped retreating. "You won't get any closer than this," he said.

Guilfoyle palmed the sweat from his forehead. He couldn't feel his legs or feet, but adrenaline kept them steady. He rested the lampstick on his shoulder like a baseball bat. "I won't let you have him, either. Maybe I don't get the prince, and Tinton don't either, but you definitely don't."

He twirled the lampstick and stepped around the table. "Kept to myself on Europa. I didn't have a whole lot but what I did have no one could take from me. I had control. I never should've come."

"So go," Horrocks said. He made fists so tight the stitches over his missing finger burst.

"Can't go back. Sold everything to outfit the *Honey Locust*. Sold everything cheap to come out here and get rich," Guilfoyle said. He pointed the lampstick at Horrocks. "You got all the good things, always. Pretty wife. The best wrecks. A mine. A fucking mine!"

He swung the lampstick through another set of shelves.

"Won't find a thing you make a mess like this," Horrocks said.

"They made Ringers here. You hate Ringers. You should be helping me. I deserve something." The adrenaline was beginning to fade. "You never should have saved me, Horrocks. Most days I wish you hadn't."

Guilfoyle raised the lampstick again and Horrocks flew at him. They fell to the floor, spinning and punching. Guilfoyle lifted Horrocks by the shirt and slammed him onto a table. Horrocks punched Guilfoyle in the chest with his bad hand. The pain immobilized Horrocks' entire arm. He leaned against the table and kicked Guilfoyle in the face. Guilfoyle snared Horrocks' foot and flipped him over the table.

Horrocks landed on his side and was slow to get up. He tried to use one of the shelves to help him stand but it caved under his weight. Guilfoyle came around the side and pinned Horrocks to the floor by bashing him with the lampstick.

"I'm hell with bats!" Guilfoyle said and kept swinging. Horrocks could feel the lampstick denting his back. He timed the swings, caught the lampstick between his left arm and his ribs and knocked Guilfoyle into a medcom with a strong uppercut.

"Look at your hand," Guilfoyle said. "Broke off one of your fingers, didn't I."

Horrocks hefted the lampstick, gauging its weight. "Wasn't you," he said.

"Oh give me some goddam credit," Guilfoyle said. He staggered forward and threw a wild punch. Horrocks swung the lampstick and crushed Guilfoyle's cheek.

This'll all be worth it when I have the kid, Guilfoyle thought. He should have let me die.

"Damn tanks is where they are," Guilfoyle said. "I see feet under there."

Guilfoyle threw more wild punches and Horrocks continued beating him with the lampstick.

"We're almost there," Guilfoyle said. His clothes were shredded. So was his face. The numbness abandoned his feet; he could feel the bones grinding against each other. His knees were in agony. Should have let me die, Guilfoyle thought. I thought I wanted to live but I was wrong. I don't want to live in pain anymore.

Guilfoyle stopped trying to dodge the lampstick. It caught him in the mouth, shattering his dentures.

Horrocks' bloody palms were losing hold of the lampstick. "Guilfoyle, back up. Back up and we'll—"

"I wish you ca liff wid a same hurt you curse me wid," Guilfoyle said and threw himself on Horrocks.

Guilfoyle was impaled on the lampstick. Horrocks dropped them both. Guilfoyle hit the floor; bits of false teeth tumbled out of his mouth.

"Horrocks," Sari said and slid the tanks out of her way. "Oh my God, Horrocks. Your back. Christ, your back."

The walls shook from the pounding outside. Chemical drums fell off the few remaining shelves.

"Nearly wrecked the whole room," Surgeon One said.

"Protecting you," Horrocks said.

Surgeon Two nudged Sari aside. "Normally we'd spend a few hours cleaning up but we have to operate immediately and this mess, it complicates things."

"Looks like only a couple operating bays are online," Surgeon One said.

"That simplifies it. Two bays. I'm sure you'll manage," Horrocks said and walked toward Sari.

The surgeons stepped in front of her.

"Horrocks, you know what we need," Surgeon Two said.

"We need stability," Surgeon One said.

"Stability," Surgeon Two said.

They approached Horrocks together.

Horrocks sidestepped them and tripped over Guilfoyle's body. "There is no more stability," Horrocks said. "You're out of work. The king's dead."

"Sari told us," Surgeon One said. "Time for a new king."

The surgeons followed Horrocks around the room like obedient pets. Horrocks tipped machines in their path.

"A new king. A replacement," Surgeon Two said.

"Not me," Horrocks said.

"We waited and waited, tried to be optimistic. That time has passed," Surgeon Two said.

"You were loyal to him, now be loyal to his memory," Surgeon One said.

"Pick someone else."

"Deadline's hours away," Surgeon One said. He motioned toward the door. "Can't tell miner from Bastard out there."

"Use the prince," Horrocks said.

"He's only just started working in the mines," Surgeon One said. "A few of us know Kingston told you all his Furnace secrets as part of your bargain. That's priceless knowledge. With the king gone, if you don't help, it'll be extinct. You've run your own Furnace for how many years now? You've managed a mine, Horrocks, you can handle nine more."

"I don't need to be made a Ringer to run the mines."

"Everyone's been through a hellish twenty days," Surgeon Two said. "They want the king back. They need the king."

"Without Kingston's secrets, without that the mines'll falter," Surgeon Two said.

"Bring me your engineers and I'll tell them," Horrocks said.

"The only reason the mines stayed so safe for so long is because everyone thought only the king knew, and he was well guarded. You'll be well guarded, too," Surgeon Two said. "You have the experience. Don't be so simple, Horrocks! You see the logic. This is the easiest solution, the best solution."

"Get away," Horrocks said.

"A new Ringer," Surgeon Two said.

"I look nothing like the king."

"That's never been a problem," Surgeon Two said.

"I'm half a head taller than him."

"We're very good," Surgeon Two said.

"Find someone else. I hate Ringers," Horrocks said and hurled instrument trays at them.

The surgeons were not deterred. "Your Furnace is in jeopardy. Sari's pregnant, isn't she? Don't you see how much she's bleeding? We'll save the baby. Consent, Horrocks."

Horrocks looked past the surgeons at Sari. She was holding onto a table. Her pants were streaked with blood.

"No one will believe it," Horrocks said.

"They'll want to," Surgeon One said. "They'll have to."

"I hate Ringers."

"Your Furnace, your wife," Surgeon One said.

"My baby," Sari said.

"Your baby," Surgeon One said.

"I can't make this decision now," Horrocks said.

"It's not yours to make and it's already been made," said Surgeon Two. "The good of the kingdom, Horrocks. The life of your child."

"I love you," Sari said. "You've made sacrifices before. Our baby."

The banging outside intensified.

"Don't worry," Surgeon One said. "No one gets in here. The door by the tanks is locked. If you locked the door from Porphyria's safe-chamber, no one gets in here."

Lost my Furnace, Horrocks thought. My coworkers. My friend Wyeth. My salvation, the king. Probably my child. Not my wife. I don't want to lose my wife.

He stared at Sari. His shoulders slumped and he nodded.

The surgeons removed hypodermic guns from their coats. When they approached Horrocks he pulled the lampstick from Guilfoyle's torso and swung at them.

"We figured—"

They'll take my face from me, Horrocks thought. Brand me someone else.

The surgeons raised their guns. "It's already been agreed, Horrocks."

What if they can't give it back? Horrocks thought. I'd be gone forever.

Horrocks swung the lampstick again, breaking one of the hypodermic guns.

"Really, Horrocks," the surgeons said.

Sari, Horrocks thought and lowered the lampstick. The surgeons fired. Horrocks passed out and crashed through a medicine cart. The surgeons struggled to lift his body off the floor. The prince helped them and they managed to lay him on a table.

"Didn't you see what that animal did to his back?" Sari said and rolled Horrocks onto his stomach. "You going to start the operation now?"

"No they won't," the prince said. "Leave him be. I'll replace the king."

"You're not even his real son," Surgeon Two said.

"I'm Porphyria's son," the prince said. "The kingdom's mine either way. The miners haven't accepted Rouen. Even if my mom's alive, it'll be easy for me to take control. The kingdom is mine. I'd rather have it as my father. It'll restore the peace sooner."

"We needed Horrocks' knowledge," Surgeon One said.

"So he'll tell me what he knows. I grew up on the Furnaces. I'll understand what Horrocks has to tell me. The managing engineers will help me with everything else."

"My baby," Sari said.

"They'll see to your child," the prince said and glared at the surgeons. "I'm the king now. They'll do what I say."

"Why did you wait so long to speak up?" Surgeon Two asked.

"I was curious if he'd say yes, and I was working up the courage to say the same thing. Yes. Horrocks has done enough for everyone. Me, not him. Me," the prince said.

"We'll have to do something about your acne," said Surgeon One.

"And your weight. And that awful hair," said Surgeon Two.

The prince got up on one of the tables. "Get started."

"Something we have to do first," Surgeon One said. "Shouldn't take long at all."

The surgeons turned on the overhead monitors and scrolled through the Furnace's rooms.

Sari stroked Horrocks' hair and whispered to him. Her voice wavered as dizziness consumed her. She hitched herself up onto the table and lay next to her husband.

The surgeons saw Tinton in the queen's safe-chamber, Rouen in the volcanic lobby. Both men were dead.

The surgeons turned on the mine-wide intercom and said, "The king's alive. We've found the king."

CHAPTER 42

"We should get started already. You know the way."

"We will," Horrocks said.

"I miss the *Moondrunk*. This ship makes me feel sleazy."

"The Bastards really did a job on the *Moondrunk*. She was in no shape."

"Could've taken the next Longliner," Sari said.

"I told you, nothing directly related to the king."

Sari's bare feet were propped on the cockpit's dashboard. She hunched forward in her chair, a bottle of nail polish in her hands.

"Hope this ship can make the trip," she said.

"It's Parish-class. Mackerracher said it could."

"That's all he said?"

"He apologized first, about the whole Mission episode. Said these ships were built for some crusade armada they decided never to send."

"If she starts breaking down we can always go to the chapel to pray," Sari said. She used the brush on her big toe.

Sari had clipped a plastic flower to the side of the viewscreen. It was the first of many trinkets she had used in her attempt at lively redecoration. Horrocks knew it would never work. The ship's personality was too stubborn. The crosses, paintings, and glassed-in Bibles refused to come off the walls. Horrocks had covered them with a torn bedsheet; that was his attempt at redecoration.

He backed up his chair and ran into some boxes marked Clothes-His, Clothes-Hers, Jackets, Dishes, Clothes-Hers, Photos. The *Honey Locust* overflowed with their boxes. Even the chapel had become a storeroom. Horrocks found it depressing the way their lives had been so easily compartmentalized.

Horrocks had left the horsehair chair on his mine. He'd tossed most of Guilfoyle's furniture. It was garbage anyway.

The mine was garbage, too. Tinton hadn't lied. The place was beyond repair.

Sari finished painting her nails and nodded at the mines on the viewscreen.

"Think he'll last? The junior king?" she said.

"A lot of bounty hunters came in off the last Longliner," Horrocks said. "Plus you've got the Bastards."

"Which I don't understand," Sari said. She blew on her wet toenails. "The doctors produced a king before the deadline. There's nothing to inherit. No one believed the Bastards who said they saw Guilfoyle kill the king."

"Nobody wanted to," Horrocks said.

"What are the Bastards still doing here?"

"They'll wait. Probably fall back on their extortion blockades for the time being."

Three paperbacks were piled on the dashboard. Horrocks had found them when he cleaned out the ship. Westerns. Elmer Kelton westerns. He thumbed through the book with the brightest cover. He was starting to get used to his missing finger.

"So he won't make it?" Sari said.

"Not our problem, kiddo," he said and put his hand on her belly. Sari's stomach had doubled in size in the three months since the prince's ascension. The flesh artists, true to the prince's word, saved Sari's baby in an operation twice as long as the prince's transformation. They sewed up Horrocks' hand as well. While Sari recuperated Horrocks revealed to the prince all the king's Furnace secrets. Together they ran through a gamut of permutations and hypothetical catastrophes. Horrocks was impressed with the boy's focus as the prince was also dealing with his mother's death and the stress of running a kingdom.

The prince relegated most of his responsibilities to various managers, made a few very public appearances to comfort the miners but knew that soon he'd have to adopt this new persona permanently. The flesh artists gave him daily mannerism training.

On the way back to their Furnace they spotted Guilfoyle's abandoned ship. It took Sari two days to burn the junk from the blocked exhausts. Horrocks spent most of those two days outside the *Honey Locust*, using the heat from the exhausts to cremate the bodies from his freezer. He also cremated the Ringer that Guilfoyle had left to starve in the storeroom.

They flew home in the *Honey Locust* and filled Guilfoyle's morgue with De Cuir and the others. Thirty-two others, in addition to the eleven bodies Guilfoyle had in there, some of them dating from the Push.

Horrocks and Sari spent the next few months on Earth, going from family to family, returning the bodies, attending funerals.

Eleven more funerals waited for them in the Deeps.

"Who are they?" Sari asked and pointed to the silver ships that congregated on the outskirts of the mines.

"Have to be scouts from Eurasian mining companies."

"More strife," Sari said.

It would be too much work, Horrocks thought. Three, four years fixing the Furnace. Fighting off the parasites and Bastards. Worrying about the baby. I relied on the king and his kingdom for too many things for too long. I never loved this business. I was a fraud, as duplicitous as the Ringers. I need to be myself. Sari thinks she'll be safer in the Deeps. We'll try it her way. We tried it mine, it didn't work. We'll try it her way.

"I hope the prince makes it," Sari said. She used a manicure pen to correct the nail polish around her toes.

One of the boxes in the kitchen fell over. Horrocks looked down through the open trapdoor. His dog looked up at him innocently.

"How long you figure it'll take?" Horrocks asked.

"Twice what it would a Longliner. Five months if Guilfoyle's Spot Drive's any good," Sari said, and thought, The baby'll be here by then. "You can start her up anytime."

"Five months with you. I don't know if I can stand that," he said.

She punched him in the arm.

Horrocks thought about the Ringers the queen had made of him. During the last three months he had thought about them a lot, and he decided he needed them back. He wasn't sure what his motive was. He knew he'd never feel whole until he went to the Deeps and caught them himself. He didn't think he would hurt them. Maybe pay to have their faces changed again. Maybe not.

I can't be afraid to leave this place, he thought. Go to the Deeps with Sari. The fucking Deeps. We tried it my way and here we are.

"We'll try it your way," he said.

ABOUT THE AUTHOR

A fan of science fiction since the time he could read, Adam Connell devoured all things genre and promptly became the oddest kid in his class. "The book that influenced me the most was *Dune*," Connell says. "It's a literary landmark. It fulfills the kind of promise that only speculative fiction can deliver, by bringing new context and meaning to age-old human issues. By that I mean without the constraints of our current social and technological climate. For the author of genre fiction, there are millions of ways to dissect humanity." Connell began writing science fiction at age fifteen, and since his graduation from college in 1995 he has written six novels—the first three have been completely destroyed to save him from future embarrassment.

Connell graduated from New York University with a degree in English and went on to a job in finance. This unusual career path was the result of happy accident, good fortune, and desperation. Throughout his seven years in finance, Connell was never completely happy. In 2002 he was contemplating a career change when his company made the decision for him. Connell was laid off with about 200 other employees.

After his "separation" from the finance industry, Connell hunted for work in the publishing field. During a phone interview with Sandra Schulberg, publisher of Phobos Books, Connell mentioned his passion for novel writing. Ms. Schulberg arranged for a second interview to be held in her office, and invited Connell to bring along two of his best manuscripts.

Instead of a job, Connell got two book contracts. The first contract was for *Counterfeit Kings*. His next novel, *Cold Tonnage*, will be published by Phobos Books in the winter of 2004. He lives in New York City. Visit him on the web at www.counterfeitkings.com.